CAN YOU GROW A POPSICLE?

Distributed to Schools and Libraries
in the United States by
ENCYCLOPAEDIA BRITANNICA EDUCATIONAL CORP.
310 S. Michigan Avenue
Chicago, Illinois 60604

Library of Congress Cataloging-in-Publication Data
Woodworth, Viki.
Can you grow a popsicle? / Viki Woodworth.
p. cm.
Summary: Illustrations and rhyming text ask several questions
about flowers, vegetables, and trees.
ISBN 0-89565-820-8
1. Gardening – Juvenile literature.
[1. Plants.] I. Title.
SB457.W66 1993   91-33167
635–dc20   CIP / AC

CAN YOU GROW A POPSICLE?

by Viki
Woodworth

THE
CHILD'S
WORLD

Viki Woodworth

Viki Woodworth graduated from Miami University in Oxford, Ohio. Though trained as an art teacher, she chose to write and illustrate children's books as a way to teach and reach children. She lives in Seattle, Washington with her husband and two young daughters.

If you plant a seed,
what will come up?

A turtle?

A flower?

A shoe
or a cup?

(A Flower)

What in your garden grows underground?

A carrot?

A popsicle?

A fish
or a hound?

(A Carrot)

What do you think can grow on a tree?

A chicken?
A monkey?

An apple
or a bee?

(An Apple)

**What will help your
plants to grow big?**

A poodle?

A clock?

Rain

or a pig?

(Rain)

If you plant a garden, what will you grow?

Vegetables.

Flowers.

Whatever you sow!

Critical Live Art

Live Art is a contested category, not least because of the historical, disciplinary and institutional ambiguities that the term often tends to conceal. Live Art can be usefully defined as a peculiarly British variation on particular legacies of cultural experimentation – a historically and culturally contingent translation of categories including body art, performance art, time-based art, and endurance art. The recent social and cultural history of the UK has involved specific factors that have crucially influenced the development of Live Art since the late 1970s. These have included issues in national cultural politics relating to sexuality, gender, disability, technology, and cultural policy.

In the past decade there has been a proliferation of festivals of Live Art in the UK and growing support for Live Art in major venues. Nevertheless, while specific artists have been afforded critical essays and monographs, there is a relative absence of scholarly work on Live Art as a historically and culturally specific mode of artistic production. Through essays by leading scholars and critical interviews with influential artists in the sector, *Critical Live Art* addresses the historical and cultural specificity of contemporary experimental performance, and explores the diversity of practices that are carried out, programmed, read or taught as Live Art.

This book is based on a special issue of *Contemporary Theatre Review*.

Dominic Johnson is Senior Lecturer in the School of English and Drama at Queen Mary, University of London, UK. Previous publications include *Glorious Catastrophe: Jack Smith, Performance and Visual Culture* (2012) and *Theatre & the Visual* (2012).

Critical Live Art

Contemporary Histories of
Performance in the UK

Edited by
Dominic Johnson

Routledge
Taylor & Francis Group

LONDON AND NEW YORK

First published 2013
by Routledge
2 Park Square, Milton Park, Abingdon, Oxon, OX14 4RN

Simultaneously published in the USA and Canada
by Routledge
711 Third Avenue, New York, NY 10017

Routledge is an imprint of the Taylor & Francis Group, an informa business

© 2013 Taylor & Francis

This book is based on a special issue of *Contemporary Theatre Review*, volume 22, issue 1.
The Publisher requests to those authors who may be citing this book to state, also,
the bibliographical details of the special issue on which the book was based.

British Library Cataloguing in Publication Data
A catalogue record for this book is available from the British Library

ISBN13: 978-0-415-65981-9

Typeset in ITC Galliard
by Saxon Graphics Ltd, Derby

Publisher's Note
The publisher would like to make readers aware that the chapters in this book may be referred
to as articles as they are identical to the articles published in the special issue. The publisher
accepts responsibility for any inconsistencies that may have arisen in the course of preparing this
volume for print.

Contents

Citation Information

The following chapters were originally published in the journal *Contemporary Theatre Review*. When citing this material, please use the original issue information and page numbering for each article, as follows:

Chapter 2
Towards a Prehistory of Live Art in the UK
Heike Roms and Rebecca Edwards
Contemporary Theatre Review, volume 22, issue 1 (February 2012) pp. 17-31

Chapter 3
The Freaks' Roll Call: Live Art and the Arts Council, 1968–73
Graham Saunders
Contemporary Theatre Review, volume 22, issue 1 (February 2012) pp. 32-45

Chapter 4
Positive Surrender: An Interview with BREYER P-ORRIDGE
Dominic Johnson
Contemporary Theatre Review, volume 22, issue 1 (February 2012) pp. 134-166

Chapter 5
The Common Turn in Performance
Gavin Butt
Contemporary Theatre Review, volume 22, issue 1 (February 2012) pp. 46-61

Chapter 6
Duckie's Gay Shame: *Critiquing Pride and Selling Shame in Club Performance*
Catherine Silverstone
Contemporary Theatre Review, volume 22, issue 1 (February 2012) pp. 62-78

Chapter 7
Frightening the Horses: An Interview with Neil Bartlett
Lois Keidan
Contemporary Theatre Review, volume 22, issue 1 (February 2012) pp. 152-160

Notes on Contributors

Julia Bardsley is an artist based in London. She was formerly the Co-Artistic Director of the Haymarket Theatre in Leicester and the Young Vic in London. Between 2003–09 she developed and performed her *Divine Trilogy*, which toured widely. Her current work focuses on the Medea myth as source material for a series of collaborative performances and videos. She is an Artsadmin Associate Artist, and received an Honorary Doctorate from Middlesex University in 2007. www.juliabardsley.net

Neil Bartlett is an artist, playwright, novelist, and director. He founded the theatre company Gloria in 1988 and was Artistic Director of the Lyric Hammersmith from 1994 to 2004. His novels include *Ready to Catch Him Should He Fall*, *Mr. Clive and Mr. Page* and *Skin Lane*. His translations and dramatic adaptations have been performed widely across the English-speaking world. www.neil-bartlett.com

Gianna Bouchard is Principal Lecturer in Drama at Anglia Ruskin University, Cambridge, UK. Her research focuses on relations between medical science, experimental theatre, live art, interdisciplinary arts practice and critical theory. Her work has been published in *Performance Research* and she has most recently contributed to the edited collection, *ORLAN: A Hybrid Body of Art Works* (Routledge).

BREYER P-ORRIDGE are a composite identity consisting of Genesis BREYER P-ORRIDGE and Lady Jaye BREYER P-ORRIDGE. Genesis BREYER P-ORRIDGE first achieved recognition with COUM Transmissions, and the bands Throbbing Gristle and Psychic TV. Lady Jaye BREYER P-ORRIDGE was a New York-based performance artist and musician. She passed away in 2007. They have exhibited internationally. www.genesisbreyerporridge.com

Gavin Butt is a Reader in the Department of Visual Cultures, Goldsmiths, University of London, UK. He is the author of *Between You and Me: Queer Disclosures in the New York Art World 1948–1963* (Duke University Press) and editor of *After Criticism: New Responses to Art and Performance* (Blackwell). He is co-director of Performance Matters, a three-year AHRC-funded research project on the cultural value of performance. www.thisisperformancematters.co.uk

Rebecca Edwards is Employer Engagement and Knowledge Transfer Manager in the Department of Theatre, Film and Television Studies at Aberystwyth University, UK. She was Research Assistant on the AHRC project '"It Was Forty Years Ago Today": Locating the Early History of Performance Art in Wales 1967–1979'. She completed her PhD at Swansea University. www.performance-wales.org

Deirdre Heddon is a Reader in Theatre Studies at the University of Glasgow, UK. She is the author of *Autobiography and Performance* (Palgrave Macmillan), and co-author of *Devising Performance* (Palgrave Macmillan). She has published many articles on the use of autobiography in performance in a variety of journals and edited collections. From 2006–09 she was the academic mentor of the AHRC Creative Fellow, Adrian Howells.

Helen Iball teaches in the Workshop Theatre at the University of Leeds, UK. She has published on writers and practitioners including Bobby Baker, Sarah Kane and Howard Barker. Her current project is *Theatre Personal: Audiences with Intimacy 1990–2010*.

Dominic Johnson is a Senior Lecturer in the Department of Drama at Queen Mary, University of London, UK. He is the author of *Glorious Catastrophe: Jack Smith, Performance and Visual Culture* (Manchester University Press) and *Theatre & the Visual* (Palgrave Macmillan) and editor of *Franko B: Blinded by Love* (Damiani Press) and *Manuel Vason: Encounters − Performance, Photography, Collaboration* (Arnolfini).

Lois Keidan is Director of the Live Art Development Agency. She was Director of Live Arts at the Institute of Contemporary Arts, London, UK from 1992 to 1997. In 1999, she was awarded an Honorary Fellowship by Dartington College of Arts, and in 2009, she was awarded an Honorary Fellowship by Queen Mary, University of London.

Brian Lobel is a Senior Lecturer at the University of Chichester, UK, and an artist whose work has been shown in the UK and internationally. He has received commissions and grants from Wellcome Trust, motiroti, Jerwood Charitable Foundation and Lower Manhattan Cultural Council. His first play *BALL* was published in 2010, and other writings have appeared in *Performance Research* and *PAJ*. He received a PhD in Drama from Queen Mary, University of London. www.blobelwarming. com

Heike Roms is Senior Lecturer in Performance Studies at Aberystwyth University, UK. She was Principal Investigator on '"It Was Forty Years Ago Today": Locating the Early History of Performance Art in Wales 1967–1979', an AHRC-funded project (2009–11). She won the David Bradby TaPRA Award for Research in International Theatre and Performance 2011. www. performance-wales.org

Graham Saunders is a Reader in Theatre Studies at the University of Reading, UK. His books include *Love Me or Kill Me: Sarah Kane and the Theatre of Extremes* (MUP) and he co-edited *Cool Britannia: Political Theatre in the 1990s* (Palgrave) and *Sarah Kane in Context* (MUP). He is Principal Investigator of an AHRC project on the Arts Council of Great Britain 1945–94.

Carolee Schneemann is a multidisciplinary artist. Her paintings, photography, performance art and installation works have been shown at major international museums, including a retrospective exhibition at the New Museum of Contemporary Art in New York entitled *Up To And Including Her Limits*. Her publications include *Cézanne, She Was A Great Painter* (1976), *Early and Recent Work* (1983), *More Than Meat Joy: Performance Works and Selected Writings* (1979, 1997) and *Imaging Her Erotics* (2003). *Correspondence Course*, a collection of her letters, was recently published by Duke University Press.

Lara Shalson is a Lecturer in Theatre and Performance Studies at King's College, London, UK. She is currently completing a book on the performance of endurance across a range of art and political contexts, from civil rights protests to performance art.

Catherine Silverstone is Senior Lecturer in Drama, Theatre and Performance Studies at Queen Mary, University of London, UK. She works on contemporary performance, especially in relation to Shakespeare, trauma, gender, sexuality, ethnicity and theatrical reconstruction. She is the author of *Shakespeare, Trauma and Contemporary Performance* (Routledge) and co-editor of *Tragedy in Transition* (Blackwell).

Rachel Zerihan is a Lecturer in Theatre at the University of Sheffield, UK. She was awarded a PhD for her thesis that examines 'Catharsis in the Works of Contemporary Female Performance'. In 2009 Rachel produced a commissioned Live Art Development Agency publication, Study Room Guide on One to One Performance, and co-edited *Interfaces of Performance* (Ashgate), an edited collection of works examining the use of technologies in contemporary performance practice.

Foreword: Live Art Performance Art Body Art

Carolee Schneemann

Live Art needs to be passionate, risky, and *not* sure of its self. Can contemporary nomenclatures absorb and integrate the materials of unprecedented influences that might define performance art?

My visual discipline developed as a landscape painter – a concentration within a perceptual focus continuously being challenged by shifts of light, the wind, the weather, or the viscosity of my paints, so that the need to respond to change within my focus prepared me for future experiences with the principles of Zen, John Cage's chance operations, the superimpositions and juxtapositions in the music of Charles Ives, and the incremental energies of collage. These early influences of physical and kinetic perceptions merged with the visual dynamics of Abstract Expressionism in painting. I experienced Pollock's fluid lines only by following the kinetic energy; I understood the strokes of oil paint on canvas as a physical 'event' when closely viewing Velázquez, as well as the paintings of Joan Mitchell. I saw Paul Cézanne's structures as analyzing a physical/optical space where the broken line shifted volumes within traditional perspectives; thus collage led directly to the fractured planes of Willem De Kooning's paintings. Within this realm in 1963, I envisioned a sequence of actions where I would spontaneously collage my body so that it became part of my painting constructions, namely *Eye Body: 36 Transformative Actions for Camera* (1963). This work also proposed the questions: Could I be both image and image-maker? Could these visual actions destabilize the pervasive traditions of male artists' configurations of the female body?

The velocity of influences that performance art contains are vast and varied, and able to absorb every possible cultural influence. Because Live Art is so permeable, so absorptive of sensory and conceptual influences, contemporary perceptual events can explode directions within the confluence of anthropology, archeology, religious iconography, Busby Berkeley, Bugs Bunny, *Breaking Bad* – that is, high art to low art in recombination, so long as the body reinvents form and conjures the contemporary meltdown: melt in, blow up.

A core development of Live Art/body art/performance art was the self-depictions and self-assertions of woman artists, who shaped the 1970s with issues that had been taboo, marginalized, or ignored. Theatre, dance and monologues melted into integrations of forbidden male issues: gay history, the disaster of AIDS, and gender and cross-gender issues. Performance art can address ritual intimacy, transformative politics, gay, lesbian, Black, Asian, and feminist material, as it shifts the scale of the body from live action to the increasing inclusion of media, including projection systems, and live feed video. Political aspects often motivate the most unexpected formal developments – breaking time, extending space. For me to leave the solitude of my painter's studio and to engage live actions in public was to inhabit an ecstatic realm of energy, which in its power is inexplicable (as in *Meat Joy*).

And I will always struggle within the contradiction of the conceptual concentration that demands solitary isolation while the performative, exposed formulation is physicalized within a community of participants, and confronts other communities. (I remain bewildered that the use of my body in performance has eclipsed the fuller scope of my constructed work, including film and video. In principle, however, the male artists who initiated what became performance art have remained identified with their paintings, sculptures, and installations.)

In the 1960s the artists envisioning happenings, events, and Fluxus were deadly against theatre. There was no concept of 'performance art' yet, but theatre had to do with perfectibility, repetition, predictability, the unitary text, and a fixed space. Everything we did came out of painting, risky invention, visions of motion, and materials. I was influenced by Claes Oldenburg's *Store Days* (1963), in which I participated the week after Jim Tenney and I arrived in New York from Illinois; as well as works by Allan Kaprow, Robert Whitman, Jim Dine, Red Grooms, and of course the courageous early actions of Yoko Ono: sensory arenas by painters extending their materials into actual space and live time. We were performing our events in lakes, and landscapes, and garbage dumps. We ended up using theatre spaces for some works if there was nothing else available, but we did not want to sit in regular seats, in a predetermined space; although there were times when we might take over a theatre and it could be quite magical – but I think it had to do with invading it, and taking over, so that we weren't accepting its traditional premises.

My years in the 1960s and 1970s in London were a time in which the city's traditional social and class structures were in a state of dissolution. Resistance to the Vietnam War activated many radical, creative Americans to come to the UK and participate in the vitality of the music, drugs, and rock and roll, including events at the Roundhouse, and raves out in the countryside. The shifts in social structures were unique and volatile. There was a constant request for my film *Fuses* (1965–1968), the unique self-shot collage of explicit heterosexual erotic pleasure. I was on panels with John Trevelyan – then Secretary of the British Board of Film Censors – as he organized major public presentations addressing issues of censorship.

I would make major works in London, including advanced performative situations. I was invited by Joe Berke to participate in the *Dialectics of Liberation Congress* at the Roundhouse in 1967, for example, alongside figures in anti-psychiatry, including Paul Goodman, R. D. Laing, and others. It would be a living, vital performance event that included street people, horses and carts, encompassing the issues of the conference. The anti-psychiatrists were enraged that a young woman they didn't appreciate was creating an overarching event that would incorporate their own texts. I was struggling against the same old unconscious male rage and fury; in this case that a young woman had been invited to absorb and reposition the issues of the *Dialectics of Liberation* – an event that was otherwise lacking in the participation of women. I also directed major media and performative works at the Roundhouse concerned with the Vietnam War, and brought information into London from the Chicago Seven, and the Black Panthers.

It's always unexpected when a particular work becomes iconic. I had no idea that *Fuses*, or *Eye Body*, or *Interior Scroll* (1975) would ever leave that small realm of the avant-garde where they originated. In terms of *Interior Scroll*, specifically, it was fortunate that Anthony McCall – my partner at the time – was there to make photographs of the performance. If he hadn't been there we wouldn't have any documentation of the event. I reconstructed *Interior Scroll* in a cave with seven women in 1995, so there is now video documentation.

The powers of photography provide a record into which we project and identify, and which we question. I am grateful for documentation of my works, and to all the photographers. In the 1960s and 70s, we did not have budgets for equipment or to hire people for documentation. Professionalism, self-promotion, polish, and predictability occur in the mid-1980s as the commodification of performance and performers takes an aesthetic value.

Contemporary historians are proposing unprecedented replications of performance art: a need for the redo, overdo, video documents, archival maintenance. The documents of historical performances can seem increasingly distanced from their cultural momentum or necessity that produced the work at the time. Their political and social contexts change – as do their psychosexual contexts and physical materials. I was invited to reconstruct *Meat Joy* (1964) in *A Short History of Performance* at the Whitechapel Gallery in London in 2002. In 1964, you couldn't say cunt, vagina, orgasm, lubricity, cum. Female personal sexuality was intimate while explicit references belonged to porno or medical science. These early taboos surrounding *Meat Joy* vitalized its demonstrative physical trust, spontaneity, and the intensive contact improvisation within the group, which was unprecedented. These actions, so central to my motives, were affecting to the original audience; but would the audience in 2002 respond to the erotic ritualized energy with an untried, under rehearsed performance group? It was a very different animal. Still, certain of my works remain central to this cultural history. Can my current installations and video works energize aspects of a culture today tottering on menace, on undeclared militarism, and on ecological disasters?

Introduction:
Live Art in the UK

Dominic Johnson

What is Live Art, what are its histories in the United Kingdom, and how might artists and scholars account for its achievements and legacies in critical terms? *Critical Live Art* establishes a series of ways of approaching Live Art in the UK as a geographically, culturally, and historically situated set of practices, across – and to some extent between – theatre, performance, and visual culture. The contributors explore the contingency and particularity of Live Art, for example by reading the specific contexts, venues, policies, and sectors that support its practices, or by rooting key works in relevant histories and discourses. The chapters and interviews demonstrate that works of Live Art often function as complex critical acts, and demand nuanced theoretical apparatuses to enable them to produce meaning. Scholars and artists labour in concert, in order to enable art to achieve its work.

Live Art questions the contexts in which it is presented. Through live performance, documentation, discussion, and other acts of dissemination and circulation, specific works of Live Art engage critically with the histories out of which they emerge, or against which they otherwise may create frictions. Live Art offers critical, political, and social rejoinders to the situations from which it frequently strikes out.

Drawing on theatre and performance studies, and art history and visual studies, the contributors to *Critical Live Art* explicitly address the historical and material conditions for the production and reception of Live Art in the UK. The recent social and cultural history of the UK has involved specific factors that crucially influenced the development of Live Art since the 1970s. These have included issues in national cultural politics relating to sexuality, gender, race, disability, cultural policy and funding, programming, and teaching in higher education. In other words, neither the creation nor experience of Live Art takes place in a social or cultural vacuum, and therefore *Critical Live Art* attempts to document what might be termed the historicity of Live Art.

In the past decade there has been a proliferation of festivals of Live Art in the UK, and growing support for Live Art in major venues. Nevertheless, while specific artists have been afforded critical essays and monographs, there is a relative absence of scholarly work on Live Art as a historically and culturally specific mode of artistic production. Artists who present their work in Live Art venues and festivals are itinerant boundary-crossers. (Indeed, the term 'Live Artist' as a discrete label is generally a misnomer, an empty signifier – one is hard pushed to think of any artist who operates solely in the Live Art sector.) It is important to ground analyses of Live Art in the precise ways the term is used in programming, and by artists, to ensure that the academic frameworks that are deployed are closely tied to the material conditions of production in the cultural sector. Particularly, the critical interviews with artists included in this collection demonstrate some of the peculiar problems that Live Art poses as a sector.

The methodological and other limitations of art history, theatre and performance studies, and curatorial practice frequently come into question in the essays and interviews collected here. Read in concert with each other, they pose a challenge to the fallacy of seeing Live Art as somehow outside the remit of one specific discipline, or outside the curatorial activities of specific traditions in the cultural industries. If the work under scrutiny in *Critical Live Art* poses methodological and political challenges to disciplinary business as usual, such difficulty is accentuated by the relative absence of attempts to clearly define or characterise Live Art in the UK as a distinct history. As Nick Kaye argued in a special issue of the journal *Contemporary Theatre Review* in 1994, Live Art in the UK may be distinct from the development of performance art in the United States, for example, partly on account of the differing histories that each set of practices tends to privilege.[1] The key survey of performance art available in 1994, Henry M. Sayre's pioneering book *The Object of Performance*, published 5 years previously, set a precedent of sorts for the emphasis on selectively privileging those instances of performance that clarified emergent understandings of a wider distribution of 'postmodern' visual art practices, including painting, photography, and sculpture.[2] The book explicitly studied American art between 1970 and the late 1980s, and apparently set a trend for the absenting of British examples from those discussed in histories of performance art. The landmark studies published shortly after Kaye's special issue include two art-historical books – Amelia Jones' *Body Art/ Performing the Subject*, and Kathy O'Dell's *Contract with the Skin: Masochism, Performance Art, and the 1970s* – and one theatre studies book, Rebecca Schneider's *The Explicit Body in Performance*.[3] All three made immense contributions to the study of performance art, have become classics in the field, and arguably have not been surpassed in more recent studies of experimental performance. However, none directly explores work by British-based performance practitioners (with the exception of O'Dell's fleeting references to Richard Long and Gustav Metzger). I am interested in what might happen to (American-centric) histories of experimental performance when confronted by Live Art in the UK.

1. Nick Kaye, 'Introduction – Live Art: Definition and Documentation', *Contemporary Theatre Review*, Special Issue: Live Art: Definition and Documentation, 2.2 (1994), 1–7 (p. 1).

2. Henry M. Sayre, *The Object of Performance: The American Avant-Garde Since 1970* (Chicago: University of Chicago Press, 1989).

3. Amelia Jones, Body *Art/Performing the Subject* (Minneapolis and London: University of Minnesota Press, 1999); Kathy O'Dell, *Contract with the Skin: Masochism, Performance Art, and the 1970s* (Minneapolis: University of Minnesota Press, 1998); and Rebecca

Schneider, *The Explicit Body in Performance* (London and New York: Routledge, 1997).

4. Cited in Marilyn Butler, 'Questioning the "Canon"', in *Literature in the Modern World: Critical Essays and Documents*, ed. by Dennis Walder (Oxford: Oxford University Press, 1990), pp. 9–17 (p. 9).

5. Adrian Heathfield, 'Then Again', in *Perform, Repeat, Record: Live Art in History*, ed. by Amelia Jones and Adrian Heathfield (Bristol and London: Intellect with the Live Art Development Agency, 2012), pp. 27–35 (p. 33).

6. See *Contemporary Theatre Review*, Special issue: Live Art in the UK, ed. by Dominic Johnson, 22.1 (2012).

7. My interview with Bardsley was previously published as 'The Skin of the Theatre: An Interview with Julia Bardsley', in *Contemporary Theatre Review*, 20.3 (2010), 340–52.

8. See Martin O'Brien, 'Treating the Body', in *Contemporary Theatre Review*, 22.1 (2012), 146–50.

The historian David Cannadine noted wryly that after the decline of British imperialism, international readers conceded the 'pointlessness of specializing in British history, now that no one but the British were interested in it.'[4] This suggestion of the negligible impression made by British histories upon international culture has, arguably, been naturalised in narratives of experimental performance culture. This is not the case for British drama, bearing in mind international scholarship on Caryl Churchill, Sarah Kane, Joe Orton, John Osborne, or Harold Pinter – to name but a few arguably canonical British playwrights. However, there is no denying the relative marginality of British experimental performance practices in histories of performance – especially those published from the perspective of art history. I hope that *Critical Live Art* may begin to unsettle and redistribute the way that the histories of performance art and Live Art are currently articulated.

Rather than re-establish a (thankfully deflated) colonial imperative, *Critical Live Art* instead seeks to address some of the unique achievements of artists working in Live Art in the UK. This partly involves a concerted attempt by all the contributors to address an expanded range of artists, often by departing from more familiar objects of study. While *Critical Live Art* does not provide an exhaustive history, it does attempt to broaden the spectrum of visible or viable artistic practices. As Adrian Heathfield has cogently argued, as a 'modest archive' of performance, any history must consider and attempt to unsettle its own 'technique of repetition', to produce archival records whose own achievements and limitations are scrutinised. An act of historical narration, he argues, should interrogate and resist, particularly, 'the unfortunate consequences of the archival impulse', which may include canonisation, political neutralisation, or other normalising effects of traditional scholarship.[5]

Background

Many of the contents of *Critical Live Art* were previously published in 'Live Art in the UK', a special issue of *Contemporary Theatre Review* I guest-edited in 2012.[6] The special issue was divided into three sections. The first section comprised eight original articles by leading authorities in the field of performance studies and Live Art scholarship. These reappear in *Critical Live Art*, prefaced by a commissioned foreword by the legendary American media artist Carolee Schneemann; and supplemented by my own chapter, which develops the original introduction towards a fuller account of the historiographical challenges posed by Live Art. The 'Documents' section of the special issue included two interviews republished here, which have been complemented by an additional interview with Julia Bardsley.[7] The 'Documents' section also included a series of images and texts by Martin O'Brien, who uses endurance to explore his experiences as a person living with Cystic Fibrosis[8]; and a critical response to a landmark symposium on Live Art authored by its co-curators, the artist-scholars Johanna Linsley and Helena Walsh.[9]

The third section of the journal, 'Backpages', included short commissioned texts and a previously unpublished report by the late

9. Johanna Linsley and Helena Walsh, 'Gobsmacked: Getting Speechless in Performance', in *Contemporary Theatre Review*, 22.1 (2012), 161–66.

10. Jeff Nuttall, 'The Situation Regarding Performance Art (1973)', in *Contemporary Theatre Review*, 22.1 (2012), 175–77.

11. Slavka Sverakova, 'Performance Art in Northern Ireland', *Contemporary Theatre Review*, 22.1 (2012), 177–80; and Laura Bissell, 'Live Art in Scotland: *The Salon Project*', *Contemporary Theatre Review*, 22.1 (2012), 180–82.

British artist Jeff Nuttall.[10] The short essays were commissioned as commentaries on aspects of Live Art that were not discussed in detail in the preceding articles and documents. For example, two short articles in the Backpages section, by Laura Bissell and Slavka Sverakova, expanded on the fuller range of locations for Live Art, by exploring the local histories of relevant experimentation in Scotland and Northern Ireland, respectively.[11] My elision of these pieces, here, admittedly reinstates some of the oversights that their initial inclusion sought to address, namely the emphasis on histories of Live Art in the UK that are limited mostly to England and Wales. Additional short pieces by Elaine Avila, Carl Lavery, Peter Petralia, and others in the Backpages section provided brief reflections on international Live Art, in order to acknowledge the scope for deploying the term outside the UK. I encourage readers to engage with these additional materials by consulting the special issue of the journal. The essays and other documents collected here should be understood in part as a spur to new archival and theoretical research into a continually expanding archive of contemporary performance.

The present collection

Critical Live Art begins with a discussion of the historiographical challenges that attend the study of Live Art. Rather than provide a history of Live Art practices, I suggest that policy, documents, and conditions of reading and reception can be addressed to distinguish between Live Art and its proximate genres or strategies – as well as to read the methodological problems posed by Live Art – as a paradoxically specific and indeterminate collection of objects of study. Insights into its particular genealogy suggest ways of acknowledging the differing approaches demanded by events and artists associated with Live Art.

The collection continues with two detailed surveys of the 'prehistory' of Live Art in the UK. In *London Calling*, Barry Miles has suggested that early countercultural achievements in the UK were centred on London, emerging from a confluence of bar and café cultures, galleries, independent bookshops, and art salons, in the 1940s and 1950s, which fostered the downward social mobility associated with Bohemian cultural development.[12] The diverse products of these social and cultural experiments would directly influence the idiosyncratic performance practices of Rose English, Ian Hinchliffe, Bruce Lacey, John Latham, Jeff Nuttall, David Medalla, or Silvia Ziranek – all pioneers of Live Art in the UK. Heike Roms, Rebecca Edwards and Graham Saunders give two striking new histories that extend Miles' narrative, by departing from his emphasis on London as the epicentre of cultural innovation.

Drawing in part from their exhaustive research project on Live Art in Wales, Roms and Edwards explain that between 1962 and 1966, UK-based artists such as Mark Boyle, Anne Kesselaar, Gustav Metzger, Adrian Henri and others set the scene for the development of Live Art as a sector, influenced by visiting European and North American counterparts such as Jean-Jacques Lebel, Allan Kaprow, and artists associated with the international Fluxus movement. A crucial achievement of Roms

12. Barry Miles, *London Calling: A Countercultural History of London since 1945* (London: Atlantic Books, 2010), pp. 69–80.

and Edwards' chapter is to shift our attention to the relatively under-acknowledged regional heartlands of Live Art, especially Cardiff and Edinburgh. Graham Saunders confirms Roms and Edwards' suspicion that the terminological shift to Live Art after around 1979 marked 'a substantial change in the infrastructural frameworks' that fostered experimental practice. Through a detailed survey of the decision-making procedures of the Arts Council of Great Britain (ACGB), Saunders demonstrates that Live Art is a historically and culturally specific development. He shows persuasively that it emerged out of the expansion of funding categories in the UK, through the formation of the ACGB Experimental Drama committee in 1970, and the recognition of Combined Arts soon after the committee's dissolution in 1973. In the process, Saunders casts new light upon the development of cultural policy in the UK in the early 1970s. His chapter will provide a solid foundation for subsequent research on under-examined artist-collectives such as COUM Transmissions, Pip Simmons Group, the People Show, and Shirley Cameron and Roland Miller.

My interview with BREYER P-ORRIDGE brings artists' own viewpoints and recollections to the discussion of 'pre-histories' of Live Art and their aftermaths. Under a previous moniker, Genesis P-Orridge was a crucial figure in the pre-history of Live Art in the UK. As my interview demonstrates, the recent work of BREYER P-ORRIDGE is perhaps conceptually apposite for a history of contemporary Live Art. Yet in their interview, the artists reject the nomenclature outright:

> By changing 'Live Art' to 'Living Art', more levels and flexibilities of meaning are aroused. Living Art implies some form of being alive as opposed to dead. The art is active and filled with potential and still evolving […]. Art, we believe, must be all-inclusive and 24/7, with its prime motivation embedded, no matter how obliquely, in every action or product.

Like the other interviewees in *Critical Live Art*, BREYER P-ORRIDGE demonstrate some of the limitations to the implicit assumptions that sustain Live Art as a sector. If Live Art is often characterised by its 'slipperiness' as a category, BREYER P-ORRIDGE are too slippery, even, for the sector as it is currently formulated. In recent years, they have performed in the UK in music venues – Genesis BREYER P-ORRIDGE was a member of Throbbing Gristle (with the former members of COUM Transmissions), and Genesis and Lady Jaye BREYER P-ORRIDGE performed in a recent manifestation of the band Psychic TV. Yet no Live Art venue or festival has produced or presented the performance-based work of BREYER P-ORRIDGE. This fact – and their dual nationalities – might render them improper for a history of Live Art in the UK, despite the crucial contributions Genesis BREYER P-ORRIDGE made to the development of performance as a cultural logic in the history of British art. I see their volatile status 'beyond the pale' as a suggestive reminder of the disciplinary, institutional, and policy-based constitutions of Live Art as a sector as opposed to a formal genre.

Chapters by Gavin Butt and Catherine Silverstone look to marginal spaces that have fostered recent Live Art, namely the club performance scene and its offshoots. Butt defines this expansion or detour as a 'common turn' in performance practices and performance studies. As Tracy C. Davis has noted, performance studies has been the scene for a dizzying sequence of 'turns': epistemic revisionisms including the cultural, linguistic, historical and performative turns. Such 'turns', she writes, are 'not accomplished simply by swivelling on one's heels and facing a new cardinal direction. As goes the body, so goes the gaze, but new conceptions of textuality and the legibility of culture send many people moving, functionally and rhetorically, in whole new ways and directions.'[13] Butt and Silverstone's chapters contribute to new 'turns', towards marginal spaces that carry their own distinctive material conditions of production and reception, and, indeed, their own peculiar pleasures.

13. Tracy C. Davis, 'Introduction: The Pirouette, Detour, Revolution, Deflection, Deviation, Tack, and Yaw of the Performative Turn', in *Cambridge Companion to Performance Studies*, ed. by Tracy C. Davis (Cambridge: Cambridge University Press, 2008), pp. 1–8 (p. 2).

Both Butt and Silverstone note the problems posed by marginality. They both observe the sublimated retention of taste cultures by the Live Art sector, and gesture to the challenging fact that Live Art is itself characterised by a specific set of inclusions and exclusions. Both scholars study relatively unfamiliar works, from the multimedia work of Mel Brimfield to the club environments of Duckie. Scholarship might valuably continue to address the relative non-participation of other forms and genres, for example new circus, vaudeville and cabaret, drag, and the wider practices of club performance. To date, these histories have rarely been acknowledged in terms of the Live Art sector's 'broad-spectrum' definition of relevant or valuable practices.

Lois Keidan's extended conversation with the theatre artist, author and polymath Neil Bartlett confirms that artists have claimed an expanded field of spaces and styles for contemporary performance. Bartlett explores his own idiosyncratic placement between and across major institutions of theatre and the itinerant spaces of Live Art. A key figure of early Live Art, Bartlett has since arguably crossed into the dominant circuits of theatrical production, typifying Keidan's own definition of Live Art as a catch-all term for artists who participate in diverse venues and contexts as they see fit. Yet Bartlett also complicates this idea. Some of his recent work, in its ambition and grandiosity, has perhaps transcended or outstripped the material possibilities of the Live Art sector. In his work and in his provocative statements to Keidan, Bartlett reveals some of the limitations and challenges faced by artists working in marginal forms and spaces.

Two further chapters, by Brian Lobel and Gianna Bouchard, rethink the politics of the body in recent Live Art, with particular emphasis on medical and biomedical practice. Lobel compares Rita Marcalo and Bobby Baker, exploring relations between disability arts and implicit acts of advocacy. Lobel argues that the reception of Marcalo and Baker's works tends to position the artists as spokespersons for constituencies outside of the direct audiences for their work, through their disclosures of illness in performance (epilepsy and mental illness, respectively). Drawing implicitly on his own artistic practice – which frequently explores his recovery from cancer – Lobel suggests that disclosure and advocacy offer both advantages and disadvantages for artists working in proximity to illness and disability.[14] For Bouchard, the formally diverse body works of Marisa Carnesky and Kira O'Reilly must be read from a historically situated perspective, because of the specific history of medical and other developments since the early 1990s. A politics of the body

14. See also Brian Lobel, *BALL and Other Funny Stories About Cancer* (London: Oberon Books, 2012).

emerges in this work, Bouchard shows, through heightened negotiations of feminist agency in performance. By appropriating divergent cultural histories and aesthetic registers, Carnesky and O'Reilly represent skin as a site of political, ethical and legal contestation. In a widely acknowledged argument, Kathy O'Dell wrote that performance art in the 1970s used 'masochism' in order to represent the contemporary splitting of the subject brought about by militarisation, especially the Vietnam War. For O'Dell, Marina Abramović, Gina Pane, Chris Burden and Vito Acconci deployed 'masochism as metaphor', creating situations of suffering 'in order to point to trouble in two interconnected social institutions: the law and the home', through artistic negotiations of the social contract.[15] Tarrying implicitly with O'Dell's earlier argument, Lobel and Bouchard suggest that Live Art in the UK may renew our understanding of social anxieties, offering new ways of thinking about the place of the body within legal, scientific, medical, and bioscientific contexts.

Carnesky and O'Reilly are fixtures of Live Art and experimental performance programming in the UK and Europe. Similarly, Julia Bardsley is widely presented, and is notable for the visual and affective power of her highly idiosyncratic work. In the third and final interview of *Critical Live Art*, Bardsley shows that artists often find themselves in volatile positions between the legacies of relatively distinct discourses and histories – for her, between those of visual art and theatre. Like Bartlett, Bardsley has vast experience as a director of repertory theatre in institutional spaces. Yet more recently, since her controversial 'retirement' from the theatre in the early 1990s, Bardsley has generally made smaller scale productions in experimental spaces, either as a solo artist or with her long-time collaborator Andrew Poppy, the iconic experimental composer and musician. Like BREYER P-ORRIDGE, Bardsley is circumspect about identifying as a Live Art practitioner, but is also intrigued by the formal and practical possibilities that it offers as a sector.

Similarly concerned with competing or otherwise dissonant histories, Lara Shalson's essay suggests a novel approach to the art-historical concept of endurance. Shalson explores the ways in which the genres, traditions and histories of theatre, specifically, endure in Live Art as a category, perhaps in spite of artists' own protestations against the perceived orthodoxy of theatrical form. In 1994, Susan Melrose argued that watching Live Art is characterised by 'the performance of a *feeling of dispossession*, staged within the property of theatre.'[16] Artificially dispossessed from familiar histories, she suggested – from visual art and theatre, but also from philosophy – Live Art offers a set of complex theoretical problems for spectators, as we struggle to define the terms of our affective engagements with performances. 'There is always more' to Live Art, Melrose adds, 'than meets the eye'.[17] Shalson argues that theatre endures as a disorganising supplement to the production of meaning in works presented in Live Art contexts, looking specifically to the work of Forced Entertainment, a British theatre company who have been a mainstay of Live Art and related programming for more than two decades.

A further 'supplement' – the production of affective relations – is the focus of a collaboratively written chapter by Deirdre Heddon, Helen Iball and Rachel Zerihan on one to one or audience of one performances.

15. O'Dell, *Contract with with the Skin*, pp. 11–12.

16. Susan Melrose, 'Please Please me: "Empathy" and "Sympathy" in Critical Metapraxis', in *Contemporary Theatre Review*, 2.2 (1994), 73–83 (p. 77).

17. Ibid., p. 81.

Comparing their differing perspectives on three one-to-one performances that they attended on a single day – as part of artist Adrian Howells' one-day festival and symposium celebrating the form at the University of Glasgow – Heddon, Iball and Zerihan account for the parallels and contradictions between audience's experiences of a single work. Their chapter usefully advances what Peggy Phelan has called 'performative writing', as a method of scholarly analysis that enacts (rather than describes) 'the affective force of the performance event again, as it plays itself out in an ongoing temporality made vivid by the psychic process of distortion […] and made narrow by the muscular force of political repression in all its mutative violence.'[18] Phelan achieved this feat through melancholic investments in suggestive resonances between, on the one hand, the tendency of performance to lose itself and, on the other, quite disparate events of death and disappearance. Heddon, Iball and Zerihan re-ground performative writing by comparing three attempts to write an authoritative account of performances that took place solely for audiences of one.

While Phelan suggests a distinction between subjective investment and political effect, I hope that the writings collected here provoke vivid collaborations between the two projects of spectatorship. Moreover, asking questions about the stakes and terms of Live Art's marginality – or indeed its institutional status – need not unsettle its claims to political efficacy. Rather, a new mode of analysis might allow a revised historiography of Live Art that opens up a fuller and more productive analysis of its cultural politics. Many of the artists under examination in *Critical Live Art* explore the precise and destabilising promises of the body, desire and pleasure, in the space of performance. Such explorations take a dizzying range of forms. Their works suggest, in manifold ways, that we should search for the bite, the flinch, and the grimace of one's confusion in the face of Live Art, and never settle for anything less, despite the consolations that more convivial forms might sometimes offer. I hope that the practices celebrated in these pages oppose the timid, predictable or otherwise conservative drifts of some contemporary art and theatre – and indeed of performance. The accounts and arguments posed here might sustain the progressive, challenging, uneasy, and antagonistic possibilities that Live Art is capable of fostering.

18. Peggy Phelan, *Mourning Sex: Performing Public Memories* (London and New York: Routledge, 1997), p. 12.

Marginalia: Towards a Historiography of Live Art

Dominic Johnson

1. This chapter was previously published in short form as 'Introduction: The What, Where and When of Live Art', in *Contemporary Theatre Review*, Special Issue: Live Art in the UK, 22.1 (2012), 1–16. I thank Maria M. Delgado for her comments towards the development of this chapter.

2. Notable recent publications include *Histories and Practices of Live Art*, ed. by Deirdre Heddon and Jennie Klein (Basingstoke and New York: Palgrave Macmillan, 2012); and the international anthology *Perform, Repeat, Record: Live Art in History*, ed. by Amelia Jones and Adrian Heathfield (Bristol and London: Intellect with the Live Art Development Agency, 2012). Many key Live Art works are folded into an interestingly

Live Art is a contested category, not least because of the historical, disciplinary and institutional ambiguities that the term often tends to conceal.[1] Live Art is used to describe a wide range of performance practices in programming at cultural institutions in the UK, and to some extent in Europe. It also describes a busy sub-discipline of teaching and scholarly publication in theatre, performance and visual studies. However, the term 'Live Art' is rarely put under critical scrutiny. When did the term first come into usage? Does it formally describe a discrete set of practices? Is it the same as or differentiated from similar terms, such as performance art or body art? Live Art poses terminological, disciplinary, discursive, and other historiographical problems. Is Live Art a style, a genre, an idiom, or a sector? To what extent do artists identify with it as a useful label for their work? And how might we quantify the debts owed by Live Art to differing formal histories, such as theatre or visual art?

Live Art is a busy and fertile sector, with a long and rich history of artists, practices, and venues. Yet it has been subject to surprisingly few attempts at historiographical analysis or expansive historical overviews. Rather than being specifically resistant to historical narration as such, Live Art has been overlooked for various reasons. It is presented in different venues with varying frequency, but leaves visual records that are scattered, incomplete, or private, and little in the way of written commentaries or reviews in newspapers and similar periodicals. The academy has begun to address Live Art in the UK as a series of important artistic strategies and processes,[2] but a number of issues still inhibit its fuller historicisation. Live Art remains in some ways a puzzle, or an enigma. This problem is in fact germane to cultural histories whose narration is troubled by 'genealogical complexity', David Savran notes.

broad, medium-non-specific survey in Sally O'Reilly, *The Body in Contemporary Art* (London: Thames and Hudson, 2009).

3. David Savran, 'The Do-Re-Mi of Musical Theatre Historiography', in *Changing the Subject: Marvin Carlson and Theatre Studies, 1959–2009*, ed. by Joseph Roach (Ann Arbor: University of Michigan Press, 2009), pp. 223–37 (p. 225).

4. For example, UK-based artists including Bobby Baker, Franko B, Forced Entertainment, Alastair MacLennan, Lone Twin, and Stelarc have coordinated their own publications, often with scholar-editors, and have commissioned writings from scholars or curators to accompany their photographic documentation of performances.

5. The earliest usage is probably RoseLee Goldberg's, in *Performance: Live Art 1909 to the Present* (New York: H. N. Abrams, 1978). The UK edition was published by Thames & Hudson in 1979, although she does not explain her usage of the specific term 'Live Art' in either edition.

6. Rob La Frenais, 'Editorial', in *The Performance Magazine* 1 (June 1979), 3 (p. 3).

7. See Richard Schechner, 'Performance Studies: The Broad Spectrum Approach', *TDR: The Drama Review*, 32.3 (1988), 7.

8. Frank Dobson, 'Life under the Tories, Part One', in *The Performance Magazine*, 1 (June 1979), 21 (p. 21).

He explain that such histories may evoke 'unusual historiographical challenges', especially when a set of practices owes its conventions and formulas to multiple and divergent genealogies, for example literary, dramatic, and popular histories.[3] This aspect of Live Art perhaps ensures its historical and hermeneutic instability.

Researching Live Art poses its own frustrations. There is a limited scope of venues for publication of scholarly articles on Live Art in the UK – for example, due to the relatively tight disciplinary focus of many academic journals. The published writing that has emerged often focuses on relatively narrow sets of artists and companies; other writings appear in well-established artists' or companies' own publications.[4] Such writings generally refrain from defining Live Art, or fail to distinguish it from similar but arguably distinct forms, sectors, or idioms, such as performance art, body art, or time-based art. How does Live Art – as a specific and potentially discrete set of practices – require or prompt a new or revised historiography? I begin with a discussion of the emergence of the term, and a commentary on the succession of challenges or refusals that followed in the 1990s.

Origins

In the United Kingdom, Live Art is a self-sufficient sector for the production and presentation of contemporary performance. However, the term had different meanings when it was first introduced in the late 1970s.[5] Its particular genealogy – as a term and as a sector – offers useful vantage points for exploring its specificity, as well as its peculiar indeterminacy. Its first usages in the UK were a result of the concerted efforts of *The Performance Magazine*, a monthly periodical that underwent shifts in editorial remits, as well as name changes, under the leadership of Rob La Frenais. In the magazine's first issue in June 1979, La Frenais wrote, 'There are still some events worth stifling a yawn for. They are difficult to pin down [...] to separate from the sludge of experience'. Giving a deceptively broad description of these events, he writes, 'they consist of people doing things in front of others. They are performances.'[6] This dryly detached statement set up what would become a familiar definition of Live Art, as a collection of fresh, new, diverse performances, with little in common other than the fact of their liveness and the peculiar pleasure experiencing the events might induce in audiences. La Frenais' definition anticipates the 'broad spectrum' approach adopted by the emergent discipline of Performance Studies, as most famously defined by Richard Schechner in 1988.[7]

Also in the inaugural issue of *The Performance Magazine*, the Labour MP Frank Dobson noted that the innovations observed in Live Art were closely related to the new social context of Margaret Thatcher's newly victorious Conservative government. Dobson described Tory arts policy as a disturbing tension between élite commitment to high art on the one hand, and 'a thundering and distinct philistinism' on the other, which could only conspire to the detriment of those who make 'unsung work'.[8] Despite these observations by cultural and political

9. Subscription advert, in *The Performance Magazine*, 7 (1980), 31.

10. Rob La Frenais, 'Live Art Has Its Day', in *Performance Magazine*, 14 (1981), 5–6.

11. *The Performance Magazine: The Regular Review of Live Art in the UK*, 12 (1981). In October of 1982, 'Regular' was dropped from the subtitle.

12. Rob La Frenais, Unpublished correspondence with the author, Wednesday 5 October 2011.

13. Robert Ayers and Nikki Milican, 'The Early Years', in *National Review of Live Art: Archive 1979–2010*, ed. by Deirdre Heddon, Jennie Klein and Nikki Milican (Glasgow: New Moves International, 2010), pp. 5–18 (p. 8). 1986 also saw the first official usage of the term in British cultural policy, when the Arts Council of Great Britain set up the Live Art Education Scheme to support artists' placements in higher education.

commentators, 'Live Art' did not appear as a term in the magazine until its seventh issue, published in 1980, in a subscription advertisement that described the publication as 'the first accessible guide to the new live art activities happening in galleries, small theatres, streets and fields all over Britain'.[9]

At the time, key artists involved in these activities included Bobby Baker, Brith Gof, Paul Burwell, Shirley Cameron and Roland Miller, Dogs in Honey, Forced Entertainment, Forkbeard Fantasy, Tina Keane, Alastair MacLennan, Jeff Nuttall, Carlyle Reedy, and Marty St. James. The advert in *The Performance Magazine* notes the diverse range of spaces being utilised by Dobson's 'unsung heroes' of anti-establishment arts, and implicitly suggests that the work is in some way specific to Britain. Articles and reviews in the magazine continue to describe the work as 'performance art' or simply as 'performance', in relative isolation from American and European contexts.

The first clear critical usage of the term in the magazine appears in late 1981, in 'Live Art Has Its Day', La Frenais' review of The Midland Group Performance Art Platform (a festival that would later adopt the new term to rename itself the National Review of Live Art).[10] In 1982, the magazine added a subtitle to its name, to become *The Performance Magazine: The Regular Review of Live Art in the UK*.[11] The term 'Live Art' was still slow to catch on as a nomenclature in the writings it published, despite a concerted editorial effort by La Frenais. 'Performance' and 'Live Art' are seemingly interchangeable at this historical juncture – although, as discussed below, the terms would become arguably more distinct in the coming years.

At the time, the term 'Live Art' offered some advantages, enabling a broader appeal and an expanded range of support structures for programmers, and for some artists. Asked about the shift, La Frenais remembers, 'I suspect it emerged as a more "inclusive" alternative in the UK to the term "performance art" which was rather specific to a type of visual art which used the body as material and whose visceral nature alienated some establishment commentators (and early funders) at the time.'[12] The former director of the National Review of Live Art, Nikki Milican makes a similar point about the use of the term in the title of the festival after 1986: 'changing the name from "Performance Art" to "Live Art" was about adopting a marketing strategy in order to develop an audience'. This strategy had a social and economic context: 'it was a very fickle time in terms of funding and we were in an extremely vulnerable situation (it was the Thatcher years) – if we couldn't prove there was an audience, we would lose our funding.'[13] The new terminology also enabled groundbreaking approaches to programming under a handy new rubric, as artists working in diverse forms could be curated alongside comparably innovative artists working beyond the formal specificities of performance art as such. For example, a commissioned installation by the filmmaker and writer Derek Jarman was programmed at the National Review of Live Art in 1989, alongside works by choreographer Anne Teresa de Keersmaeker, composer Jocelyn Pook, and performance artists such as Richard Layzell, Anne Seagrave, and Gary Stevens.

Definitions and Challenges

Despite the deliberate imperatives outlined above, in the thirty years since its introduction as a new nomenclature, Live Art has metamorphosed to suggest a new set of meanings. While an officer at the Arts Council of Great Britain (ACGB), Lois Keidan stated in her report *National Arts and Media Strategy: Discussion Document on Live Art* (1991) that 'evolutions of form, coupled with the need to acknowledge innovative challenging practices from diverse cultures beyond Eurocentric monocultural traditions' prompted ACGB's Performance Art Advisory Group, of which she was a member, to 'change our terminology from the "restrictive practice" of Performance Art to the flexibility and responsiveness of the term Live Art.'[14] Indeed, while scholars have failed to precisely define the term, the same endeavour has been the subject of serious attempts by writers of cultural policy documents, especially at ACGB in the 1980s and 1990s. 'Central to the debate on Live Art is the issue of categorisation and definition,' Keidan argues. 'For an area of practice which cuts across and subverts traditional art form boundaries, this is not a new problem,' she notes of its resistance to precise definition, 'but it continues to have serious implications for effective funding, production, representation, artistic development, education, training and critical debate.'[15]

Crucially, Keidan notes that definition, and the development of terminologies, is not a peripheral or restrictive activity, but a key way of ensuring that artists, promoters, and producers have access to ACGB's financial and infrastructural resources. Yet she also cites artist Richard Layzell's dissenting statement that the establishment's attempt to define experimental forms 'is symptomatic of the very problem that Performance Artists should be trying to overcome,' namely the urge to fix and institutionalise resistant techniques or histories.[16] This may have been the case in 1991, but I would argue that the well-meaning refusal to define Live Art remains a hindrance to artists working in the sector. The absence of clarity about what the term signifies licenses the marginalisation of unrecognised or uncategorisable work, by arts organisations and by the academy. Nevertheless, Layzell was not alone in his discomfort with the attempt to introduce 'Live Art' as a term with a fixed referent. Several years after Keidan's document, Linda Ludwin reported widespread resistance to the use of Live Art as a terminology, especially among those working in the cultural industries (whom she interviewed towards her policy document). 'The term "Live Art" was controversial', she writes, and 'was characterised during most interviews as meaningless, off-putting to audiences and too restricting for Promoters and Producers. It was not considered a neutral term, or one that was recognised outside of the sector.'[17] Ludwin also notes that its 'esoteric' or opaque connotations make Live Art seem unattractive, outlandish or unfathomable to critics, hampering the wider critical and popular reception of work staged under the banner of Live Art.[18]

Keidan's report elucidates the imperatives that drove the sector, and the arguments warranting its sustained support. The National Arts and Media (NAM) Strategy Unit commissioned Keidan's discussion document, in response to the Minister for Arts Lord Luce's instruction

14. Lois Keidan, *National Arts and Media Strategy: Discussion Document on Live Art*, Number 26 (London: NAM, 1991), p. 2. The ACGB was restructured in 1994, to become the National Arts Councils National Lottery. Since 2003, Arts Council England (ACE) has managed responsibilities for arts and culture in England. See 'The history of the Arts Council', Arts Council England website, http://www.artscouncil.org.uk/who-we-are/history-arts-council/ [accessed 24/08/12].

15. Keidan, *National Arts and Media Strategy*, p. iii.

16. Ibid., p. 1.

17. Linda Ludwin, *Working on the Cutting Edge: Sliding Down the Razor Blade of Live Art – The Training Needs of Senior Promoters and Producers of Live Art Working in England* (London: Arts Council England, 1996), p. 5.

18. Ibid., p. 16.

19. Today, there are no venues dedicated to presenting Live Art in London. There are several one-venue annual festivals in 2012 that present Live Art alongside other forms, including: Sacred at Chelsea Theatre; Burst at Battersea Arts Centre; and Sprint at Camden People's Theatre. Pacitti Company's Spill is the major festival of Live Art and related work, and is biannual at various venues in London, including Barbican, National Theatre Studios, and Soho Theatre.

20. Ludwin, *Working on the Cutting Edge*, pp. 4–5.

21. Michael McMillan, *Cultural Grounding: Live Art and Cultural Diversity – Action Research Project*, A Report for the Visual Arts Department of the Arts Council of Great Britain (1990), p. 4.

22. Ibid. He adds that a comparison of carnival and opera as comparable forms of 'combined arts' is a case in point. Opera has been continually funded since ACGB's inception through the 1946 Royal Charter, yet carnival had been deemed non-artistic, thus the latter has received less overall funding in total than Eurocentric opera companies had received in the fiscal year 1989–90 (p. 6).

23. Cited in McMillan, *Cultural Grounding*, p. 11.

24. David A. Bailey, Ian Baucom and Sonia Boyce, 'Shades of Black: Assembling the 1980s', in *Shades of Black: Assembling Black Arts in 1980s Britain*, ed. by David A. Bailey, Ian Baucom and Sonia Boyce (Durham and London: Duke University Press, 2005), pp. xi–xxv (p. xiv).

to NAM's constituent bodies (including ACGB) to prepare a national strategy for developing and supporting national arts and media sectors. She outlined achievements in the Live Art sector over the previous five years, set out its prospects, and suggested priority areas for increased support, including financial resources for individual artists, and expansions in social participation, cultural diversity, training and management, and physical infrastructure (venues). In the discussion document, Keidan is expressly concerned with the lack of a devoted venue for Live Art in London,[19] which warrants Live Art as a series of 'special events' in programmes devoted to visual art, experimental theatre, or alternative comedy. Whereas spaces for Live Art existed in regional cities – Hull Time-Based Arts, Glasgow's Third Eye Centre, or Cardiff's Centre for Performance Research being some of her examples – in London, Live Art 'belongs everywhere and nowhere simultaneously, relegated to the unmanageable status of "cuckoo style adjuncts" to more established areas of programming'.[20]

Keidan's report was also prompted by the publication of *Cultural Grounding*, Michael McMillan's influential report on Live Art and cultural diversity published the previous year. The debates over the evolution of terms to discuss Live Art and 'Black Art' are both comparable and connected, and warrant some commentary here. In his report, McMillan argued, 'Live art operates on the margins of the visual arts, because of its "avant-garde" and ephemeral nature. Yet dominant definitions of performance are eurocentric and exclude many Afro-Asian (Black) artists.'[21] Reading the work of artists of colour including David Medalla, Rasheed Araeen, Mona Hatoum, Keith Khan, SuAndi, through the critical writings of Paul Gilroy, Rex Nettleford, and Kwesi Owusu, McMillan showed that Black artists working in Live Art are located in a position of double extremity – pushed to the edges of a cultural phenomenon that is already exterior, on account of their racial identity. McMillan's report demonstrated that the emergent rhetoric of 'cultural marginality' and 'ethnic minorities' leveraged the exclusion of non-white artists from both mainstream and experimental arts, licensed by the misconception of 'Black Art' as 'a homogenous and linear culture and politics.'[22] If Live Art disregarded Black Art as self-contained, partisan, or provincial, it reduplicated the same prejudices that mainstream arts and culture wielded against Live Art. McMillan cites a presentation by Nettleford to the *Arts and Cultural Diversity* symposium (1989) in which the esteemed Jamaican scholar argued: 'A principal reason for the historical neglect of black arts has been the failure to place its achievements within the framework of a broad heterogeneous national culture, [and] the failure to regard it as an equal contribution to that culture.'[23] More recently, David A. Bailey, Ian Baucom, and the artist Sonia Boyce have reiterated these concerns, asking 'whether it is in fact possible to speak of a semicoherent arts movement organised under the signs of "blackness" and "black Britishness",' and have queried what it means for such terms 'to name the historical and conceptual site where a variegated array of artistic practices intersect.'[24]

In his report, McMillan laid the blame for marginalisation upon ACBG's policy decisions, showing that ACGB's funding conditions and

25. McMillan, *Cultural Grounding*, pp. 6-9.

definitions of Live Art 'by their nature, exclude artists not working in a "white European tradition",' the latter being typified in his report by the sculptural performances of Stuart Brisley or Gilbert and George.[25] Thus, McMillan shows that the practice of defining Live Art, Black Art, or other important cultural phenomena, can itself give unwanted leverage to the attempts to proscribe cultural diversity. In place of 'ethnic absolutism,' McMillan argues for 'trans-racial cultural syncretism', or rich dialogue and cultural appropriations across races, glasses, and generations. McMillan's reading persuasively troubles the argument, above, that clear definition enables artists' access to financial and other kinds of support.

Black Art and Live Art are both used to signify 'variegated' sectors, idioms, or genres, but only provisionally. Their elucidation as terminologies can be both efficacious and misleading, an opportunity or a hindrance, for artists, curators, and audiences. A parallel question can be asked of other shorthand labels for sectors, styles, or forms in the arts. Other scholars have explained convincingly that the project of precisely labelling or defining the terms of artistic production can have its own shortcomings, both for movements and for individual artists. For example, in the context of the artist VALIE EXPORT's documentation of her pieces in Europe in the 1960s, Mechtild Widrich argues, 'labels such as "photo-performance", or "performance for the camera" do more to obscure the complexity of the performative action that unfolds than to reveal the actual dynamics of the interaction between the piece, its context, and its audience(s).'[26]

26. Mechtild Widrich, 'Can Photographs Make It So? Repeated Outbreaks of VALIE EXPORT's Genital Panic since 1969', in *Perform, Repeat, Record*, pp. 89–103 (pp. 89–90).

It is useful to look closely at critical attempts to explain the specificity of Live Art, to explore further the apparently uncertain utility of new nomenclatures for art and performance. In a handbook about Live Art published in 1991, for example, the artist and critic Robert Ayers gave a provisional definition of the term. His essay supports abstractions familiar to contemporary discussions of performance more broadly. Ayers states that 'live art allows a direct and unmediated contact between art and audience. It requires no object – no painting, sculpture, print or photograph – it requires no equipment, no venue or agent, no intermediary of any sort to act between the person who makes the art and the person it affects.'[27] Ayers' definition suggests the transformative aspirations and anti-capitalist politics of some Live Art, yet relies on contradictory assumptions that do not hold up against the practices documented throughout his book. The practices of 'first generation' Live Art practitioners – Anthony Howell, Andre Stitt, Stephen Cripps, Anne Bean, Stuart Brisley, or Nigel Rolfe, for example, in which the artists variously manipulated furniture, power tools, fire, honey, mud, or paint – suggest Live Art in the UK was in many ways fascinated by 'painting, sculpture, print or photograph', and other objective forms that could be – and usually were – compellingly documented and archived. Moreover, the notion of an 'unmediated' representation is a contradiction in terms, for all representations are in and of themselves exercises in mediation, even if the formal strategies were unusual, original, or deliberately inartistic.

27. Robert Ayers, 'Changing People's Lives', in *Live Art*, ed. by Robert Ayers and David Butler (Sunderland: AN Press, 1991), pp. 9–13 (p. 9).

Amelia Jones notes that statements about the transcendental qualities of performance are frequently reiterated in 'crudely metaphysical' and 'heroic' celebrations of body-based practice, and these statements can

28. Amelia Jones, *Body Art/ Performing the Subject* (Minneapolis and London: University of Minnesota Press, 1998), pp. 22, 33.

function as debilitating targets for critics of performance art and body art (more so than the work itself).[28] Moreover, the idealism of Ayers' description does not sit well with the highly theatrical and dance-based practices of younger artists. This 'second generation' of Live Art practitioners was well versed in the formal languages of 'mediation' – theatre, dance, video and film – and highly dependent on specific venues or sites for the production of meaning. The disparate strategies of Pascal Brannan, Marisa Carnesky, Gary Carter, Ernst Fischer, Susan Lewis, Robert Pacitti, Sarbjit Samra, or Simon Vincenzi – all shown in London at the Institute of Contemporary Arts (ICA) in the early 1990s, around the time Ayer's essay was published – suggest the highly and effectively mediated quality of much Live Art. To be fair to Ayers, his own performance work is explicitly action-based, and often centred on the body in exhausting situations of physical endurance in suggestive attempts to overcome the spectacular, or otherwise 'theatrical' implications of overt mediation. He may have been projecting his own artistic imperatives onto Live Art as a relatively emergent phenomenon.

Live Art Today

The key difference between the terms 'performance art' and 'Live Art' today – despite being so often used interchangeably – is that in the UK, performance art is a wide-ranging formal tradition, while Live Art is a self-sufficient sector in the cultural industries. While some practitioners in the Live Art sector use performance art as a formal technique, others do not. Similarly, many performance artists in the UK do not present their work in the venues and festivals associated with the Live Art sector (Pablo Bronstein, Spartacus Chetwynd, Gillian Wearing, and Ian White are good examples). Live Art is therefore a contradictory phenomenon, both usefully anomalous and confusingly specific.

The distinction between Live Art and performance art reflects the older distinction between performance art and fringe theatre in the UK; as the pioneer Jeff Nuttall argued in a report written in 1973 (and published posthumously in 2012), the two terms may seem frequently similar or interchangeable, yet practitioners associated with each 'not only feel separate in ideology and technique, but, in fact, are separate, knowing one another not at all. They drink, as it were, in separate pubs.'[29] In his essay – commissioned by fellow artists Roland Miller and Shirley Cameron for a report to the Experimental Drama Committee of the ACGB – Nuttall proceeded to outline his own convincing understanding of the six 'groups' associated with performance art in the UK, varying from theatre-oriented artists, to agitprop 'left-wing preachers', to underground and countercultural 'crusaders', and other distinct variations on 'performance art proper'.[30]

Many artists currently active in the Live Art sector clearly adopt the formal qualities associated with performance art – as inheritors of what Nuttall calls 'the brushers and chisellers and welders and sprayers who turned to the living flesh in the 1950s'.[31] Today, such artists include Brian Catling, George Chakravarthi, Marcia Farquhar, Helena Goldwater,

29. Jeff Nuttall, 'The Situation Regarding Performance Art (1973)', in *Contemporary Theatre Review*, 22.1 (2012), 175–77 (p. 175).

30. Ibid., pp. 176–77.

31. Ibid., p. 177.

Hayley Newman, Gary Stevens, or Aaron Williamson – not least because they are more readily associated with the formal histories of fine art. They variously employ sculpture, video, and new media, or exploit the histories of Happenings, actions, or interventions, and tend to avoid the specific spaces, techniques and durations of theatre. Others in the Live Art sector draw more clearly on experimental theatre practice, and are therefore less clearly associated with the international histories and traditions of performance art – relevant examples might include Curious (Leslie Hill and Helen Paris), Robin Deacon, Rose English, Duckie, Gob Squad, Kim Noble, Robert Pacitti, or Geraldine Pilgrim. While refusing some dramatic conventions, such as characterisation, narrative, and plot resolution, they often employ the audience configurations, durations, and technical apparatuses of theatrical representation in their performances.

A further array of artists in the Live Art sector refuse the logics of performance art – and depart from Nuttall's earlier classifications – by drawing on miscellaneous disciplines such as dance, video and digital arts, cabaret, music, protest, or spoken word, such as Katherine Araniello, Dickie Beau, desperate optimists, Kazuko Hohki, John Jordan, Stacy Makishi, La Ribot, or Mehmet Sander. Any attempt to firmly distinguish between artists in this manner is perhaps reductive and instrumentalist on my part, but suggests a diversity of practices and approaches in Live Art, as a sector that sustains multiple ways of working that do not always relate neatly or closely to the legacies we have come to associate with international performance art. Finally, some artists associated with Live Art uncompromisingly exceed any attempts to fix their relations to the provisional histories I have outlined here. Good examples of such itinerant, idiosyncratic, and otherwise disruptive figures include Ernst Fischer, Oreet Ashery, Adrian Howells, Helena Hunter, Shabnam Shabazi, or Manuel Vason. They either constitute part of an exceptional, unwieldy category, or unfix the categorical imperative altogether.

Live Art is an idiosyncratic phenomenon as it includes within its purview such broad, seemingly unmanageable, and perpendicular scopes of artists and performance practices. It is this sense of miscellany and multiplicity that suggests Live Art's identity as a sector as opposed to a form, an idiom, a style, or a genre. Such an assertion is, in itself, nothing new. Deirdre Heddon notes that the Live Art Development Agency (LADA) has referred to Live Art as a sector regularly since 2001, when Lois Keidan and her former colleague Daniel Brine published the report 'Focus Live Art: The Challenges Facing Policy and Provision for Live Art in England and Looking Towards a More Sustainable Future'. Heddon notes that LADA was founded in 1999, in the immediate aftermath of New Labour's landslide victory in the parliamentary elections in 1997. Heddon ties this observation to LADA and other agencies' deployment of 'neoliberal' terms – lobbying, professional development, career trajectories, infrastructures, sustainability, partnerships, and so on – suggesting the proximities between the emergent sector of Live Art and New Labour's capitalisation on the arts as economically viable 'cultural industries'.[32]

Other writers have similarly noted Live Art's peculiar resistance to precise definition. In 1994, theatre scholar Nick Kaye observed that Live

32. Deirdre Heddon, 'The Radical Institutionalisation of Live Art? Or: Live Art is Dead', unpublished paper presented at Performance Studies international, PSi #18, University of Leeds, 28 June 2012.

33. Nick Kaye, 'Introduction: Live Art: Definition and Documentation', in *Contemporary Theatre Review*, Special Issue: Live Art: Definition and Documentation, 2.2 (1994), 1–7 (p. 1).

Art was less a form or genre than a critical lens. He writes, Live Art 'invokes a particular way of looking at work,' a 'frame' through which audiences and critics perceive an implicit vocabulary among diverse and seemingly unrelated formal activities.[33] Despite this strategic circumspection, with the possibilities for criticism and funding that La Frenais and others, above, envisioned for the new nomenclature also came an explicit set of resources, venues, agencies, markets, and organs of dissemination. 'Performance art' did not fall out of favour entirely as a term, but rather persists as a designated set of recognisable stylistic practices that circulate within the material conditions created and sustained by Live Art as a sector. A network of venues, development agencies, festivals, and other related programming circuits sustains the sector, bolstered by national arts funding programmes and imperatives in academic research and teaching.

Despite the *sectoralisation* of Live Art, many relevant artists move easily from key venues to others unconnected to the sector. There is little that is constitutively unique in the modes of production and presentation associated with Live Art in the UK, beyond the possibilities for funding and support that are sometimes available for UK-based artists, and the conceptual frameworks that are conferred upon their work by development agencies, scholars, and curators. Lois Keidan and Daniel Brine confirmed this in an interview with Ruth Holdsworth in 2006, stating, 'Live Art as a term does seem particular to the UK in the way that we mean it. [...] The practices are not unique, but the terminology is.'[34] In its most fortuitous manifestations, Live Art operates as a levelling ground, in which audiences are provided a charged space in which to experience varied, contradictory, and challenging performances. In other instances, though, the Live Art sector can also feel like a false economy – 'a tiny cottage industry at the peripheries', as Neil Bartlett describes Live Art in this book – or a parochial system for presenting work that sometimes feels unhelpfully cut off from the wider histories and conventions of artistic production.

34. Cited in Ruth Marie Holdsworth, 'Curating Risk', unpublished PhD thesis, University of Bristol, 2011, p. 10.

Between

The opening festival of the Tate Tanks performance venue in 2012 – in refurbished vaults adjoining the Turbine Hall in Tate Modern in London – was greeted with some raised eyebrows in the sector, when among an impressive roster of 41 events by international artists, only one was presented by an artist associated with Live Art in the UK (Harold Offeh's homage to the work of Vito Acconci). This striking lapse occurred in spite of the Tanks' characterisation by broadcast media as an opportunity to 'introduce Live Art to the mainstream'.[35] At least tacitly, Tate distinguished relevant visual art performance from the contemporary Live Art sector, opting instead for international visual, performance or dance artists like Tania Bruguera, Anne Teresa de Keersmaeker, Mike Kelley, Suzanne Lacy, and Boris Charmatz. So, while the striking similarities between practitioners active in the Live Art sector and those working in performance beyond the sector's remit might suggest little that is constitutively unique in the modes of production and presentation

35. *Art in Action* was the inaugural series at Tate Tanks, which ran for fifteen weeks from 18 July to 28 October 2012. See Charlotte Higgins, 'Tate Modern unlocks Tanks and introduces live art into mainstream', in Guardian (17 July 2011), 3.

associated with Live Art in the UK, ideological assumptions at the levels of cultural policy and curatorial practice in fact separate out sectors and parallel discursive histories.

In other words, Tate's dismissal of Live Art reinforces the Live Art sector's disciplinary isolation from the major institutional remit of visual art. The visual arts sector in the UK – its institutions and organs of promotion, canonicity, and sale – generally celebrates works of performance that are geographically or historically remote, yet frequently overlooks the achievements of artists on its doorstep, namely those whose provisional allegiances to Live Art seem to signal their unassailable difference. This difference conditions a type of ghettoisation, perhaps as one unfortunate effect of the Live Art sector's longstanding project of self-definition as a distinct 'cultural strategy'. As Live Art has consistently redefined itself as an independent, self-sufficient sector – through policy decisions, festivals, support networks, and institutions – it has perhaps become conspicuously easy for the mainstream of visual art and theatre to ignore its achievements.

This unhappy effect has occurred against the best intentions and valuable contributions of Live Art's most vocal and active guardians. The most influential definition of Live Art as a boundary crossing, shape shifting, itinerant set of practices is that given by Lois Keidan. Formerly a policy officer at ACGB, and later the Director of Live Arts programming at the ICA in London, Keidan is also a co-founder and Director of the Live Art Development Agency, a cultural institution in London that assists artists, programmers and funders, and houses a publishing wing and an archive. As an authority on the development of Live Art in the UK and Europe, Keidan is well placed to define the term. Influentially, Keidan defines Live Art not as a form but as a 'cultural strategy' typical of artists who refuse disciplinary and historical categories such as theatre, visual art, or dance. She writes, 'Live Art is a framing device for a catalogue of approaches to the possibilities of liveness by artists who chose to work across, in between, and at the edges of more traditional artistic forms.'[36]

Keidan has in many ways been a lone voice in defining Live Art, because of a tendency to shy away from such attempts. As a result, Keidan's cumulative efforts to define and chart Live Art have sometimes been mistaken for statements of orthodoxy. For example, Beth Hoffmann has questioned Keidan's representation of traditional art forms as foils to experimental strategies. Hoffmann argues that by positing theatre, especially, as a straw man to be demolished or negated, Live Art 'emerges not from a model of positive affinity and formal resemblance between works, but from a principle of non-identity'. Hoffmann argues this conceives theatre as a monolith, which artists subsequently profess to disrupt or abandon, perhaps lending new work a political edge or iconoclastic tenor that it may in fact lack. The tendency to describe Live Art in terms of its refusals of stable identity, she continues, rhetorically assumes 'a transgression that in turn serves as an efficacious "cultural strategy",' nevertheless obscuring the more complex relations between contemporary innovations and their historical precedents.[37]

The emphasis on Live Art as operating between – as opposed to against, outside, or regardless of – institutionalised practices has a variety

36. Lois Keidan and Daniel Brine, 'Live Art in London', in *PAJ* 81 (2005), 74-82 (p. 74).

37. Beth Hoffmann, 'Radicalism and the Theatre in Genealogies of Live Art', in *Performance Research*, 14.1 (2009), pp. 95–105 (pp. 101–2).

of unfortunate effects on histories of the sector. As one effect, perhaps, many of the key artists of the recent past have slipped from historical memory, or seem no longer relevant to the ways in which a history of contemporary performance in the UK is generally written. For example, in 1987, the Arts Council of Great Britain commissioned and published *Live Art Now*.[38] In its pages, key figures include Stephen Taylor Woodrow, Rose English, Bow Gamelan Ensemble (Anne Bean and Paul Burwell), Stuart Brisley, Alastair MacLennan, Gary Stevens, Nigel Rolfe, Dogs in Honey, and Annie Griffin. While some of these artists – Brisley, Bean, and MacLennan – are more frequently discussed in performance histories, other figures are no longer readily acknowledged. Some found fame in other fields, either on account of disenchantment with the field, or simply to pursue new interests: Taylor Woodrow and Griffin left Live Art for careers in television, and when Dogs in Honey disbanded, Stephen Jones fronted the British pop band, Babybird. Similarly, other key figures of the 1970s and 1980s gave up performance for more marketable forms, for example Brisley, Marc Camille Chaimowicz, Gilbert and George, John Latham, and Bruce McLean, who focused variously on video, sculpture, and painting. Indeed, as Richard Layzell notes, these latter artists 'emerged as closest to household names in performance art'.[39] Disconcertingly, Live Art is characterised by a glass ceiling that seems to require artists to find fame or fortune in other fields. The apparent barring of recognition in major venues is one such signal of this limitation. This institutional hostility or indifference to Live Art suggests a serious hindrance to the career development of artists working in performance. Yet it also suggests Live Art has a powerful status as a creative engine of sorts, a laboratory of ideas – even a rite of passage – that inspires the development of other more institutionally viable art forms.

In *Live Art Now*, Jeni Walwyn rejects the familiar myth of the 'death' of performance art or Live Art, noting such suspicions usually emerge from the arts establishment itself – critics, curators, and art historians – who have 'tended to treat the medium as if it was a movement which has come and gone'.[40] Its rumoured 'death', she argues, overlooks how Live Art continues to inform other media, for example through its impact upon film, dance, sound art, and sculpture. The work of Mike Figgis is a case in point. He was a member of the People Show in the 1970s, and an artist in his own right; he has since gone on to become a noted mainstream filmmaker. Similar trajectories can be seen in the careers of artists such as Franko B, Bobby Baker, Neil Bartlett, or Rose English, whose diverse careers began in Live Art venues yet embraced mainstream spaces of artistic production in later years, including museums, major theatres, and international festivals.

In the conclusion to her 1991 report, Keidan notes that the partial and selective assimilation of marginal arts practices into mainstream culture is an inevitable development. However, she adds, 'The seedbed of such work must be nurtured,' and the artists with whom experimentation originates 'must be recognised as the pioneers who chart the new territories for us all.'[41] The 'between-ness' of Live Art therefore should not be mistaken for a suggestion of its inherent marginality, or minority appeal. Tracey Warr writes that after the Performance Art Promoters Scheme was established

38. Jeni Walwyn, Tracey Warr and Gray Watson, *Live Art Now* (London: Arts Council of Great Britain, 1987).

39. Richard Layzell, 'Beginnings in Britain', in *Live Art*, pp. 25–28 (p. 26).

40. Jeni Walwyn 'Performance Art in Britain, 1985–87', in *Live Art Now*, n.p.

41. Keidan, *National Arts and Media Strategy*, p. 20.

42. Tracey Warr, 'Introduction', in *Live Art Now*, n.p.

in 1985, there was a boom in the presentation of Live Art, and huge rises in the numbers of visitors to events in a range of spaces.[42] She discusses performance events in an industrial estate in Halifax, on spare land in the Isle of Dogs, a shopping precinct in Sheffield, a park in Swindon, and disused swimming pools in Nottingham and Brighton. Other more established venues included the Royal Albert Hall, and municipal galleries like the Laing in Newcastle, or the City Art Galleries in Manchester. Despite the unusual choice of venues in many cases, Warr notes that these events were often very well attended. Shown at Southampton Art Gallery, Taylor Woodrow's *The Living Paintings* (1987) was attended by 50,000 people – more than the previous record in 1976, when the gallery exhibited the F. A. Cup. Live Art may celebrate its own 'underground' status, but it also has broad public appeal in some instances.

Walwyn notes the discursive problems Live Art poses, as a sector that has 'suffered from a burden of history, texts, teaching and funding guidelines.' 'Although [Live Art] has not died,' she continues, 'it has to a certain extent been institutionalised. It can no longer consider itself illegitimate or underground.'[43] In *Performance Magazine*, artist Rose Garrard noted a similar problem, laying the full weight of responsibility on the scarcity of knowledgeable and committed writers in the UK, which restricts artists' access to international critical reception. In a review of the Symposium d'Art-Performance in Lyon (May 1981), organised by Orlan and Hubert Besacier, Garrard argued that the work of participating UK artists such as Rolfe, Chaimowicz and Brisley (and international artists including Heinz Cibulka, Tom Marioni, and Carolee Schneemann) suffers because the art press fails to cover it. 'As a result', Garrard writes, 'the rich variety of performance art in Britain is little known abroad and has become increasingly isolated from the outside world'.[44] Moreover, she adds, 'In Britain the role of live work is often read inaccurately as polarised in opposition to the art object. The more integrated history of innovative forms in Europe creates a less paranoid approach.'[45] She asks implicitly for a wider critical understanding of the historical traditions being interrogated by a broad range of artists in the period.

43. Walwyn, n.p.

44. Rose Garrard, 'Lyon Performance Festival', in *Performance Magazine*, 13 (September/October 1981), 30–31 (p. 30).

45. Garrard, p. 31.

46. Kaye, p. 1.

47. See Michel Foucault, *The History of Sexuality, Vol. 1: The Will to Knowledge*, trans by Robert Hurley (London: Penguin Books, 1981); Douglas Crimp, 'How to have Promiscuity in an Epidemic', in *Melancholia and Moralism: Essays on AIDS and Queer Politics* (Cambridge and London: MIT Press, 2002); Tim Dean, *Unlimited Intimacy: Reflections on the Subculture of Barebacking* (Chicago and London: University of Chicago Press, 2009).

In this section, I have suggested that Live Art is frequently characterised as a set of practices that derives its political acumen from the ability to evade institutional endorsement, sponsorship, or control. If the cultural politics of Live Art is dependent on its strategically 'mobile' position between established forms, I am interested in the stakes and terms of what Nick Kaye called its 'slipperiness'.[46] What are the cultural politics of mobility more generally, from which Live Art derives its positive value as a set of practices or discourses that elude classification? Mobility has been understood as a useful tactic in cultural theory, especially for sexual subcultures. Queer theorists have argued that the frequent promiscuity of gay men's desires – a practical deployment of mobility towards the pursuit of sexual encounters – should be celebrated as a positive model for sexual ethics. Yet such a theorisation is not neatly transposable to other discourses or practices.[47]

What might be at stake in the argument that the cultural politics of Live Art emerges from its ability to evade the eye of power, below the radar of institutions, scholarship, criticism, and so on? In the UK major institutions are for the most part rather rigidly organised around particular practices or histories that are fairly narrowly defined. Live Art comes to characterise itself as an 'outcast' sector, a wayward collection of interstitial, marginalised, or failed practices. My suspicion is that this works well for curators and promoters of Live Art, who capitalise on the cachet of subversion that accompanies marginality, but it has complex material effects for artists. Caught in the interstices of institutional remits, sectors, histories and markets, Live Art practitioners do not necessarily capitalise on the suggested possibilities that marginality and mobility seem to suggest, but rather find themselves occupying a series of materially unhelpful fringe or 'ghettoised' phenomena.

The institutionalisation of Live Art also seems to suggest that mobility is inevitably a politically advantageous experience. However, it has sometimes tended to ensure the marginal status of Live Art practitioners without any of the benefits that accrue to 'properly' (sexually) marginal subjects: subcultural identification, community, agency, pleasure, and so on. Often, evading the eye of power simply means a stable position outside the archive, beyond the canon, or compensatory participation within a minor archive.

Desire and Identity

An emphasis on identity and identity politics has been a mainstay of performance art and Live Art, since the late 1960s at least. Their prevalence has intensified since the revival of antagonistic performance styles in the 'golden age' of Live Art in the UK, namely the 1990s. Yet Live Art is a 'broad church', and examinations of identity politics in Live Art have persisted amid the trend towards participatory, relational, applied, or socially engaged Live Art. My own interests and preferences generally have tended towards an investment in what might broadly be called identity-based Live Art and performance. My discussions here, and the artists I privilege in my analysis, similarly tend away from those who rely on the activations supposedly inherent in relational art. I raise this not as an apologia for the exclusions that characterise the present chapter – or the edited collection it appears in – but because the histories we may construct of a sector, a practice, a form, or a genre, are irrevocably shaped by the desires and personal imperatives that we uphold in our political and other subjective commitments. There can be no objective history of a field of cultural production. Yet it is important to attempt to be forthright about our desires, imperatives, and repressions (as much as this is ever possible), and to lay our exclusions and inclusions open to deliberation.

'Relational aesthetics' has become a buzzword of contemporary art theory and criticism since the publication of Nicolas Bourriaud's book of the same name, published in French in 1998, and in English translation in 2002. For Bourriaud, the participatory works he discusses in *Relational Aesthetics* are in many ways incompatible with formally similar performances programmed in Live Art festivals and one-off events, which nevertheless use similar tactics of appropriation and *détournement*, to involve audiences in participatory means. In Live Art examples include variations on familiar forms such as Laura Godfrey Isaacs's alternative village fêtes, Joshua Sofaer's treasure hunts, Yara El Sherbini's pub quizzes, or Richard Dedomenici's sporting event using office chairs.

Bourriaud defined relational aesthetics as 'an art taking as its theoretical horizon the realm of human interactions and its social context, rather than the assertion of an independent and *private* symbolic space'.[48] Yet Bourriaud's prime examples are institutionally endorsed artists who present participatory projects in commercial galleries, public museums, or art biennales, complicating his artificial distinction between the progressive condition of relationality and the retrograde emphasis that other artists might place on 'private', personal or otherwise 'symbolic' practices of representation. Whereas the former seemingly open up new and democratic perspectives on human interaction, Bourriaud argues that the latter are 'falsely aristocratic'. He means that modes of spectatorship emphasising seeing, hearing and feeling defer to a kind of modernist connoisseurship, wrapped up in processes of appreciation and acquisition. His account is muddied by the unresolved contradiction between the apparently anti-capitalist sensibility of relational practices – nevertheless sponsored by commercial and corporate ventures – and 'aristocratic' practices that nevertheless operate outside of capitalist logics of reception and consumption.

Claire Bishop has damningly critiqued relational and participatory art's attempts to feign a cultural politics, showing that their frequently ameliorative imperatives often work by substituting a lightweight sense of democracy for more ambivalent political investments, on the part of artists and audiences. As long as the attempt to produce (usually meagre) effects of social inclusion take precedence over aesthetic achievements, she writes, 'there can be no failed unsuccessful, unresolved, or boring works of participatory art, because all are equally essential to the task of repairing the social bond.'[49] While Bishop's contemporary examples mostly focus on gallery artists, we can add 'relational' Live Art practices quite neatly to her objects of critique. Participatory and 'socially engaged' art tends to posit transparent ideological positions, and easy solutions, she argues, and foreclose the more political efficacious modes of critical spectatorship that less palatable forms may enable. Bishop has explained these shortcomings persuasively, arguing rightly that while relational art professes political engagement, it does so by producing limited effects that are too convivial to generate realisable solutions. Of the tendency of artists and apologists to 'self-censor' the range of effects and affects they incite, Bishop writes, 'idiosyncratic or controversial ideas are subdued and normalised in favour of a consensual behaviour upon whose irreproachable sensitivity we can all rationally agree.'[50] Bishop calls persuasively for antagonistic spurs to a revivified politics of spectatorship, arguing for 'unease, discomfort or frustration – along with fear, contradiction, exhilaration and absurdity', as a potent antidote to the 'over-solicitousness that judges in advance what people are capable of coping with [that] can be just as insidious as intending to offend them'.[51] Yet Bishop's argument does not acknowledge Live Art

48. Nicolas Bourriaud, *Relational Aesthetics*, trans. by Simon Pleasance, Fronza Woods, and Mathieu Copeland (Dijon: Les Presses du réel, 2002), p. 14.

49. Claire Bishop, *Artificial Hells: Participatory Art and the Politics of Spectatorship* (New York: Verso, 2012), p. 13.

50. Ibid., p. 26.

51. Bishop, p. 26.

in the UK, either as examples of the 'over-solicitousness' of relational art, or of the progressive forms that celebrate 'unease' towards more progressive goals.

For Bourriaud, relational aesthetics emerges in the 1990s, as a decade in which art took on a utopian project: encouraging 'conviviality' and 'sociability', rather than less palatable ways of experiencing the world.[52] If the history of art and performance is opened up to an overview of practices that took place outside of the narrow confines of commercial galleries, the 1990s reflects the aggressive, distasteful and wilfully antagonistic practices that Bishop calls for, but exceeds the range of artists she deems worthy of critique. This hidden history is typified by the plenitude of performances imported into the ICA in London, especially between the years 1993 and 1996, under the inimitable influence of Lois Keidan, then Director of Live Arts Programming at the ICA (1992–97). Works by 'visiting' artists (including Karen Finley, Ron Athey, the Hittite Empire, Tim Miller, Penny Arcade, Mehmet Sander, Albert Vidal, Guillermo Gómez-Peña, or Kate Bornstein), and UK-based artists such as Franko B, Robert Pacitti, Marisa Carnesky, Giovanna Maria Casseta, SuAndi cannot be shoehorned into the amiable typology that Bourriaud provides, but relate neatly to many of the imperatives that Bishop demands from politically engaged participatory arts and performance.

Strikingly, both Bourriaud's theory and Bishop's critique achieve their divergent objectives by suggesting the supposed ineffectiveness or anachronism of identity politics. Bourriaud disregards such work with a convenient (though unconvincing) sleight of hand. He states that antagonistic work about identity politics – the cultural politics of sexuality, gender, race, or nationality – is anachronistic, at best, for 'any stance that is "directly" critical of society is futile, if based on the illusion of a marginality that is nowadays impossible, not to say regressive'.[53] Bishop makes similar arguments towards opposing ends, stating: 'sensitivity to difference risks becoming a new kind of repressive norm', and '[the] solution implied by the discourse of social exclusion is simply the goal of transition across the boundary from excluded to included, to allow people to access the holy grail of self-sufficient consumerism'.[54] As a result, a whole range of artists working with participation in Live Art towards uneasy or discomfiting politics are excluded from her history, from Franko B's iconic early one-to-one performances, to more recent participatory works by Ron Athey or Kira O'Reilly.

Bourriaud's statement is a privileged but untenable suspicion about the anachronism of particularity in an age of supposed multiculturalism, social tolerance, and improved rights for minorities. Bishop argues the inadequacy of identity politics on account of its supposed apologia for neoliberalism. Identity politics, and the art that supports its claims, are deemed politically irrelevant, formerly to celebrate convivial art, and latterly to demean conviviality in favour of antagonistic art. In both instances, however, the imperatives to trash identity and its politics are fuelled by an undisclosed taste culture, a predilection or subjective investment in favour of certain practices and against others, but one that cannot be disclosed without throwing the autonomy of the hierarchising impulse into disrepute. 'The desire to rid art of subject matter', Henry

52. Bourriaud, pp. 29–31.

53. Ibid., p. 31.

54. Bishop, pp. 25, 13.

55. Henry M. Sayre, *The Object of Performance: The American Avant-garde since 1970* (Chicago and London: Chicago University Press, 1989), p. 41.

56. Bourriaud, p. 61.

57. Amelia Jones, *Seeing Differently: A Theory and History of Identification and the Visual Arts* (London and New York: Routledge), p. 220.

58. While Bishop has not published her criticisms about Live Art, she explained her suspicions about its anachronism in 'Delegated Performance', unpublished paper presented at Performance Studies international, PSi#14, University of Copenhagen, 23 August 2008.

59. Peggy Phelan, *Unmarked: The Politics of Performance* (London and New York: Routledge, 1993), p. 148.

60. Peggy Phelan, 'Violence and Rupture: Misfires of the Ephemeral', in *Live Art in LA: Performance in Southern California, 1970–1983*, ed. by Phelan (New York and London: Routledge, 2012), pp. 1–38 (p. 9).

Sayre has written, 'to claim for it an autonomous self-reflexivity, has long been one of the primary concerns of the modernist enterprise.'[55]

Bourriaud and Bishop's accounts are, variously, manifestations of the neo-modernist refusal to disclose authorial desire. In doing so, each argument is a smokescreen for the institutional strategy that marginalises Live Art, by performing the formalist suspicion that identity-based work is autobiographical or invested, narcissistic, essentialist, marginal, elitist, or simply old hat. Bourriaud claims that 'in this day and age, feminism, anti-racism and environmentalism all operate too frequently as lobbies playing the power game' and that each cannot 'call itself into question in a structural way'.[56] The politics of this disingenuous claim have been put under devastating scrutiny by Amelia Jones in her recent book *Seeing Differently*, where she argues that theoretical accounts of the contemporary moment as 'post-identity' fail to acknowledge the persistent lived experiences of individuals who lay claim to identifications outside the hegemonic subject position of white, male, middle class privileges:

> It is not viable nor politically acceptable to state that we are post-identity in such a world in which anxieties about being human become deadly and violent behaviors toward others. [We] cannot continue to act as if issues of identification do not condition every engagement we have with art, as with culture more broadly construed and with others in general.[57]

A cliché of discussions about histories of Live Art conveniently designates identity-based performance as nostalgic, anachronistic, or irrelevant to the contemporary political or cultural climate.[58] Countering this tendency, it is important to emphasise the persistence of identity and its politics as fertile conjunctions of themes for artists and audiences alike.

Iconicity

Beyond its marginality in specific academic disciplines, Live Art also begs the question of the generic subjugation of performance more broadly, as 'the runt of the litter' in the contemporary repertoire of formal strategies, to borrow Peggy Phelan's memorable description of performance art. Phelan argues that performance 'clogs the smooth machinery of reproductive representation', as part of its 'ontological' resistance to reproduction, in visual records that attest to the fullness and density of live performance.[59] Rethinking her earlier suspicions about the ontological distinctions between photography and performance, Phelan has more recently noted, 'To consider seriously the history of live art, therefore, we must begin with the photographic arts and acknowledge the capacity to complicate the ideological and psychological difficulties raised by the ephemeral broadly.'[60] Rather than recanting her formidable earlier argument, she acknowledges that visual studies has developed useful skills that can be deployed towards addressing the major contributions that have been made in Live Art and related ephemeral or time-based practices.

Phelan's sophisticated account of the ontology of performance in *Unmarked* was a milestone of performance studies, and has definitively influenced the discipline's understanding of the distinction between the live, ephemeral event of performance, and the plastic traces that is the photographic document. As a closing remark, I suggest that the iconicity of the photographic document poses a useful means of overcoming – at least provisionally – the sectorial condition of Live Art in the UK. If the institutionalisation of Live Art as an apparently self-sufficient sector, as a theme in cultural policy, and as a funding category has had a ghettoising effect, the photographic records of Live Art are apt to circulate in seemingly less fettered ways. Photographs allow the ephemeral, sometimes marginal event of Live Art to 'speak' beyond itself, in temporal, geographical, formal terms, exceeding the bounds of the sector that has been constructed to underpin it.[61]

The two crucial photographers whose work facilitates this expansion are Manuel Vason and Hugo Glendinning. Both fulfil an iconographical function, translating the sometimes 'provincial' Live Art event into an object that travels into apparently inaccessible spaces, including magazines and other publications, galleries, and museums. Similarly, the canonical status of a handful of individual works of performance art works in the 1960s and 1970s has been ensured by iconic images that have become ubiquitous features of its written histories. Performance art in the period is arguably précised by compelling images: a stunned Chris Burden touching his left arm punctured by a sharpshooter's bullet, in *Shoot* (1971; the photographer is never named); Joseph Beuys wrapped in a felt blanket as a coyote grips it in its teeth, in *I Like America and America Likes Me* (1974; photograph by Caroline Tisdall); or Carolee Schneemann daubed in paint, reading a length of paper pulled from her vagina, in *Interior Scroll* (1975; photograph by Anthony McCall).

In terms of the iconographic translation of Live Art, Hugo Glendinning's photographs of Forced Entertainment are an enduring document of the company's work. He was also commissioned to document the performances that took place at the Live Art Development Agency's *Live Culture* programme at Tate Modern in March 2003.[62] Glendinning's photographs of artists are iconic documents, recording live events using a clean, almost photojournalistic aesthetic that reduces extraneous interference and distils the event into a series of accessible images. Manuel Vason's practice exploits the iconographical enterprise in different ways. In Vason's collaborative partnerships with artists, a performance is either restaged anew or uniquely developed, specifically for his camera. The images differ in principle from conventional documentation of performance – including Glendinning's images of Live Art events, and the canonical images of performance art mentioned above by McCall or Tisdall – in that Vason is always the sole witness to the singular live event, which takes place in a space of the artists' choosing, without the presence of an audience. His process always categorically resists the tendency to try and sum up a temporal performance in an iconic image that is deemed representative of a larger, unseen whole.[63]

This removal of the record from the traditional documentary function troubles the wishful strategy of transparency and authenticity recreated

61. Key accounts of the document's contradictory claims to iconicity and authenticity include: Philip Auslander, 'The Performativity of Performance Documentation', in *PAJ: A Journal of Performance and Art*, 84:28.3 (2006), 1–10; Rebecca Schneider, 'Performance Remains', in *Performance Research*, 6.2 (2001), 100–108 Tracey Warr, 'Image as Icon: Recognising the Enigma', in *Art, Lies and Videotape: Exposing Performance*, exh. cat., Tate Liverpool (London: Tate, 2004), pp. 30–37.

62. See Glenginning's images throughout *Live: Art and Performance*, ed. by Adrian Heathfield (London: Tate, 2004).

63. For a more detailed analysis of Vason's practice, see my 'Passing Intimacies: Manuel Vason's Photographic Encounters', in *Manuel Vason: Encounters – Photography, Performance, Collaboration*', ed. by Dominic Johnson (Bristol: Arnolfini, 2007), pp. 10–17.

in many photographic histories of performance. Moreover, it emphasises the willfully inauthentic, iconographic function I am signaling here. Vason's collaborative documents have been shown in touring solo and group exhibitions, and widely reproduced in books, magazines, and academic journals. In his most recent book *Encounters* (2007), the works of artists such as Oreet Ashery, Ernst Fischer, Alistair MacLennan, and Kira O'Reilly – all familiar participants in festivals and venues associated with the Live Art sector – rub against artists who are arguably more at home in other sectors or programming circuits: the sculptor Stuart Brisley; the drag-based visual artist and musician Vaginal Davis; South African performance artist Steven Cohen; or Los Angeles-based cabaret performers Velvet Hammer Burlesque. Similarly, in Adrian Heathfield's *Live* (2004), Glendinning's images of artists associated with Live Art, such as Franko B or Forced Entertainment, are placed alongside international performance practitioners including Marina Abramović, Chris Burden, Guillermo Gómez-Peña, or Paul McCarthy. With all the caveats that attend the discussion of images in lieu of live events, the sectoralisation of Live Art seems less precise and limiting when the works are approached through the highly mediated format of iconic images, for example in published collections.

In conclusion, the discourses that have been variously developed to discuss Live Art cannot be easily reconfigured, repealed, nor dispelled. Yet neither should they be ignored. Amelia Jones provides a striking critique of – and redress to – the exclusionary tendencies of art history, noting that the archives of Live Art and performance art can be analysed as much for what they include as for what they actively or passively exclude. 'What prompts later artists, curators, and scholars to be interested' in a particular history, she writes, 'is of course largely ideological.' Analysing examples of Live Art in LA, Jones shows that institutional archives can be suspect on account of the individual and minority histories they fail to account for. 'The rise and fall of intellectual or curatorial trends', Jones argues, 'themselves linked to generational shifts and political, economic, and social pressures, leads to the formation of certain archives and the retrieval of particular kinds of works'.[64] I hope to have shown that Live Art – as a term, as a sector, and as a peripatetic and imprecise set of artists' practices – should be discussed with attention to the real situations in which it circulates for artists and for the venues they present their work in, to ensure the progressive expansion of contemporary histories of performance in the UK. As Stuart Hall writes, 'Despite the sophistication of our scholarly and critical apparatus in art criticism, history, and theory, we are still not that far advanced in finding ways of thinking about the relationship between the work and the world,' as our sophistication is undermined either by over-determining the connection, or by suppressing the 'worldliness' of the work of art.[65] Through a renewed attention to the complex relations between art, artists, and their particular worlds, a sensitive historical awareness of Live Art may be devised and fostered.

64. Amelia Jones, 'Lost Bodies: Early 1970s Performance Art in Art History', in *Live Art in LA*, pp. 115–84 (p. 118). Jones' title refers to 'performance art', as opposed to 'Live Art'. However the two terms are potentially interchangeable here.

65. Stuart Hall, 'Assembling the 1980s: The Deluge – and After', in *Shades of Black*, pp. 1–20 (pp. 18-9).

Towards a Prehistory of Live Art in the UK

Heike Roms and Rebecca Edwards

In 1994, *Contemporary Theatre Review* published a special issue on Live Art in the UK, entitled 'British Live Art: Essays and Documentations'. In his introduction, editor Nick Kaye outlines a brief history of the term – 'Live Art' – and the field of artistic practices it had come to stand for.[1] Beginning by establishing its resistance to any formal definition as one of the defining features of Live Art, Kaye goes on to consider its historical and geographical specificity vis-à-vis its close relative, performance art. Performance art, he argues, is both a historical precursor and a contemporary component of Live Art. As a past artistic practice, performance art generated two distinct traditions, according to Kaye: a North American and continental European approach on the one hand, and a British approach on the other. The former is characterized by him as emerging in the early 1960s 'through a reconceiving of the object in sculpture, a reaching beyond the physical frame of the work in painting, through new compositional procedures in music and developments in dance'.[2] In contrast, performance art in Britain underwent a 'very different' development:

> Emerging some ten years after its counterpart in the US and continental Europe, British 'performance art' of the late 1960s and early 1970s was not only shadowed by the strength of the politically radical and largely text-based alternative British theatre, but shared some of its practices and concerns.[3]

The result was 'a "theatricality" somehow connected to and yet at one remove from the prevailing languages and practices of "theatre" and "drama"'.[4] It is from this 'uncertain point of "difference"'[5] to the

1. Nick Kaye, 'Introduction – Live Art: Definition and Documentation', *Contemporary Theatre Review*, 2.2 (1994), 1–7.

2. Ibid., p. 2.

3. Ibid.

4. Ibid., p. 3.

5. Ibid.

6. The British roots of the term 'performance art' are difficult to locate. Jeff Nuttall credits himself and Roland Miller (when members of The People Show) as having invented it 'to differentiate between what we were doing and what had always been called theatre' and cites modernist traditions of poetry and painting as inspirations (Jeff Nuttall, without title, *Studio International*, 195.991–2 (1981), 54–55 (p. 54)). The fact is that in 1973 the Arts Council of Great Britain had a Performance Art Committee (a subcommittee of its Art Panel), consisting of Miller, Adrian Henri, Gavin Henderson and Ted Little (The Arts Council of Great Britain, *Twenty-Ninth Annual Report and Accounts 1973–1974* (London: Arts Council of Great Britain, 1974)) and that from the mid-1970s on the name was firmly established in Britain (if not always appreciated by all the artists it labelled), appearing in the titles of funding schemes, festivals and publications.

7. The genealogy of the term in the USA is even less certain. RoseLee Goldberg suggests that the term 'was first used very loosely by artists in the early 1960s in the USA' but does not provide a source (RoseLee Goldberg, 'Performance Art', in *From Expressionism to Post-Modernism (The Grove Dictionary of Art)*, ed. by Jane Turner (London: Macmillan Reference, 2000), pp. 294–302 (p. 294). For an account of the history of the term see Bruce

dominant practices of theatre, he proposes, that British performance art eventually developed in the 1980s into Live Art – a development that was characterized for Kaye by a more explicit re-engagement with the formal language of the theatre that had been shadowing performance art in Britain since its emergence.

Our main interest here lies not in questions of nomenclature but in the historical trajectory that Kaye sketches out as it sums up two widely held assumptions concerning the history of performance art and Live Art in Britain: firstly, that performance art in this country has owed more to the formal vocabularies and concerns of theatre than to those of fine art; and secondly, that artists in Britain began to create works that could be characterized as performance art from around the late 1960s, a decade or so after artists in North America (John Cage, Jim Dine, Al Hansen, Dick Higgins, Allan Kaprow, Alison Knowles, Claes Oldenburg, Yoko Ono, Robert Rauschenberg, Carolee Schneemann and others) and continental Europe (Joseph Beuys, Robert Filliou, Yves Klein, Jean-Jacques Lebel, Ben Vautier, Wolf Vostell and others) began to experiment with Happenings, actions, 'dé-coll/ages' and Fluxus events. It is both these assumptions that we would like to subject to closer scrutiny in this essay. While it is correct that performance art as a term was not in established use in Britain until about the early 1970s[6], this seemed to have also been the case for North America and continental Europe.[7] The American and European performance-based, event-structured art practices of the 1950s and 1960s are now commonly regarded as performance art *avant la lettre* and are cited as milestones in most available historical accounts of the art form. This retrospective attribution is certainly not without its problems, as it risks overlooking the formal specificities and contextual contingencies of, for example, Happenings or Fluxus events by lumping them all together under the catch-all label 'performance art'.[8] But our question here is not so much whether such a rhetorical move is justified. Rather, we are asking whether, if we accept that the work of the 1960s was part of an artistic development that later came to be named 'performance art' in the USA and continental Europe (as Kaye and others have done), why do we not also claim this work for the history of performance art and Live Art in Britain?

Throughout the 1960s artists based in Britain (Mark Boyle and Joan Hills, Ian Breakwell, Cornelius Cardew, Bob Cobbing, Ivor Davies, George Brecht, Adrian Henri, Bruce Lacey, Brian Lane, John Latham, Gustav Metzger, Jeff Nuttall, Robin Page and many others) staged Happenings and Fluxus concerts, explored Event Structures and created Auto-Destructive Art demonstrations and introduced performative approaches into fields such as art, poetry, music and cinema – yet their work is these days rarely considered in the context of a history of British performance art or Live Art. Certain outstanding events have, of course, received attention: the Fluxus *Festival of Misfits* in London in 1962, the infamous 'Nude Happening' in Edinburgh in 1963 and the *Destruction in Art Symposium* in London in 1966 frequently appear as landmark events in accounts of the 1960s neo-avant-garde. They have as yet, however, to be fully claimed as belonging to the history of performance art in the UK.[9] We want to propose that, in their attempt

Barber, 'Indexing: Conditionalism and its Heretical Equivalents', in Al Bronson and Peggy Gale (eds), *Performance by Artists* (Toronto: Art Metropole), pp. 183–204.

8. Amelia Jones has proposed that the term 'performance art' is also inappropriate for a description of the body art practices of the early 1970s (which are often only accessible through documentation) as the term encompasses 'any kind of theatricalized production on the part of a visual artist' and presupposes a live event. Amelia Jones, '"Presence" in Absentia: Experiencing Performance as Documentation', *Art Journal*, 56.4 (Winter 1997), 11–18 (p. 18).

9. Early accounts of performance activities in Britain have tended to be more inclusive: see, for example, Adrian Henri, *Environments and Happenings* (London: Thames and Hudson, 1974); Jeff Nuttall, *Bomb Culture* (London: MacGibbon & Kee, 1968); and Jeff Nuttall, *Performance Art: Memoirs Vol. 1* (London: John Calder, 1979). Henri and Nuttall both locate performance within an expanded field of new forms of artistic practice, arising from painting, sculpture, poetry and music, connected in Henri's case through an address to the totality of the work's environmental dimension, in Nuttall's case through strategies of juxtaposition and the use of found objects.

10. Sandy Craig, for example, refers to 1960s performance

to identify a 'British' tradition for performance art and Live Art, many histories of the art form have tended to overlook this work, not because it occurred before the term was coined, but because it had few distinctive – or distinctively 'British' – traits.[10] It emerged in the early 1960s from international networks and collaborations, often involving precisely those artists from North America and continental Europe who, as Kaye puts it, conceptualized their practice 'against the terms and integrities of the work in art rather than in relation to "theatre" or "drama"'.[11]

This essay represents a small effort towards reclaiming the performance works of the 1960s as part of the history (or prehistory) of performance art and Live Art in Britain. The wording here is deliberate: the focus will be on the history of performance art in Britain, not on that of British performance art. The difference is subtle but important: the primary aim is not to identify a manifestation of the art form that is recognizably different from developments elsewhere. We are more interested in how some of the major international developments in artistic experimentation during the period affected – and in turn were affected by – art making in the UK, whether undertaken by artists resident here or by those coming from elsewhere. While the works of the latter may not have been 'British' by way of authorship, the conditions of their making were nonetheless often specific to Britain and its cultural, social and political make-up at the time. In a short essay of this kind we are naturally unable to deliver anything approximating a comprehensive re-appreciation of 1960s performance work in the UK. Instead, we will focus on a couple of select examples. Our primary case in point will be a little-known occasion of experimentation in the 1960s, a Happening staged in Cardiff in 1965.[12] Our purpose is to show that such work was not limited to a handful of events staged in the swinging metropolis,[13] but that it impacted on art making in Britain at the time more widely and deeply. In the context of the present special issue, our main concern thereby will be to examine the possible links that one might be able to draw between these earlier works and the emergence, twenty or so years later, of what came to be called Live Art in the UK.

The Birth Of Live Art From The Spirit Of (Anti-)Theatre?

Let's begin, though, with a comparatively well-known example of 1960s performance experimentation, often referred to as Britain's first Happening.[14] It took place on 7 September 1963 in Edinburgh's McEwan Hall, in the context of the Edinburgh Festival International Drama Conference.[15] The conference was organized by publisher John Calder and brought together a mixture of figures from the theatrical establishment of the time[16] and representatives of the bourgeoning avant-garde scene with the intention to debate the 'Theatre of the Future'. The latter contingent included, from the USA, artist Allan Kaprow, director Kenneth Dewey, critic and playwright Charles Marowitz (then resident in Britain) and, from the UK, artist Mark Boyle. According to Dewey, activities as precursors of the 'alternative theatre' that flourished in 1970s Britain, but proposes that they are 'more representative as the final flings of a European tradition of the avant-garde than as the first gestures of a full-blooded radical alternative' (Sandy Craig, 'Reflexes of the Future', in *Dreams and Deconstructions: Alternative Theatre in Britain*, ed. by Sandy Craig (Ambergate: Amber Lane Press, 1980), pp. 9–29 (p. 15)). Similarly, Catherine Itzin considers Jim Hayne's work in Edinburgh in the 1960s as fertilizing a radical theatre tradition in Britain whose proper beginning she locates, like Craig, in 1968. Catherine Itzin, *Stages in the Revolution: Political Theatre in Britain since 1968* (London: Methuen, 1980), p. 9.

11. Kaye, 'Introduction', p. 2.

12. Research on the Cardiff Happening of 1965 has emerged from our current research project: '"It Was Forty Years Ago Today": Locating the Early History of Performance Art in Wales 1965–1979', <www.performance-wales.org> [accessed 12 November 2011]. The research has been supported by a research grant from the UK's Arts and Humanities Research Council (AHRC) (2009–11). Principal Investigator: Heike Roms, Research Assistant: Rebecca Edwards, <www.ahrc.ac.uk> [accessed 12 November 2011].

13. Indeed, Henri proposes that the experimental performance work in the UK came 'from a provincial rather than a

having been asked [by Calder] to show the Drama Conference a Happenings demonstration, three of us (Charles Lewsen, an English playwright, Mark Boyle, [...], and myself) studied the Conference itself through four days. On the fifth day an eight-minute piece comprised of some fifteen events dealing with Conference themes was introduced back into the Conference. This reportage-type Happening is an alternative to writing a play or essay about the whole thing later.[17]

The 'events' or actions that were carried out in the Happening all apparently 'introduced' a version of the conference 'back into' itself that portrayed it as an outdated, museum-like set-up obsessed with limiting creative and interpretative possibilities. The planned actions included, in Dewey's own words:

A platform speaker (Charles Marowitz) making a pseudo-serious proposal that the conference formally accept, as the definitive interpretation, his explanation of *Waiting For Godot*. An audience member (Charles Lewsen) attacking the speaker for being unclear and not heroic enough. [...] A [...] tape made from fragments of speeches at the conference. [...] An actress on the platform (Carroll Baker) beginning to stare at someone at the back of the hall (Allan Kaprow), eventually taking off a large fur coat and moving towards him across the tops of the audience seats. A nude model (Anne Kesselaar) being whisked across the organ loft on a spotlight stand. [...] A sheep skeleton hung on the giant flat with Cocteau's symbol of the conference. [...] A woman with a baby, and a boy with a radio entering the hall, mounting the platform, looking at everything as if in a museum, and leaving.[18]

The Happening (not unsurprisingly) provoked a very disapproving response from the other conference participants.[19] And Kesselaar's nudity, although only visible for a few seconds, was picked up by a scandal-mongering popular press,[20] which secured the event its subsequent nickname, the 'Nude Happening'.[21]

In a recent essay on 'Radicalism and the Theatre in Genealogies of Live Art', Beth Hoffmann too begins here, at the Edinburgh Happening of 1963.[22] She subjects one of the lengthier chronicles of the event, published by Charles Marowitz in his reminiscences of Britain's art world in the 1960s, to a close reading. She teases out how the playwright's account positions the event 'as a wedge generating vituperative conflict'[23] between – what the 1960s liked to call – the theatrical 'establishment' and the newly emerging experimental 'counterculture'. Hoffmann observes that:

Marowitz seems much more concerned to emphasize the Happening's disruptive qualities, the way it negates a set of expectations about what theatre looks like, rather than to focus on the meanings that the Happening generates and how, as a form, it can be articulated into existing arts practices.[24]

Hoffmann is interested in the Edinburgh Happening as a precursor to Live Art practice, but the link she draws between the event of 1963 and

London context'. Henri, *Environments*, p. 111.

14. Henri cites earlier Happenings being created in Liverpool in 1962, 'as a result of my reading an article by Allan Kaprow earlier that year'. Henri, *Environments*, p. 116.

15. In January of the same year Jim Haynes, Calder and Richard Demarco had founded the influential Traverse Theatre in Edinburgh, which together with the International Festival (and later the Demarco Gallery) made the Scottish capital an important location for new approaches to performance.

16. Including critic Kenneth Tynan (as chair), actor Laurence Olivier, playwrights John Arden, Arnold Wesker, Harold Pinter, Max Frisch and Eugene Ionesco, academic Martin Esslin, and others.

17. Ken Dewey, 'X-ings', *Tulane Drama Review*, 10.2 (Winter 1965), 216–23 (p. 222).

18. Ken Dewey as cited in Charles Marowitz, *Burnt Bridges: A Souvenir of the Swinging Sixties and Beyond* (London: Hodder and Stoughton, 1990), pp. 59–60.

19. Allan Kaprow staged a Happening entitled *Exit Piece* (also known as *Out*) on the same day in the courtyard of the McEwan Hall; see Jeff Kelley, *Childsplay: The Art of Allan Kaprow* (Berkeley: University of California Press, 2004), pp. 93–95. There are reports that another Happening planned by Kaprow (to be entitled *Sea*) was

present practice is not based on continuities of form or style. Rather, she locates such continuities in the manner in which the work has been framed discursively. Putting Marowitz's account alongside selected writings of the past thirty years on Live Art, she concludes that:

> [s]pecifically within the British context, at least, live art emerges not from a model of positive affinity and formal resemblance among works but from a principle of non-identity, the lack of a definition outside the negation, subversion or transgression of a received practice or set of practices [...].[25]

The history of performance art and Live Art in the UK is thus for Hoffmann constituted as a recurrent discursive re-enactment of the assumed break between 'theatre' and 'performance' – figured as 'tradition' versus 'experiment' – that first entered the debate in Britain in the early 1960s. Following Hoffmann, we may therefore conclude that 1963 is the year in which Live Art was born in the UK – not as a specific artistic practice, but as a specific attitude towards artistic practice.

Like Kaye, so Hoffmann too locates this attitude in its 'uncertain point of "difference"' to the vocabularies of theatre.[26] But while Kaye dates its emergence to the late 1960s and the rise of performance art proper, Hoffmann traces it right back to the performance experimentations of the preceding period. Hers is, of course, not an art historical project but one that tries to deconstruct present taken-for-granted conceptualizations by linking them to certain genealogies of discourse formation. But it is worth asking nonetheless whether the birth of performance art or Live Art from the spirit of theatre (or rather the spirit of anti-theatre) was generally characteristic for the performance work of the period in Britain, or whether it became foregrounded at the Edinburgh Happening because of the specific placement of that event within the context of a conference devoted to theatre and drama?

To Begin Again At The Already Begun

Let's begin again, at the already begun. Two years later, in another British city, at another conference, another Happening took place. This time, it was a group of poets who convened in the Welsh capital of Cardiff for a week-long discussion on the 'status, function and future of poetry'.[27] The event, sponsored by the Gulbenkian Foundation and held at the National Museum of Wales' Reardon Smith Lecture Theatre, was part of the British government's high profile *First Commonwealth Arts Festival* of 1965, billed as a celebration of 'the diversity of [...] cultures within the overall unity of the Commonwealth'[28] and as one of the largest arts festivals ever to be staged in the UK. Cardiff had been chosen, alongside London and fellow ports Glasgow and Liverpool, to play host to a range of different cultural events (from the Sydney Symphony Orchestra to the Nigerian Folk Opera), part of which was the *Commonwealth Poetry Conference*.[29] Around sixty poets from all over the Commonwealth and the United States came to Wales (among them future Nobel-prize winner Wole Soyinka and Australian poet Les

cancelled at the insistence of conference chair, Kenneth Tynan; see Hanns Sohm, *happening & fluxus* (Cologne: Kölnischer Kunstverein, 1970), n. p.

20. Kesselaar and Calder were subsequently charged with indecency, but Kesselaar was acquitted and charges against Calder were dropped.

21. Dewey's title for the event appears in some publications as *In Memory of Big Ed*; see Allan Kaprow, *Assemblage, Environments and Happenings* (New York: H. N. Abrams, 1966), pp. 281–84.

22. Beth Hoffmann, 'Radicalism and the Theatre in Genealogies of Live Art', *Performance Research*, 14.1 (Spring 2009), 95–105.

23. Ibid., p. 96.

24. Ibid. In his account of the event Dewey seems far more concerned with notions of form than Marowitz, considering the Happening as having 'freed' text, which he identifies as one of the three 'frames' of theatre (the others being space and time). See Dewey, 'X-ings', p. 221).

25. Hoffmann, 'Radicalism', pp. 100–2.

26. Kaye, 'Introduction', p. 3.

27. Cardiff Commonwealth Arts Festival 1965, *Programme* (Cardiff: Cardiff Commonwealth Arts Festival, 1965), n. p.

28. Ian Hunter, 'A Unique Festival of Commonwealth

Murray). Their gathering was from the outset riddled with conflicts: a group of poets boycotted the event over accusations of bullying, a walk-out was staged in protest of an experimental film programme and there are stories of wrecked hotel rooms and of rampant abuse of the free food and alcohol provision. But the 'major struggle of the week', as local paper, the *Western Mail*, observed succinctly, was 'between traditionalists and the beats'.[30] The 'Beats' were a mixture of US- and UK-based poets who, influenced by American Beat poetry, closely affiliated themselves – artistically and politically – with the 'counterculture': these included Adrian Henri, Roger McGough and Brian Patten (who came to be known as the three original Mersey Poets), Alexander Trocchi, Jeff Nuttall (later founder of The People Show), Michael Horovitz, Paolo Lionni and Dan Richter.

The aesthetic and political battles that divided the conference came to a climax in the concluding event of the week, the Happening. The potential of its happening had been rumoured in the press for days, and it was once postponed, but, on the conference's last evening, 24 September 1965, the Happening, the first to occur in the Welsh capital, finally took place.[31] The organizer of the event was not a poet, but the artist Tom Hudson, newly appointed Director of Studies at Cardiff College of Art. He invited two fellow artists, Frenchman Jean-Jacques Lebel (often credited as the first proponent of Happenings in Europe) and American Fluxus-affiliate, composer Philip Corner, to join the event alongside the Beats. The proceedings kicked off with an unannounced disruption of one of the scheduled poetry readings, when a two-hundredweight pig (allegedly a Vietnamese species hired from a local zoo) was smuggled into the Reardon Smith Lecture Theatre to be presented on stage as part of a lament for the Vietnam War. The actual Happening then followed at a second site, Cardiff's Jackson Hall. This is how the *Western Mail* reporter experienced it:

> While a New York composer [Philip Corner] 'tested' domestic utensils for sound by scraping a microphone across them and pounding them with a hammer, bearded poets reclined on paper to act as human stencils last night at the paint-splashed, long-awaited festival 'happening'. Seventeen-stone Adrian Henry [i.e. Henri], of Liverpool, howled an ode across the prostrate body of a girl art student he had just 'kicked to death after partial strangling.' A woman in a transparent plastic gown jumped with paint-sodden feet into a pile of feathers and draped toilet seats, leaves and bottles on a red, yellow and blue floor mosaic made of paper. [...] Sculptor Jean-Paul Lebelle [i.e. Jean-Jacques Lebel] invited us to place our hands through a pierced screen, thus to receive a hose-pipe [*sic*] that paint had transformed into a garish python [...]. Mr. Tom Hudson, Cardiff College of Art director of studies, supervised an intricate 'aesthetic, satirical assembly line' which passed our entry tickets – humble bits of useless machinery, old clothes or beer bottles – from artist to artist around the howling room until they emerged as things of gruesome beauty. Eerie, ear-splitting noises spat from a tape-recorder as sound-tester Phillip Kerner [i.e. Philip Corner] accepted or rejected our gifts with maniacal concentration. [...] Roger McGough [...] joined [Adrian Henri] and

Image 1 Philip Corner at Cardiff Happening, 24 September 1965. Photographer unknown: photo courtesy of Tom Hudson estate and National Arts Education Archive.

Image 2 Performer at Cardiff Happening, 24 September 1965. Photographer unknown: photo courtesy of Tom Hudson estate and National Arts Education Archive.

Image 3 Performer at Cardiff Happening, 24 September 1965. Photographer unknown: photo courtesy of Tom Hudson estate and National Arts Education Archive.

Image 4 Assemblage of transformed objects at Cardiff Happening, 24 September 1965. Photographer unknown: photo courtesy of Tom Hudson estate and National Arts Education Archive.

Culture',
*Commonwealth
Journal*, 8.3 (May/
June 1965), 107–10
(p. 107).

29. Festival Directors in
Cardiff were Bill and
Wendy Harpe, later
founders of Liverpool's
*Great Georges
Community Cultural
Project*.

30. 'Fringe Events Give
Funds a Boost. Third
Week Begins "in
Black"', by Western
Mail Reporter, *Western
Mail* (25 September
1965), p. 4. The
newspaper here uses a
remark by conference
participant, poet T.
Wignesan.

31. The event has been
referred to under two
different titles: as
Assembly Line (by Tom
Hudson) and as *Welsh
Automative Salad with
Yogurt* (by Jean-
Jacques Lebel). (The
original score by Lebel
calls the event *Welsh
Automotive Salad with
Yougurt*; see Jean-
Jacques Lebel, 'Welsh
Automative Salad with
Yogurt', in Jean-
Jaques Lebel and
Androula Michaël
(eds), *happenings de
jean-jacques lebel ou
l'insoumission radicale*
(Paris: Éditions Hazan,
2009), pp. 172–75.)
These appear to have
been two different
contributions to the
same work. We have
decided therefore to
refer to the overall
event as the 'Cardiff
Happening of 1965'.

32. Michael Lloyd-
Williams, 'Poetry,
Paint and Toilet Seats',
Western Mail (25
September 1965), p. 4.

33. Michael Lloyd-
Williams, 'Girls Offer
to Dance in Nude.
Edinburgh-Style
"Happening" Is Out',
Western Mail (23
September 1965), p. 5.

jazz-poet Pete Brown on an improvised stage to yell, read aloud about death, and gnash their teeth. It all ended with the tooting of a flute from behind a curtain [...].[32]

How strong the resonances from the Edinburgh Happening still were two years later and how they influenced the perception of its Cardiff successor is evident in the press coverage. Two days before the Happening in Cardiff, the *Western Mail* ran an article under the headline 'Girls Offer to Dance in Nude. Edinburgh-Style "Happening" Is Out',[33] which claimed that two women had volunteered to re-enact Anne Kesselaar's nude appearance. As Adrian Henri has suggested, the scandalized press reception of the Edinburgh event had left such a strong impression on the popular consciousness at the time that 'the Great British Public has associated happenings with naked ladies',[34] and Kesselaar's action had turned into a set piece to be potentially re-enacted whenever 'shock' to the establishment was on the agenda. But the *Western Mail* goes on to quote Alexander Trocchi, who had also been present in Edinburgh in 1963, as talking 'nostalgically' of the prior event and turning down the offer of its re-enactment as the organizers in Cardiff were 'not out to shock for shocking's sake'.[35] This suggests that while the Edinburgh Happening, especially its status as one of the catalyst events of British counterculture, was already a moment in the past about which to feel nostalgic, Happenings remained an artistic proposition that could be explored on one's own terms. Thus, at first glance there seemed to have been many parallels with its Edinburgh precursor – its intervention into a high-profile conference event devoted to the 'future' of an art form and its opposition to the literary establishment, for example. But there were also important differences that characterized the Cardiff event.

The most striking difference is that none of the accounts of the Cardiff Happening – whether in the contemporaneous press coverage or in subsequent reminiscences by its participants[36] – ever made any reference to theatre, either as an artistic practice or as a cultural institution against whose conventions the Happening was conceived. Instead, the reference points were to do with the traditions of poetry, fine art and music. The actions carried out during the event strongly confirm this (even more so if we compare them to the ones of the Edinburgh Happening and their unequivocal reference to the conference setting itself): the use of ready-made or found objects (hosepipe, toilet seat, etc.) cited post-Duchamp developments in sculpture. The real-time application of splattering paint related to attempts to reach beyond the frame of the canvas that had grown out of action painting.[37] The pairing of words with actions and the exploitation of the sonic quality of language were foremost concerns in the developments of Beat, concrete and other forms of experimental poetry. And the manipulation of everyday sounds drew upon the sonic experimentations of John Cage (with whom Corner collaborated frequently). In his version of events, Lebel furthermore emphasizes the participatory (and political) nature of the work, which was structured around (a neo-Marxist inflected) exchange of objects of no actual commercial but highly symbolic or personal value, and which was

34. Henri, *Environments*, p. 86.

35. Lloyd-Williams, 'Girls Offer'.

36. See, for example, Nuttall, *Bomb Culture*, pp. 230–32.

37. Action painting's influence on Happenings is well documented, not least through Kaprow's seminal essay on Jackson Pollock (1958): Allan Kaprow, 'The Legacy of Jackson Pollock', *Essays on the Blurring of Art and Life*, ed. by Jeff Kelley (Berkeley: University of California Press, 1993), pp. 1–9.

38. Lebel, *happenings*, p. 172.

39. Dick Higgins, 'Intermedia', *The Something Else Newsletter*, 1.1 (February 1966), n. p.

40. Such posturing was certainly a part of the event, and other participants at the conference duly condemned the Happening as 'nonsense' and its organizers as 'degenerate freaks'. See Harri Webb in *A Militant Muse: Selected Literary Journalism 1948–80*, ed. by Meic Stephens (Bridgend: Seren, 1998 (1965; 1977)), pp. 80, 200. Yet the Cardiff Beats also aimed at wider political targets than those represented by the art establishment. A letter written to 'fellow poet' Chairman Mao (initiated by Michael Horovitz and Michael de Freitas), a petition to the Queen (authored by Paolo Leonni), a pig in lament of the Vietnam war were all part of the performative protest repertoire in Cardiff. The other poets present also represented a very different kind of

intended to mock the increasing commercialization of the art market and capitalism's veneration of the law of supply and demand.[38] Here was a group of artists from different disciplinary backgrounds who came together in a mutual 'intermedial'[39] attempt to expand the terms and vocabularies of their respective practices in performance. Their intention was not simply to stage a countercultural posturing against ideas of tradition and the establishment,[40] but also to develop further the work that had emerged from previous experimentations. Lebel, Corner, Nuttall, Horovitz, Henri and other participants of the Cardiff Happening had already made (and seen) similar performance works elsewhere. Lebel calls the Cardiff Happening 'une résonance critique, une contradiction et un contrepoint'[41] (a critical resonance, a contradiction and a counter-point) to a Happening by Kaprow entitled *Exchange*,[42] and Philip Corner remembers it as recalling 'the participation party in Dick Higgins' house in 1961'.[43]

The Cardiff Happening of 1965 therefore suggests to us that, although Happenings may have been conceptualized by Kaprow, Oldenburg, Dewey, Cage and others in reference to the vocabularies of theatre[44], their compositional procedures, participatory strategies and event-structured unfolding were employed to explore aesthetic concerns that arose from the formal languages of music, painting, sculpture and poetry as well as those (or often more than those) of the theatre. This observation may need some qualification: We do not wish to deny that (as Josette Féral[45] and others have argued) performance is always haunted by the conditions of theatricality, by certain time–space relation, mode of subjectivity and practice of reiteration that define theatre's representational operations. But as a culturally and historically specific practice or institution (whether literary establishment or popular entertainment), the theatre was not always the primary reference point when artists in Britain in the 1960s turned to an exploration of performance in their work. Instead, a great number of these artists were concerned with precisely the 'terms and integrities of the work in art' that Kaye associates with the specific performance art traditions in the United States and continental Europe.[46] Of course, in the case of the Cardiff Happening of 1965 (as was the case, for example, with the Edinburgh Happening, the *Festival of Misfits* and the *Destruction in Art Symposium*), North American and European artists (and occasionally artists from further afield) were centrally involved in the creation of the work. It would therefore be absurd to regard the Cardiff Happening as a 'British' piece of performance work. But the circumstances of its creation had much to do with the conditions of art making in Britain at the time, in particular with the major shifts that were occurring in art education and which enabled Tom Hudson to invite Jean-Jacques Lebel and Philip Corner to Cardiff on behalf of the local College of Art. It was also motivated by developments in British counterculture, which looked purposefully beyond its national borders in search for others who shared its political and artistic convictions, building international networks of solidarity and exchange. Only three months prior to the Cardiff event, on 11 June 1965, many of its participants – among them Trocchi, Nuttall, Brown, Lionni, Horovitz and Richter – had taken part in the *Poets of the*

establishment than
Tynan or Olivier (then
newly designated
director of the National
Theatre) had stood for
in Edinburgh: the
poetic orthodoxy
against whom the Beats
protested was
represented largely by
poets from Asia and
Africa, which made the
conflict between
tradition and
experimentation run
along complex cultural,
racial and religious
lines.

41. Lebel, *happenings*,
p. 172.

42. We have not been able
to find any details
about this work, and it
is possible that Lebel
misremembers the
title.

43. Philip Corner,
'Memory of the First
Happening in Cardiff
in 1964 [*sic*] – Or at
least what i remember
of my part in it',
unpublished event
score, 2009.

44. For conceptual
writings on
Happenings see
*Happenings and Other
Acts*, ed. by Mariellen
R. Sandford (London
and New York:
Routledge, 1995).

45. Josette Féral,
'Performance and
Theatricality: The
Subject Demystified',
Modern Drama, 25
(Spring 1982),
170–81.

46. Kaye, 'Introduction',
p. 2.

47. James Morrison, 'The
Beat Goes On', *The
Independent* (22
September 2005),
p. 44–45.

48. The *Western Mail*
reported from the
preliminary talks to
establish an agenda for
the Cardiff Poetry
Conference: '[I]t soon
became apparent that
there were plenty of

World – Poets of Our Time reading (also known as the *First International Poetry Incarnation*) held at the Royal Albert Hall in London. Billed as 'Britain's first full-scale "happening"',[47] the event attracted over 7000 people and manifested the size and energy of the alternative scene (and connected the British Beat poets to their American counterparts, most famously represented in London by Allen Ginsberg). Poetry had taken a central place in the countercultural movement, and Happenings had become central to the new movements in poetry.[48]

It is the relationship between the Cardiff Happening of 1965 and its predecessors that particularly interests us as it sheds some light on the way in which performance art created its own histories. What is noteworthy about the Cardiff event is its explicitly reiterative quality. The creators of the Happening seemed to have deliberately evoked a range of antecedents: from the Edinburgh Happening to the *Poetry Incarnation*, to the participatory experiments of Kaprow and Higgins. This proposes that the artists in Cardiff purposefully wanted to tap into an energy that had already been originated in other places, in this case by prior events in London, Edinburgh and New York. Within the established parameters of 'originality' that haunt all art histories, especially those of the so-called avant-garde,[49] it would mark the work out as a secondary (provincial) afterthought to the artistic revolutions staged elsewhere in the capitals of art production and thus justify its relative obscurity. But the Cardiff Happening invites us to rethink such notions of origins and originality, significance and obscurity, especially as they become closely associated with ideas of centre or metropolis and margin or copy. Indeed, even the events at Edinburgh in 1963 ('Britain's first Happening') and London in 1965 ('Britain's first full-scale Happening') were, despite their mutual claims to 'firstness', framed as demonstrations of or responses to developments in art (Happenings, Beat poetry) that were already in full swing elsewhere. This suggests that the history of performance did not merely develop in those moments when artists made works that changed the parameters of artistic practice (the moments that historical accounts of performance art have largely focused on), but also when artists elsewhere restaged those moments (or their particular take on them) in order to partake in this change and thus turn isolated events into the kinds of larger developments that we are then able to recognize as 'histories'.[50]

Infrastructural Remains

What, then, are the possible links between the performance experiments of the 1960s in Britain and the emergence, twenty or so years later in a very different social, artistic and political climate, of what came to be called Live Art? In what way can we conceive of the earlier works as a kind of (pre-)history of Live Art in the UK? We would like to take a step back from this question for a moment and consider first how we may conceptualize such links. RoseLee Goldberg, in an early essay on the subject, proposes a contextual approach to the history of performance ideas for discussion, including the topically pertinent one of whether happenings were necessary for poets'. Beata Lipman, '"Decadent" European Poetry Criticised', *Western Mail* (21 September 1965), p. 5.

49. See Rosalind E. Krauss, *The Originality of the Avant-Garde and Other Modernist Myths* (Cambridge, MA and London: MIT Press, 1986).

50. Reiterations of this kind have appeared a lot in our interviews with artists of the period, see Heike Roms and Rebecca Edwards, 'It Was Forty Years Ago Today'. Interviews with artists, administrators and audience members, accessible at the British Library Sound Archive.

51. RoseLee Goldberg, 'Performance: A Hidden History', in *The Art of Performance: A Critical Anthology*, ed. by Gregory Battcock and Robert Nickas (New York: Dutton, 1984), pp. 24–36 (p. 26).

52. See Goldberg, *Performance: Live Art*.

53. Hoffmann, 'Radicalism', p. 102.

54. Kaye, 'Introduction', p. 2.

55. Ibid., p. 3.

56. Kristine Stiles, 'The Story of the Destruction in Art Symposium and the "DIAS Affect"', in *Gustav Metzger: History History*, ed. by Sabine Breitwieser (Ostfildern-Ruit: Hatje Cantz, 2005), pp. 41–65 (p. 54).

art. She argues that this history can be regarded 'as a series of waves; successive periods when performance provided a release from the stagnation and complacency of set styles and attitudes'.[51] Consequently, as she herself had done in *Performance: Live Art 1909 to the Present* (first published in 1979), performance art's history is portrayed as a series of discontinuous developments from many beginnings, in many locations, each performing a similar disconnection from whatever is considered tradition or mainstream.[52] Following her model, the performance events of the 1960s in Britain and today's Live Art could be thought of as equivalent responses to a changed set of circumstances. It is precisely within this model of performance as a recurrent mode of transgression (which she calls, after Jon McKenzie, the 'liminal-norm'[53]) in which Hoffmann, as we have outlined above, locates a continuity that runs through the history of performance art and Live Art in the UK. Kaye, on the other hand, despite emphasizing Live Art's resistance to being characterized formally, offers some pointers towards identifying a certain formal evolution in British performance work: from the 'intuitive [...] play between image, text and narrative' and 'marked comic eccentricity'[54] of the 1970s 'toward a more direct, self-conscious address to the terms and vocabulary of conventional theatre practice'[55] in the 1980s. All three approaches provide in their different ways potentially useful insights into how performance art as an art form has developed (not just in Britain): its often discontinuous nature, but also the continuing relevance of certain formal, conceptual or even political concerns (around language, action, body, subjectivity, intersubjectivity, time, space, etc.) that can connect the work of one artist with that of another; its repeatedly celebrated 'break' with tradition which itself has now become part of performance art's own tradition; and its deep, constitutive enmeshment with the histories of other art forms which it has sought to transgress. Tracing the impact of one of the key events of the 1960s – the *Destruction in Art Symposium* in London 1966 – on subsequent artistic and social developments, Kristine Stiles has added a further factor (drawing on Hayden White's critique of the writing of history): affect. To emphasize affect, she argues, is to

> consciously shift focus from the traditional notion of factual historical data and art historical 'influence' [...] in order to attend to the tangible and intangible transference of ideas and feelings through society by emotions and actions that may result in entirely different visual and behavioral forms of cultural address, but that carry the genealogy of their prototype.[56]

A continuity of attitude to changed circumstances, a persistently reiterated conceptual framework and discourse, an evolution of formal preoccupations, the continued reverberation of certain ideas or emotions – all of these are possible models for figuring the relationship between the performance work of the 1960s and contemporary Live Art in Britain.

We want to suggest an additional aspect, which is of particular importance for our chosen example: namely the emergence in Britain in the 1960s of an infrastructural framework for performance work, which

57. Sandy Craig has analysed the rapid establishment of an infrastructure for experimental performance practice in the late 1960s and early 1970s in the UK, including new venues, new publications (e.g. *Time Out*) and the Arts Council's *New Activities* funding schemes, initiated in 1968; Craig, 'Reflexes', pp. 15–17.

58. A parallel history could be developed through Jeff Nuttall, another participant in the Cardiff Happening, and his involvement in Leeds College of Art, which became an equally important site for the training of performance artists in the 1970s. Rose English, Roger Ely, Dave Stephens, Geraldine Pilgrim and others were Nuttall's students at Leeds.

59. See Clive Ashwin, *A Century of Art Education 1882–1982* (London: Middlesex Polytechnic, 1982).

60. Mark Hudson, 'Obituaries: Tom Hudson', *Independent* (8 January 1998).

61. The 'Basic Design' approach eventually became the basis for the new Foundation Course provision in the UK in the 1960s. Its suggestion of an organic development that would take the artists from 2D to 3D to 4D, its emphasis on materials and skills and the underlying notion that there are universally applicable 'foundational' principles for art making have since been widely criticized. See David Thistlewood, 'A Continuing Process: The New Creativity in British Art Education

has impacted on the developments of future works beyond the supposed failure of the neo-avant-garde. In its long-standing theoretical attention to performance's 'ephemerality' performance theory has risked losing sight of the fact that performance does not only generate emotional and intellectual responses but often also quite tangible outcomes: networks, platforms, festivals, spaces, training programmes, funding schemes, publications and, latterly increasingly also, archives. Such infrastructures may indeed only come into view if we focus on the emergence and re-emergence of performance art in the context of one specific location, rather than track its history as a series of exceptional events across many sites. And it involves a greater appreciation of performance art's institutionalizing capacity, which runs counter to performance theory's preoccupation with the 'liminal-norm'. Instead of regarding performance art as always positioned outside of institutional frameworks, such appreciation would require a closer analysis of what kinds of organizational structures have been generated by performance artists themselves and those who have supported their work, and what sort of artistic, social, political or economic efficacy such structures have sought to engender.[57]

A close analysis of this kind is beyond the scope of this essay. Instead, we would like to return briefly to the Cardiff Happening of 1965 and sketch out its particular infrastructural remains. The event was linked, via its organizer Tom Hudson, to the history of an institution that was to play a vital role in the development of Live Art in the UK: Cardiff College of Art.[58] Hudson was appointed to the College in 1964 in the wake of a major restructuring of the art educational sector in Britain. In 1960, the National Advisory Council on Art Education, better known as The Coldstream Report, recommended the introduction of a new Diploma in Art and Design, which was to shift the emphasis from craft-based training towards a liberal education in art by including compulsory academic elements such as art history or psychology. While the old National Diploma had been awarded centrally, art colleges now had to apply individually for degree-awarding powers.[59] Cardiff College of Art was turned down in its first attempt – as a result, the College decided to appoint Tom Hudson, one of the most influential educators of the period, as Director of Studies with almost unlimited powers, a large budget and the brief to make Cardiff one of the leading art schools in the country.[60] A consummate teacher, Hudson was one of the advocates of a new approach to the teaching of art commonly known as 'Basic Design', which was inspired by the pedagogical principles of the Bauhaus and committed to the achievements of the classic European avant-garde.[61] Hudson had developed 'Basic Design' – or, as he preferred to call it, the 'Basic Course' – together with fellow artists Victor Pasmore, Harry Thubron and Richard Hamilton at Durham, Leeds and Leicester since the mid-1950s. Following the ethos of modernism, their intention was to develop a more rational approach to teaching art, away from ideas of individual expressiveness towards principles and a kind of syntax for creativity. The integration of design and industrial materials and methods was central to this new approach, and old differentiations between 'painting' and 'sculpture' were

1955–1965', in *Histories of Art and Design Education: Cole to Coldstream*, ed. by David Thistlewood (Harlow: Longman, 1992), pp. 152–68.

62. Hudson later re-engaged with performance work in the context of the performative 'symposia' that were regularly held by Cardiff College of Art in the early 1970s.

63. The move from two- to three- to four-dimensionality mirrored that of the development from painting to assemblage to happening undertaken by Kaprow and others.

64. The Tom Hudson Collection at the National Arts Education Archive, West Bretton, Wakefield, UK.

65. The workshops were held under different titles: *Action and Ideas*, or *Action/Ideas*, or *Myself and Others*. They were devised by Gingell in close collaboration with fellow teachers Di Setch and Chris Orr and former students, Andrew Walton and, in particular, John Danvers.

66. Tom Hudson too at the time increasingly conceptualized his teaching practice as a mode of performance, creating a series of lecture performances (or what he termed 'Academic Performances'), which were presented in the framework of the symposia.

67. Other art schools that influenced the development of performance in Britain, besides Cardiff and Leeds, included Bradford, Croydon,

replaced by reference to work in 'two dimensions' and 'three dimensions'.

Hudson's foray into Happenings, which he had encountered on a visit to New York in the same year he took up his post in Cardiff, was initially short-lived,[62] and he soon returned to his modernist pedagogy, built on simple experimental exercises in what he regarded as the basis building blocks of artistic practice (including point, line and colour). It seems, however, that the labour of elaborating such 'elementary' properties, especially those of space and three-dimensionality, eventually led Hudson's students towards exploring time, movement – and performance.[63] Hudson's archive contains 8 mm movies, shot in 1967, that document various 'Colour Experiments', one of which shows a group of art students staging performative interventions in the city centre of Cardiff, covered head to toe in coloured paint.[64] Performance art was then not yet an institutionally supported part of the pedagogical practice at Cardiff, but it appears that through a particular pedagogical practice performance became possible. A few years later, a more purposeful and sustained approach to teaching performance began to take shape at Cardiff. In the early 1970s, Hudson's colleague, John Gingell, ran a regular series of performance workshops at the College and at the nearby Barry Summer School.[65] These were accompanied by 'symposia', held at the Reardon Smith Lecture Theatre in Cardiff, where students, staff and guests (among them Bruce Lacey, Robin Page and Cornelius Cardew) staged performance pieces alternating with performance-lecture formats.[66] They led to the eventual institutionalization of performance art at Cardiff College of Art: in the mid-1970s, Cardiff became one of the first art schools in the UK where Fine Art students could follow a dedicated (tutor-supported and institutionally resourced) programme in time-based work (performance, film and video and sound art): the so-called 'Third Area' (or 'Alternative Studies').[67] Later rechristened 'Time-Based Studies', it was run from 1986 by Anthony Howell, one of the founder members of The Theatre of Mistakes and himself creator of a unique approach to performance pedagogy;[68] followed in 1999 by performance artist, André Stitt. Under Howell, Cardiff came to house *Cardiff Art in Time*, an influential international performance art and video festival that ran from 1994 to 1999 (and was briefly revived by Stitt in 2007), and *Grey Suit: Video for Art & Literature*, an innovative performance art and poetry magazine distributed on VHS. Performance artists that have come out of this school include Clive Robertson and Marty St James in the 1970s, Glenn Davidson and Anne Hayes in the 1980s, Kira O'Reilly and Robin Deacon in the 1990s, and Richard DeDomenici and Paul Hurley in the 2000s.

Peggy Phelan has called the attempt to create a narrative history of performance art 'paradoxical' as 'by taking a narrative form, this history risks missing the performative force of the art it seeks to comprehend'.[69] And needless to say, this particular slice of the history of performance art has not been as straightforwardly causal as our brief narration makes it out to be. Much of the work that was created by artists in the 1960s and early 1970s within the context of Cardiff College of Art was virtually unknown to those who succeeded them, despite working and studying in

Maidstone, Newcastle and Reading.

68. Anthony Howell, *The Analysis of Performance Art: A Guide to Its Theory and Practice* (Amsterdam: Harwood Academic Publishers, 1999).

69. Peggy Phelan, 'Shards of a History of Performance Art: Pollock and Namuth through a Glass, Darkly', in *A Companion to Narrative Theory*, ed. by James Phelan and Peter J. Rabinowitz (Malden: Blackwell, 2005), pp. 499–512 (p. 500).

70. See Heike Roms and Rebecca Edwards, Interview with John Danvers, Charles Garrad and Ken Hickman, Cardiff, 4 March 2010 as part of 'It Was Forty Years Ago Today'. Interviews with artists, administrators and audience members, accessible at the British Library Sound Archive.

71. There are, of course, a number of scholars who have evaluated performance work in Britain within the context of fine art discourses; see, for example, the work of Guy Brett.

the same institution. Hudson himself reportedly at first strongly resisted the attempts of students in the late 1960s to explore performance work as part of their studies,[70] and few of the students then were aware of the role their teacher had played only a few years earlier in the staging of Wales' first Happening. Throughout the near half-century since that event, performances have repeatedly challenged the institutional frameworks, health and safety regulations, examination procedures or aesthetic preferences of the College. But to acknowledge that the history of performance art is not one of easy causality does not imply that performance art has no history. In the wake of the Cardiff Happening of 1965 an institutional space began to open up in which performance art could emerge, and emerge again, and again – a space that, through its training of artists and the recurrent development of opportunities for exchange, presentation and critical discourse, has become highly influential on British Live Art in the 1980s and beyond.

Conclusion: The Beginnings And Ends of Performance's Histories

The 1960s were an important period for the development of performance in Britain. Artists from a variety of disciplinary backgrounds turned to performance in an attempt to explore and expand the vocabularies of their practice. A large number of them was therein not concerned primarily with reworking the terms of theatricality but instead responded to the formal traditions of fine art, poetry or music. Their work has so far rarely been claimed as part of the history of performance art and Live Art in Britain. We have proposed that this can be explained by the fact that the work was internationalist in nature and often involved collaborations with artists from outside the UK, so that it does not allow to be characterized as distinctively 'British'. It may also be connected with the fact that many historical accounts of the art form have been written from the later vantage point of Live Art and thus may have sought out evidence of historical antecedents for Live Art's indebtedness to the representational languages of theatre.[71] This indebtedness is unquestioned. We are not aiming to refute that the traditions of theatre have influenced the work of many proponents of British performance art and Live Art. Even stronger have been the influences of vernacular theatrical traditions, including variety and circus, on this work. It is not our intention to reinstate a modernist avant-garde genealogy at the expense of the performative traditions of popular culture and their close link with issues of class, race and gender. (Indeed, much of the 1960s avant-garde was also inspired by such traditions.) What we have been attempting to assert here is that there were (and still are) other genealogies at play in performance art and Live Art in the UK besides those of the theatre. These genealogies continued well into the 1970s and beyond: so that alongside, for example, IOU Theatre and Forkbeard Fantasy, who Kaye cites as illustrations for theatre's influence on 1970s British performance art, there were artists such as The People Show, John Fox and Sue Gill (Welfare State), Stuart Brisley, The Theatre of Mistakes, Timothy Emlyn Jones (aka Tim Jones), Rose Finn-Kelcey, Anne Bean,

72. British performance art's musical genealogy is less well known but equally important. See, for example, the Cage-influenced performance works of Gavin Bryars in the 1970s.

Nigel Rolfe, Tina Keane, Marty St James, Shirley Cameron and Roland Miller, Rob Con, Ian Hinchliffe, Roger Ely, Dave Stephens and many others whose work grew from the concerns of a visual arts-based practice. If Live Art developed from an 'uncertain point of "difference"' to theatre, it has in equal measures grown out of points of difference to sculpture, painting, poetry or music.[72]

The links between the work that emerged in the 1960s under the different labels of 'Happenings', 'Fluxus', 'Auto-Destructive Art', 'Event-Structured Art', 'Art-Events', 'Actions' and so forth, and the work created much later under the label of 'Live Art' are complex and multifaceted. One frame through which one may explore possible continuities, which we believe has been under-regarded, is that of the various infrastructures that the work has helped to generate. Indeed, it would be worth examining in greater detail whether, as we suspect, the terminological shift to 'Live Art' in the 1980s did not only mark a change in aesthetics, but also – and possibly even more so – a substantial change in the infrastructural frameworks that had supported the scene up to that point. (Take, for example, the year 1979. Not only was it the year of a significant governmental change in the UK, which ushered in eighteen years of conservative cultural policy making that would alter the conditions for art profoundly. In the field of performance art, 1979 saw a remarkable rise in the number of publications devoted to the art form, including Goldberg's first comprehensive history of performance art[73], and the first issues of two new specialist UK-based magazines, *Performance Magazine* and *P. S. Primary Source*. Performance art had evidently matured to the extent that it warranted historical evaluations of its past and critical reflections of its presence and future. Furthermore, in 1979 a number of organizations came into being (among them the *Performance Art Platform*, later renamed *National Review of Live Art*, a biannual, later annual showcase of new work that ran until 2010; and producers Artsadmin) that for the next thirty years have acted as protagonists of a newly organized scene.)

73. Goldberg, *Performance: Live Art*; Nuttall's *Memoirs* was published in the same year; Craig, *Dreams* and Itzin, *Stages* followed a year later.

And yet, while experimental performance practice in Britain over the past five decades has manifested a great ability to emerge and emerge again, generating or transforming organizational structures as it has done so, some of its histories are forced into an untimely end. And so it is that in 2010, in an attempt to rationalize its provision in a time of dwindling public funds, the Cardiff School of Art and Design (as it is now known) decided to close, after nearly forty years, its performance provision.

The Freaks' Roll Call: Live Art and the Arts Council, 1968–73

Graham Saunders

1. See Richard Witts, *Artist Unknown: An Alternative History of the Arts Council* (London: Little, Brown and Company, 1998), p. 326.

2. *The Arts in Hard Times*, Thirty-First Annual Report 31 March 1976 (London: Arts Council of Great Britain, 1976), p. 20. The Arts Council's archive is housed at the Victoria and Albert Museum's Theatre and Performance Collection at Blythe House London. The archive's holdings can be accessed online at <http://www.vam.ac.uk/vastatic/wid/ead/acgb/acgbf.html>.

3. The article is published in the 'Backpages' section of the present issue of *Contemporary Theatre Review*.

The Arts Council of Great Britain (ACGB) has been acknowledged, and credits itself as being, the enabling engine for Fringe Theatre and Live Art, which coalesced in the late 1960s and flourished during the 1970s. Even in its Dickensian-sounding 1976 annual report *The Arts in Hard Times*, Deputy Secretary General Richard Pulford could proudly declare that Fringe and Experimental Drama had been an area of exceptional growth, with subsidy rising from £223,000 in the previous year to just under £500,000. Taking into account the money spent by the affiliated Regional Arts Associations (RAA) that year the Arts Council had spent £1.5 million on a total of one hundred and six non-building-based companies.[1] In case the reader missed the full impact of this largesse, Pulford's report pointed out that such activity had scarcely existed seven years previously.[2] Yet the Arts Council's decision to fund Live Art – or Performance Art as it was frequently called at the time – was to be fraught with problems over definition, policy confusions and at times open resistance. This article will attempt to outline how policy slowly evolved during a period when definitions of what constituted performance were being completely redefined.

Jeff Nuttall's (1973) paper 'The Situation Regarding Performance Art', written for the Arts Council, was an early attempt at defining terminology, which drew attention to key practitioners and, even more importantly, unequivocally dispelled the notion that Performance Art shared any familial links to drama or theatre.[3] Nuttall points out that while the term Performance Art had been accepted from the outset in America and Europe, an anomalous situation existed in Britain where it had become associated in the minds of audiences and bodies such as the Arts Council with the growth of Fringe and Alternative Theatre. Since then, Amelia Jones locates the 1990s as the time when Performance Art was superseded by Live Art as a term in recognition of the body as central to much of its practice.[4]

The Freaks Assemble

The Arts Council's Drama Panel first became aware of stirrings after 1965 when it began to note an increasing number of applications that were non-literary, improvisational, cross-disciplinary and multimedia-based. Many of these applications made to the New Drama scheme were rejected due to its insistence that a script be submitted, although the Drama Panel did respond to this problem with an interim solution of asking its governing Council to make a general grant available to companies undertaking non-traditional forms of drama.

However, it was the closure in 1969 of Jim Haynes' Arts Lab in London's Drury Lane after the Arts Council had rejected its emergency request for a grant of £7000 that constituted what it called 'the test case'.[5] The Arts Lab had been a venue where groups including The People Show and The Pip Simmons Group could develop work without what Sandy Craig called 'the hampering restrictions of traditional theatre'[6] and in a confidential Arts Council report written at the time, entitled 'Work in Experimental Drama' there is a note of regret that the governing Council 'could not be persuaded to help this particular company [the Arts Lab] until it was too late'.[7] Yet there were those in the Arts Council who saw the refusal to fund the Arts Lab as eminently

Image 1. People Show, *People Show 44: The Flying Show* (1972) with Jeff Nuttall, Mark Long, Mike Figgis and an unidentified performer. Photo by Dirk Deleu: photo courtesy of David Duchin/People Show.

4. Amelia Jones, 'Live Art in Art History: A Paradox', in *The Cambridge Companion to Performance Studies*, ed. by Tracy C. Davis (Cambridge: Cambridge University Press, 2008), pp. 151–65.

5. 'Work in Experimental Drama' Experimental Projects Committee, Arts Council of Great Britain archive, ACGB 43/42/7, undated.

6. See 'Reflexes of the Future: The Beginnings of the Fringe', in *Dreams and Deconstructions: Alternative Theatre in Britain*, ed. by Sandy Craig (Amber Lane: Ambergate, 1980), pp. 9–29 (p. 16).

7. 'Work in Experimental Drama', Experimental Projects Committee, ACGB 43/42/7, undated.

8. Ronald Hayman, *The Set-Up: An Anatomy of the English Theatre Today* (London: Methuen, 1973), p. 29.

9. J. W. Lambert, *Drama in Britain 1964–73* (Harlow: Longman, 1974), p. 43.

10. Witts, *Artist Unknown*, p. 318.

11. Craig, *Dreams and Deconstructions*, p. 181.

12. Lord Goodman, Chairman's Report, *Arts Council of Great Britain Twenty-Fourth Annual Report*, 1969, n. p.

13. Robert Hutchinson, *Politics of the Arts Council* (London: Sinclair Browne, 1982), p. 106 (Note 18).

14. Chairman's Report, *Arts Council of Great Britain Twenty-Fifth Annual Report*, 31 March 1970, n. p.

sensible. Some were reported to have described its activities as 'immoral'[8] while in his survey of the period, theatre critic J. W. Lambert described the Arts Lab as 'less a theatrical breeding ground than an uncovenanted and bankrupt doss-house'.[9] Lambert's assessment is significant given the part he was to play in shaping Arts Council policy towards Live Art. Despite its closure, like a many-headed hydra, other arts labs mushroomed in its likeness and elsewhere throughout the UK spaces for performance became utilized in cellars, pubs and outside spaces that facilitated opportunities for collaboration between artists working in different mediums.

The Freaks Come Calling

In 1968 this new performance culture encountered the Arts Council for the first time. Richard Witts has described its policy towards drama up to this point as one of perpetuating 'the sort of theatre it had known since Hitler invaded Poland' and that when suddenly 'thespian hippies and street theatre Trotskyites started to piddle against the Council's doors [...] the department hadn't a clue how to handle them.'[10] Sandy Craig also believed that the Arts Council only reluctantly entered into dialogue following a sustained campaign by the artists own Independent Theatre Council,[11] but whatever the truth of the matter, faced by such agitating forces the Arts Council set up The New Activities Committee (NAC) (1968–70). While this marks an important moment in the history of British Live Art, the feeling of suspicion that the NAC aroused within the higher echelons of the Arts Council can be gauged by Lord Goodman's annual Chairman's Report of 1969, which is couched in the language of a well-meaning vicar who has reluctantly given over his youth club to a boisterous skiffle group. Goodman talks of the ACGB hearing about 'a group of youngsters around the country that had some new ideas' but is torn between thinking whether they were 'having us on toast' to half-heartedly wondering whether this might be the 'beginning of a new artistic era'.

Despite Goodman's open acknowledgement that 'the very word "young" [...] strikes a note of terror in all establishment bosoms',[12] in an unprecedented move the NAC recruited half its membership from artists representing the new performance culture. Yet despite the good intentions, this only served to accentuate the ideological gulf. At one point the Committee was invaded by six members of a group calling itself FACOP (Friends of the Arts Council's Operative), who declared their lack of confidence in what it dubbed 'the paunch belt'[13] (which included J. W. Lambert – an odd choice given his opinion of Jim Haynes' Arts Lab) and their replacement with an Artist's Panel. Little wonder that in its annual report of 1970, Goodman pointedly commented on the Committee's failure 'to impose discipline or control on the wilder elements of juvenile London [who...] look[ed] as though they had come down the chimney'.[14]

Nevertheless, during 1969–70 the NAC distributed £15,000 among the Arts Council's eight Regional Associations in order to promote what the Committee called 'Gatherings' in order to assess the extent of

15. Craig, 'Reflexes of the future', p. 16.

16. Baz Kershaw locates the group at the carnivalesque end of a spectrum in alternative theatre, the other end being agit prop. See Kershaw, *The Politics of Performance: Radical Theatre as Cultural Intervention* (London Routledge, 1992), p. 83. Like Welfare State, The John Bull Puncture Repair Kit mainly performed at outdoor venues and festivals and often incorporated rock music into their performances.

17. Roland Miller, 'Performance Art', 10 September 1973, p. 2. ACGB 43/42/7.

18. Chairman's Report, *ACGB Twenty-Fifth Annual Report*, n. p.

19. Robert Hutchinson, *Politics of the Arts Council*, p. 108.

20. 'Work in Experimental Drama', Experimental Projects Committee, ACGB archive 43/42/7, undated.

21. Minutes of the Experimental Projects Committee, 11 November 1970. ACGB archive 43/42/7.

22. Ronald Hayman, *The Set-up* (London: Methuen, 1973), p. 212 (Note 8).

23. Jinnie Schiele, *Off-Centre Stages: Fringe Theatre at the Open Space and the Round House 1968–1983* (Hatfield: University of Hertfordshire Press, 2005), p. 106.

experimental work being undertaken and requirements for future funding. Although Craig described the sum as 'miserly',[15] the eight Gatherings held throughout English regions were a seminal moment in the history of Live Art. The most significant of the Gatherings was the one that took place in May 1970 at Hebden Bridge in Yorkshire. Organized by Al Beach and Mick Banks from The John Bull Puncture Repair Kit,[16] many participants were drawn from many neighbouring universities and art colleges in Leeds and Bradford. Groups who performed included Sun, a group of students from the electronic music department at Leeds university, who mixed fireworks and other effects, and an early incarnation of Welfare State with John Fox, Roger Coleman and students from Bradford College of Art, who were described by Roland Miller as a 'rock group with circus-type burlesque acts'.[17] Bradford College of Art was also represented by its 'theatre' group led by Albert Hunt. Collectively, the Gatherings were to be catalysts that provided opportunities for collaboration between groups and individuals who wished to engage in performance, rather than theatre.

While these events demonstrated the existence of a new group of performers with a strong case for funding future activities, the Council's response to the NAC's report was lukewarm. Despite the Chairman's patronizing comment that Council was prepared 'to give "new activities" a sporting chance',[18] and despite accepting the majority of its recommendations based on the Committee's majority and minority reports, Council rejected the idea of allocating £100,000 to what would have to been called a New Activities and Multimedia Committee.[19] The NAC itself also failed to recommend making individual grants to artists working within multimedia,[20] and it is significant that no specific funding allocation was made to experimental projects during 1969–70.[21]

However, the Arts Council's recognition in principle to support experimental work was demonstrated elsewhere through direct subsidy on the recommendations of the Drama Panel during the NAC's lifetime. For instance during 1968–69 the Arts Council began to subsidize a number of new companies and performance spaces such as Charles Marowitz's Camden Playhouse Productions (£2355), Ed Berman's community-based Inter-Action Trust (£2300) and Tony Bicât and David Hare's touring company Portable (£89). Although no new money was forthcoming specifically for experimental work 1969–70 saw Inter-Action's budget more than treble, while Portable's modest grant of £89 expanded significantly to £2922.[22] New groups also started to receive funding including the Joseph Chaikin and Richard Schechner influenced physical performance work of Nancy Meckler's Freehold, the 'American cartoon style'[23] devised work of The Pip Simmons Group, as well as performance venues in London such as the Soho and Warehouse.

The Experimental Projects Committee

One practical response by the Arts Council to the NAC's reports was to set up what it called the Experimental Projects Committee (EPC). Described in the Chairman's Report of 1969–70 as being formed to

24. Chairman's Report, *ACGB Twenty-Fifth Annual Report.*

consider 'any activity which looks "new", in the sense that it does not fit into the pattern of the other arts',[24] its first meeting took place on 11 November 1970. The composition of its all-male committee – which included the literary academic Frank Kermode as its Chairman, actor and film director Richard Attenborough and the film/theatre producer and co-founder of the English Stage Company Oscar Lewenstein – clearly demonstrated that the experiment of parleying with young radicals during the period of the NAC was over. Lack of relevant artistic representation was raised at its second meeting by Peter Stark, (one of the founders of Birmingham Arts Lab and a lone survivor from the NAC), and while its Chairman agreed to put the proposal to Council, it was doubted whether the recommendation would be accepted.[25] The vicar was now firmly back in charge of his youth club.

25. Minutes of the Experimental Projects Committee, 9 December 1970. ACGB 43/42/7.

Firm control also extended to allocation of funds. At its first meeting the Chairman reminded members that despite the Committee's lack of budget it should proceed on the assumption that Council would find sufficient funds based on its recommendations.[26] The EPC could also recommend applications referred to them by other specialist Arts Council Panels such as Music, Art and Dance as well as from the Regional Arts Associations. Representation from members of the Literature, Art and Music Panels also meant, in theory at least, a structure was in place that enabled the multi-disciplinary nature of much of this work to be taken into consideration by the Committee.

26. Minutes of the Experimental Projects Committee, 11 November 1970. ACGB 43/42/7.

While remit and structure meant that the EPC could not be considered toothless, Council was still not immediately ready to give its new committee the same budgetary powers as more established bodies such as the New Drama Committee. However, by its third meeting on 1 January 1971 the EPC learnt that £15,000 from Council had been allocated for the financial year 1971–72, with additional funds set aside by the Drama Panel. However, it is significant that the sum allocated was the same as the initial seed corn funding given to the NAC in 1969 to finance the regional 'Gatherings', and also needs to be considered in relation to the Arts Council's allocation to New Drama that year of £57,264.

The Experimental Drama Committee

The EPC was also complemented that year by the Experimental Drama Committee (EDC) whose main function was to provide a conduit for applications that the New Drama Committee felt to be outside their remit or interests – essentially work that was non-text based and operated within a different performance context. This committee was far smaller than the EPC, comprising of six members as opposed to the EPC's eleven. Members at its first meeting included the critic and Head of BBC Radio Drama, Martin Esslin; the playwright, James Saunders; and the Arts Council's Deputy Drama Director, Dennis Andrews. Also present at these early meetings was the twenty-nine-year-old Assistant Drama Director, Nick Barter. One recurring feature that the Arts Council's archives reveal is the influence that an energetic individual could exert upon policy through their work on committees and panels, especially if

27. See Craig, "Unmasking the Lie': Political Theatre', in *Dreams and Deconstructions*, pp. 30–48 (p. 35).

the Chairman was weak, or the committee divided or lacking regular attendees. Barter, a former deputy Artistic Director of the RSC's Theatre Ground and Artistic Director of Ipswich Arts Theatre has been cited by Sandy Craig as one of the few individuals in the Arts Council who was demonstrably sympathetic to experimental performance.[27] The archives confirm this view, both through his presence on the EDC and later as Secretary for the EPC, where he championed the case for funding Live Art often in the face of inertia, bemusement and sometimes open hostility.

The differing attitudes between the conservatives and the progressives can be seen early on when the EDC was called upon to consider jointly with members of the New Drama Committee (NDC) groups and individuals it had inherited from the NAC. The aim of the NDC was to shift responsibility for these to either the EDC or EPC. When the joint panel met on 4 February 1971 applications were received from, among others, The People Show, Phantom Captain, Black Box and People, Time/Space. Members of the NDC included the writer Bamber Gascoigne, the actor Nickolas Grace, Peter James (founder of Liverpool Everyman Theatre) and the ubiquitous J. W. Lambert (who also chaired the Drama Panel, the Young People's Theatre Committee and was in addition a member of Council). Lambert's attitude towards Live Art can be gauged when The People Show announced during their interview that they wanted to move away from theatre-based work towards street shows and happenings, together with adopting a policy of not charging their audiences, Lambert recommend shifting the group away from his responsibility and onto the EPC. However, others on the joint committee such as James Saunders found the decision less easy to make, arguing that the group's activities 'merely came at one end of the spectrum of new drama'.[28] This conflict became the nub of what would ultimately disadvantage Live Art in terms of funding policy – for by refusing to recognize performance artists as belonging to a broad continuum of drama, the Arts Council continued to produce a divisive policy that artificially separated Live Art from recognized forms of performance. At the same time, lack of any clear definitions or categories led to some poor funding decisions. For instance, at the same meeting the 'fairly weird ideas' (as Martin Esslin describes them) of Neil Hornick's Phantom Captain, convinced some members that their work fell under experimental drama, yet because some of their activities involved young people their application was referred to the Young People's Theatre panel. Similarly the environmental group People Time/Space, described in the minutes as 'Roland Miller (plus four tangerine peeling students from Wolverhampton College of Design)', despite having 'greatly entertained [the Committee members . . .] did not feel it had much to do with drama as such', and their proposed Cyclamen Cyclists project to continuously tour from town to town, belonged more in the realm of 'experimental art'.[29]

28. Minutes of the New Drama Committee, 4 February 1971. ACGB 43/43/1.

29. Ibid.

While this assessment of the group's work might be a reasonable one in terms of having to provide categories, companies that followed a more recognizable theatre tradition were conspicuous in benefiting financially. Whereas The People Show's application for £2,800 was deferred until its

30. Ibid.

work (after the departure of Roland Miller to Action Space/Time and John Darling to the Yorkshire Gnomes), could be seen by the Committee, Portable saw its application for £8,970 receive unanimous approval as 'a good group who had found some excellent writers and who would use the money well'.[30] Similarly, despite impressing the Committee, the pioneering Live Art group Black Box, who had been in existence since 1965, had their application for £7,000 turned down. Their work, described by John Elsom as 'large scale images of woods, streams, pools and fountains using light projected through coloured glass as a means of changing the images and, sometimes, of telling a visual story'.[31] the Committee found 'impossible to categorize – totally mixed media, so perhaps ought to be considered [under] Experimental Projects'.[32] Black Box's later referral to the EPC also caused much wringing of hands: first of all it was recommended that both the main Art and Drama Panels discussed their application, followed by Music at the EPC meeting of 16 April. Their application was considered again on 30 April, and then referred once more – this time to the EDC, but with a recommendation that if the Art and Music Panels failed to provide funding then the application should be resubmitted to the EDC in the autumn. Such bureaucratic shuffling of applications and confusion over the terms of reference showed that despite representation at the EPC from the Art, Music and Literature Panels, Live Art's multi- disciplinarity was causing problems for the Arts Council.

31. John Elsom, *Post-War British Theatre* (London: Routledge, 1979), p. 153.

32. Minutes of the New Drama Committee, 4 February 1971. ACGB 43/43/1.

A Need For Definition

Clear terms of reference were urgently required. In February 1972 recommendations were presented to the EDC in a document put together by Nick Barter with the sub-heading, 'A Personal and Incomplete View of Experimental Groups and their Distinctive Qualities'.[33] Here Barter divide experimental performance under four distinct categories: Permanent and Semi-Permanent Ensembles; New Play Companies; Lunchtime Theatres; and Performance Artists. The first category of Permanent and Semi-Permanent Companies made up the bulk of the Arts Council's existing list of clients and included Freehold, The Pip Simmons Group and The People Show. Given the New Drama Committee and even the EDC's preference towards text-based companies, New Play Companies produced another lengthy list including Portable, 7.84 and Quipu. The category of Lunchtime Theatres also predominantly referred to theatres such as Ambiance, Basement and Soho-Poly that featured text-based work. The last category, Performance Artists, was a far shorter and rarefied group comprising of Roland Miller and Shirley Cameron's Landscape Gardening/Living Spaces, The Yorkshire Gnomes, The John Bull Puncture Repair Kit and Black Box. Points of common reference Barter identified a shared background in the visual arts, non-theatre performance venues and crossover into other art forms such as dance, music and new media. While the list can be criticized for its arbitrariness (Welfare State, despite an acknowledgement of John Fox's fine arts background categorized under Permanent and Semi-

33. "'Fringe", "Experimental" and "Alternative" Theatre Groups', 24 February 1972. ACGB 43/42/7.

Permanent companies, while The People Show according to Barter developed from performance artists into what he calls 'structured performances'), or partiality over the importance assigned to groups based around a leading director (such Nancy Meckler's Freehold, Ken Campbell's Road Show and Keith Johnstone's Theatre Machine), it did at least attempt to provide a nomenclature that demarcated between the vague terms 'new drama' and 'performance art'. Although Barter's work did something to rectify the failure of the NAC to differentiate clearly between the two forms, problems of definition would continue to be an on-going problem.

It was to be Roland Miller, one of the co-founders of Living Landscapes, who was to come closest to providing some practical remedies to the problems that the Arts Council had created for itself over Live Art. Miller, who been peripherally involved in the NAC joined the EDC in March 1972. His appointment had come about after a long struggle to co-opt sympathetic artists. Earlier in January, Barter had attempted to recruit the playwright (and member of Portable) Howard Brenton as a committee member. His reasons for declining reveal not only the sense of cohesiveness felt among his generation, but also their circumspection about directly involving themselves with the Arts Council:

> I feel too involved with the work of 'Experimental' Groups and allied to their struggles of performing [...] and just don't want to be involved in deciding who gets what share of the money cake. For example, I'm interested in Roland Miller's work, and have worked with him on a piece. And I admire Pip Simmon's work, and know him. I don't know how I'd begin saying Roland should get or not get x, Pip y.[34]

34. Howard Brenton, Letter to Nick Barter, 17 January 1972. ACGB archive 43/ 43/1.

Unlike Brenton, Miller was not afraid to make artistic judgements or provide criteria that distinguished Live Art from theatre. Within seven days of joining the EDC Miller wrote the first of two reports. The first was a set of proposals. Already by September 1972 Miller realized that an 'establishment' of groups deemed experimental by the Arts Council were in receipt of subsidy at levels that might potentially compromise newer, more genuinely experimental groups. Miller also called upon the EDC to address London bias towards the companies supported and an alternative set of criteria to Barter's classification: here, Miller categorizes groups by the background of personnel involved. These include: (a) professionals including Freehold, The Hana Nō Mask Company, The Pip Simmons Group, Portable, The Ken Campbell Roadshow, Low Moan Spectacular, Triple Action, Quipu, Recreation Ground and venues such as the Open Space, The King's Head, Basement, Soho/Poly; (b) full-time teachers and students such as Brighton Combination, Welfare State International and the Bradford College of Art who treat Live Art as part of their on-going teaching and research; (c) artists including, Living Landscapes, Oval House, The John Bull Puncture Repair Kit, Phantom Captain, The Yorkshire Gnomes and The People Show who come from non-theatrical or teaching backgrounds and whose work stands little chance 'of being

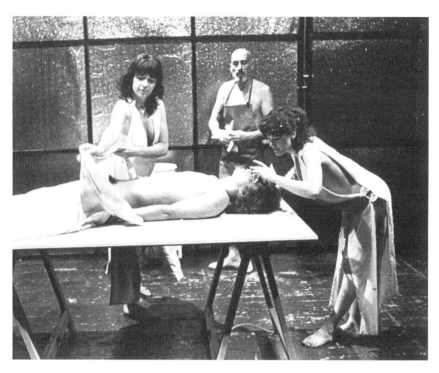

Image 2. Pip Simmons Group, *Masque of the Red Death* (Mickery Theatre, Amsterdam, September 1977). Photo by Bob Van Dantzig. © Pip Simmons: photo courtesy of the artist and Artsadmin.

35. Roland Miller, 'Proposals to the Experimental Drama Committee of the Arts Council of Great Britain', 12 September 1972. ACGB archive 43/43/1.

assimilated by mainstream theatre [or] any educational or sociological framework'.[35]

Miller concludes that groups in (a) tend to be both less innovative and also more financially demanding than those in categories (b) and (c), because of an inbuilt expectation from the Arts Council wanting to see a discernable return for their subsidy and the need for those in (a) to hit on a successful formula. Because (b) and particularly (c) work with fewer expectations from the Arts Council the chances of producing genuinely innovative work are greater. Miller also argues that group size is influential and cites Peter Brook's experiments with Artaud's Theatre of Cruelty only being realized by splitting into a smaller group within the Royal Shakespeare Company. Miller concludes by arguing that groups and individuals in (c) are also more cost effective in terms of work generated in relation to subsidy received, while their smaller size also makes them more adaptable to change. As evidence Miller calculates that his seven named groups in category (c) between them produced sixty pieces of work in the financial year 1971/72 for a combined subsidy of £3,000 as opposed to the £25,827 given to the companies and venues in (a), which during the same period produced twenty-three shows.

The following September, Miller (together with significant contributions from Shirley Cameron and Jeff Nuttall) submitted the second of his reports, this time specifically on the relationship of Live Art to the EPC.

Not only does it provide a valuable first-hand account of the development of Live Art, but it also includes a detailed directory of early practitioners and a theoretical framework that sets out a clear set of differences between theatre and performance. Miller terms these 'Declared' and 'Undeclared'. In the Declared mode intention is expressed clearly through text, director, actors, technicians and an audience who hold a number of set expectations. By contrast, for the Undeclared even the performers are unsure of the outcome of what might be an exploration of 'the dimensions and atmosphere of a building [...] a colour [...] a sound [...] a landscape [...] without fully knowing what *result* they want'. Likewise, spectators may simply be used as 'the sounding board for these reverberations'. The paper more generally also pinpoints key problems concerning the Arts Council's systems for assessing Live Art, where existing policies in Art and Music tended to fund one-off projects rather than the precedent established by the Drama Panel, which acknowledged that work by a dedicated group required long-term subsidy.[36] Yet at the same time Miller recognizes that subsidy also encourages inertia, with the tendency for individuals in established companies being reluctant to leave the security afforded by the group. Miller cites examples such as members of the Bath Arts Workshop prioritizing the Natural Theatre Company above their own interests, or Diz Wills from The John Bull Puncture Repair Kit working within the boundaries of the group rather than developing his own performance poetry.[37] Miller's chief recommendation is that the unique conditions under which Live Art operates requires what he calls a Performance Artist's Representative Committee, comprising predominantly of the artists themselves 'to serve as a clearing house and general bureau for performance art'.[38] However, by the time Miller and Cameron's report was presented the EPC itself was under threat, and performance art – which Jeff Nuttall described as 'a phrase tentatively tossed around like a cooling hot potato' – was to move out of the EPC's hands before the end of the year.[39]

In October 1973 Nick Barter wrote to the Deputy Secretary General of the Arts Council to inform him that the EPC was now in total disarray.[40] Amongst its problems were a weak Chairman in Edward Lucie-Smith and Committee members such as the poet Adrian Henri who appeared to have lost interest, while others such as the novelist Paul Bailey in his letter of resignation from the Committee found himself 'completely out of sympathy with 90% of the applicants [finding] most of their "ideas" trivial beyond words'.[41] In reply Lucie-Smith, despite Barter's complaints, comes closest to justifying both the work of the EPC and the EDC:

> You seem to me to offer a rather sweeping judgement of the EPC's work on minimal experience of its deliberations. Many of the committee's clients may be freakish [...] but many of the people who come to us have a social commitment more talked about than practiced by 'liberal' writers.[42]

Despite his passionate defence of the EPC, Lucie-Smith's letter only succeeded in producing more ferment when Charles Osborne from the

36. Roland Miller and Shirley Cameron, 'Declared and Undeclared: Two Approaches to Performance as a Technique', 3 July 1973, p. 12. ACGB 43/42/7. Emphasis in original.

37. Roland Miller and Shirley Cameron, 'Report on Performance Art to the Experimental Projects Committee', 10 September 1973. ACGB 43/42/7.

38. Ibid., p. 5.

39. Jeff Nuttall, 'The Situation Regarding Performance Art', August 1973. ACGB 43/42/7.

40. Nick Barter, Memo to Deputy Secretary General, 'Experimental Projects Committee', 30 October 1973. ACGB 43/42/7.

41. Paul Bailey, Letter to Edward Lucie Smith, 13 July 1973. ACGB 43/42/7.

42. Edward Lucie-Smith, Letter to Paul Bailey, 15 July 1973. ACGB 43/42/7.

Literature Panel, who sat on the EPC from 1970–72, unhelpfully contributed after seeing the correspondence between Bailey and Lucie-Smith,

> I have found it impossible to produce Literature Panel members to serve on that committee [the EPC] who are sufficiently gullible, or sufficiently willing to suspend their amusement [at the] total lack of talent, imagination, and even ability to express clearly the trivia cluttering up [the artist's] minds.[43]

Osborne's response, however undiplomatic is telling as it uncharacteristically lays open the feelings that may have surreptitiously shaped Arts Council policy towards Live Art since 1969.

COUM Transmissions and Genesis P-Orridge

COUM Transmissions in many ways embodied many of these prejudices. Formed in Hull in 1969 and led by Genesis P-Orridge, COUM fall into a form of Live Art described by Jeff Nuttall whereby the 'life-style of the collective [is] a creative achievement in itself' and adds 'even (hilariously) to the Arts Council'.[44] P-Orridge first approached the Arts Council for a capital grant and company subsidy in January 1973. Describing COUM as following 'no creed exactly', but one with 'roots in Zen, fun, concrete and expresses itself through every media (don't they all these days)'. P-Orridge explains that despite producing work since 1969, 'we wanted to wait till we knew we were capable of sustained and diverse creative activity'.[45] The scope and diversity of these endeavours included correspondence art, the recording of an LP and performance events including attempting to disqualify themselves deliberately from a national folk rock competition, in order – as P-Orridge explained – 'to point out some of the delusions, and contradictions of the pop industry'.[46]

Over the next month P-Orridge began sending the EPC a number of parcels containing examples of the group's correspondence art as well as artefacts, photographs and other writings. This reached such a point that Nick Barter wrote to P-Orridge asking him to 'please don't use us as an archive for all your various documents', warning that 'anything that isn't directly relevant to applications will, I'm afraid end up in the dustbin'.[47] Fortunately, this threat was never carried out and a collection of COUM's mail art and various ephemera are still held in the Arts Council archive.

COUM's approach at drawing the EPC's attention to the nature of their work still succeeded in irritating its Chairman Edward Lucie-Smith who 'was concerned by the tone of persistent facetiousness' running through their application and felt he would quickly tire of their 'avant-garde of nervous jerking'.[48] However, Nick Barter drew attention to the length of time the group had been established and argued that a small sum should be allocated to fund an on-going project that the Committee could go and see. A recommendation of £250 was agreed upon and Barter also wrote to the Yorkshire Arts Association (YAA) who had

43. Charles Osborne, Letter to Edward Lucie-Smith, 18 July 1973. ACGB 43/42/7.

44. Nuttall, 'The Situation Regarding Performance Art', n. p.

45. Genesis P-Orridge, Letter to the Arts Council of Great Britain, 17 January 1973, p. 1. ACGB 41/47/1. For an extended conversation with BREYER P-ORRIDGE (as Genesis P-Orridge now identifies), see their conversation with Dominic Johnson in the 'Documents' section of the present issue of *Contemporary Theatre Review*. pp. 134–45.

46. Ibid., p. 2.

47. Nick Barter. Letter to Genesis P-Orridge, 8 June 1973. ACGB 41/47/1.

48. Minutes of the Experimental Projects Committee, 23 February 1973. ACGB 43/42/7.

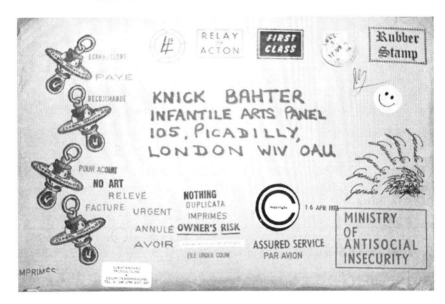

Image 3. COUM Transmissions, untitled postal art to the Arts Council (1973): photo courtesy of Tony Coult. © Genesis P-Orridge.

previously granted COUM £100 in 1972 for a show entitled *The Alien Brain* and a further £75 for another entitled *The Ministry of Anti-Social Insecurity* performed in February 1973 at the Ferens Art Gallery, Hull. This had consisted of an installation entitled 'Wagon Train', which a local review described as 'an old pram decorated in the most gaudy and bizarre manner'.[49]

The response from Michael Dawson of the YAA to Barter's enquiry about COUM's work exposes the Arts Council's ingrained prejudices, but also suggests recognition of the group's sincerity and acceptance that Live Art could encompass an artist's lifestyle. So while Dawson can describe COUM as 'inexperienced, uncontrolled and inept', he acknowledges that 'the performances are usually improvisational and spontaneous so cannot be judged in a theatrical context' and speaks about 'the group's sincerity and charm'. Dawson also recognizes that 'Genesis P-Orrridge [...] is creating for himself and his friends an elaborate life-style and if this, in itself, can be judged as a work of art then what he is doing is both thorough going and valid.' Dawson concludes with a question that also lay at the heart of Arts Council's policy towards Live Art: 'can bodies such as the Arts Council and the Association subsidise a lifestyle?' in that 'it is our subsidy up until now that has created the opportunity'.[50] Barter's response that 'it is perhaps the lifestyle of the group which might offer most' is suggestive that not everyone in the Arts Council was opposed to Live Art.[51]

P-Orridge's response to the grant of £250 was one of both 'welcoum [*sic*] support' and disappointment in that 'it seems we have to pass a kind of A Level to qualify'.[52] Yet this had been standard, if unofficial Arts Council policy from the beginning, whereby groups deemed 'experimental' were first offered modest sums and if the signs seemed encouraging more substantial amounts would be offered. Therefore

49. John Humber, 'It's Nicely Framed, But Is It Art?', *Daily Mail* (15 February 1973). ACGB 41/47/1, unpaginated clipping.

50. Michael Dawson, Letter to Nick Barter, 4 April 1973. ACGB 41/47/1.

51. Nick Barter, Letter to Michael Dawson, 18 April 1973. ACGB 41/47/1.

52. Genesis P-Orridge, Letter to Nick Barter, 26 April 1973. ACGB 41/47 /1.

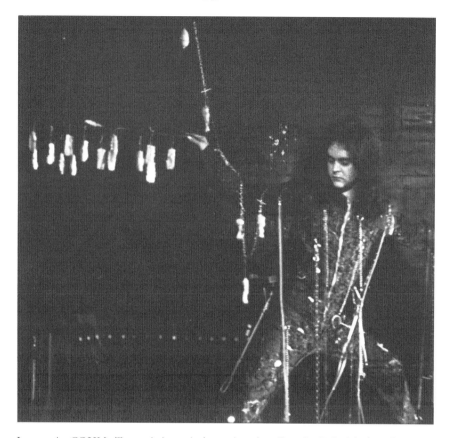

Image 4. COUM Transmissions (solo action by Genesis P-Orridge), *Through a Tamponstick Darkly* (1974) Arts Centre, Elephant and Castle, London. Photographer unknown. © BREYER P-ORRIDGE: photo courtesy Invisible Exports, New York.

Portable in 1969 received £89, followed by £2,992 in 1970, while the £150 allocated to Ken Campbell's Roadshow in 1971 rose to £1100 the following year. The same also happened to COUM, who the year after their £250 from the YAA received £1500 in annual subsidy.[53] However, by 1974 COUM were no longer receiving their funding from the EPC, or even the Drama Panel.

53. Figures taken from the Arts Council of Great Britain's Annual Reports, 1969–1974.

A Move To The Art Panel

Barter's hope (in his memo of October 1973 to the Deputy Secretary-General) that the EPC could 'limp along for two more meetings'[54] proved correct. The last meeting of the EPC took place on 14 December 1973, with many of its functions being devolved to the Arts Council's Community Arts Committee and the 'hot potato' of performance art transferred once again – this time to the Art Panel. Consequently, in 1974 groups including COUM Transmissions, Gasp, The John Bull Puncture Repair Kit, Landscapes and Living Spaces, Lumiere & Son Theatre Company, Myriad Event Structures, Situations and Real

54. Nick Barter, Memo to Deputy Secretary General, 'Experimental Projects Committee', 30 October 1973. ACGB 43/42/7.

Lifescapes and Phantom Captain all became the responsibility of the Art Panel.

55. Edward Lucie-Smith, Letter to Paul Bailey, 1 July 1973. ACGB 43/42/7.

Lucie-Smith's comment that the EPC (and by default the EDC) were 'an establishment mechanism for dealing with freaks',[55] neatly encapsulates much of the Arts Council's early relationship with Live Art. As we have seen in this broad account, evolving policy was often hampered by confusions over proper definition and lack of representation by the performance artists themselves on committees helping to shape policy. Nevertheless, groups such as Living Landscapes and COUM directly benefited from subsidy and Live Art, as part of its commitment to the 'Fringe', continued to be one of the Arts Council's notable achievements during the 1970s. However, writers and performers such as Howard Brenton and Ken Campbell who demonstrated visible connections to an existing theatre tradition were always advantaged when it came to funding, as were groups such as The Brighton Combination or Inter-action, who could demonstrate a social purpose behind the work. Live Art, where such concerns were often secondary to the work itself, were always going to be disappointed. While artists such as Roland Miller and Genesis P-Orridge were eventually recognized in terms of funding, for other groups such as The Yorkshire Gnomes and Gasp, subsidy was often based on levels that constituted little more than goodwill gestures than serious attempts at long-term funding.

Ultimately the early years of the ACGB's involvement with Live Art is one shared with many other artists between 1945–94 – essentially that of a benign benefactor; humanistic but also patrician in its tastes. Consequently it could only ever partly accommodate artists whose views differed so radically. Attempts at reaching an accommodation between these very different sensibilities is not only the story of the early years of Live Art, but how the arts in general developed under a system of public subsidy in Britain.

INTERVIEW

Positive Surrender: An Interview with BREYER P-ORRIDGE

Dominic Johnson

In their pronouncements on performance, art, history and humanity, BREYER P-ORRIDGE like to paint in broad brushstrokes. They create grand narratives about human evolution, creative potential, the politics of the body and self-determination through art. Crucially, they do so in order to urge us to attempt to replace old systems with new possibilities for change. 'Viva la Evolution!' is a key rallying cry of BREYER P-ORRIDGE, in interviews, statements and performances. Formerly Genesis P-Orridge and Lady Jaye Breyer, in recent years the artists have forgone their earlier names and public identities towards a new collective subjectivity. In tandem, the two formerly discreet individuals used cosmetic surgery, performance and other tools to produce a 'Third Being', a p-androgyne – or positive androgyne – that goes by the name BREYER P-ORRIDGE. This composite identity has obliterated the two prior individualities, towards a political exploration of the possibilities that emerge from experiments with art, science and culture. BREYER P-ORRIDGE's project epitomises and perhaps exceeds the use of performance in everyday life to blur the distinctions between art/life, even rendering such distinctions obsolete. As Laure Leber's portrait shows (see Image 1), the efforts of the surgical and other interventions have enabled the artists to achieve a striking similarity, troubling the common divisions attributable to gender, age, experience and other factors that become seemingly inconsequential under pressure from their unique 'living art' rituals.

Over a series of operations, beginning 1999, BREYER P-ORRIDGE used cosmetic surgery and body modification techniques towards a corporeal translation of the cut-up technique of William S.

Image 1   BREYER P-ORRIDGE, *Untitled* (2006): photo by Laure Leber. © BREYER P-ORRIDGE. Courtesy of the artist and Invisible Exports, New York.

Burroughs and Brion Gysin.[1] In *Breaking Sex* the two artists underwent a series of surgical procedures, including breast implants, chin, cheek and eye augmentation, dental operations and facial tattooing. *Breaking Sex* was an attempt to manifest physically 'the third mind', a concept that Burroughs and Gysin invented in the 1960s to invoke the possibilities that arise from a blurring of subjective limits through a technical approximation of collage through writing. As Gérard Georges-Lemaire writes,

> *The Third Mind* is not the history of a literary collaboration, but rather the complete fusion in a praxis of two subjectivities [...] that metamorphose into a third; it is from this collusion that a new author emerges, an absent third person invisibly and beyond grasp, decoding the silence.[2]

BREYER P-ORRIDGE followed, to the letter, this merging of subjectivities at the expense of a single authorial voice, producing the 'pandrogyne' (or 'p-androgyne'), a fleshy incarnation of the 'third mind'. They provocatively enacted Burroughs and Gysin's abandonment of inviolate works and artistic ownership, 'a magical or divine creativity that could only result from the unconditional integration of two sources' – in this case, the mirroring of bodies through surgical interventions.[3]

One of the problems with writing about BREYER P-ORRIDGE is the way in which they thread fertile fictions into their myths of self-invention. 'My original name was Neil Andrew Megson', Genesis BREYER P-ORRIDGE states. 'A couple of years ago I started to wonder what happened to Neil. I have become an artwork with no author. In a sense, Neil destroyed himself by

c-

1. For a detailed analysis of this project, see Dominic Johnson, 'Psychic Weight: The Pleasures and Pains of Performance', in *ORLAN: A Hybrid Body of Art Works*, ed. by Simon Donger with Simon Shepherd and ORLAN (Abingdon and New York: Routledge, 2010), pp. 84–99.
2. Gérard Georges-Lemaire, '23 Stitches Taken', in William S. Burroughs and Brion Gysin, *The Third Mind* (London: John Calder, 1979), pp. 9–24 (p. 18).
3. BREYER P-ORRIDGE, 'Excerpts from a Dialogue with Dominic Johnson', *Everything You Know About Sex Is Wrong: Extremes of Human Sexuality (and Everything in between)*, ed. by Russ Kick (New York: Disinformation Press, 2005), pp. 345–48 (p. 345).

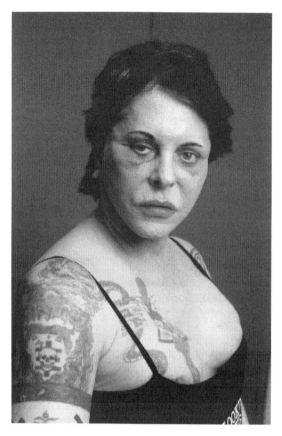

Image 2   BREYER P-ORRIDGE, *My Sacred Wound is Your Material Glamour* (2005). © BREYER P-OR-RIDGE. Courtesy of the artist and Invisible Exports, New York.

reating me.'[4] The threat the artists pose to traditional unities of biography and subjectivity were consolidated in disturbing ways when Lady Jaye BREYER P-ORRIDGE died, suddenly, of heart failure in October 2007. Since Lady Jaye's death, Genesis BREYER P-ORRIDGE identifies in the first person as 'we'. As such, their work inspires semantic trouble on several levels, from the capitalisation of their name, to the merging of singular histories into a confusingly conglomerate identity, to the surviving artist's decision to identify in the plural. According to Genesis BREYER P-ORRIDGE,

Since Lady Jaye dropped her body on 9 October 2007, we dropped using 'I' in favour of 'we' to signify Lady Jaye's continued presence in our body and personality, as well as her ongoing presence in

the Pandrogeny project – not just a nostalgic presence but a dynamic one as we continue to create works we co-created and proposed using photographic and other biological materials to realise new works.

Despite the tragedy of Lady Jaye's death, the project has persisted in a wide-ranging series of art/life endeavours. The decision to carry on the 'collaboration' functions as another way in which the artist(s) find new ways of complicating the convention methods of scholarly, curatorial and other practices of accounting for and narrating artistic achievements. Traditional modes of biography, historical summary and critical writing fail when one tries to discuss the multiple identities, harassed bodies and destitute subjectivities that p-androgyny has produced. It has proven difficult to negotiate how to refer to the artists, owing to the different ways they identify across various moments, in terms of gendered and singular or plural personal pronouns (the artists refer to themselves with traditional first pronouns in the dialogue below, but have asked that I refer to them in the plural in this introduction; Genesis BREYER P-ORRIDGE also refer to themselves in the plural in the prologue added since we conducted the interview). They have invented a string of neologisms to describe themselves and their practices. As a 'Third Being', they are both multiple and a composite, unified persona. However, language fails me in my attempts to address them clearly and concisely. I struggle in my abilities to write about them, and to describe efficiently how they constitute themselves as subjects and as artists. This is not simply a methodological burden, but a sign of their insistent refusal to allow others to assimilate them and their artistic practices into convenient systems of production, consumption and reception.

The following interview with Genesis and Lady Jaye BREYER P-ORRIDGE was conducted live at New York University in April 2007. The dialogue was presented as part of the keynote address to a symposium that explored the possibilities for subcultural practice in an age of quickening and intensifying processes of gentrification, containment and commodification.[5] In their innovations

4. Genesis BREYER P-ORRIDGE, interview with the author, New York, April 2007.

5. *After CBGB: Gender, Sexuality and the Future of Subculture* took place at New York University on 13 April 2007, and was organised by the Centre for the Study of Gender and Sexuality. I am grateful to Tavia Nyong'o and Robert D. Campbell for permission to publish an edited transcript of the dialogue. The transcript has been amended and extended in correspondence since 2007, including a prologue added by Genesis BREYER P-ORRIDGE in 2011.

across the art/life divide, BREYER P-ORRIDGE have resisted the tendency towards institutional assimilation, by exploring a form of positive cultural terrorism in and beyond performance. Here, they explain how their current project *Breaking Sex* (1999–2007) complements and extends their earlier solo and collaborative practices towards new and challenging realisations in the cultural politics of Live Art and performance. They discuss their own perceived relations to 'Live Art', and a preference for using the terminology of 'Living Art', tying *Breaking Sex* and earlier works into the historical avant-garde project. Since the mid-twentieth century, the avant-garde has attempted the 'sublation' of art into the praxis of life, in order to demolish the bourgeois institution of art as a set of practices, values and bodies of knowledge that sit apart from lived experiences.[6] Live Art and performance art practitioners in the UK have long explored the avant-garde project of bringing art into the praxis of life, for example the Living Art projects of Gilbert & George or Leigh Bowery.

Genesis and Lady Jaye BREYER P-ORRIDGE are key to histories of cultural experimentation – in the UK since the 1960s, on the one hand, and in downtown New York's club and performance scene on the other – and these histories have merged in an unprecedented experiment. The American-born artist Lady Jaye BREYER P-ORRIDGE was a formative influence on downtown performance, as a member of Blacklips Performance Cult (with Antony Hegarty), a club performance troupe inspired by Jimmy Camicia's legendary Hot Peaches. Lady Jaye was also influential as a co-founder of the House of Domination at the legendary New York club Jackie 60. Born in Manchester in 1950, Genesis BREYER P-ORRIDGE relentlessly inserted new strategies into the horizon of art and popular culture from an early age, and these included historical cultural innovations such as industrial music and body modification in the 1970s, acid house in the 1980s and, most recently, the figure of the p-androgyne.[7] I should add that the provision of

seemingly straightforward information, including the artists' personal histories, feels surprisingly awkward in the wake of the unique collaborative principles that BREYER P-ORRIDGE uphold. It is this spirit of persistent interruption, I would argue, that makes their work an apposite example of Live Art (despite their protestations about the limitations of this term), bearing in mind its frequent definition as a strategic disturbance of institutional conventions. This should hardly be surprising: a founder of the British performance group COUM Transmissions, the art/music groups Throbbing Gristle and Psychic TV, and the spoken word project Thee Majesty, Genesis BREYER P-ORRIDGE have been at the forefront of British cross-disciplinary arts for four decades. Nevertheless, many of these accomplishments have been written out of dominant histories of performance and Live Art in the UK, along with the work of a range of prolific artists who were similarly crucial to the cultural landscape of British art in the 1970s and 1980s especially. These include Shirley Cameron and Roland Miller, Pip Simmons, John Bull Puncture Repair Kit and Bruce Lacey. BREYER P-ORRIDGE discuss some of these artists as influences on their early work, primarily during the years in which COUM Transmissions were active.

'One of my main quests in life has been to take control of my own identity in a very real way', BREYER P-ORRIDGE state.[8] In their practice, this quest has involved performance art, collage, mail art, sound and music, the occult practice of Sigil drawing (inspired by the art of Austin Osman Spare) and other seemingly uncategorisable artistic pursuits. Since the public inauguration of the Pandrogeny (or Pandrogyny) project their works have focused upon video works, sculptures, installations and photography. These diverse and personally invested practices have led to the development of new modes of performance and, most strikingly perhaps, the obliteration of any feasible distinction between art and life. As BREYER P-ORRIDGE state, 'Pandrogeny is not about defining differences but about creating similarities. Not about separation but about unification, about inclusion and resolution.'[9] They clearly define the project of breaking sex as an evolutionary endeavour, to urge the body into more responsive and responsible arrangements.

6. Peter Bürger, *Theory of the Avant-Garde* trans. by Michael Shaw (Minneapolis: University of Minnesota Press, 1984).
7. See Brian Cogan, '"Do They Owe Us a Living? Of Course They Do!": Crass, Throbbing Gristle, and Anarchy and Radicalism in Early English Punk Rock', *Journal for the Study of Radicalism*, 1 (2008), 77–90; Drew Daniel, *Throbbing Gristle's 20 Jazz Funk Greats* (London: 33 1/3, 2008); Richard Metzger, *Book of Lies: The Disinformation Guide to Magick and the Occult* (New York: Disinformation, 2003); Genesis P-Orridge, *Painful but Fabulous: The Life and Art of Genesis P-Orridge* (New York: Soft Skull, 2002); Simon Reynolds, *Rip It Up and Start Again: Postpunk, 1978–1984* (London: Faber and Faber, 2006); *Modern Primitives:*

Investigations of Contemporary Adornment Rituals, ed. by V. Vale and Andrea Juno (San Francisco: Re/Search, 1997).
8. Genesis BREYER P-ORRIDGE, interview with the author, New York, April 2007.
9. Ibid.

everything about coum is true

Image 3 COUM Transmissions, *Scenes of Victory #3* (1976). Solo COUM Transmissions action by Genesis BREYER P-ORRIDGE at Death Factory, London 1976. © BREYER P-ORRIDGE. Courtesy of the artist and Invisible Exports, New York.

This politics is clearly influenced by Burroughs, who wrote of 'the feeling that the whole human organism and its way of propagating is repellent and inefficient. A living being is an artifact, like the flintlock. Well, what's wrong with the flint-lock? Just about everything.'[10] Describing the problems with early firearm technologies, and their replacement by more sophisticated machines, Burroughs continues that 'the human artifact is back there with the flintlock [...] There are possibilities of more efficient organisms. If you don't use it you lose it.'[11] The relentless deconditioning of limits has been a persistent impulse for BREYER P-ORRIDGE across forty years of creative experimentation. It constitutes a subversive bleeding across contested boundaries,

and a highly political attempt to muddle pre-conceived categories of experience. In the words of their mentor, Burroughs, after the 'Master of the Assassins', Hassan I Sabbah: 'NOTHING IS TRUE. EVERYTHING IS PERMITTED.'[12]

Prologue by Genesis BREYER P-ORRIDGE

We suppose we have exaggerated a few things in terms of this project, but that's what you do – can do – in a work of fiction (thinking of Lady Jaye's life seen as a resume). One of the first strategies Jaye proposed to me was after I complained about the tedium of doing countless repetitious inter-views for different media, because of the imposed separation of literature, music, performance, art and life. S/he suggested that, instead of retelling the same story and anecdotes ad nauseam, that we make up different conflicting answers each time we were interviewed. Through SELF-editing, cultural, social and economic pressures and intimidations alone all lives become fictional and that is before neuroses, ambitions, paranoia and mental idiosyncrasies become part of the mix. So, as all identities are fictional, active co-authorship of our Pandrogenic narrative is an essential strategy.[13]

Interview

Dominic Johnson: *How did* Breaking Sex *come about?*

Genesis BREYER P-ORRIDGE: At the begin-ning of *Breaking Sex* and Pandrogeny, Lady Jaye and I saw it primarily as an incredibly romantic thing to do – to want to become each other, to look like each other. So the very first thing that we did that was more or less permanent was I got two tattoos on my cheek – beauty spots where Lady Jaye has some, and then she had one removed on the other cheek, so that we were beginning to make our faces more superficially the same. Then she got the shape of her eyes changed so that they were more like mine, and got her nose worked on to make it like mine. Lady

10. Cited in Ted Morgan, *Literary Outlaw: The Life and Times of William S. Burroughs* (London: Pimlico, 1991), p. 352.
11. Ibid.
12. William S. Burroughs, *Cities of the Red Night* (London: Penguin, 1981), p. xviii.
13. Genesis BREYER P-ORRIDGE added this paragraph as a prologue in 2011 during the collaborative editing of the interview from the transcript into a publishable form.

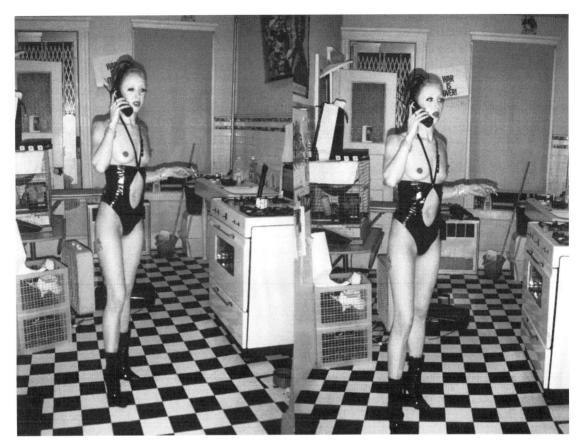

Image 4   BREYER P-ORRIDGE, *Keeping Up With the Brian Joneses* (2008). C-print on Plexiglas. © BREYER P-ORRIDGE. Courtesy of the artist and Invisible Exports, New York.

Jaye and I both got breast implants three years ago on Valentine's Day 2003 and we woke up together in the room where you come back from being under the anaesthetic, and we held hands, and as I looked down I found myself saying, 'Oh, these are our angelic bodies.' I found it really interesting that I would go to sleep and when I woke up I would not recognise the person in the mirror in the same way.

I'm just a basic heterosexual, which confuses people because it's much less common for heterosexuals to be transgender. And I'm not fully accepted by the transgender community because they don't understand why it would be an art project. We really are investigating the idea of evolution. We're challenging DNA and refusing to accept it as the programming that controls our biological life. I am a p-androgyne – a positive androgyne. A hermaphrodite by choice. Pandrogeny is a suggestion or strategy for the survival of the species. In some ways all the different projects – even the music – are about challenging the status

quo in order to change. I think change should be inclusive of other people, not exclusive.

DJ: *I'd like to ask you about the idea of allegiance, in the sense of connecting to forgotten or less privileged parts of cultural history. You've often discussed your relation to William S. Burroughs, Brion Gysin and Derek Jarman, for example. How important is it to you to connect yourself to histories of cultural experimentation?*

GBPO: People feel a kinship with what BREYER P-ORRIDGE have been doing in our various incarnations. It was the same for me when I was young in the 1960s, and I'm sure for Lady Jaye in her time. There are certain people, certain movements, usually suppressed ways of seeing the world, different ways of perceiving reality that shine like beacons because they contradict everything that's being pushed into you by the so-called normal world. I went to a very authoritarian British school that actually had a statement in their manifesto that said that art was not a real subject – parents were expected to be glad that teachers didn't waste their

Image 5   BREYER P-ORRIDGE, *Untitled* (2006): photo by Laure Leber. © BREYER P-ORRIDGE. Courtesy of the artist and Invisible Exports, New York.

time teaching us anything to do with literature or art. For whatever reasons I'm perverse and that made me want to look at literature and art as much as I could. So there was an attraction for previous manifestations of rebellion I think. If you feel rebellious against the status quo you look for commonality with other rebels. You seek them out. You ask them what it is that they're trying to say and find out if you can say something similar but in a more contemporary way. So that's how I very luckily got to know William Burroughs, Brion Gysin and Derek Jarman very early, in the period between 1969 and 1971.[14]

Burroughs and Gysin have been highly influential to us, particularly in relation to the practice of the 'cut-up'. To liberate the word from linearity, they began to cut-up texts and, incorporating random chance, re-assembled both their own and co-opted literature 'to see what it really says'. They referred to the phenomena of profound and poetic new collisions and meanings that resulted from their intimate collaborations as the 'Third Mind'. This was produced with a willingness to sacrifice their separate, previously inviolate works and artistic 'ownership'. In many ways they saw the Third Mind as an entity in and of itself. Something 'other', closer to a purity or essence, and the origin and source of a magical or divine creativity that could only result from the unconditional integration of two sources.

DJ: *Literary experimentation was very important to you. How has your work been influenced by the history of performance in the UK?*

GBPO: We began working with performance in 1965 in Solihull, Warwickshire, with dadaist street happenings like *Beautiful Litter*.[15] We scattered small cards with evocative words written on them all over town, inside cafes, bookshops, etc. and in the street. As any curious person picked up the words they were creating a haiku-like poem. All the cards picked up also 'wrote' a long poem, but one that

14. For a detailed history of this period, see Simon Ford, *Wreckers of Civilisation: The Story of COUM Transmissions and Throbbing Gristle* (London: Black Dog, 1999), pp. 1.11–2.10.

15. This section was also added in 2011, hence the shift from 'I' to 'we' in the use of personal pronoun.

nobody would ever see or hear complete. In 1969 we joined David Medalla's Exploding Galaxy in Islington and it was there that we were mutated by the rigorous aesthetics into entirely new ways of seeing what art could become. We founded COUM Transmissions in 1969 as well. Initially alone, later with John Shapeero and, as time went by, more and more people became involved to varying degrees of engagement. COUM Transmissions began to flourish in Hull in 1970–71 creating unsolicited street theatre happenings. These actions got noticed and we began to receive Arts Council bursaries and grants. We added pages to *Groupvine* [magazine] and as a direct result COUM began to be invited to participate in a lot of the Arts Festivals that flourished then. We met Roland Miller and Shirley Cameron who were very supportive of our early, somewhat shambolic events and actions. We met the John Bull Puncture Repair Kit, The Welfare State and Jeff Nuttall and The People Show during the early 1970s. We were generally surprised how many of these people were art school lecturers with very academic approaches to performance art – as it had only just been dubbed. Almost all of these groups seemed to have a pretty theatrical bent to their works with, it also seemed, a diminishing ratio of improvisation or happening. Because we were heavily involved in mail art – and through that, Fluxus our influences were more conceptual and ironic.

As time progressed we dug deeper and deeper into taboo, transgressive actions, sexuality and gender roles, primarily with Sleazy Christopherson and Cosey Fanni Tutti. We had all had the good fortune to avoid art college, so our evolution was based almost entirely upon our own communal explorations together sexually and our lengthy internal discussions about boundaries of all kinds. Who delineates them? Who benefits from social norms? Is there a valid reason for government intrusion into the privacy of our individual physical bodies? An artist's right to choose how they use and abuse their flesh was an important issue. Towards the end of COUM Transmissions the work was almost entirely about gender roles as we tried to destabilise them.

DJ: *Performance is clearly an important methodology in your practice. Do you find the term 'Live Art' relevant or useful as a description of your work? If not how would you describe your practice?*

GBPO: If you said 'Living Art' we might be comfortable with that as a term. By changing 'Live Art' to 'Living Art', more levels and flexibilities of meaning are aroused. Living Art implies some form of being alive as opposed to dead. The art is active and filled with potential and still evolving. From the artists' perspective it clarifies an important distinction for BREYER P-ORRIDGE, namely the insistence that we are living art constantly without any separation between creation of art objects, installations, films and any other useful medium available, and what are normally seen as 'domestic' activities in daily living. Art, we believe, must be all-inclusive and 24/7, with its prime motivation embedded, no matter how obliquely, in every action or product. That motivation is a positive evolution of the human species: a transcendence of current economic, social, sexual and religious mores. When you consider transsexuality, cross-dressing, cosmetic surgery, piercing and tattooing, they are all calculated impulses – a symptomatic groping towards the next phase. One of the great things about human beings is that we impulsively and intuitively express what is inevitably next in the evolution of culture and our species. It is the Other that we are destined to become.

It is important to point out that whilst we continue to develop and document performances (primarily through Sigils [*magickal* drawings], Polaroids and video), these are almost exclusively enacted in private. We use self-created rituals to see how deeply we can explore the neurosphere (the consciousness and the chemical brain), the endurance levels of our bodies and minds, and their threshold for restriction and physical limitations of our bodies. The goal is not to produce aesthetically satisfying artworks but to try and retrieve the diaphanous waves of potentially new information to explain questions such as why are we here? What other states of being are there? What is the true nature of time? What other dimensions and locations beyond our small consensus reality might exist? Pandrogeny includes every means of perception, so 'Live Art' would be inaccurate, misleading and far too constricting a term for BREYER P-ORRIDGE.

DJ: *You both bring very different histories and experiences to the project of* Breaking Sex. *Can you each say something about the preparations that enabled you to tackle such complex and provocative material?*

Lady Jaye BREYER P-ORRIDGE: Although our backgrounds are very different, Gen and I share common early childhood experiences. When we discussed our early life quite soon after we met we realised that sharing these similar experiences caused us to perceive the world in a certain way. As an extension of that some of the same artists resonated strongly with us – Marcel Duchamp, Pierre Molinier, Hans Bellmer, Stelarc and ORLAN spring to mind. Like getting hit over the head, you find something obscure or suppressed and it seems like a truth, and you ask how it could have escaped you for so long. Not all of our life experiences have been the same, naturally – we're from different generations, and from different countries, but that in many ways helps our work. It would not be a work of the Third Mind/Third Being if we saw everything identically. Sometimes our views will contradict each other, like an exception that proves the rule. Our work isn't parallel sometimes, but rather perpendicular, and forms a greater whole that covers a lot more territory.

GBPO: Jaye became very active in the downtown New York scene and alternative theatre. Do you want to mention that?

LJBPO: A lot of the work that I did when I was younger drew certain parallels to Gen's work. Had I known about Gen's work – had I been a little more worldly and sophisticated – I might not have done some of these things, knowing that they had already been done in the 1970s! But I felt a need in myself to explore certain things, and when I started reviewing Gen's early work I realised it expressed similar ideas to what I was feeling at the same age.

DJ: *To turn specifically to the Pandrogeny project, one of the most striking tensions in the work is that although it may seem at least superficially to be monstrous or horrific, on a much deeper level it demonstrates an investment in romance. Can you say something about the collision between monstrosity and romance?*

GBPO: At the very beginning before we were committed to being with each other for a long time, one of the very first times we actually met in New York I stayed at Jaye's apartment – we were still just good friends – one of the first things she did was dress me up like a little doll, in a very androgynous way.

LJBPO: It was a green crushed-velvet Betsey Johnson cat-suit.

GBPO: And a little leather skirt, with Fluevog shoes that you bought me especially.

LJBPO: Only the best.

GBPO: Only the best. So there was an immediate resonance between us that was never discussed at the beginning where we began to blend. From then on we playfully started to cross-dress with each other, and play with the idea of looking similar and not taking on traditional roles. When we got married on Friday 13 June 1995, we intuitively – without a great deal of discussion – swapped roles. I wore a white lace dress and nice white and black shoes, and Jaye wore skin-tight leather trousers, motorcycle boots, a leather vest over her naked torso revealing her breasts, and a moustache. That was the first step – a

Image 6 BREYER P-ORRIDGE, *Topless Poor-trait* (2008–2010). C-print on Plexiglas: photo by M. Sharkey, reprocessed by BREYER P-ORRIDGE. © BREYER P-ORRIDGE. Courtesy of the artist and Invisible Exports, New York.

deeply romantic urge to blend. The mutual orgasm can be a transcendent experience where two people seem to become one. Another way you can have that experience is to create a baby, which is again two people becoming one. We didn't want to have a baby, but we did want to create a new being that represented the two of us, so we took each other and started to analyse how we could play with that sense of Positive Surrender, and create a new dynamic being. That's where the more considered artistic side began.

DJ: *Would you say that* Breaking Sex *is a utopian project?*

GBPO: When we began *Breaking Sex* and as it developed into Pandrogeny both of us saw it as primarily a process of and for our own liberation from any gender or identity expectations or social conditioning. The central energy was our deeply romantic love for one another. Inevitably, as performance artists and creators who see no separation whatsoever between our daily life and the concept of 'art' we channelled our responses and observations back into our practice, and integrated documentation into exhibitions via sculptures, assemblages and photo works overlaid onto collages of original Polaroids generated by our experiments and rituals. A core part of our collaboration was always endless discussion and dialogue back and forth about the effects we were noting on ourselves, and the expanding implications we felt we were exposing.

In 1971, Burroughs charged me with a task: 'How do you short circuit control?' We came to feel that control was ultimately inseparable from information and in turn recording devices, from pre-Astoric cave paintings to the Internet to the archaeological residue recorded within the earth itself. Control, we concluded, resides biologically in and as DNA. The gender, shape, medical flaws and longevity of individual existence are pre-programmed to a large extent by DNA. We speculated that DNA itself might be the primary life form on earth, with our species as host organisms that unwittingly enabled the continuity of DNA. We saw DNA as a limiting mechanism of human existence. To contradict, interdict and deny the DNA pre-programme of our physical unfolding became both a part of our agenda personally and a symbol of our absolute rejection of any and all imposed evolution. So we began mutating towards an hermaphroditic logo of our rejection of DNA. As we became more comfortable as a third being of, at least conceptually, obliterating obvious physical and gender differences, we discovered another layer of meanings and possibilities released by our project. When you refute the control of DNA we felt you can begin to embrace a rejection of any limitations to the mutability and possibility for evolution. BREYER P-ORRIDGE have come to view the physical body as simply raw material. 'A cheap suitcase for consciousness', as Lady Jaye says.

We support all surgical or genetic advances towards self-designed futures. Why not hibernate in order to colonise space for example? Grow gills to swim underwater? Fur or feathers as fashion accessories? Central to all these various speculations was the collapse of binary systems into redundancy. We believe that as one becomes the author of one's own physical and social narrative by inclusivity instead of exclusivity, as you excise oneself from either/or, black/white, Muslim/Christian, male/female and so on you can become aware of similarities, commonality, and eventually perceive oneself as part of a 'HumanE Species'. A world embracing mutation and radical evolution will more naturally assign resources to the most advantageous aspect for the well-being of the entire species. This is a very brief explanation of our thought process. From union through and as love, to union as a demonstration of change socially, and eventually to union of an entire species perceived as one fully integrated organism with no limitation on any level of biological mutability. Self designed personally and socially in preparation for the next phase of humane evolution. The colonisation of space. The human body is not sacred, it is a tool with a consciousness. There is no reason to believe or assume that this is our finished state. This is, to BREYER P-ORRIDGE, a 'larval', initial state of being at a crossroads. We believe, with Pandrogeny, that the means of perception can be seized and become limitless, leading our species into being an inclusive, integrated organism on a threshold of unimaginable and miraculous achievements. Hence we say, 'Viva La Evolution!' Utopian? Absolutely.

DJ: *How does the political emerge from this particular sense of the utopian? I'm reminded of Burroughs' statement that 'paranoia is having all the facts', where a political statement emerges from blurring the boundaries between two opposites: the positive and the negative, loaded and neutral, romance and monstrosity.*

GBPO: Burroughs also said that if there's a situation that makes you uncomfortable, or feels threatening, look for the vested interest. Well, we felt very uncomfortable in the stereotypical roles we were assigned, in terms of gender and being biologically present. We wanted to expose the deliberate conditioning and the push towards emotional, economic and creative inertia, which serves the purposes of globalised culture. The last thing that the great corporations would like is to have a new species erupt that's based on the absolute rejection of everything inherited at birth – identity, body, social position, gender, race, humanity – a new species that has the right and the way to erase everything we were given and rebuild itself. That's where the political emerges.

LJBPO: Today I was talking to Gen about the story of Marduk and Tiamat. It's the first recorded story of how mankind was created – a Sumerian narrative about a pre-Biblical god who conquers the dragon Tiamat who represents femininity, chaos, nature and wilderness. The other gods made Marduk in the figure of a man, and gave him the power to create the world – including the first city and the first civilisation – and the power to rule its people.[16] So the very first creation story is based on control. There's an extension of the story that says

16. See Stephanie Dalley, *Myths from Mesopotamia: Creation, the Flood, Gilgamesh, and Others* (Oxford: Oxford Paperbacks, 2008).

humans were put here to serve gods and to serve kings, and fill their storehouses with grain to give them wealth. I would find some kind of change refreshing at this point.

GBPO: Gender infuses every cultural system and is a very important aspect of reassessing what it is to be present, to feel that you're alive in any particular consensus reality. Yet people often confuse gender and identity too easily. Identity is something that begins from the moment you're conceived, while you're still inside your mother's womb. Before you even come out there is the influence of relatives you've never met that you may hate when you do meet, all these things that your parents want to have happen, and their friends have investments in what you're going to be, and it just gets worse from then – school, peer groups, you're a boy so you have to hang out with the boys and do boy things, and so on. The key point about this structure is that it's fictional. If it wasn't you making all those choices up to the point you become fully self-aware, perhaps around puberty, then you've had the story of your identity written for you – a narrative written by someone else. That's just not acceptable. Everyone should have the absolute right to be the person who writes their own story and creates their own narrative. To give it away or to let it go through laziness is a tragedy. That's how we're controlled, because we let those stories become the warp and the weft of the fabric of society, and then we're stuck. So a process of deconditioning is incredibly important if you want to rebuild your own identity and write your own story.

LJBPO: It's difficult of course, because our culture doesn't accept change, and if you were to reject everything – all your family's wishes and all their dreams for you they would be hurt. We're controlled by guilt. We don't want to make changes that will make other people love us less or not accept us.

GBPO: I'm sure everyone knows about that. Everyone has to go through it over and over again. Well, there are very simple ways to change your identity. Change your name. The name is the first way that other people exert power over you. If you change your name you take on a huge challenge. Neil Megson thought he could make an artwork that was an extension of Andy Warhol's idea of the superstar, and create consciously a character as an art piece, which was Genesis P-Orridge. But Neil hasn't been seen since 1969. Gone. Subsumed.

LJBPO: And the character wasn't just Genesis. If I look at what's left of the archive, all the photographs, there are hundreds of different characters that all have very distinctive personal-

ities and represent different ideas. Sometimes they lasted for ten minutes and sometimes they lasted for a few years. It was so wonderful to see an artist who had so much to express.

DJ: *Finally, I think it's clear from the amount of exhibitions and performances that you are working on right now that there seems to be a moment for your work. I'm interested in the conditions that make the reception of work possible, but I'm also intrigued as to whether you think there's a future for subculture. Why is this the moment right for* Breaking Sex *and the emergence of the pandrogyne?*

LJBPO: In one of your earlier questions you used the word 'monstrosity'. In the past twenty years, broadcast media and advertising have become so sophisticated that ever since punk all these manifestations of subversive culture that young people especially are attracted to have been taken from the streets and repackaged, and sold back to them. Everything is a potential product, and I think that for some people we are just a little too raw and a little too hard to look at. It's going to be very hard to put our work in a box, place a little ribbon on it, and sell it. I think that's exciting because what we are working on isn't a commodity. How can you sell individuality? It's not the kind of individuality like 'I want to be different like everybody else', where a subversive style is defined for you, along with where you should go, the type of people you should hang out with, the shops you should purchase your clothing at or the kind of music you can listen too. What we're doing is much more abstract than that – you can't pin it down as easily because it covers so many bases.

GBPO: There are two lines of thinking that I'm pondering. One of them is quite simple, which is that Pandrogeny, as a word, is uncluttered by any specific connections to gender, sexual orientation or sexual preference. It's a very gender-neutral word. But it's also a very clear declaration at the same time. At the very least it gives a lot of different people a chance to discuss issues to do with the survival of the species, the way that culture is working and the changes that are happening to the way people view their bodies. If Pandrogeny does nothing else but open up debate by becoming a word that can be rebuilt from the beginning to represent a much more non-aligned view of things, then that would be important.

The second way I can respond to your question is that we're in an age where people are still driven by prehistoric genetic codes. To put it simply, when we were all running around naked trying to catch slow-moving animals in prehistoric times it probably came in very useful for the male of the species to have the fight or flight reflex in his genetic code, in order to hunt and survive. Without that primitive drive we wouldn't all still be here. We then discovered weapons and tools that helped us to kill some of those slow-moving animals, including each other. We got very excited when we learnt we could make tools, and slowly but surely over thousands of years we built this incredible, miraculous, technological environment. People can pick up little boxes and talk to somebody at the other end of the earth, they can fly, they can be in space looking down. But nobody's been bothered to check on our behaviour and move it along at the same rate. We're still genetically prehistoric. So we're in this horrible situation of a futuristic technological environment and a prehistoric band of clever apes ready to destroy each other because their behavioural responses are so polarised from the world they live in. It's an incredibly dangerous time. Dualistic societies have become so fundamentally inert, uncontrollably consuming decreasing resources and self-perpetuating,

threatening the continued existence of our species and the pragmatic beauty of infinite diversity of expression. In this context the journey represented by Pandrogeny – and the experimental creation of a third form of gender-neutral living being – is concerned with nothing less than strategies dedicated to the survival of the species.

Pandrogeny went from that deep romance that you mentioned into a discussion about identity and how it's made. That led us to realise that really the ultimate question is: evolution or not. That makes it a very volatile and exciting concept for us, which contains the seed of a discussion about survival. That's why it's resonating – people instinctively are seeing Pandrogeny as a door they can pass through in order to talk about their fears:

And then you want two
See if you could
Go right through
A thick brick wall.

The Common Turn in Performance

Gavin Butt

Histories

In a spoof TV documentary comprising part of Mel Brimfield's 2010 work *This Is Performance Art*, there are the bare bones of a now familiar story of the emergence of Live Art.[1] In a thirty-five minute video that comprises a generally irreverent look at performance history, Brimfield focuses at one point on the transition from minimalism to body art, a shift now widely acknowledged as seminal in the formation of Live Art. The move away from object-based work towards artists using their own 'live' bodies as material for art practice, is often taken alongside challenges to 'the circumstance and expectations of theatre' making Live Art a kind of doubled 'exit strategy': an exiting, that is, from the conventions of both fine art and theatre in the mid- to late twentieth century.[2] This general approach to accounting for, and defining, Live Art has been crucial to discourses around the form since the 1980s, particularly within the UK, as it has been promoted by, among others, the National Review of Live Art in Glasgow and the Live Art Development Agency in London.[3]

In Brimfield's video, this narrative of Live Art's development survives at least partially intact, but not without a few surprising twists. First, whereas the dominance of US culture in stories of post-war art might lead us to more readily expect an American artist such as Robert Morris or Bruce Nauman to embody the shift towards Live Art, it is Bruce McLean, a Scottish artist, who is given this pioneering role in Brimfield's documentary. True, McLean is an acknowledged figure in the history of performance art, and features, for example, in RoseLee Goldberg's path breaking study of the form.[4] He was also one of the artists selected to re-perform 'seminal' work at the Whitechapel Gallery's *A Short History of Performance* in 2002 alongside other performance art 'greats' including

1. *This is Performance Art: Performed Sculpture and Dance (Part 1)* took place at Camden Arts Centre, London, 8 April–8 June 2010.

2. 'What is Live Art?', from the Live Art Development Agency's website, <http://www.thisisliveart.co.uk/about_us/what_is_live_art.html> [accessed 24 November 2011].

3. I generally follow this definition of 'Live Art' in this essay. I invoke it as a generally capacious moniker designating performance art and body art, as well as other kinds of live work that set themselves apart from

Carolee Schneemann, Stuart Brisley and Hermann Nitsch.[5] Brimfield steers very far, however, from any sober estimation of McLean's canonical value, as the would-be authoritative voice-over of the documentary soon makes apparent:

> One man can lay more claim than most to toppling the unwieldy macho edifice [of minimalism] from its dusty plinth. I refer, of course, to Bruce McLean. His path to global stardom proves what the human spirit can accomplish when relentless drive and determination converge with dreams. His long and arduous journey from two-bit pub stripper collecting tips in a bucket to become one of the world's most accomplished and innovative artists is an inspiration to all who face overwhelming obstacles and challenges on the road to success.

In presenting such a deliberately hackneyed and parodic voiceover, spoken by an actor, Brimfield goes over-the-top in narrating McLean's significance and centrality to the histories of Live Art, and clues us in to her generally mischievous approach to cultural status in *This Is Performance Art*. Melding the hagiographic mythologizing tendencies of art history with the gossipy and sensationalist narratives of celebrity culture, McLean is not only championed here as the heroic challenger to the 'pompous monumentality of plinth-based sculpture' but, in addition, tales about the artist's supposed work as a stripper, his beefcake attractiveness and his womanizing with the unlikely trio of RoseLee Goldberg herself, artist Martha Rosler and pop singer Olivia Newton John are deftly, and hilariously, woven into the historical mix.

This brings us to perhaps the most striking twist to the Live Art story that Brimfield's work represents: that it incongruously drags the seriousness of performance art history into the orbit of comedy. For the most part *This Is Performance Art* is funny because it imaginatively recounts bizarre and absurdist narratives in place of 'proper' performance history. For instance, the story of McLean's pivotal role in fashioning the beginnings of Live Art is told largely by means of invented, improbable and sometimes ludicrous anecdotes about his work and its departure from minimalist aesthetics. For example, McLean is reported to have played a trick on Donald Judd, the minimalist artist, involving the release of helium into a recording studio during Judd's supposed interview with Melvyn Bragg on BBC Radio 4. We are then told that this event was picked up, and referred to as an epochal moment, by art critic Michael Fried in his now classic essay 'Art and Objecthood'[6] – again somewhat improbably re-imagined as published in the pages of British satirical journal *Private Eye*. The narrative of McLean's artistic progress goes well beyond even the most outlying regions of historical feasibility, including playful references to McLean's 'unforgettable beefcake performance' in a Levi's television advertisement, a factually 'incorrect' riff on model Nick Kamen's famous launderette strip in a watershed campaign from the 1980s.[7] Such bold offerings of avowedly illegitimate narratives are mirrored by *This Is Performance Art's* wildly inappropriate use of archival materials – deliberately mis-matching voiceover narrative and images to great comic effect: for example, an image of Egyptian pyramids flashes up

traditional forms in the visual and performing arts. However, as will become clear, what I am calling 'the common turn' takes us somewhat beyond the boundaries of even the most extended definitions of Live Art, to the culturally broader, and generalized, field of *performance*.

4. RoseLee Goldberg, *Performance Art: From Futurism to the Present* (London and New York: Thames & Hudson, 2001), pp. 177–78.

5. *A Short History of Performance – Part 1*, Whitechapel Gallery, London, 15–21 April 2002.

6. Michael Fried, *Art and Objecthood Essays and Reviews* (Chicago and London: University of Chicago Press, 1998).

7. Brimfield's work might be understood in Marc Siegel's terms as a practice of queer 'fabulation' in playing fast and loose with the requirements of historical veracity. For a related account of the historical fabulations of Berlin-based performance artist Vaginal Davis, see Marc Siegel, 'Vaginal Davis's Gospel Truths', *Camera Obscura*, 23.1 67 (2008), 151–57. On the queerness of gossip as a form of historical testimony see Gavin Butt, *Between You and Me: Queer Disclosures in the New York Art World 1948–1963* (Durham and London: Duke University Press, 2005).

on screen as documentation of minimalist artworks, or a hilariously freakish portrait of a man with staring eyes and fright hair is presented as being an image of Judd himself (see Image 1).

All this campy silliness could, of course, be seen to be the work of an artist simply mining the history of performance art for laughs. But I prefer to see in Brimfield's camping the old Christopher Isherwood understanding of the term: that 'camp makes fun *out* of something, rather than *of* it'.[8] Which is to say that rather than simply ridiculing performance history, or indeed televisual culture's attempts to tell stories about it, it makes levity the chief affective state through which Brimfield imagines her almost impossible, and yet necessary, project of what I want to call a 'common' performance history. I'm interested in how *This Is Performance Art* can be understood as a jovial attempt to take us beyond the narrow confines of specialist performance histories in order to make connections across radically unlike traditions: to tell a history – a *general, shared* history – in which narratives of ordinary and extra-ordinary performance cultures are freely intertwined. For some this may appear as highly unorthodox and indefensible, to others still a mocking, perhaps even philistine approach to history. This is because, as we shall see, *This Is Performance Art* demonstrably transgresses the boundaries of its putative subject – performance art – and above all *the taste cultures that enclose it*.

It is important, I think, to recognize how cultural taste operates in the formation of discourses of performance and Live Art, perhaps especially when we seem most blind to its shaping force on the creation of the canon's inclusions and exclusions.[9] To remind ourselves of this, one need only read Goldberg's *Performance Art: From Futurism to the Present* to become quickly aware of how value judgements shape the stories that get told. Not only are these judgements positive, as it were, in favour of the artists and works selected for consideration, but also, as the French sociologist Pierre Bourdieu reminds us, implicitly negative.[10] They are also the negative assessment of *other* works not included or analysed in the book, and of the presumptive tastes of such work's appreciative audiences and consumers. I single out Goldberg here among the countless other scholars and critics I could cite not because she is particularly discriminatory or vengeful, but simply because she occasionally makes explicit the negative determinations that underpin a 'taste' for Live Art. In a section of the book addressing Live Art post-1968 she remarks upon artists' distaste for commercialized cabaret and theatre, and affirms instead the values of a performance that cleaves towards 'art' as opposed to presumptively retrograde performance work lending itself to the market.[11] Such

Image 1 Mel Brimfield, still from *This Is Performance Art – Part One: Performed Sculpture and Dance*, 2010: photo courtesy of Ceri Hand Gallery.

8. Christopher Isherwood, *The World in the Evening* (London: Methuen, 1954), p. 125. Emphasis added.

9. Questions of taste have arguably fallen off the critical agenda somewhat in the humanities in recent years, perhaps consequent upon the waning of Cultural Studies within British and US universities, and the relative disappearance of social and economic class as a category of analysis in other fields of study. An interpretative discourse of taste has, therefore, largely retreated into the social sciences, particularly sociology.

10. 'It is no accident', Bourdieu writes, 'that, when [tastes] have to be justified, they are asserted purely negatively, by the refusal of other tastes. In matters of taste, more than anywhere else, all determination is negation'. Pierre Bourdieu, *Distinction: A Social Critique of the Judgement of Taste* (Cambridge, MA: Harvard University Press, 1984), p. 56.

11. Goldberg, *Performance Art*, pp. 177–81.

12. This is something that, for reasons of space, cannot be undertaken in this article. An initial list, though by no means representative, of some of the items which might be consulted in such a study include: RoseLee Goldberg, *Performance: Live Art Since the 60s* (London and New York: Thames & Hudson, 1998); RoseLee Goldberg, *Performa: New Visual Art Performance* (New York: Performa, 2007); *Live: Art and Performance*, ed. by Adrian Heathfield (London: Tate Publishing, 2004); Amelia Jones, *Body Art: Performing the Subject* (Minneapolis and London: University of Minnesota Press, 1998); *Out of Actions: Between Performance and the Object 1949–1979*, ed. by Paul Schimmel (London and New York: Thames & Hudson, 1998); Lea Vergine, *Body Art and Performance: The Body as Language* (Milan: Skira, 2000, orig. 1974); *The Artist's Body*, ed. by Tracey Warr (London and New York: Phaidon, 2000).

13. Sarah Thornton, *Club Cultures: Music, Media and Subcultural Capital* (Middletown: Wesleyan University Press, 1996), p. 5.

14. Gans defines taste cultures by dint of the particular aesthetic values and standards that pertain within any one, and in which certain kinds of judgement prevail. As a Leftist sociologist he predominantly conceives of these cultures as they correspond to social

a taste *for art* clusters around the supposed independence and innovativeness of artists like Gilbert and George, Stephen Taylor Woodrow and Miranda Payne she suggests, as opposed to presumptively aesthetically and politically regressive forms like cabaret. Thus Goldberg demonstrates an explicitly negative determination of Live Art taste culture, which more usually polices its borders by saying little or nothing about performance work that falls beyond its bounds.

Thinking about discourses of Live Art in this way enables us to understand how they are not at all immune from the processes of distinction so adroitly analysed by Bourdieu and others in his wake. One could, for example, look at the various histories, museum survey shows and other gallery exhibitions which have variously explored Live Art, performance art and body art over the past forty years, and chart how they might be considered as formative expressions of a highly specialized Live Art 'taste culture'.[12] One could explore the manifestly heterogeneous and protean canon of this culture, comprising a taste for experimental dance and theatre, body art, performance art, durational and other expanded art practices, and see operative within it a drive to distinguish those making, writing about, curating and going to see Live Art from 'perpetually absent [and] denigrated other[s]'.[13] These 'others' might be certain mainstream and popular forms of performance (like cabaret and stand-up comedy for example), and the values that they and their audiences might be supposed to embody. Such distinctions, and the values underpinning them, might be difficult to place within extant sociological typologies of high, middle and low culture – even though Live Art taste cleaves predominantly, of course, towards the high. Even more expanded typologies of taste cultures offered by sociologists like Herbert J. Gans, built around class, youth and racial cultures, would be unlikely to prove fine enough to catch the social and cultural specificity of Live Art cultures.[14] But it would be possible to see how, following Sarah Thornton's reading of 'distinctions of cultures without distinction', that discourses surrounding Live Art are nevertheless operative in distinguishing it and its publics from performance cultures that might, in Thornton's words, seem less 'distinguished' and rather more 'common'.[15] This notwithstanding Live Art's own relative lack of economic and symbolic capital when compared with more established and traditional forms like opera and visual art.

Within the narrow confines of this essay it will suffice to say that the capacity of Live Art's makers, interpreters and audiences to manufacture cultural distinction, is what Brimfield's work makes apparent, if not outright thematizes. What I'm interested in doing, therefore, in what follows is exploring how the artist's work, and the work of others, pushes against what I'm arguing are the largely under-examined and unspoken limits of Live Art discourse and culture. In pursuing more affirmatively an idea of 'the common' in performance – as opposed to an understanding of it as that presumptively *without* distinction – I consider the idea instead of a performance *commons*, and Brimfield and others as performance *commoners*, in order to think again about how we approach relationships between high and low culture, elite and popular, and the valued and valueless in the field of performance. This will take us, in due class. He lists them as: high, upper-middle, lower-middle, low, and quasi-folk low. Additional taste cultures he identifies as youth, black and ethnic which exhibit particular relationships to his basic typology of class-based cultures. See Herbert J. Gans, *Popular Culture and High Culture: An Analysis and Evaluation of Taste* (New York: Basic Books, 1999), pp. 100–60.

15. Thornton, *Club Cultures*, p. 5.

course, to contemporary debates about questions of cultural property, and connect what I have to say about taste culture to debates about ownership and proprietary 'enclosure'. How might taste be seen to 'enclose' the cultural field? And how might Brimfield's fantastically surreal history attempt to imagine a performance past loosened from the compartmentalizing visions and exclusionary judgements of taste cultures; of Live Art or, indeed, of popular and mainstream performance?

Perhaps the chief way in which Brimfield's work does this is by bringing into its historical purview popular performance personae considered well beyond the pale by the standards of Live Art discourse – sitting them illegitimately, and rudely, alongside canonical artists. Brimfield opens up performance history to a promiscuous connectivity of inappropriate couplings imagined by invented performance ephemera – such as a fictional billposter for *Genital Panic* (see Image 2). Painted by the artist, this is one of the many jocular documents that, along with her faux TV show, comprise the artist's unique make-believe archive of performance. In what is a knowing pastiche of variety bill fare, here we see a counter-factual imagining in which elite international avant-garde performance artists sit cheek-by-jowl with 'low' British musical and comedy acts – a kind of imaginative performance 'mash-up'. Body artist Carolee Schneemann, for example, famous progenitor of feminist performance art, shares headline double-billing with Debbie McGee, a British stage and television performer perhaps best known as the assistant and wife of 1980s TV magician Paul Daniels. According to some equally invented, and accompanying, programme notes (see Image 3), Schneemann and McGee's purportedly legendary cabaret performance 'What's in the Box?' was 'credited with bringing together some of the most influential double acts in performance history, including Barbra Streisand and Joseph Beuys; Art & Language and Russ Abbott and Elvis Costello to name but a few'.[16] We can also see further down the billing performance artist Orlan who, it is indicated, was the winner of *New Faces*, the British TV talent contest, in 1964. The gag here is that Orlan, an artist noted for multiple surgical and photographic transformations of her appearance, takes the place of the pop-

Image 2 Mel Brimfield, *Genital Panic* (2009), Gouache on paper: photo courtesy of Ceri Hand Gallery.

16. These programme notes were shown as part of 'Waiter Waiter, There's a Sculpture In My Soup – Part II', Pumphouse Gallery, London, 25 March –17 May 2009. A revised version was circulated along with *This Is Performance Art* at Camden Arts Centre in 2010.

Image 3 Mel Brimfield, '*Genital Panic* souvenir programme, Windmill Theatre', digital print, 2009: photo courtesy of Ceri Hand Gallery.

ular impressionist on this imaginative performance bill: appearing by turns as herself, as British TV comedian Eddie Large, Picasso's 'Weeping Woman' and Heinz Cibulka from one of Rudolf Schwarzkogler's actionist performances.

Of course such a billing is expressly perverse and wilfully 'wrong' in its obvious mismatches, not only of performers from different cultural life worlds, but also in its mixing up of timelines with, for example, Debbie McGee appearing at an event that is supposed to have happened in the mid-1960s, even though she didn't become a performer herself until the late 1970s. Also Orlan obviously did not win New Faces in 1964. But she *is* widely seen to have begun her career in that year, even if her surgical transformations were not to take place until 1990. Thus, there is a trickster-ish quality to this fictive document, where disregard for historical propriety nestles alongside careful and considered temporal precision in its renderings. Which is another way of saying there is evidence here of at least *some* method in the artist's madness.

Perhaps most obviously, this method is evident in Brimfield's invitation to think about the uneven history of feminism as we might track it across a common, shared field of performance practice, rather than focus our concerns on narrow performance cultures and their specific audiences. The poster certainly makes many knowing allusions to feminist performance art. The title of the show – *Genital Panic* – is borrowed from VALIE EXPORT's 1969 performance of the same name: a provocative confrontational performance in which the artist, wearing so-called 'action pants' with the crotch removed, walked through a cinema challenging her largely male patrons to confront real female genitalia rather than consume images of women on screen. This reference should be taken alongside the extended bunting-cum-tampon string which snakes out of the crotch area of a drawing of Schneemann at the top right of the poster, bearing the two legends 'What's in the Box?' and 'Here Come the Girls'. This is a deliberate, wryly 'showbiz', reference to Schneemann's *Interior Scroll* from 1975 in which the artist famously read out a feminist text inscribed on paper scroll unfurled from inside her vagina. All of this, with the presence on the roster of now canonical feminist performance artists like Orlan and Yoko Ono – as well as Schneemann – makes the piece an extended reflection on feminist art history.

Brimfield's major aim, I think, in doing so is to ponder the histories of feminism and performance beyond the confines of elite art histories by also considering a wider continuum of female performance, including low forms such as burlesque and striptease which, in the post-war world, were an increasingly important part of the burgeoning sex industries. This point is made especially powerful given that the whole performance event is imagined to have been organized under the auspices of Windmill International, the Windmill Theatre in Soho, famous for its nude tableaux vivants in the 1960s. It was also the place where many British comedians learned their trade, which Brimfield evidently wants to accord a place in her general performance history. Interesting comparisons, and cross-thinkings, are encouraged by Brimfield's approach here which roguishly insists on commonalities and connections between seemingly unlike and remote phenomena and persons. Yoko Ono's *Cut Piece* (1964), for instance, is impishly referred to by Brimfield as 'burlesque', making us rethink its stripping of the female body across both avant-garde and popular performance cultures. It poses the question: can Ono's work be quite so easily understood as proto-feminist, and counter posed so starkly to the presumptively reactionary sexual politics of burlesque? Is it defensible to carry on telling stories which position Ono's avant-garde 'strip' as both politically and aesthetically superior to that of a burlesque performer?

But what is particularly interesting for my purposes here is that this history of performance is imagined through the almost defunct art of the end-of-the-pier sign painter. Brimfield carefully and lovingly recreates that art in gouache here, giving me pause to think that one of the other things she is interested in – at least in part – are the forms of *publicity* which also comprise performance history. The hand-painted, and gaudy multi-coloured sign, is presented to us as one publicity element of *This Is Performance Art*, alongside other creatively realized forms, such as the programme notes to *Genital Panic* written in the fictive hand of the famous nightclub owner and lothario Peter Stringfellow. As I've been suggesting, Brimfield's work asks us to think historically about performance across discrete areas of practice, and across differing taste and class cultures. But perhaps more intriguingly what Brimfield's poster, and programme notes, get us to think about above all is the very interesting question of what kind of audience would attend *Genital*

Panic. How, if at all, *could* an audience exist for an event such as Brimfield imagines? Would it even be possible to have performance art devotees sitting alongside fans of Little & Large in one appreciative crowd? Doesn't Brimfield's fictive line-up summon a rather *un*imaginable audience, one that could only, in reality, succeed in alienating 'highbrow' and 'lowbrow' audiences in equal measure, due to its unorthodox and unworkable mix of life worlds?

Such questions I find particularly resonant in the field of contemporary performance at a time when, arguably, performance has come to traverse more readily what Andreas Huyssen once referred to as the 'great divide' between high and low culture.[17] This is a divide which Brimfield's work reminds us of, precisely as it strives to undermine and transgress it. Indeed the jarring juxtapositions in her work suggest that such a divide is still in place in our thinking, even some fifty plus years after the advent of Pop Art, and the cultural transformations brought about by postmodernism. We can think about this perhaps at the level of style and publics: that the work of even an artist like Andy Warhol, as he is mediated through contemporary art exhibitions and mass merchandising, has now achieved a degree of elegance and value that only attaches itself to elite culture. Of course there is much irony in this given that he was once derided in New York as the producer of embarrassingly effete and commercial drawings of shoes. Nevertheless, his work now circulates almost unproblematically as a sign of postmodern cool for a knowing group of consumers.

Brimfield's work has none, or little, of this cool and is sometimes deliberately crass and goofy – as in the live part of *This Is Performance Art* performed at the Camden Arts Centre in London in 2010. In an extended re-enactment of works by fictional performance artist Alex Owens, a dance troupe performed a kind of aerobics routine on and around minimalist plinths, all the while accompanied by a live band who sang pop songs such as Olivia Newton John's 'Physical' or numbers from the musical films *Fame* and *Flashdance* (see Image 4).[18] Here minimalist performance met pop in a way that could only result in bathetic hilarity. Whereas Warhol may now, in the twenty-first century, seem sophisticated, cool and knowing – elegant even – the overriding effects of Brimfield's meetings of avant-garde and popular seem to be either comedy or embarrassment. Whether comic *or* embarrassing depends on whether or not one recognizes oneself in the work's address – whether you laugh along *with it*, complicit in its conceit, or feel embarrassed for the artist and the crass collision of worlds she brings about. Which, of course, is to ask the question: *Who* is this work for? Who might appreciate the ethos that so obviously disrespects the sanctity of high and low taste, and chooses instead to take pleasure in both, or indeed in the *debunking* of both? In what kind of a public arena might such work have currency and value, and be judged affirmatively and enjoyed?

Publics

One way of answering this question is to turn my attention to the public sphere surrounding the diverse and heterogeneous field of queer and

17. Andreas Huyssen, *After the Great Divide: Modernism, Mass Culture, Post-Modernism* (Bloomington and Indianapolis: Indiana University Press, 1986).

18. The name of the performance artist 'Alex Owens' is borrowed from the name of the lead character in *Flashdance* played by Jennifer Beals.

19. I use 'queer' and 'feminist' here only as rough markers of identity. These are not necessarily the best descriptive terms to describe the performances that I go on to characterize here, nor are they words necessarily embraced or preferred by the artists themselves. Indeed, as will become clear, some of this work might be understood as being actively involved in a struggle to reformulate the terms of contemporary politics and performance.

20. Duckie are self-styled 'purveyors of progressive working-class entertainment' based in London who have been organizing club nights and special performance events in the UK and internationally since 1995. They run a regular weekly club and cabaret performance night at the Royal Vauxhall Tavern in South London, see <http://www.duckie.co.uk>. Club Wotever started in London in 2003 in order to provide an open, 'wotever' platform for a range of performance approaches by, and for, variously gendered and sexualized individuals, see <http://woteverworld.com/>. Eat Your Heart Out is a collective of performers based in London and founded by Scottee in 2008. They are driven by a provocative needling of the Live Art establishment and a desire to bring performance to new audiences. See <http://eyho.org.uk> for more details. Information on Bird

feminist performance in contemporary London.[19] I'm thinking here of an efflorescence of work which has largely developed on the metropolitan club and cabaret circuit in the first decade of the twenty-first century. Comprising work across different 'scenes', and playing to different though often overlapping audiences, this work can be broadly characterized by the ways in which it engages with established genres of popular performance – from stand-up comedy and variety, to cabaret and drag – while working simultaneously, and creatively, with experimental forms more associated with avant-garde theatre and Live Art. In many ways, this work stands as actual embodiment of the kinds of connection between genres and performance life worlds that Brimfield envisages in *This Is Performance Art*. While I don't have space to offer an exhaustive sociology of such developments here, it should suffice to say that this work largely clusters around, or is associated with, particular clubs in London such as Duckie, Bird Club and Club Wotever, and performance collectives such as Eat Your Heart Out.[20] Individual performers I am thinking of here are largely young or early career, and include Bird La Bird, Dickie Beau and Scottee among others. Older, more established performers, such as David Hoyle and Lois Weaver, have also found ready artistic compatriots in this broad and wide-ranging field

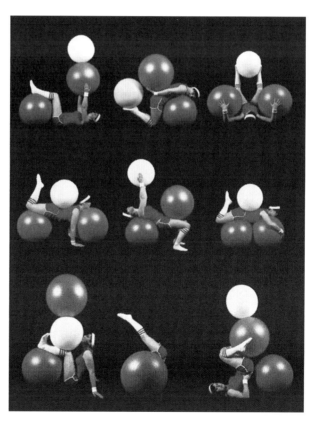

Image 4   Mel Brimfield, *This Is Performance Art: BODY/ROCK*, production still, 2010: photo courtesy of Ceri Hand Gallery.

Club can be found at <http://www.birdclub.org.uk/> and in the remainder of this essay. All links active as of 14 November 2011. Vikki Chalklin is undertaking PhD research work on the above groups in the Department of Media and Communications, Goldsmiths, University of London. I am indebted to her work, as well as to discussion with other students in the graduate seminar 'Trashing Performance', in developing the ideas in this essay.

21. Bird La Bird claims an experience of David Hoyle's work, then performing in the 1990s as The Divine David, as formative in her own development as performance artist; interview with author, 14 May 2010. For inter-generational relations between femme performers, see the FeMUSEum project led by Lois Weaver along with Bird La Bird, Amy Lamé and Carmelita Tropicana <http://www.thisisperformancematters.co.uk/words-and-images.post92.html> [accessed 14 November 2011].

22. *Gay Icons* was held at the National Portrait Gallery, London, 2 July–18 October 2009.

23. Comedians involved included Simon Munnery, Kevin Eldon, Tony Law, Josie Long, Helen Lederer, Isy Suttie and Rachel Pantechnicon.

of performance practice, which in many ways, can be regarded as building upon, and extending, their work of the 1980s and 1990s.[21]

In the context of this essay – and in lieu of any more extended analysis – it is important to state that this wave of what I want to call culturally promiscuous performance work has been enabled, I think, by the increasing tendency of performers to work freely across traditional disciplinary divides between theatre, dance, visual art and club performance. To some degree this perhaps reflects the success of a broadly defined idea, and protean practice, of 'performance' in loosening up institutional fiefdoms, and guarded areas of specialization in cultural programming.

An artist like Bird La Bird, for example, is perhaps best known in London right now as the organizer and self-styled 'mama' of Bird Club, a cabaret night for queer femmes, or to use Bird's preferred English vernacular, queer 'birds'. Until recently Bird Club was held on a monthly basis, somewhat ironically, at the Bethnal Green Working Men's Club in East London. But Bird has also been involved in femme activism, both as a graphic artist, as well as organizer of events such as the first ever Femme Pride. In 2009 she performed in the august surroundings of the National Portrait Gallery, which only very recently opened its doors to queer performers, including Dominic Johnson and David Hoyle, who performed in a series of events programmed to coincide with the *Gay Icons* photography exhibition.[22] Bird performed in a gallery space in front of a hang of the gallery's permanent collection on what was styled as an evening club event, complete with DJ Mark Moore playing club tunes for all visitors entering the cavernous ticketing arena.

My point here is simply that Bird's work circulates from club, to street, to gallery in a manner that has become more commonplace in contemporary performance culture, particularly with the artists associated with the above development of performance practice in London. Mel Brimfield's work is not really part of this broad field of work because the artist is very much art gallery-based and does not have a club performance profile; Brimfield does however have something of a burgeoning profile on the comedy circuit with works like *Intergender Wrestling* held at the London Word Festival in 2011. This piece involved many stand-up comedians and played to a mainly comedy audience, both of which are largely remote from the Live Art scene.[23] My point in bringing artists such as Brimfield and Bird together in this essay is to suggest how they share a promiscuity of cultural reference points in their work, as exemplified in Brimfield's cheeky couplings of Debbie McGee and Carolee Schneemann, which, in turn, can be taken to evidence a broader expressive ethos made out of an increasingly 'common' bank of performance resources. These similarities might be emboldened by the cultural itinerancy of both performers' works, and might be taken as marking an aspiration to forge a common language in contemporary performance, one worthy of the name by dint of being shared by all rather than exclusive property of any particular social class or cultural group.

Bird La Bird, like Brimfield, is an artist who draws freely from avant-garde and popular performance in the production of her work. For instance the tongue-in-cheek performance of feminine, if not feminist, authoritarianism in her 2009 *Femme Police*, borrows from an early 1980s *Two Ronnies* comedy sketch on British TV. *The Worm That Turned* was itself a (reactionary?) skit on female empowerment with the TV actress Diana Dors playing the leader of a group of feminist fighters who had snatched political power from men in a military coup, forcing them into subservience and requiring them to wear women's clothes. Bird's version, devised for Duckie's *Gay Shame Goes Girly* celebrations at the Brixton Academy in London, was similarly ironic as her army of femmes policed the club's punters for any signs of deviation from desired forms of femme display (see Image 5).[24] Of course, there is an arguably more progressive dimension to Bird's camping than there is in the *Two Ronnies* original, highlighting the tyranny of gender norms both inside and outside queer and feminist communities, and the problem of exclusionary forms of political togetherness. Even so, the mode of engagement is far from soberly earnest and puts Bird's performance very far indeed from the hyper-seriousness required by performance artists such as Yvonne Rainer in her now famous, almost puritan, 'no' manifesto which has sustained so much Live Art since the 1960s.[25]

Bird's work is not constrained by such an avowedly serious approach but neither is she simply producing work that is *other* to seriousness, work that is simply flip or trivial, or which belongs properly in the category of the low as opposed to the high. Instead *Femme Police* plays its part in the production of a performance public forged out of references and forms across a broad range of performance practice; from elite to ordinary, high to low, serious to light, and valued to valueless. This is so because *Femme Police* is not only a re-tread of the *Two Ronnies*. It also reprises something, again, of VALIE EXPORT's *Genital Panic* in its performance of feminine/feminist/queer rage – both in its nature as performance provocation to audience members and its imaginative embodiment of female power.[26] This derivation of performance address from both high *and* low traditions is also evident in the work of London-based performer Scottee. In reviews his work is often likened to that of avant-

Image 5   Bird La Bird, *Femme Police*, Gay Shame Goes Girly, O2 Academy Brixton, London, 4 July 2009: photo Christa Holka.

24. *Gay Shame Goes Girly*, O2 Academy Brixton, London, 4 July 2009.

25. Yvonne Rainer, 'Some Retrospective Notes on a Dance for 10 People and 12 Mattresses Called *Parts of Some Sextets*, Performed at the Wadsworth Atheneum, Hartford, Connecticut, and Judson Memorial Church, New York, in March, 1965', *The Tulane Drama Review*, 10 (Winter 1965), 168–78.

26. This exploration of 'terrorist' feminism is even more marked in Bird's performance as Birdie Solanas, the bastard offspring of Valerie Solanas, in her *Up Your Art* (2009).

garde forbears Leigh Bowery or Divine, and one could even add Paul McCarthy, given Scottee's embrace of carnivalesque excess in his work (his corpulent form is frequently made to explode and leak on stage). But when asked about his influences, Scottee is as concerned to enumerate figures of pop and small screen fame among his formative influences as he is avant-gardist ones, including singers and actresses 'Lisa Stansfield, Dawn French, Diana Dors, [and] Hattie Jacques'.[27]

All of this could be seen as evidence, of course, of Scottee and Bird's common tastes: that they, along with Mel Brimfield, exhibit a rather plebeian interest in low culture – that they are, as the saying goes, *common as muck* in situating their work within popular genealogies of influence. This we might extend to an understanding of their art as common in the received, and largely pejorative sense of the word: as in a sneeringly snobbish contempt or disgust for 'the common' as vulgar, coarse or even indecent. This might be particularly pertinent to Bird La Bird who not only addresses her audience in a thick Scouser accent riddled with expletives, very far from the received pronunciations of southern English and the etiquette of polite society, but sometimes makes work explicitly about what Mikhail Bakhtin would call the 'lower bodily stratum'.[28] But to do so would be to throw one's weight behind a persistent and heinous form of class distinction that affirms the rarefied values of elite culture through a contemptuous and stereotyped dismissal of 'common' traits and values.

Instead, it is my contention that the works of Bird and Brimfield et al. do something with low taste *as it meets the practices of elite culture* – including those of Live Art. Their work, I argue, exhibits a common *ethic* in its approach to such cultures, and strives to forge a contemporary performance public in which 'common-ness' comes to be a virtue rather than a value to be derided or critiqued. What I'm angling at is, importantly, not any 'reverse' working-class or populist snobbism *against* the elite – either in the work of these artists or in my argument. My use of the term 'common' in this essay is closer to understandings of the term that currently circulate in debates about the politics of ownership, especially in relation to ideas of cultural and intellectual property.[29] Here discussion of 'the common' takes us back to seventeenth-century English understandings of 'the commons' (with an 's') indicating the earth's natural resources: including 'the land, the forests, the water, the air, minerals, and so forth' which were understood as there to be enjoyed by all.[30] This was a common form of ownership which is distorted when it is appropriated as *property*: because that which should be the province of all, shared by and open to all, becomes exclusive to the one who owns it. For philosophers Michael Hardt and Antonio Negri, in their ongoing intellectual collaboration in rethinking democratic politics after the failures of communism in the twentieth century, this early historical understanding of the commons becomes particularly pertinent in our contemporary world where, for example, the share-ability of products on the Internet (such as on peer-to-peer file sharing sites) comes to challenge the exclusivity of capitalist private property. They argue that challenges to, for example, record companies' ownership of music through people's everyday use of global internet technologies, indicates a

27. Ben Walters, 'Scottee Interview', *Time Out London*, 18 January 2010, <http://www.timeout.com/london/cabaret/article/732/scottee-interview> [accessed 14 November 2011]. I'd like to thank Jay Stewart for drawing my attention to this article.

28. See Mikhail Bakhtin, *Rabelais and His World* (Bloomington: Indiana University Press, 1984).

29. There are many voices in this debate. Perhaps some of the most prominent are those of Michael Hardt and Antonio Negri, *Commonwealth* (Cambridge, MA: The Belknap Press of Harvard University Press, 2009); and Lewis Hyde, *Common as Air: Revolution, Art, and Ownership* (New York: Farrar, Strauss and Giroux, 2010).

30. Michael Hardt, 'The Common in Communism', in *The Idea of Communism* ed. by Costas Douzinas and Slavoj Žižek (London and New York: Verso, 2010), pp. 131–44 (p. 136). Thanks to João Florêncio for directing me to this source.

burgeoning common ownership which can be taken alongside contemporary legal challenges to the copyrighting and patenting of knowledge of the natural world by corporations. Hardt and Negri therefore place their (communist) faith in a struggle for the common as understood as that shared by, and accessible to all. For them, a politics of the common is one driven by forces that seek to take back natural, and human resources such as intellectual, creative and technological innovations into common ownership, a politics that works to combat the appropriation of the commons in the form of property. Whether private property of the individual or corporation, or public property of the State, this property is precisely what the struggle for the 'commonwealth' seeks to overcome. As Hardt himself suggests, it puts the common (back) into communism.[31]

31. Ibid.

For Lewis Hyde, in his fascinating account in *Common as Air*, the politics is less communist and more democratic republican, one which seeks to secure the public good by an appropriate balancing of different types of *access* to commonly held resources – whether these be for example of a private individual or corporation, or common. Hyde's argument is against the balance tipping too far towards the privatization of such assets, which has the effect of limiting access and 'enclosing' the commons by, for example, legal means such as copyright, patents and licences. In many ways Hyde sees this encroachment as a modern day echo of the private enclosure of common land in the traditional English commons, a move which was habitually resisted by commoners themselves re-asserting their rights of access by 'beating the bounds' – physically removing any fencing encroaching upon the boundaries of common land.[32] When I say, then, that Bird and Brimfield's work adopts a common ethic in approaching a diverse bank of performance traditions and expressive resources, I mean to characterize them as creative *commoners*, beating back the metaphorical fencing and lines of demarcation which might carve up the cultural 'field'. They utilize their diverse languages and references *freely* and *non-exclusively*. Their work does not draw upon particular performance traditions to make them the narrow 'property' of specific taste cultures – whether popular or high cultural. Instead in drawing their energies from different, sometimes toxically related, cultural registers, Bird and Brimfield can be seen to solicit a performance public in which it is possible to speak or act without regard for the exclusionary operations of taste culture, and the social divisions and stratifications that taste sustains. Instead their work 'speaks' through the resources of a broad performance continuum, shared and open to all. It is imagined that one might *not* have to lay claim to the sanctity of this or that tradition, or choose as one's own a 'proper' or legitimate heritage – one proper to, or indeed the property of, elite or popular culture. This, I think, is what then appears as goofy in Brimfield's work, or punky in Bird's, as the disregard for cultural propriety manifests itself at the level of performance affect.

32. Hyde, *Common as Air*, pp. 32–44.

This finally brings me to the paradoxes involved in the production of such a common performance public. As the work of Michael Warner has demonstrated, a public is a rather virtual thing as it 'only exists by virtue of being addressed'.[33] This imaginary public, in which the social

33. Michael Warner, *Publics and Counterpublics* (New York: Zone Books, 2002), p. 67.

divisions brought about and maintained by taste have no place, can be seen to exist in some tension with – or even be contradicted by – the *actualities* of audience response. For instance, Brimfield's work, even though arguably 'non-exclusive' in being driven by the common impulse set out thus far, ironically requires a very specialized set of knowledges in order to 'get it', in order to identify the work's various references and laugh at its in-jokes. One would, for example, need to know who *both* Debbie McGee *and* Carolee Schneemann are in order to access the work's peculiar brand of comedic juxtaposition. The ideal viewer of Brimfield's work, therefore, is necessarily someone conversant with both lowly celebrities and 'highbrow' avant-garde figures – making for a rather specialized and limited target audience.[34] Similarly Bird and Brimfield's work is also demonstrably local, if not stubbornly parochial, in its references and therefore remains somewhat out of reach for non-British viewers and audiences – or at least those unfamiliar with British popular culture. All of this illustrates something very paradoxical about the common impulse as instituted in the art and performance I have explored here: namely that the call to build a common public might – in actuality – be answered, or appreciated, by a narrow, even select band of viewers and followers.[35]

Coda

This does not, however, deter Bird La Bird from making a work that further explores the value of the common in her 2011 performance *The People's Pussy*. Bird takes to the stage in red and gold military jerkin and bloomers-cum-culottes and, in an opening monologue, reflects upon the use of the word 'cunt'. Much used in activist speech in protests over the UK coalition government's cuts to the welfare state in 2010 and 2011, such uses of the word have habitually been prefaced by the word 'Tory'. Bird goes on to suggest, to great comic effect, that 'the next time you say Tory cunt, leave my cunt out of it. Because there's nothing Tory about my cunt [. . .] My cunt says get your thieving fucking Tory hands off our NHS you robbing bastards!' Beyond its rousing, and simultaneously hilarious polemical address, this is interesting as a performance meditation on the use of the word, on who 'owns' it, and on what the politics of using it might be. Bird lays an insistent claim to her *own* cunt here, and what it purports to 'say' – to reclaim the term (and the organ?) from its more derogatory, sexist overtones still at play in Left speech denigrating the forces of the political Right.

But there is more. Bird then goes on to claim that 'her' cunt 'is a communist!', after theatrically ripping off her bloomers to reveal a furry muff between her legs in the shape of a red star (see Image 6). She then goes on to place a microphone in front of her genital region, and – in homage to feminist artists like Annie Sprinkle and Karen Finley before her, as well as to popular traditions of left activism – Bird's cunt proceeds to 'sing', kazoo-style, the tune of *L'Internationale*, to which audience members joyfully sing along. As it does so, the performer is accompanied on stage by a small troupe of cheerleaders with flags in hand, each

34. It is possible, following Gans and other sociologists of culture, to think about Brimfield, Bird and their appreciative audience members (among whom I count myself) as cultural *omnivores*. This allows us to see them and their work in the context of broader convergences taking place between differing taste publics in recent western culture. This is a rich, and complex, direction of thought but not one that I have the space to take up in this essay. See Gans, *Popular Culture*, pp. 8–13.

35. John Waters is aware of this paradox when he writes that 'a filth movement for the next century [. . .] will claw its way down the ladder of respectability to the final Armageddon of the elimination of the tyranny of good taste' (p. 296). The paradox lies in Waters' recognition that his semi-ironic call for such a movement will only be answered by a small band of freaks; that the movement itself will become its own select culture with Waters himself as its 'cult leader'. See John Waters, 'Cult Leader', in *Role Models* (London: Beautiful Books, 2010), pp. 293–317.

Image 6   Bird La Bird, *The People's Pussy*, Royal Vauxhall Tavern, London, 8 January 2011: photo Stuart Lorimer.

36. The *Cunt Cheerleaders* were a performance group comprising Cay Lang, Vanalyne Green, Dori Atlantis and Sue Boud associated with Womanhouse at Fresno State College.

bearing a single red letter sewn into their shirts, 'C', 'U', 'N', 'T', thus directly referencing the early 1970s feminist art movement.[36] So, as the performance unfolds, the ownership of 'Bird's' cunt becomes progressively more complicated. It quickly moves from being 'hers'– in the sense of privatized individual ownership – to becoming, simultaneously and additionally, a communist and a feminist cunt *as well*. Such a multiplication of claims to 'cunt identity' are made manifest by Bird's on-stage appearance which recalls both that of the feminist performance artist (in defiantly making the cunt spectacular) and, quite literally, the *sans-culottes* of French revolutionary history. But the final twist comes at the end of the performance when Bird turns her behind to the audience, revealing a comic-style plastic sphincter sewn into sheer leggings (see Image 7). Bird announces:

A little voice piped up from the back, and it was my arsehole, and she said, 'Cunt I may well be full of shite but I'm not just that I'm textured and multi-layered and I'm tired of being oppressed. C'mon cunt, let's form a coalition. You and me together it'll be fun. And we can overthrow the government!'

Image 7   Bird La Bird, *The People's Pussy*, Royal Vauxhall Tavern, London, 8 January 2011: photo Louise Brailey.

Immediately after this Bird disrobes some more, the disco lights go on, and the artist and her fellow performers dance merrily to the sounds of The Beatles' *Revolution*.

The People's Pussy is a richly comic performance, and an apposite work to close this essay with. Not in the least because, as the title of the work suggests, it is a performance exploration of *the people's* pussy, of what it might mean to lay claim to the pussy in the name of the people – in the name of a non-exclusionary politics of the common. Like the other works considered above, it is a work that demonstrates a promiscuity of high and low references, and a genre bending mix of avant-garde performance art, stand-up comedy and club performance. Plus it riotously overspills, and ignores, the established boundaries of taste. But perhaps, above all, what makes *The People's Pussy* an appropriate coda to what has gone before is that it also points to how the common impulse in performance might not only transgress boundaries of taste, but also forge connections across extant political identities and communities too. The work is a comedic exploration of this: a call for activists of varying political type to find common cause. For not only does Bird call for a broadening of the politics of the cunt to include feminists and Leftists, she also re-positions the arsehole, that over-determined locus of gay-male desire and politics, in her world-making re-imagining of 'revolutionary' bodies. *The People's Pussy*, then, might stand as testament to the morphing of the signifiers of political identity, including bodily iconographies, in a bid to make them non-exclusive and open to a politics of the common – clearly a laughing matter for Bird and the ebullient members of her audience.

Duckie's *Gay Shame*: Critiquing Pride and Selling Shame in Club Performance[1]

Catherine Silverstone

1. I'm grateful for comments I received on an earlier version of this article presented at the Department of English Literature Seminar Series at the University of Edinburgh (November 2010) and for invaluable feedback from Jen Harvie, Dominic Johnson, Julia Cort and the two anonymous reviewers for *Contemporary Theatre Review*. I'm also grateful to Simon Casson, Amy Lamé and Robin Whitmore for being so generous with their time and to Bryon Fear and Christa Holka for permission to reproduce their images.

2. *Gay Shame*, <http://duckie.co.uk/generic.php?id=66&submenu=shame> [accessed 12 November 2011].

As I entered the Coronet on 5 July 2008 for an event entitled *Gay Shame: Duckie Gets Macho*, I was presented with a wad of nine-shilling notes and a programme. Stencilled with the word 'SHAME', the programme was printed to resemble a crusty orange and brown leather wallet and advertised a range of stalls where I might part with my newfound currency, which was, literally, as 'queer as a nine-bob note'. Inside the venue, clubbers were confronted with what Duckie, the event's producing company, describes as 'an interactive nightclub-theatre with the aesthetics of a giant fucking mini-cab office: sticky, brown, stained, a bit pongee and distinctly lacking a feminine touch'.[2] As detailed in the programme we could visit 'The Straightening Salon' created by Susannah Hewlett and Hannah Eaton, which promised that participants could become 'hetero-sexual with this reprogramming treatment'; subject ourselves to Thom Shaw and Ryan Ormonde's 'Hazing, fagging and cruel schoolboy rituals' in 'Jobs for Fags'; and attend Chris Green's 'Real Man Workshop', which offered a 'life-changing 15 min men-only workshop' investigating what 'homosexuals [can] learn from the unreconstructed old-fashioned male'. These spending opportunities, along with some thirty others, co-existed alongside more predictable nightclub experiences such as drinking, dancing and live performances. One year later I found myself having a similar experience as I attended *Gay Shame Goes Girly*. On entering the much larger venue of the Brixton Academy I was again presented with a programme but this time it resembled a pink clutch purse, which opened to reveal an image of a wolf's mouth, all teeth and tongue. The programme yielded Green Shield Stamps and revealed that we might visit Johanna Linsley's 'House of Hysteria' and receive a diagnosis, pay to paint a vagina on a take-home piece of silk at Brian Lobel's 'Georgia's O' (or earn some money by modelling our own) or visit Scottee's 'Abortive Tapestry' and sew a backstreet abortion, amidst the panoply of some forty entertainments. In contrast to the rougher and dirtier aesthetic of the previous year's *Duckie Gets Macho*, *Gay Shame Goes Girly* was designed around a series of elegant interlinked shop fronts, with the style influenced by Dior's post-war New Look fashions and Cecil Beaton's photographs (see Images 1 and 2).[3]

3. Short films of the *Macho* and *Girly* events can be viewed at <http://duckie.co.uk/generic.php?id=66&submenu=shame> and <http://duckie.co.uk/generic.php?id=96&submenu=shame&special=_girly respectively> [accessed 12 November 2011].

Image 1 Setting up *Gay Shame Goes Girly* (2009) at the Brixton Academy. Image © Christa Holka.

Image 2 *Gay Shame Goes Girly* (2009) in full swing at the Brixton Academy. Image © Christa Holka.

4. 'Duckie: The Vision Thing', <http://www.duckie.co.uk/generic.php?id=41&submenu=vision> [accessed 12 November 2011].

5. *Gay Shame and Lesbian Weakness* (1998) took place at the New Connaught Rooms in London's West End.

6. Arts Council England (ACE) has funded Duckie since 2002/03 as a Regularly Funded Organisation, and through Grants for the Arts and, from 2012/13 as a National Portfolio Organisation (NPO). Between 2003/03 and 2007/08, Duckie received approximately £62,820 per year, with an additional Grant for the Arts of £79,903 offered in 2005/06. From 2008/09 to 2011/12, Duckie received approximately £146,940 per year (ACE, Freedom of Information request (FOI), July 2011). From 2012/13 until 2014/15 Duckie will be funded as one of ACE's new NPOs, with a cash percentage change of –2.3 per cent and a real percentage change of –11 per cent over this period ('National Portfolio Funding', <http://www.artscouncil.org.uk/funding/national-portfolio-funding/> [accessed 12 November 2011]).

7. Dick Hebdige, *Subculture: The Meaning of Style* (London: Routledge, 1979), p. 103.

8. Rachel Zerihan, 'Gay Shame', *Dance Theatre Journal*, 23 (2009), 16–22; Zerihan, 'Gay Shame Goes Girly', *Dance Theatre Journal*, 24 (2010), 11–15.

Duckie Gets Macho and *Gay Shame Goes Girly* were the final two events in the long-running *Gay Shame* club nights, which were produced by Duckie, the London-based, self-styled '"purveyors of progressive working class entertainment" who mix live art and light entertainment'.[4] From 1996 to 2009 (with one exception in 2007), these events took place on the same night as London's Gay Pride festivities, held annually on the first weekend of July. The early *Gay Shame* events – entitled *Gay Shame and Lesbian Weakness*, neatly inverting the slogan 'Gay Pride and Lesbian Strength' familiar from Pride marches – took place, with one exception, at the Royal Vauxhall Tavern (RVT) in South London.[5] These events were run using a format similar to Duckie's regular Saturday club nights that have been running in the same venue since 1995, where a bar/club environment is punctuated by a series of stage performances. The popularity of these early *Gay Shame* events, coupled with funding from Arts Council England (ACE), enabled Duckie to shift the event in 2004 to the Coronet, a converted cinema in Elephant and Castle (capacity: 2000) and in 2009 to the larger Brixton Academy (capacity: 3000), both in South London.[6]

In this article I want to consider *Gay Shame*'s ironic engagement with (gay) consumerism and shame. *Gay Shame* offers a playful yet trenchant critique of gay consumerism, especially as it is manifested in aspects of contemporary Pride events. To borrow Dick Hebdige's arguments from a different context, *Gay Shame* works through the form of the interactive performance marketplace to create a subcultural style that is predicated on the staging of 'conspicuous consumption' such that consumer strategies are posited as resistant to, rather than endorsing, 'more orthodox cultural formations'.[7] Modelling a fantasy of 'queer consumption' that works to resist (gay) consumerism, *Gay Shame* does not, though, as its creators are aware, sit wholly outside the system it seeks to critique. Further, the creation of Duckie's 'subcultural style', which ironically embraces 'gay shame' in the service of entertainment and pleasure, also works, potentially, to homogenise and exclude. The events also exhibit a more complicated relationship to 'gay pride' than the oppositional phrase 'gay shame' and the events' 'shaming' of the commercial aspects of Gay Pride and mainstream gay culture would initially suggest. *Gay Shame*'s co-opting and reclaiming of scenes of historical (and present day) 'gay shame' – suicide, gay bashing, psychiatric diagnosis, for example – seem to emerge from a position of relative pride and safety, of the type that discourses of gay pride and Pride events seek to foster.

Through this analysis, I want to insert Duckie's *Gay Shame* events into a critical conversation about 'gay shame' from which it has been conspicuously absent as it has been from critical attention more generally – Rachel Zerihan's richly evocative reviews of the *Macho* and *Girly* events excepted.[8] It is notable that two recent substantial books on 'gay shame' – David M. Halperin and Valerie Traub's collection *Gay Shame* (2009), which stemmed from a conference at the University of Michigan in 2003 and Sally Munt's *Queer Attachments* (2007) – do not refer to Duckie's *Gay Shame*.[9] Even allowing for the timeframe of academic publishing, this elision speaks to the primarily North American

9. *Gay Shame*, ed. by David M. Halperin and Valerie Traub (Chicago: Chicago University Press, 2009); Sally Munt, *Queer Attachments: The Cultural Politics of Shame* (Aldershot: Ashgate, 2007).

10. See for example Judith Halberstam, 'Shame and White Gay Masculinity', *Social Text*, 23.3–4 (2005), 219–33; Hiram Perez, 'You Can Have My Brown Body and Eat It, Too', *Social Text*, 23.3–4 (2005), 171–91; and Mattilda Bernstein Sycamore, 'Gay Shame: From Queer Autonomous Space to Direct Action Extravaganza', in *That's Revolting! Queer Strategies for Resisting Assimilation*, ed. by Mattilda Bernstein Sycamore (New York: Soft Skull Press, 2008), pp. 268–95 (pp. 284–86). Halperin and Traub also address the tensions that the conference generated around race and activism in their introduction 'Beyond Gay Pride', in *Gay Shame*, pp. 29–33.

11. See for example Sarah Thornton, *Club Cultures: Music, Media and Subcultural Capital* (Middletown: Wesleyan University Press, 1996); Fiona Buckland, *Impossible Dance: Club Culture and Queer World-Making* (Middletown: Wesleyan University Press, 2002); and Silvia Rief, *Club Cultures: Boundaries, Identities and Otherness* (New York: Routledge, 2009).

12. Simon Casson, interview with the author, 28 October 2010. Unless otherwise indicated, all quotations from

focus of Halperin and Traub's collection (the conference it arose from was also criticised for its failure to address ethnicity and activism adequately).[10] It also points to how club performance tends not to be included in discussions of popular entertainment. Indeed, Munt offers adept readings of several television shows – *Queer as Folk* (1999), *Six Feet Under* (2001–05), *Shameless* (2004–) – alongside a critique of shame in various institutional structures, including the academy, but the site of the club is missing, an absence that is not anomalous, even as club culture (but not usually club performance) is the subject of critical attention in sociology, queer, performance, cultural and media studies.[11]

To write about club performance is, then, an attempt to identify the kinds of cultural work that a club might do. This work is wrought from my own memories of the nights I attended and documentary traces (flyers, photographs, programmes, 'pink' currency, press coverage, web archives) of the events. I'm interested in what this detritus and interviews with the producer, hostess and designer might suggest about the club's politics, pleasures and displeasures. I'm all too aware, though, that my reading of the events is necessarily selective and the academic discourses in which I am engaged (cultural studies of consumption, queer studies and affect studies) don't always speak as fully as they might to the affective experiences that the event offers to its performers and participants. I want now to establish more fully the terms of *Gay Shame*'s ironic critique of gay consumerism, focused on Gay Pride events, in the context of other related organisations and events before turning my critique towards *Gay Shame*.

*Shame*ful Origins and Counterparts

Duckie and *Gay Shame*'s co-creator and producer, Simon Casson recalls that *Gay Shame* was born out of dissatisfaction with mainstream Gay Pride events. He describes how he attended Gay Pride in London in 1994 with 'loads of corporate sponsorship everywhere and terrible music and people being fucked on drugs' and remembers a friend saying that 'if there was a march going in the opposite direction called Gay Shame I'd be on that one, and it just stuck'.[12] This resonates with José Esteban Muñoz's contemporaneous joke with a friend about holding a '*gay shame day parade*', where the fantasy is more elaborate:

> loud colors would be discouraged. [...] Shame marchers would also be asked to carry signs no bigger than a business card. Chanting would be prohibited. Parade walkers would be asked to maintain a single file. Finally, the parade would not be held in a central city street but in some back street [...] While we cannot help but take part in some aspects of pride day, we recoil at its commercialism and hack representations of gay identity.[13]

Casson similarly asserts that Duckie and *Gay Shame* were 'part of a zeitgeist that was in opposition to the mainstream gay scene [ ] particularly [...] the gay male scene. We were against body fascism, materialism, house music, ecstasy, superficiality'. Amy Lamé – Duckie

Casson are from this interview. Duckie's co-producer is Dicky Eton who is responsible for financial and production management and related areas.

13. José Esteban Muñoz, '"The White to Be Angry": Vaginal Davis's Terrorist Drag', *Social Text*, 52/53 (1997), 80–103 (p. 96). Emphasis in original.

14. Amy Lamé, interview with the author, 13 January 2011. All quotations from Lamé are from this interview.

15. *Gay Shame*, 2004, <http://duckie. co.uk/generic. php?id=34& submenu=shame> [accessed 12 November 2011]. Robin Whitmore, interview with the author, 12 November 2010. All quotations from Whitmore are from this interview.

16. *Gay Shame*, <http:// www.duckie. co.uk/generic.php? id=105& submenu=shame> [accessed 12 November 2011].

and *Gay Shame*'s co-creator and hostess – also identifies how '*Gay Shame* came out of the commercialisation of Pride and the rise of the pink pound and our [...] desire [...] to reject that ultra-capitalist view of the commodification of sexuality'.[14] This kind of opposition can be seen from the first *Gay Shame* events, which included performers such as David Hoyle (or The Divine David, as he was then known), Chris Green and Ursula Martinez, mimicking what Casson describes as 'diva pop stars' and satirising the commercialism of Gay Pride, with lines such as 'Hello, my name's Fluffy. I believe in gay pride. Buy my new record'. At these events Lamé says she would also 'deliver these political diatribes from the stage and we'd always have some kind of quiz and performance that was really trying to say something about the state of shame and the state of the pink pound'.

Duckie's critique of the commercialisation of aspects of mainstream gay culture is, however, most clearly evidenced when *Gay Shame* shifted from the RVT to the Coronet and the Brixton Academy. Four of these five events took the form of an interactive performance marketplace designed by Robin Whitmore. At the first of these events in 2004, consumers were enjoined to 'Spend [their] pink pounds at the consumerist (f)unfair' and Whitmore says that he wanted the marketplace to 'have this feeling of a funfair that had been salvaged from a skip after a holocaust'.[15] The bracketed first 'f' suggests that 'funfair' is turned into an 'un'-funfair, highlighting the 'un*fair*ness' in the distribution of capital and access to resources inside and outside gay communities and reinforcing the event's description of itself as 'our annual festival of homosexual misery'.[16] Participants at these events were issued with currency designed by Bryon Fear which, as well as nine-bob notes and Green Shield Stamps, included pink pounds for 2004's *Gay Shame* (see Image 3) and pink Euros for 2006's *Euroshame*, which coincided with Pride London's EuroPride. In addition to spending their currency on a wide variety of performance stalls, clubbers could also take the opportunity to earn more money through performing certain tasks, such as low-paid work at *Gay Shame Goes Girly*. In the final two events, clubbers were encouraged to consume

Image 3 One Pink Pound, currency for *Gay Shame* (2004). Image © Bryon Fear.

17. Flyer, *Gay Shame: Duckie Gets Macho* (2008), <http://www.duckie.co.uk/generic.php?id=96&submenu=shame&special=_girly> [accessed 12 November 2011].

by the taglines 'Duckie turns consumers into real men' and 'Ladies are powerful consumers!'[17] In its comic promise of transformation, the first tagline suggests that identity is formed through consumption. The second identifies a niche market of women consumers and points to how consumption can provide the ground for agency, although the promise of 'low-paid work' identifies the grim irony that that not all 'ladies are powerful consumers'. The performances staged at *Gay Shame* – situated at the margins of theatre and performance cultures by virtue of their status as club performance and association with live art, revues, 'light entertainment' and 'low' performance forms – emerge as ideally suited to critique mainstream gay consumerism. That is, their form and aesthetic is intimately tied to the force of the critique. The fleeting or throwaway performances for sale in the club, where the sale is foregrounded, thus offer an ironic commentary on the invitation to consume that pervades many mainstream Pride events.

The playful acts of purchase also highlight how various constituent aspects of identity, especially sexuality, are contingent upon and implicated in circulations of capital. Drawing on John D'Emilio's classic argument in 'Capitalism and Gay Identity' a case can be made for how capitalism enables the production of contemporary western understandings of gay identities. He argues that:

18. John D'Emilio, 'Capitalism and Gay Identity', in *Powers of Desire: The Politics of Sexuality*, ed. by Ann Snitow, Christine Stansell and Sharon Thompson (New York: Monthly Review Press, 1983), pp. 100–13 (pp. 104–5). Emphasis in original.

> [o]nly when *individuals* began to make their living through wage labor, instead of as parts of an interdependent family unit, was it possible for homosexual desire to coalesce into a personal identity – an identity based on the ability to remain outside the heterosexual family and to construct a personal life based on attractions to one's own sex.[18]

19. Lisa Peñaloza, 'We're Here, We're Queer, and We're Going Shopping! A Critical Perspective on the Accommodation of Gays and Lesbians in the U.S. Marketplace', *Journal of Homosexuality*, 31 (1996), 9–41; Alexandra Chasin, *Selling Out: The Gay and Lesbian Movement Goes to Market* (New York: Palgrave, 2000); Katherine Sender, *Business Not Politics: The Making of the Gay Market* (New York: Columbia University Press, 2004).

As identities and communities start to solidify they can be niche marketed, exemplified by the concurrent rise of the phenomenon of niche marketing alongside the emergence of social movements from the mid-1960s, as Lisa Peñaloza, Alexandra Chasin and Katherine Sender note in their studies of gay marketing.[19] The marketing and associated products in turn work to iterate and then calcify certain conceptions of identity to the necessary exclusion and marginalisation of others, highlighted by the extent to which gay marketing has focused on what Peñaloza describes as 'pervasive images of white, upper-middle class, "straight looking" people at the expense of those more distanced from and threatening to the mainstream, such as the poor, ethnic/racial/sexual minorities, drag queens, and butch lesbians'.[20] Further, D'Emilio notes that 'while capitalism has knocked the material foundation away from family life, lesbians, gay men, and heterosexual feminists have become the scapegoats for the social instability of the system'.[21] So while capitalism creates possibilities for gay agency and subjectivity, these opportunities are not evenly distributed and the opportunities for agency may be heavily circumscribed, as the *Gay Shame* events work to show.

20. Peñaloza, 'We're Here', p. 34.

21. D'Emilio, 'Capitalism and Gay Identity', p. 109.

Advertised as 'a creative rebellion against the banalities of the mainstream Gay Pride festival and a satire on the commercialisation of our community', *Gay Shame* can thus be situated alongside other subcultural projects within queer communities that work to critique the

22. *Gay Shame*, <http://www.duckie.co.uk/generic.php?id=96&submenu=shame&special=_girly>. See Kaffequeeria, <http://www.kaffequeeria.org.uk/home.htm>; Get Bent, <http://www.get-bent-manchester.com/> [accessed 12 November 2011].

23. Sycamore, 'Gay Shame', p. 269.

24. Gay Shame SF, <http://www.gayshamesf.org> [accessed 12 November 2011].

25. While Lamé recalls that members of the US Gay Shame collective attended Duckie's early *Gay Shame* events, Bernstein Sycamore's account of the emergence of Gay Shame in New York and San Francisco doesn't acknowledge a connection. Bernstein Sycamore does, however, claim that '"Objective" history is a cruel lie, and I'm not interested in perpetuating such viciousness' ('Gay Shame', p. 268).

26. Outrage!, 'An Open Letter to the Pride Trust, August 1997', <http://rosecottage.me.uk/OutRage-archives/pride97.htm>. See also Outrage!, Open Letter from OutRage! to the Pride Trust, 18 July 1996, <http://rosecottage.me.uk/OutRage-archives/qintelpt.htm> [accessed 12 November 2011].

27. Miranda Joseph, *Against the Romance of Community* (Minneapolis: University of Minnesota Press, 2002), p. xxiii.

corporate consumer culture of Gay Pride and mainstream gay culture and their associated gender and sexual stereotypes, such as Kaffequeeria, a Manchester-based collective, and the 2007 Get Bent Festival, also held in Manchester.[22] Perhaps the most widely known of these counter-Pride movements is the *Gay Shame* collective that emerged in Brooklyn in 1998 and is now based in San Francisco (other similar groups have formed in Toronto, Santa Cruz and Sweden). The collective began as a festival that sought, as one of its founders Mattilda Bernstein Sycamore writes, 'to create a free all-ages space where queers could make culture and share skills and strategies for resistance, rather than just buy a bunch of crap'.[23] It has since developed into a year round 'queer extravaganza' that uses 'direct action' in the effort to create 'a new queer activism that foregrounds race, class, gender and sexuality, to counter the self-serving "values" of gay consumerism and the increasingly hypocritical left'.[24] While there are clearly affinities between the US-based *Gay Shame* collective and Duckie's *Gay Shame* nights with respect to the critique of (gay) consumerism and their efforts to 'shame' consumerist elements of Gay Pride, there is no direct collaborative relationship between these groups.[25] In addition, Duckie's *Gay Shame*, through the content of some of its performances, is interested not only in a critique of (gay) consumerism but also in the shame of certain aspects of queer histories, as I will explore below, marking an important difference between these organisations.

The broadly concurrent emergence of 'gay shame' events and organisations in the mid- to late 1990s as identified above speaks to a growing dissatisfaction with the commercialisation of gay identities and communities, strikingly marked by aspects of Pride events of the same period. In London the Pride event, which has been beset by financial difficulties indexed by the changes in its organising bodies, became increasingly commercialised from the early 1990s. The events run by the Pride Trust (1992–97), concurrent with the emergence of *Gay Shame*, also attracted criticism from the queer activist group OutRage!, who wrote letters to the Pride Trust in 1996 and 1997 to protest against 'the recent trend to dumb-down and de-gay Pride', signalled by the increased number of corporate sponsors and performers who weren't explicitly committed to gay and lesbian equality.[26] When London Mardi Gras took over running the event (1999–2003), following the voluntary liquidation of the Pride Trust, the post-parade party became ticketed. This exemplified, in starkly literal terms, how the experience of 'pride' had become a saleable commodity; it was only when Pride London, the charity that has run the event since 2004, took control that the post-parade event resumed being free. The commercialisation of Gay Pride events contrasts sharply with the event's earlier incarnations from the first London Pride march in 1972 and for the years following. These events were concerned primarily with marching to effect social and legal changes and to create a visible 'gay community', even as articulations of 'community' inevitably 'raise questions of belonging and of power', as Miranda Joseph notes, and to which I will return below.[27] Having established the terms of *Gay Shame*'s ironic critique in the context of concurrent events and organisations, I want now to turn my critique towards *Gay Shame*, specifically with respect to the possible pleasures and tensions that inhere in the types of consumption that it invites.

Selling *Gay Shame*

A consideration of what it might mean to sell 'gay shame' necessitates some consideration of what shame might be. In its most straightforward formulation, shame, as Eve Kosofsky Sedgwick summarises, 'as opposed to guilt, is a bad feeling that does not attach to what one does, but to what one is'.[28] Drawing on the work of theorists and psychologists of shame, particularly Silvan Tomkins and Michael Franz Basch, Sedgwick describes how shame in its proto-form emerges between three and seven months in the infant, just after the infant begins to recognise the faces of its caregivers. As Basch explains, '[t]he shame-humiliation response, when it appears, represents the failure or absence of the smile of contact, a reaction to the loss of feedback from others, indicating social isolation and signalling the need for relief from that condition'.[29] Similarly, for Tomkins, '[s]hame is both an interruption and a further impediment to communication, which is itself communicated'.[30] Shame thus indicates a form of communication in a moment of a break in communication, with the imprint of the blush perhaps its most arresting signifier. In Sedgwick's words the blush, lowered head and averted eyes are 'semaphores of trouble and at the same time of a desire to reconstitute the interpersonal bridge'.[31] But how might these theoretical conceptions of affect be helpful in considering *Gay Shame*, especially as the events don't explicitly, insofar as my reading of its documentary traces suggest, engage with this kind of theoretical terrain?

Michael Warner writes that he doesn't 'believe that this psychological tradition [of shame] can be a sure guide to the politics of shame' but doesn't want 'to dismiss this train of reflection out of hand'.[32] Like Warner I don't think that theories of affect can be simply applied to phenomena such as *Gay Shame* as an explanatory mechanism for the work of the event, political or otherwise. And yet, I think there is critical purchase in considering *Gay Shame* in relation to theories of affect. Specifically, if shame is thought of as a turning away, a response to a failed attempt at communication, which still betrays a desire for communication, *Gay Shame* works in bold and assertive terms to short circuit this failed communication through its invitation for a community (or communities) to form under the sign 'gay shame'. Here I'd suggest that 'community' is variously conceived by the club's participants not only in response to the shaming of aspects of Gay Pride but also in terms of the acknowledgement and refusal of 'gay shame', or the 'bad feeling' that can inhere in the formation of queer subjectivities in part due to juridical, religious and social prohibitions and their associated 'turning away' from queer subjects. In its ironic revelling in a conception of shame – embodied by its tagline of 'our annual festival of homosexual misery' – *Gay Shame* works to create individual and collective pleasures. This is achieved through reclaiming and occupying terms of abuse and

28. Eve Kosofsky Sedgwick, 'Queer Performativity: Henry James's *The Art of the Novel*', *GLQ*, 1 (1993), 1–16 (p. 12).

29. Michael Franz Basch quoted in Sedgwick, 'Queer Performativity', p. 5.

30. Silvan Tomkins, 'Shame – Humiliation and Contempt – Disgust', in *Shame and Its Sisters: A Silvan Tomkins Reader*, ed. by Eve Kosofsky Sedgwick and Adam Frank (Durham: Duke University Press, 1995), pp. 133–78 (p. 137).

31. Sedgwick, 'Queer Performativity', p. 5.

32. Michael Warner, 'Pleasures and Dangers of Shame', in *Gay Shame*, ed. by Halperin and Traub, pp. 283–96 (p. 289).

violent elements from queer cultures and histories by which queers have been shamed and subjected but not redeeming them entirely. For Sedgwick shame is not a 'toxic' part to be expelled, as is often the purview of therapeutic and community-building projects such as Gay Pride and Black Pride. Rather, '[t]he forms taken by shame [...] are instead integral to and residual in the processes by which identity itself is formed'.[33] Through the use of irony, *Gay Shame* works to keep both these possibilities in play, invoking and rejecting 'gay shame'. The use of irony which, in its simplest form, as Claire Colebrook summarises, relies 'on the audience or hearer recognising that what the speaker says can *not* be what she means', operates at *Gay Shame* both to invite an acknowledgement *and* disavowal of that which is said.[34] The ironic revelling in 'gay shame' is shadowed both by its very real histories and effects and a rejection of that which is enacted, which, perhaps ironically given the event's name, is enabled by a discourse of pride. This is perhaps most striking in 2005's death-themed *Gay Shame* and in two stalls from the 2004 and 2008 events.

Gay Shame (2005) was designed by Simon Vincenzi and described as a gay grand guignol that 'helped put gay rights back by 50 years'.[35] The event included ten staged gay suicides, which modelled different strategies for dying (e.g. drinking bleach, stabbing, swallowing pills), followed by ten funerals, where coffins were carried aloft accompanied by a dance and a band. A wake was also held on the upper level of the club where clubbers could partake of ham sandwiches and sympathy. More explicitly than many of the marketplace stalls, this *Gay Shame* directly addressed the extreme consequences of a 'bad feeling' about what one is (or might be), with the suicides referencing the comparatively high suicide and attempted suicide rates for LGBTQI (Lesbian, Gay, Bisexual, Transgender, Queer and Intersex) individuals (especially youth) compared to their heterosexual counterparts.[36] Performed for a crowd, some of whom may have lost friends or family members to suicide or contemplated it themselves, the suicides stand as a grim, perhaps even grotesque or 'bad taste', reminder of violent aspects of queer histories (and presents). In the relative safety of the club, the performance of death also works, ironically, to affirm life and to reject the deathly suicidal spectacles. The 'live' performances of suicide and the presence of the club's participants who party on (perhaps paying attention, perhaps not) in the shadow of these *Shame*ful faked deaths thus stand as a darkly ironic challenge to histories of suicidal despair and death more generally that have so often been the narrative templates for the representations of queers, especially in theatre and film.[37]

Engaging a different form of violence, at *Gay Shame* (2004) clubbers could spend six pink pounds to be gay bashed at a stall designed and run by Bryon Fear. Simply titled 'Gay Bashing' and employing the tagline 'Get Beaten, Look Cool', the stall took the form of a makeover. Participants were then photographed as if for a police mug shot (see Image 4) and the images were turned into greeting cards that mimic clichéd holiday postcards and tourist T-shirts, with the line 'I was gay bashed at Gay Shame'. Here the homophobic act of violence where one is assaulted and shamed for what one is (or might be), is turned back on

33. Sedgwick, 'Queer Performativity', p. 13.

34. Claire Colebrook, *Irony* (London: Routledge, 2004), p. 16. Emphasis in original.

35. *Gay Shame*, 2005, <http://duckie.co. uk/generic.php? id=59&submenu= shame> [accessed 12 November 2011].

36. See Ann P. Haas et al., 'Suicide and Suicide Risk in Lesbian, Gay, Bisexual, and Transgender Populations: Review and Recommendations', *Journal of Homosexuality*, 58.1 (2011), 10–51.

37. See for example Alan Sinfield, *Out on Stage: Lesbian and Gay Theatre in the Twentieth Century* (New Haven: Yale University Press, 1999); and Vito Russo, *The Celluloid Closet: Homosexuality in the Movies*, rev. edn (New York: Harper & Row, 1987).

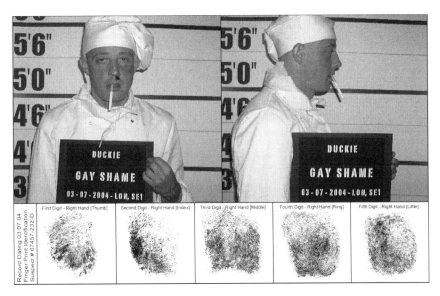

Image 4 Tom Norrington-Davies photographed for Bryon Fear's stall 'Gay Bashing' at *Gay Shame* (2004). Image © Bryon Fear.

itself such that the mark of the bashing – the sign of one's shaming – is made visible, by choice, through the (comparatively) non-violent art of make-up. The mug shot at once references the historical criminalisation of homosexuality in the UK and its attendant public shaming and reclaims this history in terms of style, where the bashing is recast in terms of 'cool' and fetishised in the memento of the photograph and the card.

Moving from the physical to the psychological, Susannah Hewlett and Hannah Eaton's 'The Straightening Salon' (2008) alludes to historical (and present day) violence done against queer people through the criminalising and pathologising of same-sex desire and behaviour, such as the inclusion of 'homosexuality' as a disorder in the American Psychiatric Association's *Diagnostic and Statistical Manual of Mental Disorders*, which wasn't removed until a revision to *DSM-II* in 1973. 'The Straightening Salon' invited participants to assume a condition of shame that was then 'expelled' through the reprogramming treatment as they were shown images of heterosexuality. The willingness of clubbers to submit to the straightening salon – the queue was so long I gave up – again identifies a pleasure (also evident in the popularity of 'Gay Bashing') in claiming that which medicalisation, along with other cultural practices (e.g. juridical, religious), have made shameful. To submit to the straightening, with *Clockwork Orange*-style reprogramming and tropes of medical authority – the performers were dressed in white coats – is also to acknowledge and mock the authority of their real world counterparts.

In performances such as these, combined with seductively comic marketing, *Gay Shame* works, through irony, both to announce and distance itself from the 'bad feeling' that has historically been constituent of the formation of queer identities in the face of various prohibitions.

Gay Shame also enables the production of a community of performers, participants and spectators who are invited to take pleasure in a series of disidentifications from heteronormativity, from the commercialisation of aspects of mainstream Pride events and from gay and mainstream consumer cultures more generally. At *Gay Shame*, shame is, in effect, hinged to the production of pleasure, rather than displeasure or the 'bad feeling' by which it is more commonly known. Shame is here embraced, perhaps paradoxically, as a form of pride. Indeed Sedgwick, influenced by Tomkins, suggests that 'shame and pride [. . .] are different interlinings of the same glove'.[38]

In arguing for the potential efficacy of *Gay Shame*'s ironic turn towards shame, my intention is not to denigrate the political and social efficacy of 'pride', especially as I've suggested that the ethos of pride, at least in part, enables *Gay Shame*'s acknowledgement and disavowal of shame. Further, the discourse of pride has been, and still is, enormously powerful in addressing homophobia, effecting legal and social change and providing a positive sense of identity and community for many individuals. Rather, the ironic turn towards shame that the *Gay Shame* events offer invites a consideration of how shame might also be harnessed in the service of individual and collective pleasures. In so doing the club creates space for the production of alternative identities, communities and style outside those marked, for example, by aspects of mainstream gay culture, even as these too are marked by tensions, as I will now explore.

*Shame*ful Jokes?

Gay Shame's ironic critique of the processes of consumption by which identities are, at least partially, formed is not, however, without limitations or tensions, especially with respect to irony, homogenisation and gender. Colebrook asserts that:

> [a]t the very least, irony is elitist: to say one thing and mean another, or to say something contrary to what is understood, relies on the possibility that those who are not enlightened or privy to the context will be excluded.[39]

In its ironic revelling in shame and deployment of the market stalls, *Gay Shame* works to create an elitist community of sorts that 'gets' the joke and works to exclude those who are not similarly enlightened, even allowing for the fact that the joke is writ large and is often explained in quite literal terms as my discussion of the marketing identifies. *Gay Shame*'s opposition to mainstream Pride events also runs the risk of homogenising these events as consumerist orgies peopled by gay clones of the kind Casson describes, when Pride marches have historically included many charities and work-place organisations. Further, some of the people who attend these events also attend *Gay Shame*, and Pride crowds, in the UK at least, often exhibit more diversity in terms of age, ethnicity, geography, education, disability and class than the relatively homogenous communities that tend to form in opposition to 'the mainstream'.[40]

38. Sedgwick, 'Queer Performativity', p. 5.

39. Colebrook, *Irony*, p. 18.

40. Halberstam makes a similar point about the diversity of pride events ('Shame and White Gay Masculinity', p. 223).

The tensions that developed in response to the *Gay Shame* events emerge, however, perhaps most clearly with respect to *Gay Shame Goes Girly*. This shows how Duckie's use of irony carries the potential for offence, especially when members of the community invited to form around the joke reject this invitation, specifically when what is said is taken to be what is meant. Whereas *Duckie Gets Macho* was advertised as a condemnation of masculinity and offered a series of jokes, which mostly coalesced around a set of stereotypes of a pre-metrosexual male – typified by images of George Best, Giant Haystacks and John Prescott, among others, printed on the advertising flyer – *Gay Shame Goes Girly* was billed on a flyer in the following terms: 'After last year's comic condemnation of masculinity comes this summer's celebration of femininity' in the form of a 'a pro-femme funfair for chicks and chaps'.[41] For the first time the event was billed as a 'funfair' (not (f)unfair) and as a *celebration* of femininity rather than a festival of homosexual misery. But the terms of that celebration warrant further analysis. In a preview article of the *Girly* event in the *Guardian*, Maddy Costa asks: 'Can a show put on by two gay men really reflect what it's like to be a woman?'[42] To some extent the question posed by Costa misses the point: Duckie employed a range of artists with various gender and sexual (dis)identifications and *Gay Shame Goes Girly* aimed to explore conceptions of femininity which don't, of course, have to be attached to biological women. Costa's question does, however, speak to a concern about how – and by whom – women are represented and the place of differing understandings of femininity in the production of gendered and sexual identities. Indeed, Lamé suggested that 'there was a real problem from the beginning of the conception of the idea and it was very much being run by men'.

In order to address these issues, a series of 'femininity salons' were run to create dialogue between men and women involved with and interested in the project on the subject of femininity. Duckie also ran two public talks in association with Lois Weaver at Queen Mary, University of London. These were advertised in the programme as addressing the 'politics & poetics of femininity in the queer community'; one night was titled 'Girls Night' and the other 'Boyz Night'. While these salons and talks seem to have been born, at least in part, out of tensions surrounding representations of women and femininity, they also identify a commitment to engaging with these issues and the politics of representation, although these events didn't necessarily resolve the tensions. Indeed, in her otherwise positive review, Zerihan notes that she felt the *Girly* event was more of a 'boy's [*sic*] party and although the subject was femininity, I felt, at times, that women became object(s) of ridicule and analysis', which chimes with my own experiences of some elements of the event.[43] It wasn't always easy to see how stalls such as Scottee's 'The Abortive Tapestry' or The Bears' 'Care Bears' Girly, Sissy-Play Party', where participants were immobilised in boxes before being given an uncompromising 'girly make over', worked to 'celebrate' femininity. In this respect the event was perhaps more successful at showing how women have been oppressed through economic and cultural pressures and how femininity, variously defined, is both embraced by and rejected from some queer subcultures. Zerihan's comment about *Gay Shame Goes Girly*

41. Flyer, *Gay Shame Goes Girly* (2009).

42. Maddy Costa, 'In Search of their Feminine Side', *Guardian*, 3 July 2009, <http://www.guardian.co.uk/lifeandstyle/2009/jul/03/gay-shame-femininity-duckie-brixton> [accessed 12 November 2011].

43. Zerihan, 'Gay Shame Goes Girly', p. 15.

being more of a boys' party also identifies, on one level, the gender differential that operates in the club; it attracts more men than women, although it does employ a significant number of women artists. Zerihan's comment also identifies the risks that attend the ironic or parodic project that can be extended to other aspects of the *Gay Shame* events, even as they also offer an incisive political critique in the context of what Casson describes as a 'fun nightclub' environment.

For instance, *Euroshame*, with its issue of pink Euros and the 'European Union of Duckie' passport/programme, neatly critiques Pride London's EuroPride event in the same year, which worked to produce a pan-European gay community, with London as its primary market. The staging of 'asylum seekers' who were not allowed past the entrance lobby offered a commentary on the politics of inclusion and exclusion that pervade conceptions of the nation state, citizenship and the formation and development of the European Union. The nation-themed stalls – assemble flat pack furniture in Sweden, get mugged in Albania or take a simulated car ride on Polish roads – pleasurable though they may be, risk reiterating (and potentially reinforcing) the stereotypes from which they derive their ironic/comic force. Further, the performance of the asylum seekers, who as Lamé recalls, attracted donations of 'real world' money as some clubbers thought 'they were real', invites consideration in terms of the ethics of staging the pain of others as spectacles for entertainment (or misfired entertainment). Thus the joke can sometimes perform additional violence and produce exclusions and marginalisations of its own, as indicated by Zerihan's and my own occasional sense of ridicule in relation to the *Girly* event, which sits, sometimes uneasily, alongside the pleasures and political critique that the club offers. If the events work to ridicule or parody the mainstream, they are also enmeshed in some of its structures, as I will now explore.

Queer Consumption: *Gay Shame* Consumes Itself

Posited as a resistance to (gay) consumer culture, *Gay Shame* does, of course, participate in the system it seeks to critique. Participants pay to enter the venue and consume beverages; thus, in structural terms, it resembles other post-Pride club nights. Further, the event is expertly marketed and the increasing sizes of the venues stand as testament to the success of Duckie's marketing and the strength of the brand *Gay Shame*. This is a brand of subcultural gay clubbing that tends to appeal, as Whitmore puts it, to a 'slightly arty punky crowd [...] people who think a bit and [...] who feel slightly not included [...] slightly outside the main commercial gay world'. In effect, *Gay Shame* sells its consumers pleasures that arise from situating itself as alternative to the mainstream. In so doing it creates opportunities for alternative forms of queer community to take shape and solidify, although these communities also run the risk of homogenising difference, internally and externally, and are also marked by tensions.

In its playful critique of consumption, *Gay Shame* offers, then, what I'd describe as a model of 'queer consumption'. In literalising the 'pink pound' it offers a fantasy of a queer economy that is outside the grip of mainstream (gay) consumer culture, embodied by aspects of Pride events of the period. Further, in its creation of a community of ironic consumers who spend currency that has no 'real world' value, it works to mock the structures of consumption that pervade 'real world' economies. That said, currency does still change hands and products and services are purchased. Crucially, though, the queer economy proposed by *Gay Shame* is not self-sufficient and is buoyed up by financial support from ACE. As Lamé puts it:

> [In] the weird market economy of the arts [...] if we actually set the ticket price at the price that we needed to cover all of our costs [...] without any arts funding you'd be paying upwards of £85 [rather than £15 for a ticket ...] It is a fully contained economy but it's a little false bubble economy and it's playing with the ideas of economy because the real economy is nothing like that [...] and nobody would come if you had to pay £85 for a ticket.

In this formulation, the fantasy queer economy of *Gay Shame* is significantly dependant on external funding (ACE, rather than corporate sponsorship) in order to sell its product at a competitive 'real world' price. In addition, the price of entry, though significantly cheaper than it otherwise would have been without ACE funding, is still sufficiently expensive to exclude a lower socio-economic demographic. *Gay Shame*'s critique of mainstream Pride events is, then, both subject to (it still needs to sell tickets) and not subject to (it is funded by a government body) the kinds of economic pressures to which the events it critiques are subject. *Gay Shame* is thus both implicated in the structures it seeks to critique but immune, to a certain extent, from the market forces that no doubt drive certain Pride events towards corporate sponsorship in order to be viable.

As well as offering a critique of mainstream consumer culture, *Gay Shame* also incorporates, with characteristic knowingness, its own critique. The programme for 2009 notes that 'We are all Consumers', highlighting how the community created by *Gay Shame* is not outside the structures it seeks to critique. Further, with the 2009 club night billed as the 'last ever', Casson says that 'we're aware that – eventually – we'll become as predictable as what we're fighting against – and we don't want that to happen'.[44] In Duckie's decision to end *Gay Shame*, this final act of non-performance offers an audacious refusal of the mechanisms of consumerism, especially as *Gay Shame* has not yet exhausted its market and ACE funding. Additionally, for both Casson and Lamé, some of the impetus for fighting against mainstream Pride events has dissipated, partly as a result of the shift away from ticketed post-parade events and a perception that the level of corporate sponsorship has declined. *Gay Shame* might thus be said to occupy an ambivalent relationship to mainstream events. As Casson puts it, 'it's not something that we want particularly to attack but neither do we particularly want to be a part of it'. Further, Lamé notes that Duckie declined the offer to be an official Pride party, not least because some of the door charge would have to be

44. Casson quoted in Steve Gray and Peter Lloyd, 'Shame, Shame, Shame', *Pink Paper*, 9 June 2009, <http://news.pinkpaper.com/NewsStory.aspx?id=1021> [accessed 12 November 2011].

paid to Pride London. *Gay Shame* sits, then, alongside the mainstream but refuses assimilation.

Although the need for *Gay Shame*'s critique of consumerism is perhaps less urgent than when the events began, the need for such work is not yet over, as recent queer critiques of Pride in Europe (particularly in Germany) attest. The force of the critique has shifted (though not entirely) from consumerism to what Jasbir K. Puar terms 'homonationalism', where '[n]ational recognition and inclusion [...] is contingent upon the segregation and disqualification of racial and sexual others from the national imaginary'.[45] Judith Butler's 'Refusal Speech' – 'I must distance myself from this complicity with racism, including anti-Muslim racism' – exemplifies this critique in response to the award of a 'Civil Courage Prize' by Berlin's Christopher Street Day Pride event. Butler effectively shames the host organisations for their refusal 'to understand antiracist politics as an essential part of their work' and praises several groups affiliated to Berlin's *Transgeniale* CSD, or alternative to the main CSD event, 'that fight against homophobia, transphobia, sexism, racism, and militarism'.[46] As homonationalism emerges as Puar notes, in part, as 'the result of the successes of queer incorporation into the domains of consumer markets and social recognition in the post-civil rights, late twentieth century', its critique is necessarily implicated in the critique of consumption and the privileging of productive consuming subjects at the expense of those who are elided and excluded from such opportunities.[47] And in these critiques, perhaps something of the spirit of the political impetus that animated Duckie's *Gay Shame* events lingers still.

The Rehabilitation of *Gay Shame*: *Gross Indecency* and *This Is Not Gay Shame*

I want to finish with a postscript on Duckie's rehabilitation of *Gay Shame* albeit outside the structure of the *Gay Shame* club nights. On London Gay Pride night 2010, Duckie produced a new club night entitled *Gross Indecency*, which was billed as a 'Pre-Gay Lib Gay Club', at the Camden Centre in North London.[48] The conceit was to 'turn back the clock' and stage 'an authentic London club night set some time in the early-1960's when to be a homosexual was to be a criminal', before the 1967 Sexual Offences Act made it legal for two men over the age of 21 to have sex in private in England and Wales.[49] Patrons (as we were designated) were instructed to wear 1960s clothing and were issued with keys and code words to facilitate our entrance into the club, mimicking some of the London underground gay clubs of the 1940s and 1950s. (A booklet of interviews with people who attended these clubs, compiled and illustrated by Robin Whitmore, was also distributed on the night). The evening included a performance of a police raid in which clubbers were told that under the Criminal Law Amendment Act 1885 we were 'all under suspicion of gross indecency', as was the licensee, Amy Lamé.[50] This Act expanded the scope for the criminalisation of homosexuality as Section 11, subtitled 'Outrages on Decency', states that 'any act of gross indecency' (not just buggery, which was subject to a separate law)

45. Jasbir K. Puar, *Terrorist Assemblages: Homonationalism in Queer Times* (Durham: Duke University Press, 2007), p. 2.

46. Judith Butler, '"I must distance myself from this complicity with racism, including anti-Muslim racism": "Civil Courage Prize" Refusal Speech, Christopher Street Day', 19 June 2010, <http://www.egs.edu/faculty/judith-butler/articles/i-must-distance-myself/>. For a discussion of *Transgeniale* CSD see Ute Kalender, 'Queer in Germany: Materialist Concerns in Theory and Activism', in *Queer in Europe: Contemporary Case Studies*, ed. by Lisa Downing and Robert Gillett (Farnham: Ashgate, 2011), pp. 71–84 (pp. 79–81).

47. Puar, *Terrorist Assemblages*, p. xii.

48. *Gross Indecency*, <http://www.duckie.co.uk/generic.php?id=104> [accessed 12 November 2011].

49. *Gross Indecency*, <http://www.duckie.co.uk/generic.php?id=104> [accessed 12 November 2011].

50. For a short film of the raid see 'Duckie Gets Raided by The Police', <http://www.duckie.co.uk/generic.php?id=104> [accessed 12 November 2011].

51. R. W. Burnie, Section 11, *The Criminal Law Amendment Act, 1885: With Introduction, Commentary and Forms of Indictments* (London: Waterlow & Sons, 1885), p. 67.

52. Equality Act 2010, <http://www.legislation.gov.uk/ukpga/2010/15/pdfs/ukpga_20100015_en.pdf> [accessed 12 November 2011]. Section 28 of the Local Government Act 1988, 'Prohibition on Promoting Homosexuality by Teaching or by Publishing Material', <http://www.legislation.gov.uk/ukpga/1988/9/section/28#section-28-enacted> [accessed 12 November 2011]. Section 28 was repealed on 21 June 2000 in Scotland and on 18 November 2003 in the rest of the UK.

53. *This Is Not Gay Shame*, <http://www.duckie.co.uk/generic.php?id=123&submenu=latest> [accessed 12 November 2011].

54. Ibid.

between men 'in public or private' was punishable by imprisonment 'for any term not exceeding two years, with or without hard labour', exemplified by the trial and conviction of Oscar Wilde.[51] The accusation of 'gross indecency' in the club was met with cheers, jeers and boos from the crowd as if we were revelling in the faux illegality and shamefulness. Here the ironic shaming of the *Gross Indecency* crowd in the reading of the Act was embraced. This kind of response is no doubt in part shadowed by the safety of the knowledge that the legal protections for those of us who identify as having same sex 'sexual orientation' (the wording in most recent legislation) in the UK have improved immeasurably since 1967, especially since the turn of the millennium with the repeal of Section 28 – the Conservative Government's 1988 legislation that sought to limit the 'promotion' of homosexuality by local authorities including in educational contexts – and the introduction of a range of equality legislation concerning the age of consent, same-sex partnerships, employment and the sale of goods and services.[52] As if to reinforce the more benign legal and social environment of the present, and the safety of the *Gross Indecency* club in particular, the threat of the police raid was neutralised, as the performers turned from accusation to the performance of a sexy, dance routine set to Frankie Valli and the Four Seasons' *Walk Like a Man*, choreographed by Luca Silverstrini. *Gross Indecency* provided an opportunity to historicise how legal discourses worked to institute and police what might be described as 'gay shame', where one is punished or shamed for what one is, notwithstanding how legislation fails to account for the complexity and multifariousness of sexual practices and identifications. To return to a pre-1967 world marks a break, of sorts, with that world, as there is no risk of arrest in the club and attendant public shaming. But the club's glamorous aesthetic (white shirted bar staff, a piano bar, beehive hair salon), designed by Laura Hopkins and Simon Kenny, also seems traced by a residual sense of nostalgia for the secrecy and risk that attended these underground clubs.

If *Gross Indecency* worked to historicise what Lamé describes as 'the history of shame', Duckie's 2011 event, *This Is Not Gay Shame*, looked to its own archive. Duckie's website notes that '[b]ecause we are in the middle of our Barbican run of Lullaby, Duckie are not doing a big Gay Pride bash this year'.[53] Instead it ran a larger version of its usual Saturday club night at the RVT with an outdoor stage and performances from *Readers Wifes Fan Club*. In the name's echo of René Magritte's ironic statement '*Ceci n'est pas une pipe*' ('This is not a pipe') beneath an image of a pipe in *The Treachery of Images* (1928–29), Duckie plays with the form and origins of its own *Gay Shame* performance history. It offers its own nostalgic return to the early events held at the RVT between 1996 and 2003 but also marks a difference to those events and the larger-scale events at the Coronet and the Brixton Academy. It both is, and is not, *Gay Shame* as Duckie has previously branded it. With the reassurance on the website that in 2012 'we will carry on the tradition of running an alternative big do on Pride night', Duckie once again situates its night as oppositional to the mainstream, although the nature of the opposition isn't yet, at the time of writing, articulated in contrast to the earlier events.[54] The fact that Duckie chose not to run a large club event for

55. ACE awarded Duckie £152,171 in 2010/11 and £141,671 in 2011/12 (ACE, FOI request, July 2011); Joseph, *Against the Romance of Community*, p. xxv.

2011 (or in 2007) also speaks to the competing demands on funding, marked by a decrease in its ACE grant, once again showing 'the inevitable implication of community in [financial] capital', as Joseph argues.[55] That is, the *Gay Shame* events and the subcultural communities that they foster are, in part at least, facilitated by the availability of capital and inhibited by its lack.

In this article, then, I've sought to show how Duckie's *Gay Shame* events (and codas to these events) offer, primarily through the form of the interactive marketplace, a trenchant critique of mainstream gay consumer culture, embodied by the commercial aspects of Pride events, especially from the mid-1990s to mid-2000s. In the ironic revelling in shame, which perhaps paradoxically seems to take place from a position of pride that the events ostensibly disavow, *Gay Shame* also invites the creation of subcultural communities. These communities can, though, produce their own forms of homogeneity in terms of demographics and style, which can work to exclude and marginalise some subject positions in the process of affirming others. In their inventiveness and ironic playfulness these events also offer the fantasy of a model of queer consumption that resists some of the imperatives of mainstream gay consumer culture. This fantasy is, though, shadowed both by the fact that *Gay Shame* participates in the system it seeks to critique and also the financial realities of cuts to the ACE budget, which affect not only Duckie but also its subcultural and mainstream counterparts. Duckie's *Gay Shame* club nights offered a vital critique of gay consumerism while sometimes probing painful aspects of queer histories (and presents) in the context of a pleasurable club experience. But as queer people can contribute to systems of production and consumption that reinforce the unequal distribution of capital, coupled with the prevalence of homophobic violence and the rise of homonationalism, the challenge now is to find new and still more inclusive ways of resisting inequality and violence. And in this work, something of Duckie's capacity for playful, irreverent and incisive critique might prove generative.

INTERVIEW

Frightening the Horses: An Interview with Neil Bartlett

Lois Keidan
(Edited and with an introduction by Dominic Johnson)

Neil Bartlett is an innovative and prolific director and playwright, and a distinguished novelist, translator, activist and performer. In his work across a staggering range of forms, including theatre, solo performance, drag, video and the novel, he is characteristic of a central tendency in Live Art, namely the capacity to choose whatever medium suits his needs in a specific project. As he explains in this interview, Bartlett is motivated by an attention to the needs and investments of audiences, and the precise capabilities and potentialities of venues.

His early solo and group performances were staged at London's Institute of Contemporary Arts, Drill Hall and Battersea Arts Centre, as well as touring to arts centres and fringe spaces across the UK, and in Europe and North America. Key productions include *A Vision of Love Revealed in Sleep* (1987) (see Image 1). In 1988, he founded Gloria, and the company created and toured fourteen projects over ten years; their final production, *The Seven Sacraments* at Southwark Cathedral (1998) was a paean to the paintings of Nicolas Poussin, co-produced by Artangel. Other major productions were presented at the National Theatre, Royal Court, Lyric Hammersmith, Blackpool Grand, as well as alternative spaces for performance such as the Royal London Hospital in Whitechapel.[1] Throughout his work, there are deliberate challenges to divisions of genre between high and low, between traditional and experimental theatrical practice. A central technique in his work across performance and literature involves charged collisions between distinct historical moments, for

example the affective shuttling between late-nineteenth- and late-twentieth-century gay London in his groundbreaking scholarly novel *Who Was That Man? A Present for Mr. Wilde* (1988).[2]

Throughout the 1980s and 1990s, Bartlett was an influential activist and lobbyist for lesbian and gay rights and AIDS awareness. In 1983, Bartlett worked with gay community theatre company Consenting Adults in Public, to stage and tour Louise Parker Kelley's *Anti Body*, the first play produced in Britain to address the AIDS crisis. He was also a speaker at the *Sex and the State* conference in Toronto in 1985, worked behind the scenes on London's first International AIDS Day (1987), participated in the campaign against Section 28 and appeared at benefits and rallies at Trafalgar Square, Hyde Park and Royal Albert Hall. HIV/AIDS specifically influenced his writing and performance, including his series of short polemic television and video pieces including *That's What Friends Are For* (1988), *That's How Strong My Love Is* (1989) and *Now That It's Morning* (1992).

In 1994 he was appointed Artistic Director of the Lyric Hammersmith theatre in London. Over a ten-year period, he transformed the venue into one of the most respected theatres in London, combining an eclectic and consistently challenging programme, a radical pricing policy and the work of a pioneering education department to build slowly a genuinely diverse audience. The range of his directing work at Hammersmith included popular Christmas shows and musical theatre, as well as radically reconceived revivals and collaborations with other leading theatre-makers of his generation

1. See Neil Bartlett, *Solo Voices: Monologues 1987–2004* (London: Oberon, 2005).

2. Neil Bartlett, *Who Was That Man? A Present for Mr. Wilde* (London: Serpent's Tail, 1988).

Image 1 Neil Bartlett, *A Vision of Love Revealed in Sleep* (Part Three, Drill Hall, London, 1989). Photographer unknown. © Neil Bartlett: photo courtesy of the artist.

such as Robert Lepage, Improbable Theatre, Kneehigh, Frantic Assembly and others. In recognition of this work at the Lyric, he was awarded the OBE in 2000. In addition to his creative refashioning of the organisation, Bartlett led the structural transformation of the building by architect Rick Mather in 2004. Bartlett left the Lyric in November 2004, with a farewell revival of Molière's *Don Juan*. He has since resumed his career as an independent theatre-maker and freelance director, creating work for the Royal Shakespeare Company, the American Repertory Theatre, the Abbey in Dublin, the Aldeburgh Festival, the Brighton Festival, the Manchester International Festival and the Royal Vauxhall Tavern. His production of *Or You Could Kiss Me* opened at the National Theatre in October 2010, in collaboration with Handspring Puppet Theatre, the South African company behind the West End and Broadway play *War Horse*.

Bartlett is also an acclaimed author. *Ready To Catch Him Should He Fall* was Capital Gay's Book of the year for 1990 and *Mr. Clive and Mr. Page* (1996) was nominated for the Whitbread prize in

1996. His most recent novel, *Skin Lane* was nominated for the Costa Book Award in 2007.[3] His translations and dramatic adaptations of works such as Honoré de Balzac's *Sarrasine*, Alexandre Dumas' *Camille*, Racine's *Berenice*, Heinrich von Kleist's *Prince of Homburg* and Jean Genet's *Splendid's* and *The Maids* have been performed widely across the English-speaking world.

In conversation with Lois Keidan,[4] Bartlett returns to his early years as a performance-maker, and discusses some of the key differences and similarities between the early 1990s and the present. Many of the questions emerge from a consideration of an issue of *Performance Magazine* that Bartlett guest-edited in 1987. In the interviews he conducted with drag performers Lily Savage and

3. Neil Bartlett, *Ready To Catch Him Should He Fall* (London: Plume, 1992); *Mr. Clive and Mr. Page* (London: Serpent's Tail, 1996); *Skin Lane* (London: Serpent's Tail, 2008).
4. The interview took place in London on 24 March 2011, and lasted several hours. The full recording and unedited transcript of the interview is available in the Live Art Development Agency Study Room.

Image 2 Neil Bartlett with Robin Whitmore, production photo, *That's What Friends Are For* (Channel 4, 1988). Photographer unknown. © Neil Bartlett: photo courtesy of the artist.

Ethyl Eichelberger, Bartlett explored the differing personal origins, traditions, uses of material, relations to style and characterisation, themes such as gender and sexuality and other problems raised by Live Art. By choosing two very different artists, bound by their mutual use of drag in performance, Bartlett commented subtly on the differing histories, contexts and material conditions of production for Live Art and performance art in the UK and the USA. Often, the two interviewees' responses are uncannily similar, while at other times they give opposing responses. For example, asking both artists if 'playing in drag ever feel[s] like an act of revenge', Eichelberger responds, 'No. I've been lucky. I don't feel the need for revenge in my life', adding that in drag, 'You feel beautiful even though you know you aren't.' Savage answers the same question by stating:

Yeah, it's delicious. Sitting up there and slating what you hate, in a packed pub, saying things, [it's] *bliss* [...] when you're on about some wally like James Anderton [former Chief Constable of Manchester, who famously said that people with AIDS were 'swirling in a cesspit of their own

making'], just pulling him down, and you've got like 200 people full of scorn and derision for this man, and you're at the helm, it's lovely.[5]

Despite the superficial similarities between Eichelberger and Savage, the incompatibility of these two perspectives suggests some of the tensions and possibilities of Live Art as a 'cultural strategy', as discussed below.

Lois Keidan: *I want to begin by discussing the issue of* Performance Magazine *you guest-edited in 1987, when the wonderful Steve Rogers was editing the magazine.[6] A useful way to start a discussion about the development of Live Art, including experimental, independent, non-mainstream performance in the*

5. Neil Bartlett, 'Ethyl and Lily: Speaking Your Mind', *Performance Magazine*, 48 (July–August 1987), 20–26 (p. 26). This copy is available in the Live Art Development Agency's Study Room in London.
6. Steve Rogers (1955–1988) was one of a series of editors of *Performance Magazine* (its subsequent editors were Rob La Frenais and Gray Watson). Rogers founded the Performance Platform (subsequently renamed the National Review of Live Art [NRLA] in 1986) at The Midland Group Arts Centre, Nottingham and served as its director from 1979 to 1981.

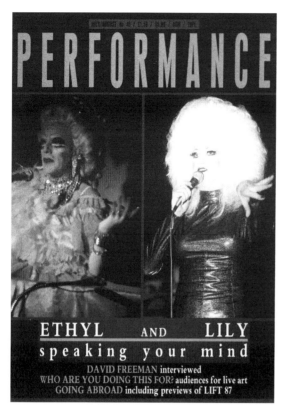

Image 3 Cover of *Performance Magazine* 1987. Photo of Lily Savage (right) at the Hippodrome, London (photo by Mark Cairns) and Ethyl Eichelberger (left) as Elizabeth I (photo by Lynn M. Grabowski). Used with permission of Rob La Frenais, former editor of *Performance Magazine*.

UK, *could be around three trajectories from that issue: one, the 'cover stars' of the special issue; two, a map of the scene in the UK at that time in the late 1980s, and how you see the shifts that have taken place between then and now; and three, your path since then, including your negotiation of a range of different contexts.*

The cover stars of the magazine were Ethyl Eichelberger and Lily Savage. Lily Savage (or rather, Paul O'Grady) is now as mainstream as it gets.[7] Eichelberger remains a huge influence of a different kind across the cultural landscape, since his death in 1990. What do their different statuses say about the history of performance and Live Art in the UK?

Neil Bartlett: I can only talk about what they meant – and mean – to me. I vividly remember editing this edition of the magazine. When Steve

asked me to do it, my reply – which may sound faux naïf, but it's not – was the same as it would be now: I don't really know about that stuff. I'm too busy making my own work, like most people. Perhaps some people in the 'proper', fine art end of Live Art tradition and practice think about categories, labels, funding categories, but I'm driven by only two things: my own internal journey as an artist (and I use the term 'internal' advisedly); and the circumstantial clutter of doing one job after the next job after the next job: in other words, what gigs are around, what possibilities or colleagues are around. So I remember saying to Steve, I'm not really a performance artist, I don't really know about performance art, and I remember him asking me (in an effort to get me to admit that I *did* know something about it I suppose) who I might like to write about. So I proposed Lily Savage and Ethyl Eichelberger, because they are two great performers, both of whom I had seen, and I thought they'd make a fascinating pair, because they're both ostensibly from the same tradition, but never would have heard of each other at that point, not least because Ethyl was from New York and Paul O'Grady was working at the Royal Vauxhall Tavern at that point.[8] But even if they had been in the same city, I'm not sure that the kind of popular working-class drag act like Lily Savage would be familiar with Ethyl, much like I'm not sure that the queens who are working in the chorus of *Priscilla: The Musical* know David Hoyle, or vice versa.

At that point in my own work I was avid for influence. When you're young – in 1987 I'd only been making my own work for five years – you see someone and you think 'Oh God, that's it, that's the way to do it'. When I saw Ethyl I was just bowled over by her. I didn't know that such a creature could exist, and likewise when I used to go and watch Paul at the Vauxhall Tavern. They're both performers of genius. They were both taking a certain set of conventions and doing something extraordinary with them: Ethyl's chosen theatre of war was American high-glamour drag (he paid the rent as a Broadway wig artist); and Lily was a working-class stand-up pub drag act.

As I remember it, when I met them they both asked me 'so what is Performance Art?' I interviewed Ethyl in a dressing room at Charles Ludlam's Theatre of the Ridiculous, and we spent most of the time talking about theatre history and

---

7. Paul O'Grady MBE has hosted two popular programmes on terrestrial British television channels: *The Paul O'Grady Show* on Channel 4 from 2004 to 2009; and a nighttime celebrity chat show *Paul O'Grady Live* on ITV1, since 2010.

8. The Royal Vauxhall Tavern is a popular performance space and club in South London, with a highly active schedule of nightly cabaret, performance art and music events, catering primarily to LGBT audiences.

especially queer theatre history. In contrast, all of Lily's material at the Vauxhall in those early days was about his family and life in Liverpool. I remember him doing a demonstration of how to disable your electric meter with a hatpin so you wouldn't have to pay for your electricity – relevant because most of his audience was on the dole. There was a terrific sense of working within an existing form, but neither of these people were coming from an academic background – they hadn't studied performance art or been to drama school. They were shining examples of how you could take something and turn it inside out through sheer wit, energy and talent as a performer. Ethyl went a long way before she died. The last time I saw her she was playing at the Lincoln Center [New York] in a production of *The Comedy of Errors* by The Brothers Karamazov. She made her entrance through the auditorium: she rushed down the steps, through the audience and cart-wheeled onto the stage, wearing a strapless 1940s ball gown, four-inch heels and playing the accordion at the same time. It's very difficult to cartwheel while playing the accordion, but she did it! When you've got that kind of talent you can play a bar, you can play the ICA [Institute of Contemporary Arts in London] or the Lincoln Center.

LK: *What I think was seminal about this issue of* Performance Magazine *was that having Ethyl Eichelberger and Lily Savage as the cover stars really represented the possibilities of Live Art. I define Live Art not as an art form but as a cultural strategy. So for me this issue of the magazine epitomises the idea that Live Art can create a context that will bridge very different worlds – that can include the practices of Ethyl Eichelberger and a particular theatrical tradition, and Lily Savage who was working in a stand-up drag tradition.*

NB: But in what parallel universe could you say that Lily Savage was a performance artist? For me my heroines and heroes are simply great performers, delivering great moments of performance that I have watched. Genre doesn't bother me very much. I don't have a hierarchy.

LK: *I think that Live Art says that there are relationships across and between practices, which are really important, and that different ways of approaching and contextualising performance can open up a range of different possibilities. I think Live Art offers a context and a set of discourses with which to talk about Lily Savage as well as Ethyl Eichelberger, as well as you. You also negotiate different contexts.*

NB: I'm increasingly less sure that I do negotiate them. I just think I crash from venue to venue. I am restless because I am dissatisfied.

LK: *What kinds of audience relations are you offered or denied by these different contexts? I'm thinking of the piece you presented at Duckie's* Performance + Cocktails.[9] *Would something like that be possible within the National Theatre, or does Duckie offer you a different kind of conversation with a different kind of audience?*

NB: Well, I recently worked in both of those venues in the course of the same week, and in one important respect, the relationship with the audience wasn't that dissimilar. The piece that I recently did at the National [*Or You Could Kiss Me* with Handspring Puppet Company, 2010] ran for six weeks, and the first three weeks were very tricky, because the audience was the National's pre-booking audience who come to see everything, and a lot of them were mortified, basically because it wasn't really a play, or because it was gay, or South African, or because the collision of performance styles in the piece was just too weird. Then gradually those people went away and other people started to come who'd actually booked to see *this* show, because either they knew some of the artists involved, or they were intrigued by the subject matter, or their friends had heard about it. Gradually the show changed, and for the last three weeks it became an event and there was a conversation with the audience that was genuine. The audience for the Duckie event, similarly, was also self-selecting. Apart from the odd person who just came because they were with their mate, I would imagine that every single person in that room had a degree in theatre or performance or something similar, or was a practitioner. That was also a barrier that had to be broken through.

You have to be aware of the limitations and the possibilities. When I made the piece at the National I knew who would come, so my main concern was that I had to have an overwhelming emotional impact on the people who *would* come. Likewise at the Royal Vauxhall Tavern. In theory, when I'm writing, I don't think about the context – I'm just writing, following my own instincts, tastes and excitements as an artist. But in practice – well, for instance, I am currently writing a new script for the Abbey Theatre in Dublin based on *The Picture of Dorian Gray* by Oscar Wilde – which I am looking at for the second time in my career. And all the time I'm preparing the project, I am very conscious that I'm being offered the chance to put the queer (for want of a better word) bleeding heart of that text –

---

9. *Performance + Cocktails* was a short season of Live Art and performance art at the Royal Vauxhall Tavern, from 24–27 August 2010, curated by Duckie's Simon Casson.

slap-bang-wallop, blood everywhere – on the stage of the National Theatre of Ireland, at a time in Ireland when everything is up for change. I have a hunch that this particular audience will embrace that proposition. When I started I was working in a very different context in terms of perceptions of gay writing and gay culture, and now – well the idea that now I can orchestrate a celebration of a queer text so wicked and poisonous and fucked up and self-destructive it can hardly breathe, and in the context of this particular audience – that's an absolute joy.

So, my point is, clearly I *do* think about this question of the audience. My ten years of work at the Lyric, for instance, was all about dismantling categories of audience. We never told people what they were coming to watch – we never labelled the work as experimental posh, popular, costume drama or radical gay theatre. We were removing obstructions to access. We wanted people who would never normally go see a pantomime – because they could say that it has nothing to do with innovative theatre and performance – to go and see *Cinderella* reworked by Improbable. Pantomime is one of the most brilliant art forms this country has ever produced. Bored with neo-realistic dramatic writing? Go to the panto. Go see [the pantomime dame] Clive Rowe at the Hackney Empire and just think. And equally, if you thought you couldn't go and see Performance Art, then we wanted you to find yourself watching Justin Bond do a Sophie Tucker song.

Another way of saying this is that one is continually trying to sabotage things. You certainly sabotage your career, because in order to have a career – as opposed to a series of jobs – you have to have consistency. You have to really be paying attention to see any consistency in my career at all. You can, but you have to know it almost as well as I do.

LK: *But that's why you're so influential.*

NB: No, I'm invisible. I'm very happy to be a cottage industry.

LK: *You're phenomenally influential, even to artists who have possibly never heard your name. If there is a bridge from the underground to main-stream programming, you constantly cross that bridge backwards and forwards. There has been an institutional embrace of Live Art – both ways – and that's a cause for celebration and also a cause for lots of handwringing.*

NB: I disagree if you think that these shifts are taking place at the centre of the culture. I think we're a tiny cottage industry at the peripheries.

LK: *I want to ask you about the relationship between the institutional and countercultural con-*

texts of Live Art. This opens up broader conversations and publics, but does the institution also blunt the teeth of the work it presents?

NB: Blunt the teeth? I think you'd be hard-pressed to say that it necessarily does. The honest answer is I don't know, because I'm not attached to any one institution.

LK: *This leads onto another question about the ways contexts to some extent determine audiences.*

NB: No, not 'to some extent' – contexts *completely* determine audiences. The audience is determined by the venue, not by the artist, unless the performer is very famous. Lily Savage could play wherever she wanted and people would go, whether it was the Royal Vauxhall Tavern or the Royal Albert Hall. It doesn't matter where Björk plays, because people will go. But that's not the type of cultural operation that we're talking about. Audiences go to venues. This is something that people don't talk about enough. Audiences think they're choosing a certain play, or a certain performance or a certain ballet, even a certain performer, but in fact, most of the time they are choosing a venue – even when the venue is a 'non-venue', where you're dealing with a site-specific work. You're not really booking to go and see Punchdrunk, for example; what you want to see is a weird event in an old office building. There's a conversation between the artist and the venue, but when I say it's the venue that decides the audience the point I'm making is that people persistently, stubbornly – and in my opinion foolishly – don't pay enough attention to how much the venue deter-mines the experience of the audience. And it's who you're sitting with that determines that experience, above all.

I wanted to do the work I was making in my early twenties – which was very queer – because I was queer. I was painted, I was powdered, I was queer. To go back to the question of context, I had to ask myself where I was going to present that work. Did I want to be in a room full of other guys who shared the 'cultural tradition' that I was working in – although I would never have used that phrase – or did I want to do it in the streets and frighten the horses? I did both of those things, but the point I'm making is that the question was really *concrete* for me. I *had* to think about the context and the audience for my work, not least because if I performed my work in front of the wrong audience I would get assaulted. That makes things beautifully clear; it's a very un-academic question. You don't get booed …

LK: *You get the shit kicked out of you.*

NB: Yes. A really big part of this period of my life and my work was working with and alongside

Image 4 Bette Bourne and François Testory in Neil Bartlett's *Sarrasine* (1990). Photo by Sean Hudson. © Neil Bartlett: photo courtesy of the artist.

fabulous women, like Annie Griffin, Baṇuta Rubess, Anne Seagrave, Rose English – to name a few. And they asked parallel questions: where can I do my work and have a good time doing it? Where are the spaces, the headspaces but also the literal spaces? What venues and audiences were going to give a woman a gig if she wants to play Macbeth (which Annie did, in a show I was in too)? Where were we going to do that?

LK: *I would also say that performance and Live Art have been crucial in terms of shifts in and around identity politics: queer, gender and race politics. Performance has offered a cultural framework to look at and create a platform for new articulations and new constructions of identity politics more generally.*

NB: I would express the same thing much more simply: that happened because everyone self-identified as a misfit or a freak. The connection between queer and feminist politics was basically: I'm a queen, she's a woman, and we're working together. Of course, it was very contested and fragmented. Things flew apart. But it was an experimental space in which you found out about what worked and what didn't work, both for you as a person and for you as an artist.

LK: *Do you have any thoughts about whether or not the 1980s was particularly fertile for performance and Live Art, and what might be the broader shifts between then and now?*

NB: If what we wanted was the right to make art on whatever scale we saw fit, we've won. I've just done a queer love story in a very complex and difficult performance language and it was commissioned and paid for by the National Theatre. The lead performer in the piece was Adjoa Andoh, and she also has her roots very firmly in small-scale, radical theatre, and we both hugged each other on the opening night and said we could not believe that it was happening. In the 1980s that show would have been on at Battersea Arts Centre – though I have to say that for me it isn't true that the object of the exercise was to get myself to the National Theatre. For me it isn't a one-way journey. One is always just trying to find the possible place for a work. It's about choice and it's about rights of access for artists. When I look back to the 1980s, I remember we wanted to be taken seriously, funded seriously, and now it seems to me you can't say that if you're queer, a woman, a freak or an experimental artist, all doors are closed. I'm not saying that there are no barriers – I'm not naïve about that – but the doors are all pretty battered. The people who have got the money and the spaces know about us. That's a big shift.

LK: *In closing, I wonder if you could talk a little more about what performances influenced you, and the moments that have been important to you?*

NB: Going to see Tina Turner at the Edinburgh Playhouse on her first comeback tour [in February 1984] when everyone thought Tina Turner was dead. That was one of the greatest performances I have ever seen. All the queens – Ethyl Eichelberger, Regina Fong, Bette Bourne, Lily Savage, John Kelly, David Hoyle, Justin Bond – an extraordinary tradition of great artists. Pina Bausch. . .

This is going to make me cry now. Talking about this just makes me feel very old.

No Man's Land [by Harold Pinter] at the National Theatre, with John Gielgud, Michael Feast, Terence Rigby and Ralph Richardson [in 1975]. Unforgettable. The first British production of *Follies* [by Stephen Sondheim] at the Shaftesbury Theatre. Rose English at Theatre Workshop in Edinburgh. There are hundreds and hundreds – a long and diverse list of people who have inspired me.

In terms of cultural moments, I think about being outside the Astoria in 1982 and stepping over two people who were fighting in the gutter, and it was Boy George and Marilyn, and thinking 'Oh god, this is fabulous!'

1982 and 1983 is when I started making work with other people. Before Gloria,[10] and before *Pornography* in 1983,[11] there was something called the 1982 Company. I was with seven other people touring the country together in the back of an old van. We went to Germany and we went to North America, doing weird and wonderful, collectively devised productions of a very obscure early Brecht

play, and an even more obscure late-nineteenth-century Latvian feminist melodrama – a truly great play by a playwright called Aspazija [1868–1943]. That was a real 'moment'. 1982–83 was an extraordinary time in London – it was extraordinary because I was twenty-three, twenty-four, but it was extraordinary because we had learned the great lesson of punk: that you could just do it. If you wanted to set up a theatre company, you just did it. The dole was still fairly easy to get. There was the Enterprise Allowance Scheme.[12] There was also a large network of small-scale arts centres around the country. I can remember getting the numbers of small arts centres and phoning them, and saying we were doing a Brecht play, describing the set and saying we all have funny painted faces and it's all marvellous and a terribly important play about the debilitating effects of late capitalism, and we'll do it for twenty-five quid.

LK: *That's a really important moment for the current generation of artists to look back on, in terms of the current crisis over arts funding in this country. Hopefully there's going to be a re-politicisation of the younger generation, because of the fact that there just aren't going to be enough resources to go around. Artists are going to have to be more inventive and creative.*

NB: What I would say is: Learn how to exploit whatever opportunities there are. Don't assume there aren't possibilities. There are lots of cracks in any system, and you can always get in somewhere. The system is so complex and so fragmentary. People, and fashion, and money, and opportunities all move very fast. You've got to be *feral*.

LK: *Today for me really marks a moment and I have to ask you to comment on it.*

NB: Elizabeth Taylor died.[13]

LK: *Exactly. Hers were some of the greatest performances of the twentieth century and I wanted to know your response.*

NB: I was really struck yesterday by how much the news of her death touched me. One, I remember when she spoke out about HIV and AIDS, and she put her money where her mouth was – and it really mattered. Her saying that she didn't think President Bush could even spell AIDS

---

10. Bartlett co-founded the theatre company Gloria in 1988 with producer Simon Mellor, composer Nicolas Bloomfield and choreographer Leah Hausman.

11. Bartlett devised and directed *Pornography: A Spectacle*, an ensemble performance that was presented at London's ICA, and subsequently toured ten cities in the UK and Canada in 1983–84.

12. The Enterprise Allowance Scheme was set up by Margaret Thatcher in late 1981 to provide a weekly allowance of £40 to those setting up new businesses, in a bid to support private entrepreneurship in the United Kingdom.

13. Dame Elizabeth 'Liz' Taylor was a British-American film actress, co-founder of the American Foundation for AIDS Research, and a gay icon; she died of congestive heart failure on 23 March 2011. This interview took place the following day, on 24 March 2011.

was just fantastic. Everything in this country was so chilly – all icebergs and tombstones, and hate and sneering, and hospital wards and horror-show. Just to have that big, warm, big-breasted, big-eyed, big-haired wonderful woman saying 'my friends are dying' was really important. Two, the moment in *A Place in the Sun* (1951) when she kisses Montgomery Clift and says 'Tell mama' in close-up, I think that's the most beautiful close-up in cinema.

If you see *A Place in the Sun* on the big screen, when that moment happens, you just want to die.

LK: *What do you hope your influence might be on younger generations of artists?*

NB: I don't ever think about it – you have to think you have stopped in order to think about influencing people. Most of the time I feel that I haven't really started. I'm still waiting to get out of my apprenticeship.

Spokeswomen and Posterpeople: Disability, Advocacy and Live Art

Brian Lobel

1. In their publications and online materials, the Live Art Development Agency (London) describes Live Art as a 'cultural strategy to include ways of working that might otherwise be excluded from a range of curatorial, cultural and critical frameworks', <http://www.this isliveart.co. uk/about_us/what_ is_live_art.html> [accessed 1 May 2011].

Artists with illness and disabilities have often used Live Art as a performance mode. As a strategy, Live Art often problematises the presence of the body, highlighting an awareness for how bodies are watched and policed by others.[1] Embracing a history of feminist and queer theory, Live Art has placed significant value in the cultural politics surrounding illness and disability. This article will demonstrate what might be at stake when different cultural sectors are invested in the form and tenor of a piece of Live Art. I will argue that this interface usefully informs current debates around illness and disability. Beyond looking at the politics of conflicting viewpoints and the representations of artists with disabilities, by looking at reviews and online responses to the work, and through interviews with both practitioners this article will provide insight into perceptions of Live Art in the UK, its presumed or critiqued exclusivity and the relationship between artists, advocates and the 'community'. Because both case studies I examine involve significant audience interaction with the marketing and press around the work, I will be considering responses to, and providing readings of, these marketing materials as much as to the live performance or gallery exhibition themselves. In this article, I will critically analyse *Involuntary Dances* (2009) by Rita Marcalo, and the exhibition of *Diary Drawings* (2009) by Bobby Baker in hopes of exploring the complicated relationship between artists creating work about illness and disability and organisations which claim to speak on behalf of, or in the interest of, those same illnesses and disabilities.

Epilepsy as Art? Rita Marcalo and 'The Community'

In November 2009, Rita Marcalo's work became the subject of an international controversy that brought to the forefront the relationship between institutions, advocacy organisations and independent artists. When I spoke with Marcalo in April 2010, she was only just beginning to digest all that had happened. Marcalo's dance trilogy *Involuntary Dances* was a personal investigation into her experience of living with epilepsy. Her artist statement for *Involuntary Dances* reads:

> [M]y body is about control. I have spent years training it so that I gain 'mastery' or control of it. However, there are these episodes in my life where I don't have any control over what my body does, the movements it does.[2]

2. 'Frequently Asked Questions', Bradford Playhouse Home page, <http://www.bradfordplayhouse.co.uk/rita/faq.htm> [accessed 5 May 2010].

In *Involuntary Dances* (Bradford Playhouse, 2009), the first piece in the trilogy, Marcalo's exploration of bodily control resulted in the creation of a 24-hour performance in which, locked in a cage, she participated in all the activities she normally avoids in order to prevent seizures, including drinking alcohol, denying herself sleep and staring at flashing lights. A month earlier she had discontinued her anti-convulsive medication. Her participation in these activities was an earnest attempt to induce a seizure that would then be filmed by the audience. The journey and production of *Involuntary Dances* is documented by an online review by Jo Verrent, who intersperses the atmosphere of the intimate performance at the Bradford Playhouse with her own real-time responses to the work.[3] Because I was not at the performance event, for the sake of this article I rely on Verrent's account and my interview with Marcalo to evidence what happened in the space that evening.

3. Jo Verrent, 'Review: Jo Verrent sees Rita Marcalo's *Involuntary Dances*', *Disability Arts Online*, 12 December 2009, <http://www.disabilityartsonline.org/?location_id=1110> [accessed 18 January 2010].

While Marcalo thought the piece assuredly would make people uncomfortable, she expected the work would receive local press and perhaps interest as far as Leeds. When Epilepsy Action put out the

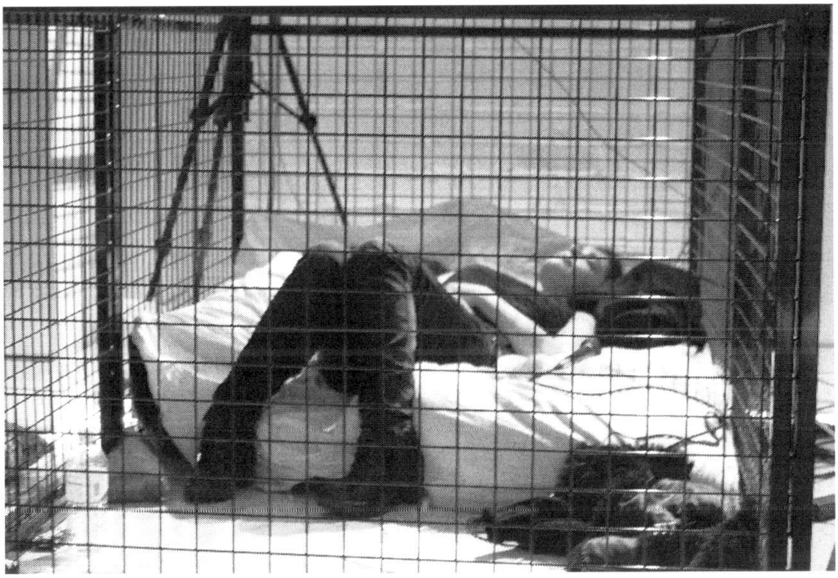

Image 1   Rita Marcalo, *Involuntary Dances* (2009): photo by Andy Wood. © Rita Marcalo.

following position statement on the work, however, international broadcast media reported on the performance:

> We recognise that everyone is free to make choices about their own health. However, we are very concerned that a person with epilepsy would stop taking their anti-epilepsy medication voluntarily in order to induce a seizure. This is potentially very dangerous and something we would strongly urge this person not to do. Seizures can bring with them the risk of injury from jerking or falling and, in the worst cases, death.
>
> People with epilepsy should not make any changes to their anti-epilepsy medication without consulting with their doctor first.
>
> It is also concerning that the performance could influence others to do something similar. At the very least, the performance should carry a health warning advising people that they should not attempt this themselves under any circumstances.
>
> We've had several complaints about this. I'm sure that many of our members would also consider the performance inappropriate.[4]

4. Epilepsy Action, November 2009, <http://www.epilepsy.org.uk/about/positionstatements/ritamarcalo> [accessed 5 April 2010].

By finishing the above position statement with the statement 'I'm sure that many of our members would also consider the performance inappropriate', Epilepsy Action makes a claim to community that needs commentary. By positioning themselves as an organisation representing a number of members (the exact number is unclear) who have complained (the number of complaints is also unclear), the organisation implicitly makes an assertion that there is a 'community' that Marcalo has offended. The language is subtle, but the image conjured, particularly from the statement's last sentence on propriety, is that there are a group of people – who are affected by, and work on issues surrounding, epilepsy – who are in strong opposition to Marcalo's performance. While the statement refrains from saying that all people with epilepsy would consider the performance inappropriate, there is a strong indication, with even the existence of a position statement on this matter, that there is a group identity associated with Epilepsy Action's membership that maintains (and in this case polices) the tone of conversation around epilepsy.

5. Miranda Joseph, *Against the Romance of Community* (Minneapolis: University of Minnesota Press, 2002), p. vii.

6. Ibid.

In *Against the Romance of Community*, Miranda Joseph demonstrates that the invocation of community, 'almost always invoked as an unequivocal good', can represent a destructive and divisive force.[5] While I will use the term 'community' throughout this article, I will do so with the un-stated, but ever present suffix '-as-they-define-it' in hopes of appreciating that the various parties' invocations of community are always done as they – and not necessarily others – define their community. Joseph argues for a more rigorous engagement with 'community', and provides numerous examples of how 'many of those to whom an identity is attributed do not participate in communal activities'.[6] Marcalo's performance, I will argue, highlights the consequences a non-participant might face. However, among the various responses I will explore, Epilepsy Action may have legitimate and well-considered arguments against Marcalo's artistic methodologies. This article will consider how *Involuntary Dances* – or simply its threat – was able to catalyse the presence of conflicting narratives about epilepsy in the public discourse. As the media response to *Involuntary Dances* was significantly more far-reaching than the performance itself, this article will investigate these responses as an essential and meaningful part of Marcalo's performance.

For Marcalo, *Involuntary Dances* represented her first project about epilepsy and she describes the work very much as a process of 'coming out' that was not dissimilar to her coming out as a lesbian. Perhaps, as with many others exploring new identities or identities for the first time, the process of coming out is not without its own growing pains, and people do not necessarily understand or embody the accepted norms or shared history of the broader community associated with this new identity. While Marcalo found a sharp metaphor for herself with the voyeurism of having her body watched and policed, when looking for an origin of the critique of Marcalo's work, many emails received by Marcalo indicated that people were critical of the work as a reiteration of the historical trope that people with epilepsy are to be caged and treated like freaks.[7] Verrent's online review neatly captures another potential offence Marcalo's work caused, referring to the 'imagined Disability Arts Rulebook', which polices such performances:

> [The Rulebook says] 'Thou shalt only produce work that relates to your experiences as a disabled person according to the social model of disability', 'thou shalt not produce work that relates to pain or fatigue or anything that speaks of disability in a way that could be interpreted as weakness'.[8]

Marcalo's performance inside a cage is seemingly discordant with Epilepsy Action's stated goals of 'increasing the understanding and knowledge of epilepsy by encouraging research and helping people with epilepsy achieve their full potential', especially if their position statement suggests that her performance would encourage people with epilepsy to discontinue their medication which, according to their research, could lead to death.[9] Although Marcalo never styled herself as a spokesperson for epilepsy, when she was quoted as saying she hoped her performance would 'raise awareness' about epilepsy, critics and those inside the epilepsy community jumped to action. 'If she wants to raise awareness', one online posting said, 'there are more tasteful ways of doing it'.[10] The job of raising awareness, even in the broadest usage of the term, seems to fall under the explicit remit of organisations like Epilepsy Action and falls nebulously inside the remit of artists creating work about a given topic. While *Involuntary Dances* was about epilepsy, it was, for Marcalo, also an exploration of the desire to look and the marginalisation of disabled bodies.

For Epilepsy Action, it is not in their stated remit to respond directly to these issues. It is only in their remit to look after how epilepsy (as a specific condition) is translated to a general public. The vision of Epilepsy Action, in this regard, according to their website, is 'To live in a society where everyone understands epilepsy and where attitudes towards the

7. Rita Marcalo presented anonymised email communication related to *Involuntary Dances* as part of the Live Art Development Agency's *Access All Areas* symposium in March 2011. A recording is available in the British Library Sound Archive, London.

8. Verrent, 'Review: Jo Verrent Sees *Involuntary Dances*'.

9. Epilepsy Action, <http://www.epilepsy.org.uk/research/earn.html> [accessed 5 May 2010].

10. Response to Jonathan Brown, 'Artist To Have Epileptic Fit Live on Stage', *Independent*, 20 November 2009, <http://www.independent.co.uk/arts-entertainment/art/news/artist-to-have-an-epileptic-fit-live-on-stage-1824122.html> [accessed 5 May 2010].

11. Epilepsy Action: Objectives <http:// www.epilepsy. org.uk/about/ objectives. html> [accessed 1 May 2011].

12. All quotations from Marcalo and Baker, unless otherwise stated, are from my interviews with the artists, conducted, respectively, in April and February 2010.

13. See, for example, James Sturcke, 'Epilepsy charity condemns posting of seizure clips on YouTube, *Guardian*, 19 May 2008, <http:// www.guardian.co.uk/ society/2008/may/ 19/health.internet> [accessed 22 January 2012].

14. Responses to Verrent.

15. Ibid.

condition are based on fact not fiction.'[11] In an interview, Marcalo discusses this impasse:

> I said something about raising awareness – and that just got taken and repeated all sorts of times. When I spoke about raising awareness, I was talking about how [the performance] came from the point of view as a person with epilepsy and looking at notions of voyeurism in our culture – looking at this idea that you're not allowed to see, you want to see, everybody wants to see [...]. So when I was talking about awareness, I was talking about a cultural commentary point of view, as an artist that's what I do [...] but then it became this other thing.[12]

From the quote above, it is clear that it was the word 'awareness' ignited tensions between Epilepsy Action and Marcalo, as awareness – as defined by Epilepsy Action – was very different than the kind of awareness to which Marcalo alluded, and which may even have eluded her. A performative interest in cultural misunderstandings of epilepsy may have been a key area of exploration for Marcalo, although it is hard to tell if this is realised upon reflection on the piece, or if these cultural misunderstandings or histories became apparent only after the critique was articulated. In the performance, Marcalo distinctly did draw a reference point for the work to recent stories of people non-consensually documenting and uploading to YouTube videos of people having seizures;[13] however, these historically embedded narratives were not referenced, neither in our interview nor in writings about the work.

The audience for *Involuntary Dances* became split in two: between those who looked at the piece as an artistic exploration; and those who believed the work, foregrounding the epileptic body, was exclusively about epilepsy in society. The splitting of the audience allowed for two different kinds of solo performances to take place: that of Rita Marcalo; and that of the multitude of online commentators who posted their opinions about Marcalo's performance to blogs, reviews and articles. If Marcalo was capable of telling her story in the abstract language of Live Art, commentators were sure to make their arguments known: narratives about experiences with epilepsy began appearing on the Internet. Regardless of tone, nearly every commentator invoked personal perspectives to justify their anger or their support for the work. In response to Verrent's review, Brian Newman writes: 'As a person who has had seizures since the early 80s [...] the idea of inducing an uncontrolled seizure in a steel basket scares me'.[14] Others defended her work using the same claim to authenticity, as demonstrated by Peter Street who writes, 'Rita Marcalo should really be congratulated. She has given birth to a freedom we with epilepsy have been seeking for years'.[15] Responding to an article in the *Daily Express*, a comment entitled 'Mother's Outrage: Epilepsy as Art? I Don't Think So!' dramatically demonstrates the difficulties faced by families – in this case a mother who cares for her son who suffers severe seizures. The commentator writes:

> I AM OUTRAGED THAT THIS WOMAN IS TRYING TO TURN EPILEPSY INTO AN ART PERFORMANCE JUST TO GET £14,000.

MY SON WHO IS NOW 25 HAS BEEN SUFFERING WITH EPILEPSY FOR THE LAST 10 YEARS AND I HAVE WITNESSED 100'S OF SEIZURES ALL OF WHICH I FIND VERY DISTRESSING. IT HAS VIRTUALLY DESTROYED HIS LIFE.[16]

16. Response to Paul Jeeves, 'Epilepsy: Rita Marcalo Receives Grant to Induce Fit on Stage', *Daily Express*, 20 November 2009, <http://www.express.co.uk/posts/view/141313> [accessed 10 January 2010]. Emphasis in original.

Such a personal interjection demonstrates the lengths the work's virtual audience went to have their voices heard.

Solo performance, as a genre, has garnered critical attention in relation to feminism and movements, which encouraged marginalised individuals to claim territory for themselves. However, the reaction to Marcalo's work demonstrates dissatisfaction with this perspective: if one voice is to speak, the criticisms seem to say, it should be a voice that adequately represents the community. If an overwhelming majority of people living with epilepsy trust organisations like Epilepsy Action to represent their interests, Marcalo's actions become invasive and/or destructive. This again highlights Marcalo's original intention for the piece in that she was only aiming to explore her personal experience with epilepsy for the first time. Faced with this knowledge, the questions for those inside a defined community may become: How much individual action do we allow in this community when people see themselves as exceptions to the larger political issues at hand? How much do we allow before we intervene?

In our interview, Marcalo discusses the reactions from people doing institutionally based work on anti-stigma campaigns and raising monies for epilepsy research. One trope she heard from many institutions was that she had erased years of education and her performance reiterated the painful history of human display popular during the nineteenth century. If she, as a newcomer, highlighted only voyeuristic aspects of how people with disabilities are policed, she may leave unconsidered a rich body of work that has brought up similar issues. In this way, *Involuntary Dances* ruffled the sensibilities of established epilepsy communities whose activity in advocacy campaigns has necessarily included significant amounts of time considering how their own bodies are watched by an uneducated public. Rosemarie Garland Thomson describes this phenomenon quite pointedly:

> Those of us with disabilities are supplicants and minstrels, striving to create valued representations of ourselves in our relations with the non-disabled majority. This is precisely what many newly disabled people can neither do nor accept; it is a subtle part of adjustment and often the most difficult.[17]

17. Rosemarie Garland Thomson, *Extraordinary Bodies: Figuring Physical Disability in American Culture and Literature* (New York: Columbia University Press, 1997), p. 13.

Although Marcalo is not newly disabled, her work demonstrates a first attempt to disclose her epilepsy professionally. Marcalo's creation of the work may be a subtle part of the adjustment process that Garland Thomson describes, although it was clearly not subtle enough for those with epilepsy who may be comfortable with the political implications of themselves becoming unwitting spectacles.

While the freak show is a trope that has been explored in work related to disabled and colonial subjectivities – in particular by Petra Kuppers' discussion of Mat Fraser's work *Sealboy: Freak* (2001) – Marcalo's approach to 'freakdom' may have been too subtle to be read as an

18. Petra Kuppers, *Disability and Contemporary Performance* (New York and London: Routledge, 2003), p. 31.

attempt to problematise such a discourse.[18] Marcalo performed the work in a relatively small theatre for a small audience, so the audience's gawking may not have felt particularly intense or threatening. Compared to Coco Fusco and Guillermo Gómez-Peña's performance *Two Undiscovered Amerindians* (1992) – in which the couple displayed themselves as recently discovered peoples locked in a cage in the foyers of major natural history museums – the context of Marcalo's work felt intimate, lessening the obvious comment on the policed, othered, subject. If Marcalo fails to frame her critique of the freak show as boldly as *Sealboy: Freak* (which features an impersonation of sideshow star Stanley Berent) or *Two Undiscovered Amerindians*, she is undoubtedly engaging with the theme of voyeurism and its relation to current discourses on surveillance and disability. What *Involuntary Dances* does uniquely, however, is engage with these discourses as they relate to epilepsy, a generally invisible disability much less instantly readable as Fraser's physical or Fusco's racial non-normativity. By displaying the epileptic body as freak, even when not in the midst of a seizure, Marcalo's performance inserts herself, as a woman with epilepsy, into discourses previously reserved for those with physically non-normative characteristics.

19. Marcalo at *Access All Areas*, 2011.

While much of the anger around her performance was prompted by its play on the theme of the freak show, according to emails received by Marcalo, or the performance's encouragement of discontinuing medication, much news was also made about its £14,000 cost, which funded the yearlong development of the trilogy of work.[19] The controversy was framed by newspapers like the *Daily Express* and online commentators as a waste of money which could or should have gone to epilepsy research or social services for people with epilepsy. As the aforementioned mother writes, 'THE ARTS COUNCIL SHOULD GIVE THIS MONEY AND INDEED ANY SPARE CASH THEY HAVE TO ONE OF THE EPILEPSY CHARITIES WHO WILL PUT IT TO GOOD USE UNLIKE MISS MARCALO'.[20] If *Involuntary Dances* was an advocacy campaign with which people agreed, they might not have a problem with the expenditure, but Marcalo herself never made a claim that the money was related to epilepsy research nor was it funded, by Arts Council England, to explore a specific medical agenda. Although it may be possible that Marcalo's work was of increased interest to the Arts Council because of its potential to promote social inclusion of people with disabilities, evidence for this, according to Marcalo, was never made readily obvious. Because commentators, such as those above, felt the message of Marcalo's work was disagreeable and/or potentially destructive to people with epilepsy, audiences viewed funding for the project through the lens of how epilepsy funds were depleted to fund *Involuntary Dances*.

20. Response to Paul Jeeves, 'Epilepsy'.

A critique of Marcalo's work may be made as to why the 'awareness' that she mentions – awareness about the cultural issues surrounding epilepsy – cannot be mobilised in the manner promoted by Douglas Crimp. The activist aesthetic he espouses in his reading of ACT UP and Gran Fury's installation *Let the Record Show...* (1987) moved work about HIV/AIDS beyond expected dichotomies of work being either

21. See Douglas Crimp, *AIDS: Cultural Analysis/Cultural Activism* (Cambridge, MA: MIT Press, 1988).

22. 'Frequently Asked Questions', Bradford Playhouse home page, <http://www.bradford playhouse.co.uk/rita/faq.html> [accessed 5 May 2010].

23. Response to Tanya O'Rouke, 'Controversial Epileptic "Fit" Performance Ends in Failure', *Telegraph & Argus*, Bradford, 12 December 2009, <http://www.the telegraphandargus.co.uk/news/local/localbrad/4790933. Dancer_Rita_takes_a_step_into_the_unknown/> [accessed 18 January 2010].

24. Garland Thomson, *Extraordinary Bodies*, p. 15.

'humanising' (of people with HIV/AIDS) or 'fund raising' for a cure.[21] Marcalo could have, similarly, demonstrated how cultural stigma around epilepsy has tangible destructive results, although it affects people on a very different scale and time schedule than was being discussed by Crimp during the early years of the HIV/AIDS epidemic. The claim could also be made, however, that my even suggesting a necessity to engage with epilepsy, as a subject matter and in such a way, may be an ableist comment expecting artists with disabilities to create in relationship to a disability arts community. It may be telling that Marcalo consistently looked to the examples of Franko B and ORLAN when defending her use of the body, in sharp contrast to choosing, as exemplars, prominent artists who have engaged their work in a disability arts context like Mat Fraser or Alison Lapper.[22] Because Marcalo did not previously think of herself as an artist with a disability, her models appear to be drawn from body-based practitioners whose work is statedly not (first and foremost, at least) about awareness-raising, even if they do raise awareness in the way about which she and not the online commentators were speaking.

While those offended by Marcalo's performance suggest she was encouraging people with epilepsy to discontinue their anti-convulsive medication, Marcalo never felt as though she was using her performance to relate to an epilepsy community, either real or imagined. As she readily admits,

> I hadn't thought about how this work was going to fit in with [discourses about disability] or not [. . .]. I wasn't there as a disabled person, this was on my way in [. . .]. I suppose what I am trying to say is that I was aware of [the discourses] but I hadn't located myself in them.

It was this process of locating-oneself-while-creating that seemingly offended those inside the epilepsy community and it is assuredly ethically complex territory. Marcalo's presentation of email communication with advocacy organisations at *Access All Areas* (March 2011), done without didactic framing and with inclusion of very considered critiques against *Involuntary Dances*, evidences that Marcalo is open to a critique of this process, if not still being protective of her own performance work.

Because Marcalo had not previously interacted with the epilepsy communities, people seemingly resented the tenor of her work and questioned her authenticity. Responding to issues of authenticity, many online commentators wrote about whether Marcalo was actually epileptic, if her seizures had ceased, or if the performance was a hoax. 'Probably isn't even still epileptic, but recovered', one voice writes in response to the *Telegraph & Argus* newspaper's post-performance coverage, 'it does happen and people paid to view such a sham'.[23] The severity and regularity of her epilepsy is something Marcalo herself commented on, saying 'Up until [the performance], I felt like I didn't have the right to call myself a disabled person because my epilepsy is for the most time controlled. It didn't feel like my identity.' When considering definitions of community as it relates to a disability context, Garland Thomson writes that '[o]nly the shared experience of stigmatisation creates commonality'.[24] Although both Marcalo and many of her critics are people living with epilepsy, the range of seizures and levels of severity and regularity make Marcalo and many commentators' experiences of epilepsy different, thus raising the question of the efficacy of Marcalo aligning with a community with which she has little in common.

The questioning of 'who's in and who's out' is perhaps a symptom of invisible disabilities like epilepsy or mental illness, and it remains difficult territory, especially considering how Marcalo previously 'passed' as non-disabled as a conscious professional choice. Self-definitions and disclosure of disability status can relate directly to access to resources (for example, receiving free prescriptions or not), privileges and oppressions, and inclusion or exclusion from epilepsy-related and more general populations. Perhaps because of this, this inter-community conversation seems unsurprisingly policed with a suspicious, or even aggressive tone. Keeping in mind these questions, and a broader look at Live Art in the UK today, it is essential to remember that very few people actually saw the live work, and that the majority of the comments were not in response to the live work or documentation of the live work, but rather the mere suggestion of the live action taking place. However, *Involuntary Dances* usefully incited a community into critical self-reflection and effectively brings to the foreground how the authority of the solo performer, or of the evidentiary 'I', can create tensions. These are heightened when members of seemingly similar populations are invested in protecting their individual interests – be they artists, advocates or people with a unique bodily experience and a story to tell.

Bobby Baker and the Minefield of Language

> Bobby Baker is a woman and an artist. She is commonly described as a performance artist or live artist, and is one of the most widely acclaimed and popular performance artists working today [...] Over the past 11 years she has periodically gone mad and is an active campaigner for more acceptance of and human rights for people categorised by society as 'disordered'.[25]

Bobby Baker is comfortable talking about mental illness, but has not always been. If *Involuntary Dances* marked Rita Marcalo's 'coming out' about epilepsy in 2010, Baker's 'coming out' happened in 2000 with *Pull Yourself Together*, her performance intervention in which, strapped to a flatbed truck driven around Central London, Baker shouted 'Pull yourself together' to passersby to promote Mental Health Awareness Week.[26] In ten subsequent years of creating work about mental illness, Baker's explorations have been both public and private, resulting in her most public work to date, *How to Live* in 2004, and her most private, eleven years of diary drawings which were only made public in 2009. In both of these cases, Baker has consciously considered her audience in the work-creation process, but not always in the same way. Through a consideration of Baker's engagement with the Wellcome Collection when creating and presenting the exhibition and book *Diary Drawings* in

25. Wellcome Collection, <http://www.wellcomecollection.org/whats-on/events/bobby-baker-in-conversation.aspx> [accessed 6 May 2010].

26. Bobby Baker and Clare Allan, 'Pull Yourself Together', in *Small Acts: Performance, the Millennium and the Marking of Time*, ed. by Adrian Heathfield (London: Black Dog Publishing, 2003), pp. 128–35 (p. 131).

2009, I hope to provide a second example of how the relationship between artists and advocacy organisations can be crafted.

During an interview I conducted with Baker in April 2010, she framed her conception of audiences in the language of 'theory of mind'. Theory of mind is the psychological discourse – or 'jargon', as Baker describes it – of how people implicitly respond to their projections of the judgements of others. Such a consideration of the audience has always been characteristic of Baker's work, but when creating *How to Live* she states that she felt more conscious of the position than before. Her consciousness, however, was not from the point of view of a mental health advocate, but rather as a woman uncomfortable disclosing her mental health status and negotiating multiple audiences at all times. It was perhaps because of her nondisclosure that her approach to her implied audience was polyvalent. First there was her family, who knew extensively about her background. Second, there were the doctors with whom she was collaborating on a performance about Dialectical Behavioural Therapy (DBT), only some of whom knew about her treatment course. Third, there was the audience of producers, directors and marketing staff at the Barbican, few of whom Baker informed about her mental illness. Finally, there was the traditional audience, the 1000 people each night at the Barbican who were coming to see her largest performance to date.

Created in 2004, *How to Live* was developed in consultation with Dr Richard Hallam and followed Baker as she described her personal re-imagining of DBT.[27] Baker positioned herself as psychologist in the performance and enacts her therapy on a pea, played by a pea on a string. While the pea occasionally interjects its own thoughts or protestations, the stage picture is that of a dominating medical institution towering over a (mostly) helpless pea. The performance contained many signature elements for Baker, and in particular included the performance being built around short vignettes, each with their own signifier, ultimately building to a fantastical or transformative conclusion. In this case, each of the vignettes was one of eleven strategies for 'how to live', each with a distinct title – when put together, the titles formed an acrostic, revealing the ultimate strategy of Baker's therapy course: W.A.T.C.H. Y.O.U.R.S.E.L.F.

Baker readily admits that the show was dangerous to her mental health – the pressures of performance were great and the conversations around the work were challenging. While the work was not framed as being as clearly autobiographical as her previous performances, it wasn't not about her either. Although the marketing material attributed the inspiration of the work to Baker's own experience with DBT, the piece demonstrated a silence around the severity of her mental illness and ambivalence about her personal relationship to the treatment course. The stigma around mental illness presumably kept her from being open about her treatment course at that time. It was this uncertainty, Baker says, which led ultimately to the tone of the work being as cheering and optimistic as it was; she states,

> The whole process was very risky for my health, but I was sort of on this mission. But at the same time, with this kind of determination and some

27. John Daniel, 'How to Live', in *Bobby Baker: Redeeming Features of Daily Life*, ed. by Michèle Barrett and Bobby Baker (London: Routledge, 2007), pp. 246–50 (p. 247).

kind of necessity to do it, [I had] this extraordinary energy [...] Funny enough that what happened was this kind of phenomenally cheering show [...] I did protect those people who saw the show from [knowing] how ill I was [...] There was this unconscious need for them to see how I learned to cope with those 11 skills, to get a sense of poignancy with the patient and the image of the pea [...] To say that this pea was me.

Unlike Marcalo, Baker made very few strong statements and presented few controversial images surrounding DBT and mental illness more generally. As she was exploring her relation to discourses about mental illness, she used a light touch and ambivalent position to explore how society views issues around mental health.

After *How to Live*, Baker became more active in mental health advocacy. She described how her role, or the sense of her role, shifted: 'I found myself really caught up in being a spokesperson and I got so politicised. I was a fountain of facts, all I could do was quote statistics.' The sentiment Baker discusses here demonstrates how she conceived that the process of being a spokesperson and activist precluded her from being an artist at the same moment. Quickly, her identity became exclusively that of a spokeswoman for mental health. Baker's shift away from performing, however, was brief, and she soon discovered her role in mental health communities might be more complex. About her identity as a spokeswoman she said,

I finally got [to realise] 'Hey, I'm an artist. I'm an artist, actually.' There are people who do [service user representing] really well [...]. I'm this, and if things work, I'm funny. That's all I can do. That's my contribution.

The relationship between Baker's activist self and her artist self came together with her 2009 exhibition *Diary Drawings* at the Wellcome Collection, the exhibition space associated with the Wellcome Trust which funds extensive biomedical research as well as scientific and artistic collaborations. While the decision-making process before exhibiting all of her drawings from her private collection was not easy, Baker's history with mental illness had, by 2009, been long public. Her involvement with the community (as she defined it) made her responsiveness and interaction with her audience even more loaded – she now knew the needs of the community and the tenor of public discourse. In practical terms, Baker was able to play very much to the expectation and needs of the audiences: she created a box for private comments to be shared with her, chose a large selection of books about mental health and featured a list of resources. With such a public dissemination of the work, her conception of the exhibition's implied spectator was even more loaded, with Baker feeling an increased responsibility for those audiences who were also mental health service users.

For the framing of the work, Baker attempted to control as much of the marketing of the work as she was able. It was here that the most interesting conflicts arose which may be the most telling of a relationship between an artist and an institution. Because Baker had been previously funded by the Wellcome Trust to create *How to Live*, there was little fear

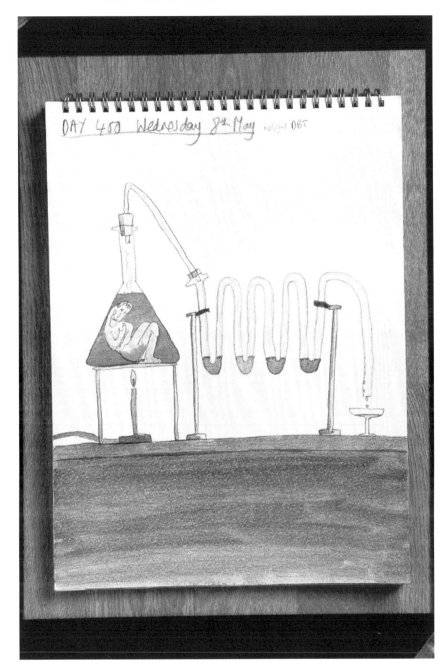

Image 2. *Diary Drawings: Day 400.* Helpful DBT. © Bobby Baker 2009. Photograph
© Andrew Whittuck.

that her work would be critiqued as illegitimate. In addition, the 'I' that
she used in this case was clear from the large amounts of drawings (158
of 700 created were displayed) and from the texts that would
accompanying the drawings as captions. But Baker was particularly
aware that this was not a performance in which, outside the captions, she

had an opportunity to speak directly to an audience. Additionally, the Wellcome Collection's large-scale marketing efforts (including advertisements in Underground Tube stations) would ensure that Londoners, even if they didn't see the exhibition, would be confronted with the mental health issues present in *Diary Drawings*.

In contrast to the case of Rita Marcalo, where it was Epilepsy Action policing the tenor of the conversation about illness, it was Bobby Baker who was the policing force in *Diary Drawings*. Although Baker is purposefully precocious and politically incorrect in her language – her biog above using the term 'gone mad' – she was exacting in the language that she felt was appropriate for all press materials associated with the exhibition. She states,

> You know, if it's your story you can say 'bonkers' or 'I'm a nutter'. And it was an interesting education process for all of us, because I had to make it clear if it's in inverted commas then you can use that language. The language was the hardest [issue]. All of us kept an eye on those words. Do you say mental health 'problem'? Mental health 'difficulty'? It's such a minefield, and I have strong feelings about it.

The marketing staff at Wellcome Collection seemed responsive to Baker's leadership on such issues. Because the Wellcome Collection lacks the specific remit of Epilepsy Action, they can allow for more diversity as to what modes of representation are appropriate. And most empowering, as happened in Baker's case, the Collection can refer to the individual creator herself to see what makes her comfortable regarding tenor. There are a number of factors at work here, including the notoriety of the artists, the intensity (or presumed intensity) of the performance work presented by either Baker and Marcalo and the fact that the Wellcome Collection and Epilepsy Action are very different organisations, and organisations which had different stakes in the work. The Wellcome Collection, as a private charity supporting informal and formal learning and stimulating interest in biomedical science through the arts, is different to the advocacy-led Epilepsy Action. In Baker's case, the Collection was funding the exhibition, while in Marcalo's case, the organisation was responding to complaints from its membership. While I do not mean to flatten these differences between Baker and Marcalo, for the sake of this article, I hope to highlight them and explore how two artists negotiate their relationship with advocacy and organisations quite distinctly.

Entrusting the tone of the work to Baker, as the Wellcome Collection did in the marketing of the exhibition, came with an unforeseen difficulty, however, in that Baker was constantly associated with the mental illness that made up the core of *Diary Drawings*. Although Baker acknowledges a continued awareness of her mental illness, the severity of her mental illness has now passed. According to Baker, her history with mental illness resulted in the marketing team treating her with the soft touch befitting someone currently with severe mental illness. Discussing Arlene Croce's refusal to review Bill T. Jones' *Still/Here*, Petra Kuppers makes the critical point that Croce, by refusing to review work by

28. Kuppers, *Disability and Contemporary Performance*, p. 53. See Arlene Croce, 'Discussing the Undiscussable', in *The Crises of Criticism*, ed. by Maurice Berger (New York: The New Press, 1998), pp. 15–29.

29. Bobby Baker, *Diary Drawings: Mental Illness and Me* (London: Profile Books, 2010), p. 212.

30. Newcastle University, <http://www.ncl.ac.uk/events/public-lectures/item.php?bobby-baker-artist> [accessed 5 May 2010].

terminally ill dancers, 'homes in on an underlying cultural assumption: people who are defined by their bodies are trapped by them'.[28] In the case of Baker and *Diary Drawings*, the producers may have fallen into this mode of thinking, over-determining their awareness of her history with mental illness and viewing her exclusively through that lens.

Baker's reliance in the Wellcome Collection to listen to her ideas was of critical importance when considering her role as an artist and as an advocate for mental health awareness. In contrast to Marcalo, Baker does define her work and her talks as advocating for disability awareness. In the final pages of the publication that accompanied *Diary Drawings*, Baker ensures that her politics around mental illness are not ambiguous, writing 'Mental illness and its treatment is a subject that provokes strong feelings and, like others, I have strong opinions about what could help. There isn't room to fit them all in here.'[29] She proceeds to make six lengthy prescriptions for the improvement in mental health services.

Before giving a large, public lecture at Newcastle University, Baker was at first displeased when the event's organisers had changed her usual biographical statement (at the top of this section) by saying that 'This lecture addresses the long period of intermittent depression that led to her *Diary Drawings* exhibition at the Wellcome Collection, London', replacing Baker's assertion that she has occasionally 'gone mad'.[30] By removing 'gone mad' from the text, Baker's initial hesitation was that the statement read too dryly, or not as an artistic statement in its own right. This displeasure, however, gave way to a mindset that sees Baker thoroughly in the camp of explicit advocacy, and choosing to be an advocate over, at this specific moment, being an artist with complete editorial control. About Newcastle, she said:

> It would have worked [...] but what they said was that it was World Mental Health Day and they didn't want to offend anyone. They wouldn't have done, but they didn't know what they were getting. And I was quite accepting. I was sort of annoyed and then I thought 'hang on a minute – people still are very embarrassed about this – and it's a shocking subject and have a bit of humility, or patience'.

While Baker clearly believes in an open tenor about mental illness, she also firmly believes that, for the goals of the advocacy campaigns in which she participates, certain things are negotiable. This is not to say that Baker would always allow her biographical statement to be changed in any way. In Newcastle, however, artistic control gave way to patience as Baker seemingly understood the nature of the Newcastle talk and saw the talk as an opportunity to forward anti-stigma work. It was not that Baker was no longer an artist; rather, her relationship to mental illness and advocacy impacts upon her relationship to the art world. As the label in the back right hand corner of *Diary Drawings* summarises such a relationship, in the area reserved for ISBN codes and subject summary: 'Arts/Psychiatry', suggesting a useful conjunction between these two discourses.

Conclusion

I have attempted to account for what is at stake when artists interact with institutions, and specifically the nebulous nature of both the terminology (awareness, community, advocacy) and the artists' approaches themselves. This ambiguity, however, might be the strongest asset of both the work, and the theory about the work. Didacticism in performance work is particularly difficult ground, which is not to say that work with a stated and explicit agenda is not useful – it can be, as performance activists like Reverend Billy can perhaps attest to.[31] But there seems to be something about 'awareness' – its porous nature, its indeterminateness – which seems well suited to performance, as an exploration of bodies in space in front of an audience. Anti-stigma campaigns attempt to shift the slow-moving ship of public opinion around myriad issues. Similarly, performance work which reflects upon certain lived experience – in hopes of, as Marcalo says, raising awareness of the cultural perspectives affecting how people with disabilities are watched or policed – demonstrates an openness for both the performer and the many audiences that the work produces.

Although performers might be very responsive to the needs and goals of a community, as Baker clearly demonstrates, the work continues to allow for multiple interpretations and considerations by an audience consisting of the 'general public'. By watching the relationships between artists and the institutions working around issues such artists reflect upon, it may be possible to see where lines are drawn. Seeing where the lines are drawn doesn't end stigma around epilepsy, mental illness or non-normative bodily experience more broadly, but it can help the communities involved to self- or collectively reflect, or to encourage dialogue around issues which may have stagnated, including discourses around voyeurism, the freak show and disability. It is undeniable that Marcalo raised awareness about epilepsy, and that Baker raised awareness about mental illness, with their respective works. The precise results of such awareness are, however, indeterminate. I do not wish to imbue this indeterminacy with a sort of power, privileging performance above other forms of activism or advocacy. Rather, I hope that through exploring Marcalo and Baker's works in relation to their own stated goals around advocacy, I have identified some of the strategies, negotiations and dilemmas unique to this brand of advocacy and, when not explicitly participating as advocates, this brand of performance.

31. Reverend Billy, *What Should I Do If Reverend Billy Is in My Store?* (New York City: The New Press, 2003).

Skin Deep: Female Flesh in UK Live Art since 1999

Gianna Bouchard

The decades at the turn of the third millennium in the UK have been a time of various scandals, controversies and court cases that have drawn attention to the ethical and legal status of the human body in various contexts. Medical, scientific, artistic, social and legal affairs have all played a significant part in raising profound and complex questions relating to issues of consent and ownership of the body. Seemingly innate rights to physical integrity, to agency over one's body, to respect of and the autonomy of both the living and the dead body, and the 'property' of one's body have come under serious stress at the turn of the twenty-first century. As the body has become increasingly exploited, manipulated, commodified and commercialised by biotechnologies, so unease has escalated about control over and proprietary interests in all bodies, both human and non-human. A series of controversies has led to an on-going debate and a re-evaluation about such fundamental questions as: do we own our bodies; what rights do we have over them in various social, medical and legal contexts; and, what principles can or should be applied to answer and clarify these dilemmas?

As a cultural practice focused on 'the exploration, use and examination of the human body', Live Art is uniquely placed to respond to, challenge and intervene in these debates.[1] Artists such as Franko B, ORLAN, Stelarc, Kira O'Reilly and Ron Athey have produced work that tests the limits of the body and, at times, the human, while claiming a stake in their own physicality and materiality. In these contexts, Live Art can erode and undermine the perceived creeping loss of agency over our bodies, reclaiming them from the dominant discourses of medicine and science.

In the last twenty years, we have been explicitly confronted by issues of personal agency and property in the body from a number of perspectives.

1. Adrian Heathfield, 'Alive', in *Live: Art and Performance*, ed. by Adrian Heathfield (London: Tate Publishing, 2004), pp. 7–13 (p. 11).

These have included organ retention scandals, the auctioning of a kidney on eBay, the imprisonment of a sculptor for the theft of human remains, legislation such as the Human Tissue Act 2004 and the establishment of the UK National Crime Intelligence DNA Database. Given the social, cultural, ontological and epistemological tensions involved, the politics of these scenarios, and others like them, are often highly charged and multifaceted. Individual and societal interests are inevitably interlaced in these moments and provoke debates around issues such as autonomy, consent, dignity, identity, privacy, accountability and religious and moral values.

Live Art has the potential to translate and transform these anxieties and controversies into lived, experiential works of affective and meaningful art. In its capacity to reveal the often invisible and unremarked ethical dilemmas or blind spots in cultural practices, Live Art can be a powerful means of intervening in these contexts and of reflecting back on them in productive ways. Certainly, as Nancy Scheper-Hughes argues, in 'society and the global economy "the body" is generally viewed and treated as an object, albeit a highly fetishized one, and as a "commodity" that can be bartered, sold or stolen in divisible and alienable parts', so the need to understand these dynamics, and critique them remains vital.[2]

This essay will argue that, at the turn of the twenty-first century, particular female Live Art makers working in the UK have sought to reflect on and articulate questions and challenges concerning these disputes and accelerating concerns. The work of Marisa Carnesky and Kira O'Reilly will be examined here in the context of these issues. By inserting their bodies, identities and, more specifically, their skin into these polemics, the practices of both artists have offered divergent ways of contemplating what is at stake in some of these biopolitical arenas; in particular, they make the female visible in relation to the ethical, social, and legal status of the human body. By offering their skin to sight in various ways, both have offered ways to think through their flesh to the politics and ethics of consent and proprietary rights in the body. Ultimately, their work is about the boundaries of self and identity in relation to the increasing objectification and commodification of the body, particularly in relation to biopolitics.

There are no property rights over bodies in English common law, due to the longstanding 'no property principle', which 'posits that something can be either a person or an object – but not both – and that only objects can be regulated by property-holding'.[3] Bodies, therefore, are 'not the subject of property rights in any conventional sense'.[4] This means, for instance, that there is no legal right to sell body parts; as bodies are not owned, they are, therefore, not divisible or disposable for financial gain. The 'no property principle' was initially invoked in relation to corpses in the late seventeenth century but this continues to be applied and tested in contemporary legal cases, such as that of the British sculptor Anthony-Noel Kelly in 1996. Kelly had paid Niel Lindsay, a laboratory technician at the Royal College of Surgeons in London, to remove anatomical specimens from the collection so that Kelly could make casts of the body parts for display as part of an art exhibition. Kelly and Lindsay were charged under the Theft Act 1968; their lawyers built a 'no property

2. Nancy Scheper-Hughes, 'Bodies for Sale – Whole or in Parts', *Commodifying Bodies*, ed. by Nancy Scheper-Hughes and Loïc Wacquant (London and New York: SAGE Publications, 2002), pp. 1–8 (p. 1).

3. Donna Dickenson, *Property in the Body: Feminist Perspectives* (Cambridge: Cambridge University Press, 2007), p. 4.

4. Ibid., p. 3.

5. Rohan Hardcastle, *Law and the Human Body: Property Rights, Ownership and Control* (Oxford and Oregon: Hart Publishing, 2009), p. 32.

6. Ibid.

7. Dickenson, *Property in the Body*, p. 16.

8. Amelia Hill, 'Our Lives Are About Alice – That's Why I Am Selling a Kidney', *Observer*, 22 February 2004, <www.guardian.co.uk/uk/2004/feb/22/health.healthand wellbeing> [accessed 25 August 2011].

9. Oliver Burkeman, 'Anything Goes', *Guardian*, 20 September 1999, <www.guardian.co.uk/theguardian/1999/sep/10/features11.g2?INT CMP=SRCH> [accessed 25 August 2011].

10. Alistair Campbell, *The Body in Bioethics* (London & New York: Routledge), p. 18.

11. Ibid., p. 15.

12. Ibid.

13. Catherine Waldby and Robert Mitchell, *Tissue Economies: Blood, Organs, and Cell Lines in Late Capitalism* (London and Durham: Duke University Press, 2006), p. 19.

14. Dickenson, *Property in the Body*, p. 4.

15. Ibid., p. 25.

16. Claudia Benthien, *Skin: On the Cultural Border between the Self and the World*, trans. by Thomas Dunlap (New York: Columbia University Press, 1999), p. 2. In terms of female artists working in the 1960s and 1970s who challenged representations of women, Gina Pane, Marina Abramović and

principle' defence that 'body parts were not property, and therefore were not capable of being stolen'.[5] The court dismissed this and convicted the pair. At appeal, it was found that 'parts of a corpse are capable of becoming property within section 4 of the Theft Act if they have "acquired different attributes" through the application of skill (such as dissection or preservation techniques) for exhibition or teaching purposes'.[6] As the stolen items were prepared specimens, Kelly was sentenced to nine months' imprisonment and Lindsay was given a six-month suspended sentence. Due to the application of the 'work and skill exception', the two men were convicted of the theft of body parts. As Donna Dickenson points out, however, this legal 'exception' protects medical staff and researchers rather than patients or the original source of the material.[7]

In a collision of medical, legal and digital ethics around issues of property and ownership in the body, in December 2003 the Internet auction site eBay was used to advertise the sale of a human kidney. A father from south-east England had placed the advertisement in the hope of raising money for his daughter who required medical treatment for cerebral palsy.[8] In a similar auction on the site in the USA in 1999, bids for a kidney rose to an astonishing $5.75 million, but both company policy and juridical rulings were cited to prohibit the sales.[9] American and English law share a common understanding that it is illegal to sell body parts under the 'no property principle' and, therefore, the auctions were never completed. These instances, and the wider debate about organ and body trading, signal social anxieties relating to a 'potential dehumanization of the self, by treating it as no more than a rational negotiator in a society dominated in all its aspects by market values, including the monetizing of parts of the human body'.[10] Alistair Campbell argues that there is an 'essential relationship between ourselves and our own bodies'; we cannot, therefore, treat the body as we would 'a tract of land or a library of books'.[11] Campbell suggests that we should perhaps look to 'other types of human right, notably those which protect the privacy, dignity and inviolability of the individual person'.[12] If the human body is 'the locus of absolute dignity, and that dignity involves the preservation and protection of integrity', then that 'dignity is destroyed if any part of the body is assigned market value and rendered alienable'.[13]

The heightened awareness of the current potential to turn our bodies into objects of property is a contemporary controversy. There is a fear that 'commodification of the body appears to be the way in which it transforms us into objects of property-holding, rather than active human subjects'.[14] At a deeper level, medical ethicist Donna Dickenson is concerned with the underlying gendered dimension of this commodification: 'All bodies are at risk from commodification, but women's bodies are most at risk. Not only are they richer in "raw materials" than men's bodies; women are also more routinely expected to allow access to their bodies'.[15] This condition of accessibility and objectification has been critiqued since the 1960s in female Body Art and Live Art practices, where women have articulated challenges to these patriarchal economies via their skin, as their canvas and 'place of encounter'.[16] Marisa Carnesky

Carolee Schneemann are key examples. See also: Rebecca Schneider, *The Explicit Body in Performance* (London and New York: Routledge, 1997); Tracey Warr and Amelia Jones, *The Artist's Body* (London: Phaidon Press, 2000); Amelia Jones, *Body Art/ Performing the Subject* (Minneapolis: University of Minnesota Press, 1998); Kathy O'Dell, *Contract with the Skin* (Minneapolis: University of Minnesota Press, 1998).

17. Marisa Carnesky, *Carnesky Productions*, <http://www.carnesky.com/productions.html> [accessed 10 April 2011].

18. On the history and politics of the sideshow and circus, see: Rosemarie Garland Thomson, *Freakery: Cultural Spectacles of the Extraordinary Body* (New York: New York University Press, 1996); Michael M. Chemers, *Staging Stigma* (New York: Palgrave Macmillan, 2008); Ricky Jay, *Learned Pigs and Fireproof Women* (New York: Villard Books, 1986); Ricky Jay, *Jay's Journal of Anomalies* (New York: Quantuck Lane Press, 2003).

19. The tattoo was created by Alex Binnie at Into You, London, funded by an Arts Council grant. Binnie's then-wife, Nicola Bowery (formerly the wife of Leigh Bowery) made the sequinned costume worn by Carnesky in her Whore of Babylon vignette in the same show. Thanks to Dominic Johnson for these extra notes.

20. Marisa Carnesky, *Jewess Tattooess*, performed at the ICA, London 1999.

is one such contemporary artist who continues this lineage of utilising the body surface to recuperate personal agency and ownership over one's physical self. For example, in her work *Jewess Tattooess* at the Institute of Contemporary Arts (ICA), London, in 1999, the significance of the female body in relation to questions of property and self-determination was explored through a particular religious ideology that poignantly intersects with these wider issues.

Carnesky describes herself as a show-woman, whose performances combine forms of popular entertainment, such as magic and illusion, fairground, circus arts, burlesque and waxworks, into multimedia spectacles and surprising encounters with peculiar pleasures and horrors. *Jewess Tattooess* specifically engaged with 'the Jewish taboo against body art, looking at the cultural and religious implications of a Jewess who chooses to become heavily tattooed' through a mix of performance, film and music.[17] Carnesky wanted to explore the Torah's prohibition against body modification and agency over her own body, as both a Jew and a woman, in relation to being tattooed. Through an examination of this religious imperative, the piece has strong resonances with bioethical debates around consent, ownership, and the integrity and dignity of the body, and more specifically, the female body.

The work unfolds over the course of an hour through a series of episodes, interjected with projected films and text. The textual placards are designed in silent movie style, explaining and enlivening the onstage action. The second such caption is titled 'Jewess Tattooess' and invites the audience to see 'the human exhibit'. Carnesky's presence on stage is through a series of brief narratives and actions that draw on a variety of references – mythological, fantastical and Biblical – about such diverse women as Lilith, Red Riding Hood and Eve. Also staged are women from the circus and fairground, as Carnesky reclines on a bed of nails (see Image 1), while eating an apple, and, from where she seemingly levitates.[18] As the 'tattooed lady' from the sideshow, she reanimates a number of fictions and prohibitions against women, such as the menstruating female, who is outcast and rejected by certain patriarchal structures.

The final sequences then emphasise social and religious taboos against the female body in focusing more specifically on her tattooed flesh. Following the levitation scene, Carnesky removes a long, white night-dress to reveal her naked body to the audience. Although her tattoos have been displayed in the projections, this is the first time the audience have witnessed them in the flesh. The symbol and myth of the female as demon and serpent that she has explored throughout is etched as a fabulous green and red dragon on her back, over her buttocks and extending down her arms and legs.[19] She dances seductively to animate this legendary creature that is tattooed on her and, as she moves, the dragon undulates and ripples, as though alive on her back. She declares to the audience that she commands 'respect of her bare back' and that she is a 'human exhibition', displaying 'my instrument, my largest organ – my skin'.[20] A projection of a rabbi affirms that the body should not be tattooed in the Jewish faith, following Leviticus 19. 28: 'You shall not make gashes on your flesh for the dead, or incise any marks on

Image 1   Marisa Carnesky, *Portrait for Magic War* (2007): photo by Manuel Vason. ©
Marisa Carnesky. Courtesy of the artist.

yourselves. I am the Lord.' The show ends with Carnesky undertaking a
live tattooing action on herself, as she marks repeatedly the flesh of her
left thigh with the star of David.

Carnesky's performance addressed the complexities at stake in debates
about the status of the body, where bodies are shown to have vastly
different meanings and values across a variety of social, cultural, political,
religious and economic structures. Her tattooed, female body, dignified
and beautiful, works as a counterpoint to and reflection on social and
medical attitudes to the body that can be instrumentalist, rather than
recognising the body's intrinsic worth as the signifier of a person, a life
and an identity.[21] What Carnesky revealed here is the difficult relation-

21. D. Gareth Jones and
Maja I. Whitaker,
*Speaking for the Dead:
The Human Body in
Biology and Medicine*
(Farnham: Ashgate,
2009), p. 36.

ship between notions of property or ownership of the self, and property in the physical body. As noted by John Locke, in his *Second Treatise of Civil Government* (1690):

> every man has a property in his own person: this no body has any right to but himself. The labour of his body, and the work of his hands, we may say, are properly his. Whatsoever then he removes out of the state that nature hath provided, and left it in, he hath mixed his labour with, and joined to it something that is his own, and thereby makes it his property.[22]

Reverberating with the 'work and skill exception' in the Kelly case examined above, Locke clearly differentiates between property in the self and property in the actual body. Thus, as Dickenson summarises, 'the liberal basis of a right to property is thus intimately linked to self-ownership; it derives from the connection between our value-creating labour and our agency, although not from our ownership of our physical bodies'.[23] In covering her torso with an imposing tattoo, Carnesky has, quite literally, drawn and made visible the agency she has over her own flesh and the Lockean idea of property in the person, in contradistinction to the legal 'no property principle' in the physical body. This is reinforced and re-activated in the final moments of the piece, where Carnesky undertakes live tattooing in front of her assembled audience.

In revealing her flesh, Carnesky confirmed the skin as the site of personal identity and individuality, heightened by the imposition of the extraordinary and permanent dragon tattoo, alongside the smaller tattoos added during the live performance. These marks reclaimed her body as her own, from social prohibitions against the female, from religious taboos as a Jew and from various legal strategies adopting the 'no property principle'. Carnesky's skin in performance became the place of re-assertion of self-ownership and agency. That this is female skin is even more poignant when addressing issues of property, rights and subjectivity, given women's long-term exclusion from full notions of self-ownership.

The terms of this exclusion are complex, involving historical and cultural practice, politics, philosophy and the law, but Dickenson helpfully summarises the relations between women's historical lack of access to property rights and their agency thus: 'It is because they [women] are propertyless that they are not construed as political subjects; it is because they are not accorded the status of subjects that they hold little or no property'.[24] This circular problem then has a direct bearing on issues of property, ownership and agency in relation to biotechnology, where tissues are routinely disaggregated from the body. For women, this is particularly significant in terms of reproductive technologies, where 'we are now witnessing the extraction of surplus value from women's reproductive labour, or the extrapolation from women's propertylessness under the domestic mode of production even when the production is no longer domestic'.[25] Although not directly concerned with biomedical practices, Carnesky's work does seem to address these issues consistently by attending to feminist concerns around the body, property and ownership. For instance, her later work,

22. John Locke, *Second Treatise of Civil Government* (1690), Chapter 5, Article 26, <http://libertyonline.hypermall.com/Locke/second/second-frame.htm> [accessed 28 April 2011].

23. Dickenson, *Property in the Body*, p. 39.

24. Donna Dickenson, *Property, Women and Politics* (Cambridge: Polity Press, 1997), p. 6.

25. Dickenson, *Property in the Body*, p. 56.

26. Thanks to Dominic Johnson for drawing my attention to these provocative connections in Carnesky's later works.

27. Dickenson, *Property in the Body*, p. 19.

28. See Stuart Millar, 'Organ Removal Scandal Widens', *Guardian*, 6 December 1999, <www.guardian. co.uk/uk/1999/ dec/06/stuartmillar ?INTCMP=SRCH> [accessed 25 August 2011].

29. The legal and ethical complexities around organ acquisition and retention have a long and interesting history, and are suggested in Carnesky's *The Quickening of the Wax*, Chelsea Theatre, London, 2010. Here she explored the controversial legacy of Madame Tussaud, who was apparently called upon in the French Revolution to make death masks from guillotined heads, sent to her from the place of execution. See Marina Warner, 'Anatomies and Heroes', in *Phantasmagoria* (Oxford: Oxford University Press, 2006), pp. 31–44.

30. Waldby and Mitchell, *Tissue Economies*, p. 34.

31. Hardcastle, *Law and the Human Body*, p. 4.

Girl from Nowhere (2003) explored women's migratory journeys from East Europe to the West and encountered 'disappeared women', while *Carnesky's Ghost Train* (2004) explicitly drew attention to sex trafficking and lost daughters.[26]

In the same year as Carnesky's *Jewess Tattooess* was staged, attention was drawn to a growing scandal centred on the Royal Liverpool Children's Hospital, Alder Hey, signalling a different set of approaches to the question of the status of the body and its ownership, this time in specifically biomedical contexts. Despite the urgency of the situation, given the rapidity of biotech developments, there is a worrying lacuna in the law about what property rights one can claim over one's own biological materials: 'in law something can be either a person or an object but not both, although human tissue and genetic material partake of both categories'.[27] English law has tended to steer away from property rights in relation to separated human tissue and has focused instead on personal rights and particularly the principle of informed consent. In 1999, a public inquiry was already underway into the paediatric cardiac surgery unit at the Bristol Royal Infirmary, which revealed the retention of organs and tissues – without informed consent – at the post-mortems of children who had died following heart surgery. This inquiry then uncovered similar practices operating at Alder Hey, where the retention of organs was happening on a large scale.[28] It materialised in 1999, that a senior pathologist had directed the systematic removal and storage of almost every organ of every child at post-mortem in the hospital, for the purposes of research and training. Parents, relatives and the wider public were outraged by the seeming lack of respect implicit in the actions of medical staff and hospital administrators that left parents unaware of the removal of their children's organs, believing that they had buried complete bodies at their funerals. When it was revealed that there was no active research programme within the Alder Hey pathology unit, the storage of the organs appeared to be even more unjustified.[29]

What this controversy clearly signalled was a significant disjuncture between the needs and rights of grieving parents and relatives, and the assumed medical imperative for research and education. The biopolitics of this scenario, and others like it, such as tissue banking and organ donation, are complex. Tissue economies 'bring with them variously ontological values around identity, affective values around kinship, aging and death, belief systems and ethical standards, and epistemological values and systems of research prestige, as well as use values and exchange values'.[30] The ensuing ethical and legal debate focused on appropriate treatment of the dead body, particularly that of the dead child, and on issues of consent.

Since the first mapping of the human genome was completed in 2000, the value of biological materials has increased significantly, so the clarity of the legal status of any removed or separated tissues is ever more pressing in order to prevent the wholesale commodification of the body.[31] In an attempt to close some of the legal loopholes, to ensure the protection of patients' rights and to improve ethical standards in biomedical practice, UK civil legislation followed the

32. See Dickenson, *Property in the Body* and Hardcastle, *Law and the Human Body* for extensive analyses of the current legal situation, its implications and potential remedies.

33. Jennifer Willet, 'Bodies in Biotechnology: Embodies Models for Understanding Biotechnology in Contemporary Art', *Leonardo Electronic Almanac*, 14 (2006), 1–8 (p. 2).

34. Ibid., p. 4.

35. See Rachel Zerihan, 'Revisiting Catharsis in Contemporary Live Art Practice: Kira O'Reilly's Evocative Skin Works', *Theatre Research International* 35 (Spring 2010), 32–42. See also J. L. Turk and Elizabeth Allen, 'Bleeding and Cupping', in *Annals of the Royal College of Surgeons of England* 65 (Spring 1983), 128–31 for an extended examination of these practices in medical history.

36. Kira O'Reilly, unpublished correspondence with the author, 26 September 2011. Thanks to O'Reilly for her notes and thoughts on this essay.

37. SymbioticA, <http://www.symbiotica.uwa.edu.au> [accessed 3 April 2011]. O'Reilly, unpublished correspondence with the author.

38. Kira O'Reilly, 'Marsyas – Beside Myself', in *Sk-interfaces*, ed. by Jens Hauser (Liverpool: FACT and Liverpool University Press, 2008), pp. 96–101 (p. 97).

Bristol and Alder Hey organ retention inquiries with the revised Human Tissue Act of 2004. This sought to clarify the regulation of biological materials removed from dead and living bodies. Based on the principle of consent, it rendered illegal the removal and storage of human tissue and organs without appropriate, informed consent, and it outlawed organ trafficking and DNA 'theft'. In other words, the law again favoured personal rights over a property model, a situation that some legal experts and medical ethicists find unsatisfactory, suggesting a combination of both would offer more clarity and protection for all involved.[32]

In all of these debates and politico-legal processes, however, it is easy to lose sight of the actual bodies; biotechnology can be a sanitising discourse that erases the 'wet, bloody, unruly, and animal from mass imaginations of the biotech future' and thereby 'skewing public interpretation [of the] complex bioethics involved'.[33] Jennifer Willet argues for an 'embodied model for biotechnology', which can help 'to develop more open, complex, participatory, and less sensationalized and digitized versions of biotechnology'.[34] She identifies positive moves towards this embodied practice in the realm of bioart that engages with, explores and challenges biotechnology within artistic and embodied contexts.

Drawing together Willet's desire for embodied responses to new technologies and Dickenson's concern over the invisibility of the female in bioethics, I will now move to analyse *inthewrongplaceness* (2005 09) by UK artist Kira O'Rcilly. O'Reilly's history as a solo performer includes one-to-one work and a number of pieces that involve cutting her skin and other forms of fleshy intervention. For instance, *Bad Humours/Affected* (1998) utilised the early medical practice of applying leeches to the body to let blood, while *Wet Cup* (2000) explored 'wet cupping', another means of bleeding for therapeutic purposes.[35] These actions 'referenced' historical practices of phlebotomy, but do not 'co-operate with the economies of medicine' and through them O'Reilly began to address female subjectivity, memory, the materiality of the body and its traces.[36]

Preceding the creation of *inthewrongplaceness*, O'Reilly had undertaken an eight-month residency in 2003–04, titled *Marsyas – Running Out of Skin*, with SymbioticA, a research laboratory in the School of Anatomy and Human Biology at the University of Western Australia. Describing itself as 'an artistic laboratory dedicated to research, learning, critique and hands-on engagement with the life sciences', artists experience working with wet biology (meaning hands-on experimentation with biological materials) in order to explore its uses and potentials through creative inquiry.[37] For O'Reilly, this was an obvious step in developing her own practice, from working with the 'trace and residue of the body' to a direct engagement with 'tissue culturing and engineering skin' grown from her own body. As her application for funding stated, she sought to 'work with a bodily materiality that originates from *her* body but has a continued *living* existence and proliferation *in vitro*' which could open new possibilities for her practice.[38]

The residency project potentially involved O'Reilly undertaking biopsies of her own skin, which she was then to engineer *in vitro* through a process of tissue culturing to a design derived from traditional lace-making techniques. Although O'Reilly received ethical approval to create tissue cultures from her own skin, she never actually did so as she was unable to obtain a satisfactory sample. O'Reilly describes this as 'ironic', given that many of her previous works relied on an 'unskilled, DIY approach [to similar procedures], by either having other artists make cuts' on her body or by doing it herself.[39] Her preparatory training in tissue culturing procedures required her to practise biopsies and cell harvesting on pigs in the first instance. The pigs were recently slaughtered as part of a research programme on asthma at the same life sciences department. O'Reilly's writing on her experiences when working with these newly slaughtered animals is very revealing of the tensions she felt between following a rigorous research methodology, fascination in the process and the horror and shame of undertaking animal research. From a list of scientific procedures that she followed in a step-by-step experimental approach, she ends up vividly engaging in the embodied affect of dissecting pig's carcasses:

When my clumsy blade accidentally tears her gut I see pig's breakfast spill
In my mind's eye I see my breakfast spill.
Following the pig biopsy I feel deeply ashamed.
You stupid, stupid cow.[40]

Emerging from this research and biotech processes, O'Reilly then made the performance *inthewrongplaceness* in 2005, commissioned by HOME, London (see Image 2), and since re-performed in a variety of locations.[41]

A durational work of between four and six hours, *inthewrongplaceness* was subdivided into ten-minute, one-to-one encounters for each audience member. Before entering the space, the audience read instructions about the time limit, and were informed that they were free to move around the space and that they 'may touch the human animal and the non-human animal'.[42] Each participant had to put on latex gloves and spray them with ethanol prior to going in, following biohazard procedures from laboratory and surgical settings that help to prevent cross-infection and contamination. Inside the space, O'Reilly spent the time moving and interacting with a female pig cadaver.

The archival images of the work draw attention to the skin of these females, as their flesh crosses, interacts, connects and separates, blurs and becomes distinctive again. The non-human and human are sometimes indistinguishable in their skins, exploring their relationality and shared embodiment within similar membranes. Similar in colour, texture, suppleness, folds and creases, the sow skin stands in for the human, just as it did in the laboratory for O'Reilly's preparatory training, before she experimented on her own flesh. Here, as in Carnesky's piece, the skin is the place of encounter in a work that explores confluences of debates and understandings and perceptions of the status of the body.[43] Unlike Carnesky's dragon tattoo, which covers the vulnerable body with its reptilian scales and confirms her selfhood, O'Reilly's naked skin is a

39. For further details about the process of tissue culturing, see Oron Catts and Ionat Zurr, 'The Tissue Culture and Art Project: The Semi-Living as Agents of Irony', in *Performance and Technology*, ed. by Susan Broadhurst and Josephine Machon (Basingstoke: Palgrave Macmillan, 2006), pp. 153–68; and Adele Senior, 'In the Face of the Victim: Confronting the Other in the Tissue Culture and Art Project', in *Sk-interfaces*, pp. 76 83.

40. O'Reilly, 'Marsyas', p. 97. Emphasis in original.

41. O'Reilly has also performed other works with pigs, such as *Falling Asleep with a Pig* (Arts Catalyst/A Foundation, London, 2009). See Bryndís Snaebjörnsdottir and Mark Wilson, 'Falling Asleep with a Pig (Interview with Kira O'Reilly)', *Antennae* 12 (Spring 2010), 38–48.

42. O'Reilly, 'Marsyas', p. 101.

43. O'Reilly notes that 'the pigs' bodies were 'always [obtained] fresh from an abattoir, and, therefore, with their innards removed'. This creates a 'huge and open cavity', which many 'participants chose to investigate'. O'Reilly, unpublished correspondence with the author, 26 September 2011.

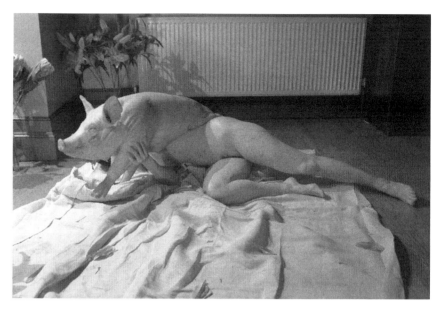

Image 2   Kira O'Reilly, *inthewrongplaceness*, HOME, 2005. Photograph © Manuel Vason. Courtesy the artist.

44. O'Reilly, 'Marsyas', p. 97.

45. Jennifer Parker-Starbuck, 'Pig Bodies and Vegetative States: Diagnosing the Symptoms of a Culture of Excess', *Women & Performance: A Journal of Feminist Theory*, 18 (2008), 133–51 (p. 145).

46. O'Reilly, 'Marsyas', p. 99.

47. Ibid., p. 98.

permeable boundary between interior and exterior, rejecting the notion that the skin 'is an impenetrable container of a coherent or fixed "self"'.[44] She opens the way to the post-human possibility of hybridisation and the melding of human and non-human in single bodies and entities, re-membering the sow in a performance where 'the pig is mourned, grieved with and perhaps seen as more than a "wasted" body'.[45] But she also performs, acknowledges, mourns, explores and wrestles with the impending interchange of bodies and the loss of individual subjectivities within the elastic parameters of biomedicine.

Exposing the dialectics of care that are invested in tissue cultures in the laboratory, O'Reilly found herself 'making fiercely tender and ferocious identifications with the pig, imaginings of mergence with the pig, co-cultured selves, and to cultivate and nurture pig bits for months'.[46] Implicit in such responses and part of O'Reilly's engagement with biomedicine is the principle of consent. Her own consent form is included in her textual piece *Marsyas – Beside Myself*, where she confirms an understanding of the risks involved in her skin biopsy and that she is 'informed' to a level with which she is satisfied.[47] This formal presence of consent, however, clearly reveals the gaping absence of it in relation to others, who are unable to give their agreement. Without examining the specificity of animal rights issues here, this work signals weaknesses in the idea of consent. For instance, the UK Human Tissue Act 2004 tried to reform the legal regulation of biological material separated from dead and living bodies by using informed consent as the governing principle. Critics, however, argue that this sidesteps the issue of clarifying property rights in the disaggregated tissue. As Dickenson notes, informed consent 'gives limited protection because it ignores the imbalance of knowledge

48. Dickenson, *Property in the Body*, p. 18.

in favour of the doctor [...] and has little to say about the situation of growing commodification'.[48] O'Reilly's own consent form says nothing about possible 'downstream' storage or use of her skin biopsy by the researchers or whether she has the right to request the removal and/or destruction of her sample in the future. Can this really be classed as informed consent as it only deals with the immediate clinical procedure? Once her skin sample has been removed, scientists can identify it as 'abandoned' and no further consent is required for anything that might be done with it. O'Reilly would have no further rights over the tissue.

Perceptions of biomedicine's dilution of property rights in our bodies and concomitant loss of identity have led, argues Dickenson, to widespread 'fear of the feminisation of property in the body', where male and female bodies are subjected to objectification and commodification in equal measure by the new biotechnologies. What O'Reilly exposes as a female performer could equally be applied to the male body, when the focus is on biological tissues: 'Fear of feminisation and the sense of losing a property in the body are most pronounced where both men and women are the "sources" of tissue, as in genetic patenting and biobanking.'[49] The bias and historical continuum is clear for Dickenson, in that the 'taking of solely female tissue does not provoke such widespread coverage and concern'.[50] As biotechnology has continued to undermine and supplant the apparent limits of the human through the last twenty years, so these performative instances of materialising female flesh can be read as responding to these encroachments and dilemmas. Intervening in the objective and analytical discourse of biotechnology, O'Reilly embodies, in Willet's terms, 'both the power and importance, as well as the harm and humility in instrumentalizing living systems'.[51] O'Reilly's performance of her female body, alongside and co-mingling with the carcass of a porcine sow, is therefore significant in re-framing the female in relation to biotechnology and recuperating women from the often invisible contexts of scientific research. Dickenson argues throughout her book, *Property in the Body*, that in much biotechnology, but more specifically in reproductive technologies, the 'lady vanishes', as the female is rarely mentioned and her rights largely ignored in favour of the rights of the embryo.[52] The visibility of the female body through the skin in such Live Art practice is also an oppositional force to the scientific and masculinised contexts of biomedical research, where the potential generative force of the female is set against the artificial and constructed interventions of science.

49. Ibid., p. 8. Gene patents can be obtained for specific, isolated gene sequences, for the chemical composition of a genetic sequence or for the processes of extraction of a gene. Biobanking refers to any archive of biological specimens used for research and experimentation. The UK established its first biobank in 2007.

50. Ibid.

51. Willet, 'Bodies in Biotechnology', p. 6.

52. Dickenson, *Property in the Body*, p. 56.

Circulating fears and concerns about the meaning and implications of such biotechnologies as stem cell research, xenotransplantation and, ultimately, the perceived power of science over life itself, were confronted and physicalised in O'Reilly's *inthewrongplaceness*, which addressed the complexities of biomedicine and its ethical dilemmas, for the artist, the scientist and the public. Involving a consideration of co-cultured tissues and the possibility of hybridisation between human and non-human, the work pointed forwards to future potentialities, suddenly realised in 2008 when scientists in Newcastle, UK, created the first animal–human hybrid embryo. The research team inserted human DNA from a skin cell into an enucleated cow ovum and activated growth via an electric shock. The

53. Alok Jha, 'First British
Human–Animal
Hybrid Embryos
Created by Scientists',
Guardian, 2 April
2008, <www.
guardian.co.uk/
science/2008/
apr/02/medical
research.ethics
ofscience>
[accessed 25 August
2011].

54. Benthien, *Skin*, p. 86.

55. Ibid., p. 89.

56. Dickenson, *Property in
the Body*, p. 180.

hybrid was 99.9 per cent human and 0.1 per cent animal and it stayed alive for three days, by which time it had divided into thirty-two cells. Denounced as an affront against human dignity and likened to the monstrosity created in *Frankenstein*, the resultant outcry was led by the Catholic Church.[53] Advocates, however, claimed potential health benefits if the research could produce human stem cells without human embryos being involved and stressed that the embryos must be destroyed within fourteen days of creation under UK law, so that they can never become viable, thereby negating the nightmare vision of Frankenstein's monster.

Returning to the skin as canvas and place of encounter, the skin is where '"woman is woman", and where she is defined by the sheath-façade that surrounds the body'.[54] Her only other anatomical meaning comes from 'the dark and muddy breeding ground in the depths of the body'.[55] As Carnesky and O'Reilly make visible and critique these gendered identifications, so biomedicine continues to deny women 'credit for their agency and intentionality in what their bodies do and produce, as in the laborious processes involved in the donation of ova or the additional risk and effort to produce cord blood'.[56] For Dickenson, these new technologies simply re-iterate old patterns of objectification and commodification of female bodies. But she does find hope in the fact that all bodies are now being feminised by the biotech industry, meaning that the male body is likewise under threat and garnering much needed attention in relation to these issues. Perhaps the exposure of the male subject to these interventions will provide a more equitable and gender-cognisant ethical framework from which to consider the use and exploitation of all bodies – female, male, human and non-human.

Whatever the future of the technologies and the debates, the works examined here are fully resonant with the controversies and anxieties being formulated and circulating in the UK in the last fifteen years in response to questions about ownership of the body. The performances by Carnesky and O'Reilly are highly significant in embodying these dilemmas and the increasing blind spots of social, political, ethical and biotechnical conceptions of the body.[57] If the lady is vanishing in biopolitics, then these Live Art makers have made strong visual and conceptual recuperations of the female in relation to a range of urgent issues around consent, proprietary rights in the body, tissue culturing and questions of self- and human identity. Through, on and over their skin, they have performed some of the most pressing bioethical questions that we have faced in the UK and continue to face as we progress into the twenty-first century. Their critiques, reflections, challenges and provocations have offered ways back to the flesh and the body, to the intimate and the personal, and to the materiality of the female, while opening the debate once more to the ethical and the social.

57. Much work on the
subject of female
agency and subjectivity
in relation to
biomedical practices
and ethics focuses
solely on ORLAN,
providing a wide range
of analysis but which
neglects other female
artists whose work is
relevant and vital to
the debate. See
*ORLAN: A Hybrid
Body of Art Works*, ed.
by Simon Donger and
Simon Shepherd with
ORLAN (London and
New York: Routledge,
2010).

INTERVIEW

The Skin of the Theatre: An Interview with Julia Bardsley

Dominic Johnson

In recent performance in visual art, there has perhaps been a curatorial shift away from practices that privilege spectacle, excess and crisis, in favour of aesthetically muted, politically undemanding, or otherwise hospitable styles. Major institutions of art have welcomed performance works that facilitate easy participation, such as Rirkrit Tiravanija's cooking demonstrations or Thomas Hirschhorn's themed libraries. Julia Bardsley is exemplary for her refusal of such tendencies, staging difficult intimacies, troubled identities, and uninhabitable spaces in performance. As such, major institutions of art have often sidelined Bardsley's work, in a time when visual spectacle and challenging politics are often superseded by more palatable, 'relational' disturbances. The contemporary institutional suspicion about spectacle has come about for several reasons; these include a cultural discomfort about the rise of high-budget, low-impact spectacular entertainment in film and theatre, and critical concerns that spectacle may be a key means for the production of de-politicized citizens in late capitalism, through to insidious developments including broadcast media tactics, advertising, and party-political spin-doctoring. However, as the novelist and cultural commentator Bruce Benderson argues, 'if the Spectacle actually is a hypnotic means of social control, its critics would best seek to subvert it by exaggerating, rather than trying to

excise, its energy and vulgarity'.[1] Since the mid-1990s, Bardsley's work has been exemplary in its pursuit of such a strategy.

Bardsley's work as a director in the 1980s and 1990s has informed her spectacular theatrical aesthetic, and especially her reliance on persona and elaborate costuming. From 1985 to 1989, her early works included devised productions for dereck, dereck, the theatre company she co-founded with Phelim McDermott (later a co-founder and artistic director of Improbable). As Joint Artistic Director of the Haymarket Theatre, Leicester (1991-93) and the Young Vic Theatre, London (1993-94), Bardsley directed highly experimental versions of major plays from the canon of western theatre. At the Haymarket, these included adaptations of T. S. Eliot's *The Family Reunion* (1992), Federico García Lorca's *Blood Wedding* (1992), Dylan Thomas' *Under Milk Wood* (1992), and *Macbeth* (1993). At the Young Vic, Bardsley remounted her own adaptation of Emile Zola's novel *Thérèse Raquin* (1993) and directed a controversial production of *Hamlet* (1994). As Bardsley explains, her early work was notable for its foregrounding of the machinery of the theatre, a highly experimental approach to canonical texts, and an attempt to produce highly charged experiences for audiences through the use of visual elements inspired by the Eastern European avant-garde. Specifically, the work of theatre artist Tadeusz Kantor has been very influential. As he wrote in 1955,

Dominic Johnson, Lecturer in Drama, Department of Drama, School of English and Drama, Queen Mary, University of London, Mile End Road, London E1 4NS.
Email: d.f.johnson@qmul.ac.uk

1. Bruce Benderson, 'Surrender to the Spectacle: The Value of Entertainment', *Parallax*, 11.2 (2005), 36-43 (p. 36).

Space which retracts violently
condenses forms [...]
to the limits of the 'impossible'.
In this dreadful
movement
the speed of making decisions
and of interventions [...]
constantly grazes
risk.[2]

For Kantor, the use of theatre as an artistic medium enables a contestation of the normative limits of creative practice, expanding the perceived autonomy of artistic forms. He foregrounds the 'risk' for performers and audiences alike in theatre that privileges spontaneity, towards a celebration of creative activities that work by 'refusing all rational classification'.[3]

For Bardsley, Kantor enabled her to recognize the ways in which the classificatory function of major institutions of theatre restricted the potential of the theatre artist. As Bardsley explains, her frustration at theatre's institutional limitations led her to abandon her directing career, towards an auteur practice in performance that merges experimental theatre, sculpture and installation, live art and performance art. The first steps in this shift involved retraining as a visual artist, and a series of performance interventions with her designer at the Young Vic, Aldona Cunningham. The theatre critic Lyn Gardner reported:

Bardsley and Cunningham decided to effectively kill themselves off and disappear into one of their own fictionalised narratives. After *Hamlet* they were no more [...] It was around this time that a pair of dark-haired, partially deaf identical twins began to be sighted at theatres around the country. Invariably these theatres were either staging productions of *Hamlet* or productions with some tenuous connection: Robert Lepage's *Elsinore* or Agatha Christie's *The Mousetrap*.[4]

Bardsley has since re-established herself as one of the most idiosyncratic artists in the UK. Her recent pieces are immersive, spectacular and unnerving.

The intense atmospheres of her theatrical worlds often involve multiple spaces of performance, special effects, video projections, and sound environments created by her long-time collaborator, the legendary British composer and sonic artist Andrew Poppy.

For the past five years, Bardsley's main project has been *The Divine Trilogy* (2003-09), a series of three spectacular immersive performances exploring disaster, horror, esotericism and disease. Bardsley invents catastrophic personae, including the morbid jester of *Trans-Acts* (2003), the toothless, hare-lipped soothsayer of *Almost the Same: Feral Rehearsals for Violent Acts of Culture* (2008), and an evangelical, yellow-eyed cowboy of the apocalypse in the final instalment, *Aftermaths: A Tear in the Meat of Vision* (2009). In this last piece, Bardsley stirs up her audience with glossolalia and enraged commandments to touch her glowing wounds, and feel her pain, accompanied by sidekick personifications of the four plagues from *The Book of Revelation*. Bardsley is masterful in her staging of bodily re-invention, transforming herself through prosthetics, brilliantly detailed costumes that complement and extend the shape of her body, and stylized performance. Her costumed body is endlessly phantasmagorical: sprouting horns, emerging from a sequinned chrysalis, grunting in the darkness, or babying mummified hares. Throughout her work, Bardsley explores the troubled agency of a body bound into perpetual catastrophe.

Indeed, Bardsley creates works that centre on provocative and challenging themes. Her works are by turns playful and disturbing, producing intensely powerful, difficult experiences for audiences. In this interview, conducted in London in December 2009, Bardsley considers the key methodologies, techniques and artistic strategies that she has developed, across a profoundly diverse and influential career, in and beyond the theatre.

Dominic Johnson: *What do you find interesting in theatre, when it is at its best?*
Julia Bardsley: For me personally, theatre is interesting when there are two things happening. You enter a world of fantasy and wonder, and you are transported in a magical sort of way. As an audience member and a maker, what I am after is a sensation that bypasses the intellectual and hits somewhere else. I don't want audiences to sit back and be detached. I am interested in a physiological sensation. At the same time, I want to see the workings of the theatre, in a way that doesn't undermine the fantasy.

2. Tadeusz Kantor, 'Representation Loses More and More Its Charm', in *Theories and Documents of Contemporary Art: A Sourcebook of Artists' Writings*, ed. by Kristine Stiles and Peter Selz (Berkeley and Los Angeles: University of California Press, 1996), pp. 58-59 (p. 58).
3. Ibid.
4. Lyn Gardner, 'Now You See Them', *Guardian*, Wednesday 13 October 1999. http://www.guardian.co.uk/culture/1999/oct/13/artsfeatures2.

Image 1   Julia Bardsley, *Macbeth* (1993); Photo: Stephen Vaughan.

DJ: *When you were Joint Artistic Director at the Haymarket and Young Vic Theatre, how did you bring those two elements together in the productions you directed?*[5]

JB: A lot of the time I was taking well-known texts, like *Macbeth*, which is relatively familiar territory for many audiences. Because it's familiar, they perhaps don't really listen to it, or fully experience the text. *Macbeth* is an incredibly extreme piece of work, and at Leicester (1993) I wanted to comment on the nature of the theatre space, the arena of the theatre as a place of violence, where the performers or actors are under the control of the director.[6] I placed myself, as director, in the role of performing the witches, so that the theme of destiny in the play related to the director's control over the space of the theatre and the performers. The battleground was the battleground of theatre. Simultaneously, I wanted the audience to enter the fiction as well, by creating moments of wonder and transformation. I extended the temporal qualities of the theatre. Usually in theatre there is a comfortable time that events take, so the murder of Lady Macduff – I had her being drowned – went on and on and on, until it went beyond 'proper' theatre time. The mechanics of the theatre – the lights, the bars, the scenery itself – was an imposing force, so that they became visible, acting on the performance space. The theatre itself became the place where ideas, emotions and violence were being played out. So I have always been interested in the meeting of those two elements, the fantasy or the fiction, and the reality of actors on stage and an audience in the real space of the auditorium. At Leicester, particularly, I was interested in bringing this challenge to

5. The Haymarket was a major repertory theatre in the Haymarket Centre in Leicester, a large city in the East Midlands. The theatre closed in 2006 after financial problems, and re-opened as Curve in 2008. The Young Vic is a well-regarded theatre in London's South Bank. It presents a range of work from classic plays to new writing and popular theatre, traditionally for young and diverse audiences.

6. For her production of *Macbeth*, Bardsley used a cast of eight performers, amalgamating some characters and cutting others. The production was notable for its use of video, evocative lighting, and sound by Andrew Poppy. For a commentary on this production, see Helen Manfull, *Taking Stage: Women Directors on Directing* (London: Methuen, 1999), pp. 130-32. As well as directing and designing the production, Bardsley played the amalgamated role of the three witches.

143

audiences who perhaps hadn't had that experience in the theatre.

DJ: *How did you become disenchanted with the theatre, if that is what happened?*

JB: I think I did become disenchanted, because the institution of British theatre has a particular history, one that is based in literature. What I was seeing from Europe, especially from Poland, was a type of theatre that wasn't purely literary, even though language was a part of it. I saw something else, where a person working in theatre could be seen as an artist, unlike in the British theatre scene where a director is seen as some sort of careerist. If you were a British director, it felt as though it wasn't legitimate to do other things as well – make installations, for example. It felt very limiting. I really admired people like Tadeusz Kantor, who was devising and performing in his pieces, but was also a sculptor, where his sculptures informed his performance work. I experienced a kind of suspicion and resistance in my desire to explore ideas and expand the notion of what theatre could be. I wanted to be a theatre artist, and it seemed very difficult to do that within an institutional theatre environment. The restrictions are partly economic. If you are running a building, the main imperative is to make the books balance, and that has a very negative effect on creativity and experimentation.

DJ: *Did you feel that there were specific institutional limitations on departures from the text and from a literary model of theatre?*

JB: Not in Leicester, because I actually had a fantastic time there, and I did some work that I am very proud of – quite extreme work for a regional repertory theatre. Problems arose more in London, where the controlling structures of the institution started to dictate what I could and couldn't do artistically. They were more clearly horrified about a director tackling a text from the theatrical canon, and doing some sort of interpretation of it, even though I don't think the interpretations I was doing were particularly radical. But there's a sense that you are not allowed to touch these sacred cows, which is mad really, as it is only material, and up for grabs. My production of *Hamlet* [Young Vic Theatre, 1994] was a celebration of theatre – that was my interpretation of the material – but in some quarters it didn't go down very well, because they thought I wasn't being reverential enough to the text, even though I was trying to do what I thought was a careful reading of the text, trying to understand the material itself rather than what the play has come to mean.

DJ: *How did you make the move out of the institutional space of theatre into a different space?*

JB: I just totally stopped making theatre. I say I retired from the theatre. I thought, I'm not going to do it any more under these circumstances; I want to make theatre but on my own terms – I don't want to do it this way. I did lots of courses: printmaking, jewellery, metalwork and woodwork, and entered a studio workshop environment, without any real idea of where it would lead. While I was printmaking, I started to think a lot more about objects and their presentation, which led to the solo installations *The Error Display* (1996) and *Punishment & Ice Cream* (1999).[7] I also explored film and video. I made my first film, which was a 16mm project called *Snow* (2000), based on a short story by Ted Hughes.[8] The story is about visual perception and seemed to be a good starting point for thinking about what film is – starting from the idea of light through the projector. I stopped thinking about performance and started working much more in visual art, until I got a Nesta Fellowship [National Endowment for Science, Technology and the Arts, 2001], which meant I had three years of support with no prescriptions about a final outcome. It was a fantastic opportunity to ask questions about myself: What am I? What do I do? What is my relationship now to theatre? It was through that process that I came to the realization that I am many things: a photographer, a performer, a theatre-maker, a sculptor, a video artist. It's fine to be all these things, but I had a problem with it for some reason. It's as if you need to fix on one role, but it's the ideas that should tell you what form to work in. The ideas will tell you they need to manifest in one medium or another.

DJ: *At what point and to what extent did the discourses and histories of live art become useful?*

JB: At the time I didn't think about it in that way, but in retrospect I can see that the context of live art is incredibly generous, particularly in terms of the people who are involved in that arena. Suddenly a dialogue about form, ideas, process and serious critical analysis – elements that have always been part of fine art discourse – were here naturally

---

7. *The Error Display: A Presentation of Remaining* was an Alternative Arts Project installed in a disused shop at 26 Chiltern Street, London in February 1996. *Punishment & Ice Cream: Ruminations on the Rod and the Cone* was presented at The Gallery, Central School of Speech and Drama, London in February 1999.

8. *Snow* was the British Council's official entry for international film festivals, and was shown at the Greenwich Film Festival, Edinburgh International Film Festival, Madrid Experimental Cinema Festival, and elsewhere, including the National Review of Live Arts screening programme. It is distributed through LUX (London).

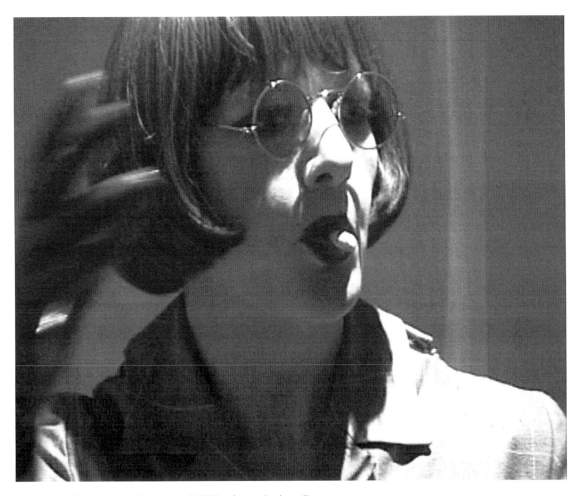

Image 2   Julia Bardsley, *Trans-Acts* (2003); photo: Andrew Poppy.

applied to performance. In the theatre it sometimes seemed that you were just making shows in a few weeks, and then you would put them on, and then you started the next show. There was no real space or precedent for having dialogues with audiences or other people working in the theatre, no real desire to have conversations about its place in a wider cultural context or the directions it was moving formally. I stumbled into the live art scene, really, through Nikki Milican [Artistic Director, National Review of Live Art, Glasgow], who had seen the work and has given a space for it over the years.[9]

People within live art seem so alert and curious but also enormously generous with their time and commitment to the work and ideas. I had never had that kind of dialogue before and I found it extremely stimulating, and very supportive. But it was never a conscious move into that territory.

DJ: *Another aspect of live art that is very useful is the fluidity of relations between the UK and*

9. The National Review of Live Art (NRLA) is the longest-running festival of performance art and live art in the UK, and celebrated its thirtieth anniversary in 2010. It is run by Artistic Director Nikki Milican OBE. Each year, the festival presents five days of performances by established artists, talks, lectures and panel discussions, a platform of work by emerging artists, and artist-run workshops. It is presented annually at the Arches in Glasgow, with additional events at Tramway, the Centre for Contemporary Arts (CCA) and other venues. Bardsley presented work at the NRLA in 2002, 2005, 2008 and 2010. For a review of Bardsley's 'hour and a half tour-de-force' performance of *Trans-Acts* at the NRLA in 2005, see Jennie Klein, 'Genre-Bending Performance', *PAJ: A Journal of Performance and Art*, 28.1 (2005), 58-66 (p. 64).

Europe, in terms of the festival circuits, which comes back to your earlier point about the insularity of the theatre.

JB: I think the festival circuit is vital. When I was working in the theatre everything was so isolated. You worked on your own production and didn't really brush up against other works or other people. The European festivals that I have been involved in have all been incredibly stimulating, and have actually been the place where I've met

UK artists. That was how Robert Pacitti [Artistic Director, Spill Festival of Performance, London] saw *Trans-Acts*; we didn't know each other, and it took a foreign festival to bring us together. The first Spill Festival [2007] was a really wonderful context for *Trans-Acts*, because Robert didn't mind talking about theatre – he didn't set up an antagonistic relation between live art and theatre. For someone like me who came from the theatre, I could have felt like an interloper, but the context was totally supportive. It was through Spill that I met Kira O'Reilly. I was already really fascinated by Kira's work, particularly her work with animals. From the outside it would seem that our work couldn't be further apart. Kira's work deals with the real, and I deal with the body in a totally artificial way – everything I do is artificial and constructed, and deliberately *not* real. So when she came to see *Trans-Acts* I was very nervous, because I was putting spikes through my tongue using fakery, whereas she uses real wounding in performance. I was worried she'd feel I was belittling her way of working. The next day we both attended a symposium as part of Spill, had lunch together, ended up not going back for the afternoon session, and spent the rest of the afternoon talking, realizing that we had much in common, even if the outcome of what we do is very different. That new friendship continues to be really important to me and to how I see my work.

DJ: *You have used animals in your own work, from the taxidermy hares in* Almost the Same *to the pantomime horse in* Improvements on

Image 3   Julia Bardsley, *Almost the Same: Feral Rehearsals for Violent Acts of Culture* (2008); Photo: Simon Annand.

Nature: A Double Act (2009).[10] *Could you say something more about the use of animals in your work?*

JB: I remember when I was very little we had a German shepherd dog that gave birth to eleven puppies. My mum and dad ran a café at that time and there was an upstairs room covered in newspaper, and the dog was there with all the puppies. I must have been about three, and I would nuzzle up with them while they were feeding, and I remember the smell of the milk and their fur, their sweet breath. So there is a connection with the animal, a sense of missing my animal side. Through culture and socialization you are not allowed to access that animal nature. I think I feel that restriction quite keenly. *Almost the Same* was an opportunity to explore that feral and uncultured side – a healthy chance to howl.

DJ: *Many of your pieces seem to explore that tension between fantasy and the visceral, where a flight of fancy gets pulled down to a horror of the body.*

JB. Yes. I think performance is always about a tension between those two poles: the glitter, glamour and beauty of diamonds, fur, leather – our adornment with skins, cultured, tamed and appropriated from nature – and the real meat of what it means to be an animal, the blood, shit and piss, which is as much its own sort of pleasure, the

mucky, dirty side. I am pulled between the sheen and gleam of the surface and the shit on the underside – the meat being turned inside out. I like the coexistence of those two textures. There's something very exciting about it. *Almost the Same* came out of the very animal experience of a miscarriage I had in rural Portugal. It's the most primal, feral, visceral experience I've had. It was a bodily process that was happening, over which I had no control. It was like I was both outside of myself and simultaneously truly being my physical, animal self; watching and experiencing the phenomena of the meat that we are, the meat that we produce inside our bodies and the amount of meat that can be expelled. Similarly, later, when I was in the development stage of *Almost the Same*, I did three days of durational performances at the Camden Arts Centre. On the last day I ended up spending two or three hours just dribbling and spitting into a bowl, and I was amazed at how much stuff the body can generate. Where does it come from, and how is it possible for the body to generate material like this? These are physical things that you don't have conscious or cultural control over, that remind you of the *meatiness* of the flesh, of your insides, and your organs at work.

DJ: *There seems to be a sense, then, that if there is monstrosity in your work, there is a meeting between the monstrous or horrific and the everyday or pedestrian. Live art often tends towards that space, where intimacy becomes frightening (such as in the one-to-one performances of Kira O'Reilly or Franko B), or where beauty is separated from horror by a skin of sorts (for example in the work of Ron Athey or Ernst Fischer). This leads into a question about* Aftermaths, *the final instalment of* The Divine Trilogy, *which explores the idea of apocalypse. Can you explain what that concept means to you?*

JB: I was interested in apocalypse as a celebration, as a revelation, or what it is to reveal, which is what theatre is, to see and to show. The spectator is there to see something revealed, in the same way that an autopsy is an opportunity for seeing inside the self. For me the apocalypse is about spectacle – vision in all its connotations, including prophecy (which is what the *Book of Revelations* is deemed to be) and other ways of seeing, where the imagination is an inner eye. *Aftermaths* is all those things thrown together, tying up apocalypse, carnival and celebration – a Bacchanalian idea of apocalypse as letting go, release, to get to somewhere that is ecstatic. I've been looking back and thinking, in a sense, how I failed to reach the level of ecstasy I intended for that piece. I've been to gigs where I have danced for hours –

10. *Almost the Same* is the second instalment in *The Divine Trilogy*, and has been presented at: City of Women Festival, Ljubljana, Slovenia; Queer Zagreb, Croatia; Chelsea Theatre, London; KANART, Lisbon; and NRLA, Glasgow (2008); and at Laboral Teatro, Gijon, Spain (2009). The performance is divided into three sections, and begins with the audience standing in a triangular formation on the stage, watching Bardsley perform a striking solo in the theatre seats. Swapping places, moving through three versions of the same costume – wearing wrestling boots, leggings, a gimp mask and a wig, in black, red and white – Bardsley interacts with a video image of herself with broken teeth and a hare-lip, as well as projected wordplay and mathematical diagrams. Major themes of the work include monstrosity, horror, disaster, and a negotiation of the desire to return to a more feral, animalistic state of things. On the programme for *Almost the Same*, Bardsley describes the work as 'a theatre of dirt, an ark of collapse', appositely describing its highly affective and uncanny evocations of a disastrous devolution into crisis. After the performance, the audience is invited onto the stage to examine its remains. *Improvements on Nature* was made in collaboration with Andrew Poppy, and commissioned by Chelsea Theatre in 2009. Bardsley and Poppy perform variations on the characters of Mary Shelley and Charles Darwin, inspired by an anecdote that tells of Shelley's *Frankenstein; or the Modern Prometheus* (1818) being found beside Darwin's deathbed. Bardsley and Poppy's performance centres around the figure of a horse, manifested through a skull used as a prop, a sculpture of dissected toy horses, and a brilliantly executed pantomime horse that the performers come together to stage in the final moments of the work, picked out in eerie darkness by black light against a grid.

like Underworld at the Roundhouse (2008) – where I was totally transported but inside something, and felt so released, and free, and out of my body. I wanted that to happen for the audience in the theatre in *Aftermaths*.[11] I don't know whether it is the conventions of theatre that tames that experience, or there weren't enough people crammed together or if the material is not familiar enough to get the audience to an ecstatic state. It's quite a task. People become familiar with music by having it in their homes. They can listen to it again and again, and a particular type of music will therefore belong to a particular moment in your life. Gigs draw on shared memories, but the audiences that come to the theatre are much more disparate – there's no commonality in the sense that you get at a gig.

DJ: *Your work often involves a sense of the magical and the occult – for example, the use of sacred shapes, geometries and equations in* Almost the Same *– and perhaps cults, which your work also flirts with.*

JB: Yes. I would still love to do something where the audience was really transported, and where we reached an ecstatic moment together, because in a sense that is the ritual of theatre, a group of people coming together towards a unique experience. Jim Morrison of The Doors talked about gigs as a secular ritual where everybody was working towards some sort of ecstatic state, which music can do in a way that is much more difficult for performance. There must be ways to do it but I haven't tapped into them yet.

DJ: Almost the Same *and* Aftermaths *are striking for the ways in which you create different configurations for audiences. For example, in* Almost the Same, *you begin the performance in the seats, with the audience on the stage in a triangular formation,* *and then physically move the audience from the stage to the seats, and then back again, transforming the set into an exhibition.*

JB: Sitting in the seats can be quite passive, both intellectually and physically. The lights come down and you become anonymous, so I like to highlight the mass, as well as the body of the spectator. I am specifically interested in what it means to be an audience in an auditorium, and the configurations of theatre spaces – the wings, backstage, the gods – the physical shape of the theatre. If you have these conventions, it's not just a case of accepting them as conventions, but of using their power to try and find a way to alert an audience to the fact that they *are* an audience, as part of a mass, and as individuals who have an effect on the performer and the performance.

DJ: *Do you feel that, as a theatre artist, you have a responsibility towards 'audience development'? What is your response to this terminology?*

JB: It's a difficult phrase. Audience development relates to funding criteria. I am not sure I have any responsibility for creating the context through which theatres garner new audiences or find the younger generations who will come and see the work. In a sense I'm not sure that's my role. Obviously I want people to see the work and I know that if they did – even if it's not something they would normally come to – they would get something out of the experience. The audience is crucial, because without it you don't have a work. That's why I concentrate on alerting the audience to their responsibility within the piece, by making sure they know they are part of the work. I'm not talking about audience participation in the crude sense, but without the audience there is only actions and lights and sound. Theatre needs that meeting of the public with what has been private. The work happens when those two things come together. It's in the public performance that I start to understand what the piece is about, because until then I am just working with material. The audience starts to shape it, to make sense of it, because the performer's concentration works in a different way in front of an audience, and something else starts to occur in the space. In some ways I hate audiences, because they don't always concentrate very well. I don't mind disruption, or heckling – I've had to deal with that quite a lot, even in conventional theatre. When I did *Macbeth* we had lots of people shouting out, and leaving, which was great because it meant that they were really feeling something, even if it was something negative.

DJ: *Live art that draws on theatre often seems polarized in its relations to audiences, between a*

11. *Aftermaths* is the third and final part of *The Divine Trilogy* and has been presented at Laban, London during Spill Festival of Performance (2009) and NRLA, Glasgow (2010). Audience members are provided with a dress code of funeral black, and give a small black offering before the start of the work. In the performance, Bardsley's persona is that of a male evangelical soothsayer, parading on an imposing black and neon cross structure, around which the audience congregates. Intermittently, four other performers join Bardsley, dressed in costumes that recall the more excessive, prosthetic looks of Leigh Bowery or Matthew Barney. Four large screens display projected video images of mobile meat sculptures and superimposed text. Andrew Poppy is installed near one arm of the cross, mixing live sound to which Bardsley responds. As Bardsley explains, the energetic performance attempts to whip up her crowd into a manic, ecstatic state. After the live performance, the four 'plagues' surround the space as living sculptures, and a framed collection of the collected black objects is auctioned and sold to the highest bidder.

desire for alienation and a desire for easy participation. On the one hand there is an attempt to withhold pleasure, and on the other, an urge to love or support an audience. I think your work intervenes in that polarity.

JB: I have a tendency, though, of trying to please an audience too much, or of over-narrating the work. I try to knock it out of myself. Coming from a narrative or story-telling tradition, it has been very hard to get away from guiding an audience through a piece, which in a way only appeals to the intellectual level. Now I am much more interested in giving them a physiological experience. By offering elements that do have a structure, but one that is buried, the audience have to piece together what is offered. Starting with *The Divine Trilogy*, especially after *Trans-Acts*, and definitely in *Almost the Same*, which was closest to what I wanted to achieve, I've begun to deliberately avoid helping the audience in that way, to pull away from my own explanatory tendencies.

DJ: *Can you describe your process of making? Where does your initial idea come from, and how do you develop it to the finished performance?*

JB: It doesn't usually begin with one single idea, but four or five that are swimming around, including something that is happening at the moment, politically or socially, or something I have read, or an image, or a flavour of an atmosphere, or just a desire to explore materials. I'll spend a couple of months reading and make notes, pursuing the ideas separately without knowing how those four or five disparate things might eventually come together into some sort of whole. It's very important that they stay discrete, so they don't get watered down, and keep their individual strength. When I transcribe my notes I'll start to see how some of the ideas cross-fertilize, or make marriages in some sort of way. I'll start doing some drawings, including maps of the space, configurations of the audience, and general ideas about how the conceptual work can be translated into a spatial dynamic. This phase involves processes of translation, so that the work doesn't remain at the level of concepts but will begin to move into questions about materials, space, shape or bodily forms. I also start making objects as well. Although I find the process of research exciting, you can get so bogged down in reading that there comes a time when you have to move out of your head and into your hands. I start gathering the lexicon or vocabulary of materials. Will it be fur, wax, honey, gold leaf, bones, plastic? What tones might they be? As I begin to make objects, I simultaneously start to sketch out a visual score, to understand how the

piece will work temporally – what sections there might be, their tenor, how one section might move into another. The piece then starts to take shape, to become more concrete, and I can get garments and set elements made. Parallel to that, I have conversations with Andrew [Poppy] about the sonic dimension, which is incredibly important for me. Without that, the performance wouldn't work, because the sonic space holds everything. Andrew will work on his own – I usually won't listen to anything and he'll only see a few things that I am working on. Towards the end of the process, Andrew will play through the material he's generated and we'll start to place it in the project score. The objects that I have made will often end up in an exhibition or installation, as a precursor or epilogue to the performance, to allow the audience a way into what I have been thinking about during the process. The objects might not necessarily appear in the piece, or be clearly connected to it, but they will have participated in the thinking process. That has always happened – even when I was in college I would provide a prologue by presenting the objects I had made. The receptacle of the theatre isn't big enough to contain everything I want to do and say, so the work tumbles out into different forms, and has to be expressed in some other way like sculpture or installation.

DJ: *Do you rehearse?*

JB: In the conventional theatre, of course, a director will work with the cast for three weeks to reach a cohesive interpretation of a text, but one of the most fantastically revelatory aspects of solo performance is that you can almost dispense with rehearsal. To me this has been a total joy, because I really loathe rehearsals – the idea that you have to find cohesion before the work is presented to an audience. For me, performance is about non-cohesion, the coexistence of elements that don't necessarily fit together, but when put together make another world that has meaning, but which the creator/performer has no control over. Not rehearsing is about relinquishing some of that control. Of course, I still set up a structure, and there are fixed elements, like the video, but within the structure I am free to do whatever I want. The audience will accept what you offer them as belonging to the work, and read it as what was intended.

DJ: *How much will a piece change or develop during a run—for example, the parts of* The Divine Trilogy?

JB: They change in a fantastic way. Except for *Trans-Acts*, I haven't performed them nearly enough to know fully what the performance is. Certainly with *Almost the Same* and *Aftermaths*, I feel that they have just started. The piece really grew when I did a run of six performances of *Almost the Same* in an old veterinary training hospital in Lisbon [KANART 2008]. It felt very different to the first performance in Glasgow [NRLA 2008], where I wasn't really *inside* it, whereas now there are sections where the physical quality of the performance is very extreme. I reached a point where I understood much more clearly the differences between the three sections, 'Nigredo', 'Rubedo' and 'Albedo', and the different qualities of the personas in each part. I felt much freer in the performance, and Andrew did live mixing of the sound in response to what I was doing in the space – or he would try something new and I would respond to that. Marty [Langthorne] would follow the developments with the lights, freewheeling a bit. The performance is more clearly live, happening in the moment, even though there is a base structure. This way of making, performing and developing the work has been a revelation and a source of creative liberation for me.

DJ: *How do you review the process, and the work itself? Do you work with the documentation in order to develop a live piece, or to review the results?*

JB: I try not to review video documentation in that way, because the third eye makes me self-conscious of my performance. The way that the performance feels, and the response of the audience, is never registered on video, so that documentation will always be infused with disappointment. I think the reviewing process happens while I am performing, because with each new presentation of a piece, with a new audience – especially if I am doing two or three performances a day, like in *Trans-Acts* – what tends to happen is that you find something new and can implement and develop it immediately in the next performance. Almost naturally, I also shed things that don't work. A section will start to morph, through accumulation and shedding, as the reviewing process happens in front of the audience.

Image 4   Julia Bardsley, *Aftermaths: a tear in the meat of vision* (2009); photo: Simon Annand.

DJ: *Is 'stage presence' a useful term for thinking about your work?*

JB: Stage presence isn't a term I would use. I prefer to think about quality of concentration, because I think any performer who has stage presence is really working with points of concentration. That's what I understand from performance – a quality of concentration that occurs when a performer focuses on something internally, and that informs the quality of the external presentation.

DJ: *Do you therefore not believe in stage presence, in terms of the ability of a body to attract and keep an audience's attention, in a way that is open to scrutiny but seems almost magical? Ron Athey talks about 'psychic weight', as the way in which a body can wield its experience as it presents itself to an audience.[12] When you perform, perhaps stage presence is a difficult term because it sounds innate, but in your performances – especially* Almost the Same *– there is a sense in which your body captures and holds attention, in an almost 'mystical' way.*

JB: Stage presence is key to performance if you are asking an audience to stay with you, watch you, and be with you. But although the power to hold people might lead to a seemingly mystical reading of the body in the space, I think it is achieved through practical means. It's a combination of, as you say, 'weight' – the history and experience of a body – and the performer's concentration with the action that is being undertaken. This is not necessarily concentration on the thing itself. Sometimes powerful concentration – and in turn its effect on an audience – can come from focusing on thoughts, internal elements of which the audience aren't aware. Audiences are acutely aware of being transfixed, or drawn to watching – they don't need to know what's motoring that action, as long as the concentration exists. Without that concentration, the performance is flabby. It evaporates because there is nothing holding it. With a lot of live art, which is often action-based, and concerned with rarefied space and action, those qualities of concentration become even more important, as there are less trappings – music, environment, lights, set, costume – to support the body. Kira O'Reilly's work is very interesting, not least because she has a very particular and acute quality of concentration.

DJ: *Perhaps persona is a more relevant term than stage presence?*

JB: Persona emerges from the release of not being yourself, or of simultaneously being yourself and other. I always say, perhaps flippantly, that I wouldn't ever go on stage without a wig. The wig is a mask that gives me permission to do things that I would never do as my bare self. So I prefer using a persona, instead of the theatrical idea of taking on a character; persona is much less anchored, more fluid and ambiguous than a fixed character. Persona enables me to take an aspect of myself, which is then pushed in a different or more extreme direction. The baseline is that the persona is a version of me, and in the pieces I often reveal myself, Julia. This returns to my earlier point about the suspension of disbelief, where the audience will engage with you as a persona but, underneath, always knows the fact of who you are and that the persona is a fiction, a construct. I like to maintain a tension between those two identities.

DJ: *In your work, there are scenographic techniques that I find very interesting. Two elements that recur in your work are the setting up of grids – on floors or on walls – and the use of scrims or screens between the performer and the audience.*

JB: The grid has a very practical function. Historically it is has been used to demonstrate optics and perspective in painting, and to show scale. I use the grid as an anchoring device, to fix something. In *Foolish Suicide Attempts* (2003) or in the black-and-white pinhole photographs from *Trans-Acts*, the grid is a fixed point across which the action takes place. Without it, the movement that happens over the photograph wouldn't register in the same way. The grid relates to the audience's point of view, the fixed place of the camera. The pinhole photos are taken over very long exposures – eight minutes long, divided into sections. You open up the aperture of the pinhole camera and photograph the grid for one and a half minutes, and then close the aperture. The grid remains on the image, and anything you photograph afterwards – the movement – is layered onto the fixed point of the grid, because the image making happens in-camera. In *Improvements of Nature*, we build a grid at the back of the space over which the movement of the pantomime horse can then register in the darkness. It is also connected to honing down the space – in forensics, 'walking the grid' is a term for surveying the crime scene, noticing all the details within a fixed square or rectangle of ground. At primary school we were taken on field trips where we

12. Ron Athey, 'In Conversation with Dominic Johnson', *The Pigs of Today are the Hams of Tomorrow: Live Lab Symposium*, The Brewhouse, Plymouth Arts Centre and Marina Abramović Institute for the Preservation of Performance Art, Plymouth, 22 January 2010.

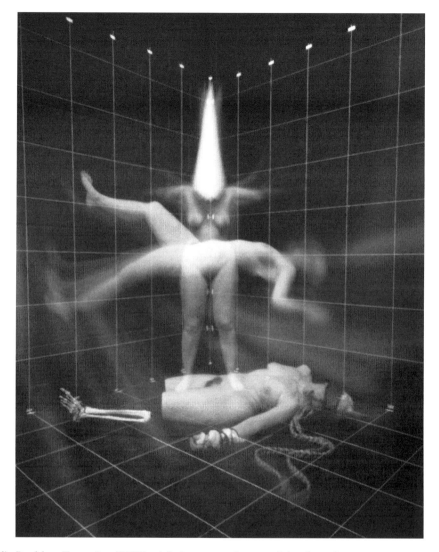

Image 5   Julia Bardsley, *Trans-Acts* (2003), pinhole camera photograph by the artist.

placed a metre-square ruler on the ground, and you noted everything that existed within your square of the grid. In the same way in the theatre, the grid acts as a framing device. I'm very interested in containers, the box, or the display of things – not even necessarily what's in the box – but how something is displayed or presented. The container or the box works to contain the scattering of the objects that I carry out in performance. A grid prevents the scattering from being arbitrary, but instead registers the location of things. The scrim is also practical. In *Almost the Same* I wanted to include video, but I didn't want the tyranny of the white projection screen at the back of the space. The black gauze

allowed me to integrate the video into the piece as a cohesive element. I also didn't want the information in the video to be simply a light source – even though that can be interesting as well. The gauze becomes a surface where the pre-recorded performance co-exists with the live, but where one doesn't dominate the other. Anywhere there is black in the projected image will allow the live presence in the space to show through, and you get a strange, hallucinogenic state, where the audience can't quite understand what is the projected image and what is live. It's a pantomime technique – characters are lit from behind gauze to create a sense of wonder. It's an old trick from the theatre, but it allows me to include video, and have a dialogue between a persona I'm performing live and another persona that has been pre-recorded.

DJ: *In Almost the Same, the gauze is then lifted to allow the audience to pass through the division between the two spaces. It seems to speak to the centrality of clothing the body in the piece, but the gauze also becomes a skin between the audience and the performer – a skin that breaks. It comes back to your earlier idea that the theatre and the body both work by containing two very different states – the beautiful and the horrific, where one is always on the verge of tipping into the other.*

JB: The gauze does function like a skin – a skin between them and me. It alerts the audience to a division or containment, creates an alertness that the audience is against the performer. The ritual of performance is almost gladiatorial. There's an expectation that the performer will give the audience whatever it is that they need, something to take them out of themselves, a revelation, but the performer can never quite live up to the audience's expectations. There is a scapegoat mechanism to the theatre, the crowd versus the individual. In *Almost the Same* it was important that there was a confrontation at the beginning between the audience and me. They're in the performance space and I'm in 'their' space. In the end there is an invitation, which is a way of demonstrating that the theatre is a construct, and that we are all in this together. I can lift the veil and take the division away, re-open the stage and invite the audience into the once-sacred performance space. We're ultimately not separate – we're the same, and we're in the theatre space trying to sort something out together, and that's why we come together in this ritual of witnessing performance. I don't know why else we would do it. Why do you go and see performance?

DJ: *I agree that there is an allure in the tension between letting go and being allowed into the machinery of the theatre. That's why there is something deeply unsatisfying, for me, in naturalistic theatre, where any failure in the machine is ignored, smoothed over, or disregarded as mere embarrassment. Live art often seems to call into play its own impending failure.*

JB: That's why I am drawn to live art, and feel very at home in it as an arena. The prospect of things falling apart, and of trying to get to the place where we are on the edge of total incomprehension, but still holding on – there's something life-affirming in that situation. The theatre is a safe space for witnessing failure. We should embrace failure, and accept that it is part of the process, and part of our selves. Maybe we can see mortality as the failure of life. If so, I think the arena of art is the only place to explore and to witness this.

On the Endurance of Theatre in Live Art

Lara Shalson

1. Beth Hoffmann, 'Radicalism and the Theatre in Genealogies of Live Art', *Performance Research*, 14 1 (2009), 95–105. The language of 'breaking' runs throughout Hoffmann's essay. For the particular phrase 'breaking with', see p. 104.

2. Ibid., p. 102.

3. Ibid., p. 100.

4. On the historical connections between the terms 'Live Art' and 'performance art', see Hoffmann's discussion of the switch in nomenclature from the Midland Group in Nottingham's 'Performance Art Platform' to the National Review of Live Art, which grew out if it (p. 100). For the tendency to refer to 'Live Art' and 'performance art' together, see for example, Adrian Heathfield's

In a recent article exploring the place of theatre in genealogies of Live Art, Beth Hoffmann characterises the history of Live Art in the UK as one of repeatedly 'breaking with' theatre.[1] She argues that '[l]ive art has long spent a great deal of time citing its "visual base" and defining itself against the texts, narratives, actors and directors of theatre'.[2] In this, Hoffmann sees the discursive history of Live Art as largely continuous with that of performance art: 'live art,' she writes, 'has generally preferred a fine art to a theatre genealogy, especially the familiar one narrated in [RoseLee] Goldberg's scholarship on the history of performance art'.[3] As historically related yet distinct terms, 'Live Art' and 'performance art' are frequently invoked together.[4] Yet, the history that Hoffman herself recounts of Live Art defining itself in (albeit negative) relation to theatre could also be cited as one of the things that distinguishes the discourse on Live Art in the UK from discourses on performance art elsewhere. After all, if Live Art cites its 'visual base' as the marker of its opposition to theatre, performance art has more often been characterised as turning to performance in a break with the conventions of the 'visual arts' themselves.[5] As Nick Kaye suggests in his introductory article to *Contemporary Theatre Review*'s 1994 issue on 'British Live Art', it is Live Art's 'sense of relationship yet distance, of a "theatricality" somehow connected to and yet at one remove from the prevailing languages and practices of "theatre" and "drama"' that marks a key difference between it and the performance art practices of North America and continental Europe.[6]

Hoffmann frames her argument in response to a 2008 polemic by Tim Etchells in which he suggests that what might unite the diverse practices of Live Art is 'an investment in "breaking" theatre'.[7] She reads this phrase as expressing a desire to break *away* from theatre. However, the introductory essay, 'Alive', in *Live: Art and Performance*, ed. Adrian Heathfield (New York and London: Routledge), pp. 7–13, where Heathfield states that the book is 'about the "genre" of performance and Live Art' (p. 7).

5. In particular, performance art is frequently described as effecting a break with modernist formalism. See for example, Henry M. Sayre, *The Object of Performance: The American Avant-Garde since 1970* (Chicago and London: University of Chicago Press, 1989); and Amelia Jones, *Body Art/Performing the Subject* (Minneapolis and London: University of Minnesota Press, 1998).

6. Nick Kaye, 'Live Art: Definition and Documentation', *Contemporary Theatre Review*, 2 (1994), 1–7 (p. 3).

7. Hoffmann, 'Radicalism', p. 98. Hoffmann is responding to Etchells' description of '*a desire to remake theatre and performance in some way – a picking up of the form, a delinquent turning it over. To break it. To open the space, as if it might be better broken, or wired a different way. To make new tools out of old ones.*' See Tim Etchells, 'Step Off the Stage', *The Live Art Almanac*, ed. by Daniel Brine (London: Live Art Development Agency, 2008), pp. 7–15, (p. 12). Emphasis in original.

8. Etchells, 'Step Off the Stage', p. 11. Italics in original.

language of breaking might also be interpreted differently. Etchells aligns the desire to break theatre with the relation of a child to a toy. He associates the approach that asks 'how can I break this?' with curiosity and vigorous will. And although he does suggest that this question might stem from 'an enjoyably careless assumption that the thing might not matter that much (might not be that precious) in its unbroken form', he also associates this approach with the work of the scientist who knows that 'trying to establish what something *is* could also involve an attempt to discover its limits, its edges, and the full extent of its capacities in any number of directions'.[8] Here, the effort to 'break theatre' is less a move away from theatre than a sustained and repeated investigation of its mechanisms, as when one attempts to 'break a game' or 'break a code'. To push theatre to its limits, to separate it into pieces, to scrutinise its components – and to return to these endeavours again and again – is not to dismiss theatre so much as to persevere in a difficult relationship to it.

Approaching Live Art's relationship to theatre along these lines, I want to suggest that theatre persists as an object of endurance in Live Art. That is, I want to propose that theatre can be understood both as something that is *endured by* and that *endures within* Live Art. Key to this argument will be the work of Forced Entertainment (the theatre company for whom Etchells is artistic director), a company that has had a central position within the Live Art sector for over two decades and whose work constitutes a significant part of the discourse on Live Art. But first, I would like to consider what is at stake in pursuing this argument. For starters, to propose an understanding of Live Art as a category of practice that, while closely connected to performance art, also has an enduring relationship to theatre is to suggest that the discourse on Live Art might allow us to navigate differently a conversation about the distinctions between theatre and performance art that has been ongoing in theatre and performance studies for several decades. Rather than simply being another permutation of that same debate – where theatre on the one hand is opposed to 'performance' (whether 'performance art' or 'Live Art') on the other – Live Art, as a third term, might provide a different perspective on the 'theatre versus performance art' debate. To pursue this possibility won't be to settle what is already largely considered to be an impossible distinction, nor do I intend to claim a privileged position for Live Art as a discourse or practice. What I do hope this avenue of thought might offer is an opportunity to reconsider some of the assumptions that often accompany these distinctions and some of the things that can be obscured by them. In particular, assumptions about *endurance* as a performance practice will be shown to be central to theatre/performance art debates. To navigate these debates differently, then, will also be to suggest ways of thinking about the performance of endurance through terms other than those usually offered within them.

Enduring Distinctions Between Theatre and Performance Art

Performances involving pain, discomfort or hardship are frequently at the heart of distinctions between theatre and performance art. In Jon

9. Jon Erickson, 'Performing Distinctions', *PAJ: A Journal of Performance and Art*, 21.3 (1999), 98–104 (p. 98).

10. Ibid., p. 98.

11. Peggy Phelan, *Unmarked: The Politics of Performance* (London: Routledge, 1993), p. 152.

12. Nicholas Ridout, *Stage Fright, Animals, and Other Theatrical Problems* (Cambridge: Cambridge University Press, 2006), p. 5.

13. Ibid., p. 170, n. 14.

14. Abramović, Schneemann, Burden, ORLAN and Acconci were all included in Exit Art's 1995 Endurance exhibition; Goldberg includes Athey's work within her discussion of 'endurance art' in *Performance: Live Art since 1960* (New York: Harry N. Abrams, 1998), p. 99; Nitsch is included in a similar list of names of artists known for 'staging performances that demanded extreme physical endurance' offered by Martin Kemp and Marina Wallace in *Spectacular Bodies: The Art and Science of the Human Body from Leonardo to Now* (Berkeley: University of California Press and Hayward Gallery, 2000), p. 154.

15. Marvin Carlson, *Performance: A Critical Introduction* (London and New York: Routledge, 1996), p. 103.

16. Marina Abramović in Nick Kaye, *Art into Theatre: Performance Interviews and Documents* (London and New York: Routledge, 1996), p. 181. Ridout also quotes this passage to

Erickson's account of a conversation among various artists about the differences between these two forms, only one category troubles the group's conclusion that it is 'impossible to distinguish performance art from theatre'.[9] As Erickson writes in parentheses, 'the only exception [he] could think of would be the literal and experiential character of endurance and body art'.[10] Erickson distinguishes endurance and body art on the basis of their literalness, but the idea that it is literal (rather than metaphorical) has often been considered the differentiating feature of performance art in general. It is precisely the rejection of illusionism, the creation of a fictional world and the conventions of role-playing in favour of the direct presentation of the performer him or herself in an acknowledged performance situation in which actions are not imitated but 'really done' that has usually been understood to characterise performance art as distinct from theatre. But, Erickson is not alone in suggesting that practices involving bodily endurance might go furthest in asserting the literal over the metaphorical. For Peggy Phelan, too, arguing that 'performance approaches the Real through resisting the metaphorical reduction of the two into the one,' it is 'specifically, a genre of performance art called "hardship art" or "ordeal art" [that] attempts to invoke a distinction between presence and representation by using the singular body as a metonymy for the apparently nonreciprocal experience of pain'.[11]

Insofar as performance art is associated with attempts to invoke the 'real' in performance, practices of endurance are frequently central to descriptions of performance art *tout court*. Indeed, when the distinction between theatre and performance art is drawn in terms of the latter's claims to the 'real', it is often artists who engage in endurance-based practices who are named. For example, Nicholas Ridout supports a statement about the 'antitheatricality of much performance art, with its conventional insistence on the presentation of "realness" rather than the representation of the real'[12] with a footnote in which he writes, 'I am thinking here of performance's tradition of emphasising real bodily presences as exemplified in the work of, inter alia, Marina Abramovic, Carolee Schneemann, Chris Burden, Hermann Nitsch, Ron Athey, Orlan, Vito Acconci'.[13] It is, I am suggesting, no coincidence that all of these artists can be described as engaging in endurance practices.[14] Endurance-based performances are frequently pointed to as quintessential examples of performance art. As Marvin Carlson notes, of the various forms of performance art that emerged around 1970, 'certainly the part that attracted the most attention from the media and the general public, were those pieces that went beyond everyday activity to push the body to extremes or even to subject it to considerable risk or pain'.[15] At the same time, Ridout's comments remind us that the effort to invoke the real in performance through bodily endurance has also often been associated with antitheatricality. Certainly, statements such as Marina Abramović's (in an interview with Nick Kaye) that 'theatre was an absolute enemy. It was something bad, it was something we should not deal with', lend credence to this view.[16] Thus, the distinction between theatre and performance art is routinely based in practices of bodily endurance, and such practices are commonly described as antitheatrical.

support his discussion
of 'the antitheatrical
positions adopted by
[...] advocates of
performance art's
"real"', in *Stage
Fright*, pp. 16–17.

17. Erickson, 'Performing
Distinctions', p. 98.

18. Herbert Blau, *The Eye
of Prey: Subversions of
the Postmodern*
(Bloomington: Indiana
University Press,
1987), p. 164.
Emphases in original.

19. Philip Auslander, *From
Acting to Performance:
Essays in Modernism
and Postmodernism*
(London: Routledge,
1997), pp. 3–4.

20. Ibid. (quoting
Diamond), p. 4.

21. Elin Diamond,
'Introduction', in
*Performance and
Cultural Politics*, ed.
by Elin Diamond
(New York:
Routledge, 1996),
pp. 1–12 (p. 4).
Emphasis added.

22. Ridout, *Stage Fright*,
p. 14.

23. Ibid., p. 13. Emphasis
added.

24. Ibid., pp. 13–14.

While claims about performance art's literalness or 'realness' have been at the heart of its distinction from theatre, throughout the 1990s with the influence of poststructuralist theory a great deal of energy was spent refuting the possibility that performance art is any more 'real' than theatre. Erickson himself swiftly hastens to undo the distinction he puts forward, writing immediately afterward, 'but even they [endurance and body art] become theatricalized in their mode of presentation'.[17] An early statement along these lines comes from Herbert Blau in 1987. In an oft-quoted passage, he writes:

> There is nothing more illusory in performance than the illusion of the unmediated. It can be a very powerful illusion in the theater, but it *is* theater, and it is *theater*, the truth of illusion, which haunts *all* performance whether or not it occurs in the theater.[18]

Ten years later, Philip Auslander would quote from this passage in order to support the statement 'it may not even be possible, within Western culture, to think "performance" without thinking "theatre," so deeply engrained is the idea of theatre in both performance and discourse about performance'.[19]

To support his argument further, Auslander also quotes from Elin Diamond's introduction to the 1996 volume *Performance and Cultural Politics*, from a section headed 'Performance/Theater': '[T]heater is the repressed of performance,' he writes.[20] Yet returning to Diamond's text, one discovers that Auslander *represses* half of Diamond's statement. The complete sentence from Diamond reads, 'Without resolving this dialectic, we might observe that if contemporary versions of performance make it the repressed of conventional theater, theater is *also* the repressed of performance.'[21] Recalling the first half of Diamond's statement opens up other insights than that all performance is ultimately theatrical. For if performance art in its most recognisable form involves the performance of endurance (as I've been suggesting the discourse on performance holds out), certainly we could say that theatre in its most recognisable form represses the endurance it entails.

A recent strand of discourse has focused more on this second implication, asking what happens when, instead of glossing over the labours of theatrical production, we acknowledge the difficulties and discomforts of the theatre situation. Here, rather than all performance becoming legible *as theatre*, theatre becomes legible as always involving the literalness of performance: labouring bodies, live co-presence, objects that are what they are even as they do the work of representation. Along these lines, in a book devoted to things that make us uncomfortable in the theatre – 'the apparently marginal or unwanted events of the theatrical encounter [...]: stage fright; embarrassment; animals; the giggles; failure in general'[22] – Ridout argues that performance art and the discourse surrounding it have something to show us about theatre: 'performance [is] that which allows us to see theatre *as itself*, by showing it turning itself inside out and revealing its operational guts'.[23] But, for Ridout, performance does not 'just arriv[e] like a deus ex machina either to save theatre's day or to put a stop to the whole sorry affair'.[24] Rather, he suggests, what we discover when we see theatre turned inside out is that '*performance was here all along*', already present in 'all those things that theatre would rather not own up to'.[25]

Importantly, for theorists and practitioners interested in the literalness of the theatrical event, theatre is often associated with the very same endurance-based artists from which it is specifically distinguished in other contexts. For instance, in a recent book, Sara Jane Bailes takes up the concept of 'performance theatre' from Elinor Fuchs to describe work that 'bears some similarity to the conventional theatre of dramatic texts in situating the theatrical event in an imaginative world [yet...] is like performance art [...] in its continuous awareness of itself as performance, and in its unavailability for re-presentation'.[26] In her introduction, Bailes draws a link between the work of Forced Entertainment, Goat Island and Elevator Repair Service (the three companies considered in her book) and performance artists 'whose practice has focused intensively on the physical limits and extensions of the body'.[27] She follows this characterisation with a long list of names: Marina Abramović and Ulay, Carolee Schneemann, Hannah Wilke, Ana Medieta, Chris Burden, VALIE EXPORT, Joseph Beuys, Vito Acconci, Bruce Nauman, and Tehching Hsieh, as well as Mona Hatoum, Nao Bustamante, Karen Finley, ORLAN, La Ribot, Stelarc, Kira O'Reilly, Franko B, Ron Athey and Bobby Baker. Her list is dominated by artists whose work involves practices of 'puncturing, probing, scarring, cutting, or suturing flesh,' and 'exhausting the body through repeated physical activity or an imposed situation of duress or (en)duration'.[28] Practices of endurance, then, are repeatedly key to understanding the relationship between theatre and performance art: endurance is either the limit that distinguishes the two forms or the principal point at which they overlap.

Yet, even in discussions that strive to think about theatre and performance art as intersecting forms, as Ridout and Bailes do, endurance tends to remain on the side of 'performance' where it continues to signal the 'real'. This becomes clear if we consider another important contribution to the conversation I've been tracking here: Hans-Thies Lehmann's *Postdramatic Theatre*.[29] For Lehmann, postdramatic theatre (a category within which Lehmann includes a number of artists working within the context of Live Art in the UK, including Forced Entertainment) is the name for 'the area of overlap between theatre and Performance Art'.[30] Similarly to how I have characterised Live Art, Lehmann describes postdramatic theatre as existing in an ongoing troubled relationship to theatre. Indeed, he chooses the term 'postdramatic' precisely to indicate that this 'new theatre' continues to have a relation to dramatic theatre (which, Lehmann points out, is for most people theatre *tout court*). He writes, 'the limbs or branches of a dramatic organism [...] are still present and form the space of a memory that is "bursting open" in a double sense'.[31] In its persistent link to drama, postdramatic theatre also seems to be theatre at the *breaking point*:

> *post*dramatic theatre, again and most definitely, does *not* mean a theatre that exists 'beyond' drama, without any relation to it. It should rather be understood as the unfolding and blossoming of a potential of disintegration, dismantling and deconstruction within drama itself.[32]

25. Ibid., p. 13. Emphasis added.

26. Sara Jane Bailes, *Performance Theatre and the Poetics of Failure: Forced Entertainment, Goat Island, Elevator Repair Service* (Abingdon and New York: Routledge, 2011), p. 21. Bailes is quoting Elinor Fuchs, *The Death of Character: Perspectives on Theater after Modernism* (Bloomington: Indiana University Press, 1996), p. 80.

27. Bailes, *Performance Theatre and the Poetics of Failure*, p. 8.

28. Ibid.

29. Hans-Thies Lehmann, *Postdramatic Theatre*, trans. by Karen Jürs-Munby (Abingdon and New York: Routledge, 2006). It is worth noting that the English translation of Lehmann's text has been critiqued for abridging the German original. See Elinor Fuchs' book review in *TDR: The Drama Review*, 52 (2008), pp. 178–83 (pp. 181–82). My discussion of Lehmann's text refers solely to the English translation.

30. Lehmann, *Postdramatic Theatre*, p. 137.

31. Ibid., p. 27.

32. Ibid., p. 44. Emphases in original.

Much like Etchell's description of Live Art as an attempt to break theatre – to open up a space within its broken form – Lehmann associates postdramatic theatre with the dismantling and deconstruction of drama from inside.

However, while the disintegration that Lehmann describes stems from a continuing relationship to a dramatic theatre that has not been forgotten, postdramatic theatre also seems to break *away* from this theatre (which is for most people theatre *per se*) in what translator Karen Jürs-Munby calls a 'turn to performance'.[33] It does so insofar as '[p]ostdramatic theatre is the replacement of dramatic action with ceremony'.[34] Moving away from the creation of a fictive cosmos towards an emphasis on the theatre situation itself, the 'performance text' of postdramatic theatre 'becomes more presence than representation, more shared than communicated experience, more process than product, more manifestation than signification, more energetic impulse than information'.[35] Postdramatic theatre's 'changed use of theatre signs leads to a blurred boundary between theatre and forms of practice such as Performance Art, forms which strive for an experience of the real', according to Lehmann.[36]

Postdramatic theatre thus blurs with performance art insofar as it *strives for the real* as opposed to the dramatic theatre, which *excludes the real*. Here, Lehmann offers a useful alternative to the usual account of the distinction between theatre and performance art. For, what he suggests is not that performance art *is* real, while theatre is purely representational (a false distinction that has been repeatedly debunked); it is that dramatic theatre typically seeks to *exclude* the realities of the theatre situation, while performance art dwells on them.[37] One need only consider the Royal Shakespeare Company's announcement, following the disclosure that the skull being used during its 2008 production of *Hamlet* was the skull of composer and pianist André Tchaikovsky, that it would no longer use Tchaikovsky's skull because it was 'too distracting' for the audience (only to later reveal that they continued to use the composer's skull anyway) to see this logic of concealing the real at work.[38] The real is excluded because it risks distracting the audience away from the fictional world of the drama. And it is because the realities of the production of theatre are meant to be excluded that these realities most often emerge in 'mishaps' and 'embarrassing mistakes',[39] in those situations that interest Ridout and Bailes, when the theatrical machine fails and the fictional world of the theatre falls apart.

For Lehmann, what is unique about postdramatic theatre is that the real does not emerge by accident, but is sought. It is no surprise that the performance art with which Lehmann associates postdramatic theatre in its striving for the real involves 'the transgression of socially repressive norms through the experience of *pain* and *danger*'.[40] Once again, the performance of endurance becomes key to distinguishing Lehmann's preferred performance form from dramatic theatre. For instance, in describing the physicality of postdramatic theatre, he writes that it 'stands out in the hard, even physically dangerous actions of the players',[41] and further on, he asserts that 'the postdramatic body offers the image of its *agony*'.[42]

As is often the case in writing about performance art, for Lehmann, the witnessing of enduring bodies is key to the politics of postdramatic

33. Karen Jürs-Munby, 'Introduction', in Lehmann, *Postdramatic Theatre*, Introduction, pp. 1–15 (p. 4).

34. Lehmann, *Postdramatic Theatre*, p. 69.

35. Ibid., p. 85.

36. Ibid., p. 134.

37. 'Aesthetically and conceptually the real in theatre has always been excluded' (ibid., p. 101).

38. I am grateful to Aoife Monks for making me aware of this story. Monks discussed this scenario in her paper, 'The Secret Life of Actors', Queen Mary, University of London, 30 March 2011.

39. Lehmann, *Postdramatic Theatre*, p. 101.

40. Ibid., p. 140. Emphasis added.

41. Ibid., p. 97.

42. Ibid., p. 163. Emphasis in original.

theatre. As opposed to the 'mimesis *of* pain' in dramatic theatre, which leads spectators to a 'painful empathy with the *played* pain', Lehmann argues that in postdramatic theatre, 'when the stage is becoming like life, when people really fall or really get hit on stage, the spectators start to fear for the players'.[43] However, while Lehmann takes it for granted that 'the observation of violence leads to feelings of responsibility and the need to intervene',[44] he also suggests that the politics of postdramatic theatre stem from an *ambiguity* about the need to intervene. As he writes, 'The novelty resides in the fact that there is a transition from *represented pain* to *pain experienced in representation*. In its moral and aesthetic ambiguity it has become the indicator for the question of representation'.[45] As indicator of the *question* of representation, the observation of bodies in pain is the moment at which the representational status of what is seen becomes uncertain. The theatre context produces an '*indecidability* whether one is dealing with reality or fiction'.[46] Through the experience of not knowing how to respond, spectators come to recognise that no form of viewership is ever neutral, including theatre spectatorship. For, when spectators have cause 'to wonder whether they should react to the events on stage as fiction (i.e. aesthetically) or as reality (for example, morally)', their usual disposition – 'the unreflected certainty and security in which they experience being spectators as an unproblematic social behaviour' – is unsettled.[47]

It could seem as though this undecidability were a crucial difference between postdramatic theatre and performance art. After all, we are often told that performance artists employ bodily discomfort as a means of participating absolutely and unquestionably in the real as opposed to in representation. (Chris Burden's statement that 'getting shot is *for real*. There's *no element* of pretense or make-believe in it', comes to mind, for example.[48]) Yet, one could argue that undecidability about how to respond is a key feature of performance art, too. Erika Fischer-Lichte, for instance, argues that Marina Abramović's *Lips of Thomas* (1975) plunged spectators into a crisis of how to respond precisely because it produced a rift between what she calls 'aesthetic and ethical demands': to respond aesthetically and respect the autonomy of the artwork would be to allow the artist to continue to harm herself; to respond ethically by putting an end to her suffering would be to risk destroying the artwork.[49] Ultimately, although Lehmann seems to distinguish the functioning of the suffering body in postdramatic theatre from its functioning in performance art, he emphasises practices of endurance and reads their meanings in terms similar to the discourse on performance art. In both readings, the enduring body brings about an 'irruption of the real'[50] within an aesthetic context, resulting in uncertainty about how to respond.

Enduring Theatre

I am interested in another approach to the question of what happens when endurance practices enter the theatre. Whereas for Lehmann, the introduction of endurance into the theatre is key to a shift *away* from the mimesis of dramatic theatre towards 'the non-mimetic principle in

43. Ibid., p. 166. Emphases in original.

44. Ibid., p. 103.

45. Ibid., p. 166. Emphasis in original.

46. Ibid., p. 101. Emphasis in original.

47. Ibid., p. 104.

48. Burden cited in Carlson, *Performance*, p. 103. Emphases added.

49. Erika Fischer-Lichte, 'Performance Art – Experiencing Liminality', in Marina Abramović, *7 Easy Pieces* (Milan: Charta, 2007), pp. 33–45 (p. 35).

50. 'Irruption of the real' is Lehmann's phrase. See, in particular, the section of *Postdramatic Theatre* titled, 'Irruption of the Real' (pp. 99–104).

51. Lehmann,
    Postdramatic Theatre,
    p. 122.

postdramatic theatre',[51] I am interested in what happens when theatre's mimetic practices themselves become the stuff of endurance. In thinking along these lines, endurance doesn't enter as an implicit synonym for 'performance' or as a sign of theatre's 'turn' to performance (a turn that always risks being read as a turn *away* from theatre). Rather, it enters as a method of intense engagement with theatre's mimetic practices themselves. In this way, theatre itself becomes an object of endurance.

Of course, to write about theatre as an object of endurance is to risk accusations of hyperbole. It is to risk being thought histrionic. This is appropriate. For, it is precisely when theatricality goes too far that it becomes difficult to bear. To write of the endurance of theatre is to resist from the start a sense that *real* endurance is only involved in situations of extreme bodily pain, exhaustion, or discomfort. It is to resist the assumption that degrees of difficulty are readily determinable, or that the line between genuine suffering and 'playing for sympathy' is always easy to draw. Rather than situating endurance as what distinguishes the 'real' of performance from the pretence of theatre, this reading asks what it might mean to endure the imitated, the rehearsed, and the repeated; to take theatre literally, and to remember that such wilful acts of endurance are also acts of love. After all, the toys we break through persistent use are often the toys we care about most.

I situate this reading at a point where theatre and performance art could appear to diverge most clearly. For Lehmann, a key difference between performance art and postdramatic theatre is the latter's repeatability. 'While actors want to realize unique moments,' he writes, 'they also want to *repeat* them'.[52] As opposed to actors who desire to repeat, performance artists, according to Lehmann, seek absolute, and therefore unrepeatable, transformation, through their art. Specifically, performance artists seek 'self-transformation'.[53] As Lehmann writes, 'The artist – in Performance Art noticeably often a female artist – organizes, executes, and exhibits actions that affect and even seize her own body.'[54] The emphasis on unrepeatable self-transformation leads Lehmann to 'consider the performance of public suicide as the most radical perspective of performance, an act that would be unclouded by any compromise through mere "theatricality" and representation and which would represent a radically real, present (and unrepeatable) experience'.[55] Here, death becomes a kind of 'ideal' towards which performance art involving pain or discomfort reaches. There are a number of issues raised by this description, which might give us pause. We might, for instance, reflect on the centrality of female artists within Lehmann's depiction of performance art. We might also consider the ethical implications of the suggestion that public suicide could be the most fully realised form of such performance. In the context of the present discussion, I would only suggest that such a claim about performance art is only possible insofar as the performance of death is a limit case for the dramatic theatre, too. That is to say, a logic that aims towards 'actual death' only becomes the (troubling) distinguishing feature of performance art (that which would finally distinguish the 'real' from the 'representational') insofar as 'staged death' is a distinctively troublesome feature of theatre.

As opposed to the finality of actual death, the performance of death on stage refuses singularity. We know without a doubt that the actor will rise

52. Ibid., p. 137. Italics in
    original.

53. Ibid.

54. Ibid.

55. Ibid., pp. 137–38.

56. 'It is not the knowledge that you are doing something, or even that you are doing something for an audience, it is the knowledge that you are repeating something which is the problem with theatre' (Ridout, *Stage Fright*, p. 19).

again and, in all likelihood, repeat the performance the next night. Thus, although repetition is one of the uncomfortable things about theatre that we try to ignore according to Ridout[56] (reminding us that it's not just performance art that is aggrieved by repetition), the performance of death makes the fact of repetition glaringly apparent. At the same time, performed death makes the act of mimesis all too obvious. Death is difficult to stage convincingly: The corpse on stage continues to breathe so that what is represented by the body is simultaneously contradicted by it. Even if it doesn't involve any tricks of the stage – retracting knives, fake blood, false blows – performed death always risks being stagey, fake. Ironically, in order to ensure that the suspension of disbelief is not interrupted, scenes involving death *must* make their staged nature apparent; there can be no fear among the audience that the actor has actually died. The reality of the theatre situation must be made apparent just enough to preserve the illusion of the drama. In this delicate balance, theatricality risks its own undoing. For, either possibility – becoming distracted by the fact that the actor has not actually died and is lying there breathing, or, becoming distracted by the fear that the actor may have actually died – risks overturning the theatrical illusion and making us uneasy in the theatre. Because of this, the performance of death is a particularly productive site for taking theatre literally, and for considering how this taking literally of theatre might make it into an object of endurance in live art.

'Every Death Scene Twice, Three Times'[57]

57. Judith Helmer and Florian Malzacher, 'Plenty Leads to Follow. Foreword', in '*Not Even a Game Anymore*': The Theatre of Forced Entertainment, ed. by Helmer and Malzacher (Berlin: Alexander Verlag, 2004), pp. 11–26 (p. 20).

58. Tim Etchells, *Certain Fragments: Contemporary Performance and Forced Entertainment* (Abingdon and New York: Routledge, 1999), p. 116.

59. See *Showtime* (1996); *(Let the Water Run Its Course) to the Sea That Made the Promise* (1986); *Some Confusions in the Law About Love* (1989); *Spectacular* (2008); and *Who Can Sing a Song to Unfrighten Me* (1999).

Stage death is a prominent feature of Forced Entertainment's work. As Etchells notes, 'almost every performance stacks a new corpse behind them'.[58] Across the company's oeuvre, death has been performed as extravagant excess and as a matter of course, messily and tidily, ludicrously and often movingly. Death has taken shape as the contents of a tin of spaghetti clutched to a player's belly, as ketchup flung about the stage, as white skeletons painted on black tracksuits, as the simple act of falling to the ground, the word 'DEAD' written on a blackboard.[59] Death is rarely a singular event for Forced Entertainment. The performers die only to be resurrected again as death is rehearsed, repeated, and copied. In the company's 2008 'theatre performance', *Spectacular*, the performance of death becomes a central act of endurance for performers and audience alike, and it is to a consideration of this piece that I would like to turn for the remainder of this essay. Of course, Forced Entertainment are well known for their extended durational performances, works of six to twenty-four hours which push at the conventional limits of theatrical duration, and it might seem likely that a consideration of endurance in their work would begin with works such as these. However, it is precisely the entrance of endurance in this 'theatre performance' (the company's name for pieces devised for theatre spaces, which run a more conventional length of around ninety minutes), that interests me here.

Spectacular, performed by Robin Arthur and Claire Marshall, is built around the conceit that on *this* night of the performance, nothing is going as it usually does. As the show begins, the lights come up on a

60. Throughout, I have used the performers' first names in keeping with the company's practice in performance. The use of these names intentionally does not distinguish between the performer and the persona performed.

stage bare aside from a microphone stand downstage right. Robin[60] enters hesitantly, dressed in a Forced Entertainment skeleton costume, and, after a pause, starts haltingly to explain that '*normally*' the show begins differently: 'normally' there's a warm up act; 'normally' there's a four piece band in the corner; 'normally' there are some potted plants on stage (to make the space 'a bit more human'); and 'normally' there's a staircase descending from the back curtain down which Robin enters. Thus begins a seventy-five-minute narration of a performance that will not be seen this evening: a show that is described variously as more 'hardcore', 'confrontational', and 'shocking' than the present performance; a show that, because of its difficulty, causes some audience members to leave within the first ten minutes; a show that fills its spectators with nostalgia and disappointment, makes them miserable and reduces them to helpless laughter; a show that includes, in addition to the band and the 'warm up guy', such 'spectacular' elements as a number of dancers dancing across the stage in simple, symmetrical formations, and a classic spotlight gag in which the spotlight, like a character, searches for someone to illuminate.

61. All quotes are my transcriptions from the published DVD recording of the production. I have attempted to preserve the feel of the hesitations in speech, but the 'ums' and 'ahs' may not be exact transcriptions.

This show also includes a death scene. Fifteen minutes into Robin's monologue, Claire enters the stage space dressed in jeans and a T-shirt, walks up to the microphone (which until now has not been used), apologises for interrupting Robin, and announces that she would 'like to do my dying now [...] my big death scene'.[61] As Robin responds hesitantly, 'Uh, yeah. Well, ... right, okay. Um ... do you want me to carry on with this, or just, um ...', Claire begins what will be a sixty-minute death scene: crying out in agony, clutching at her belly, throwing herself to the floor, and writhing about in pain. It is the beginning of a performance of dying that will continue in ebbs and flows for the remainder of the show, while Robin carries on describing the performance that would 'normally' be taking place, reflecting on his own experience of it (the bits he likes, the bits he wishes would move more quickly, the parts he begins to tune out), and periodically interrupting himself to respond to Claire's performance with criticism, praise, and suggestions for improvement.

62. That it is the *staging* of death that is difficult is emphasised early in Claire's performance when Robin suggests to her that her performance would be 'better' if the audience could see her face. At this suggestion, Claire painfully turns her head while her body remains facing away from the audience, contorting herself into a precarious and uncomfortable position.

The mimetic nature of Claire's convulsions are highlighted from the start, not only by her announcement of the act beforehand, but by the fact that she enters and begins her death scene just as Robin is describing the *actual* bodily effects of being onstage. As he recounts, by this point in the show some audience members have usually walked out, and his hands begin to tremble. Once his hands begin to shake, his breathing starts to go, he explains, holding up his hand to show the audience these nervous effects. The actual bodily effects of being onstage are thus contrasted with the staged bodily effects that Claire performs next to him. Of course, the contrast is raised in order to be complicated: even Robin's 'real' trembling is staged and therefore possibly 'faked', and as Claire continues to 'do her dying', the labour of her breathing and the difficulty of her movements begin to seem more and more genuine. In both cases, the performers' bodily discomfort is directly related to the labour of mimesis.[62]

The performance of death becomes an act of endurance not because the performer approaches a condition of almost actually dying, but

Forced Entertainment, *Spectacular* (2008). Photo by Hugo Glendinning. © Forced Entertainment. Used with Permission.

because the mimesis itself is pushed beyond conventional limits. Much like endurance-based performance art works in which a single idea or rule is carried through to the point of exhaustion, Claire performs the act of dying until she has worn it out completely. In this, her performance bears resemblance to performance art pieces such as Marina Abramović's *Freeing the Voice* (1976), in which Abramović lay on her back screaming until she lost her voice. Yet the emphasis of Claire's performance remains throughout on 'faking' it. For the audience, the performance becomes difficult not because it becomes more believable or because the audience begins to fear for Claire's well-being, but because it pushes a scene that would typically be at the peak of dramatic interest to the point of potential boredom, while simultaneously demanding our attention throughout. Endurance doesn't irrupt in the theatre to take us away from mimesis but arrives as an effect of dwelling on it.

While Claire's sixty-minute performance of dying shares formal similarities with some forms of performance art (the pedestrian clothing, the simple structuring rule, the matter of fact approach, the extended duration), it is also, as a death scene, quintessentially melodramatic. And, while Claire's death throes are largely 'non-matrixed', to use Michael Kirby's term – that is, they are not performed in the mode of a fictional character or in relation to a fictional sense of time or place, but are enacted by the performer in the here and now in a task-like manner – they *are* performed within a theatrical context, and a fictional narrative inevitably

63. See Michael Kirby, 'On Acting and Not-Acting', *TDR: The Drama Review*, 16 (1972), 3–15.

emerges through the interaction of the two performers.[63] In this metatheatrical narrative, Claire is positioned as the performer who is overly invested in her death scene, while Robin emerges as the unlikely 'hero' who carries the show despite everything else failing to materialise as it should. Part of Robin's authority comes from the fact that, unlike Claire who commits fully to her melodramatic performance of death, Robin distances himself from his role as a figure representing death (he is dressed as a skeleton). Robin displays a healthy scepticism about theatre, and this makes him seem particularly perceptive about it. Early on, he expresses doubts about 'the whole edifice of theatre', worrying aloud about the fact that he is a man of forty-five, not a child of eight, dressed in a skeleton costume when 'it's not Halloween, is it?' He worries about the potential excesses of theatre, and his responses to Claire's performance are generally complimentary when it is quiet and subdued and disapproving when her performance becomes too overwrought. In his critique of that which is melodramatic, we confront a form of antitheatricality within theatre.

When performance art is described as antitheatrical, it can seem as though this places it in opposition to the theatre. Yet, theatre has its own antitheatrical prejudices. If performance art has often been accused of antitheatricality for its interest in the real over the simulated; dramatic theatre has often been antitheatrical in its preference for the realistic over the melodramatic or obviously stagy. As Tracy C. Davis and Thomas Postlewait note, 'realism and theatricality set up a *binary configuration* in modernism, with realism aligning itself with the idea of "artless" art'.[64] Pointing out that for many people, 'theatricality is "the mode of excess," realized preeminently in melodrama', they state that 'melodrama was the temptation to be resisted by the new realist writers' at the end of the nineteenth century, while 'the campaign for natural or realistic acting also set itself against melodrama'.[65] Insofar as dramatic theatre continues to be dominated by realism (and a rejection of melodrama), one could say that theatre itself is antitheatrical.

64. Tracy C. Davis and Thomas Postlewait, 'Theatricality: An Introduction', in *Theatricality* (Cambridge and New York: Cambridge University Press, 2003), pp. 1–39 (p. 12). Emphasis added.

65. Ibid., p. 21.

But this isn't about turning the tables and redirecting accusations of antitheatricality away from performance art back towards theatre. Rather, I want to suggest that an entanglement with antitheatricality – an inability to get away from a discomfort with that which is deemed 'theatrical' – might be a point of intersection between theatre and performance art. This is something, I propose, that *Spectacular* demonstrates. Etchells claims that what he appreciates in performance is something *opposed* to theatricality:

> I am very attracted to things that are what they are, and I am very attracted to moments where what's happening is what's happening. (Laughs.) A certain kind of 'it is what it is what it is what it is'. For me there's an inherent ugliness in theatre because it is always trying to do something to you. It wants something. So I would use the word theatrical in a derogatory sense: Something that is trying too hard to affect you and is distorting itself by doing this.[66]

66. Adrian Heathfield, 'As if Things Got More Real: A Conversation with Tim Etchells', in '*Not Even a Game Anymore*', pp. 77–99 (p. 91).

Here, Etchells opposes a literalist approach (where 'it is what it is what it is what it is') with theatre, which not only asks people and things to be *other* than what they are, but which also attempts to manipulate spectators in the process: to *do* things to them and *get* things from them. Etchells also expresses a distaste for spectacle, and shortly afterward in the same conversation he dismisses conventional forms of beauty, saying: 'It's spectacular, and I think the world has enough of that. I'm only interested in beauty if I can see the work put in to make it.'[67] Here, spectacle is linked to a form of theatricality that conceals its methods and techniques in order to produce a 'seductive' display. But theatre and spectacle are not synonymous. Sometimes theatre resists spectacle, and sometimes spectacle is immodest in displaying all that has gone into it. Indeed, it is some of the slippages between anti-theatricality and anti-spectacularity that *Spectacular* offers up for consideration.

67. Ibid., p. 92.

Spectacular gestures towards a range of theatrical forms – from the low-tech haunted house aesthetic suggested by Robin's skeleton costume, to the dancing girls with their silver dresses and pink ostrich feather headpieces, to the jokes told by the warm-up guy, to the melodramatic death scene performed by Claire. What we learn from Robin's narration is that all of these elements 'normally' come together in something of a 'spectacular', or variety show, which for some untold reason isn't happening tonight. One could read *Spectacular* as an overt and prolonged rejection of 'spectacular' forms of theatre: it mocks that which passes as spectacular (the costumes, the symmetrical dance formations, the spotlights, the stairway entrances, the musical flourishes) by describing and refusing to render these things, and it distorts theatre's attempt to move its spectators by pushing Claire's over-the-top performance to excruciating extremes. Read this way, Robin's rejection of Claire's stagy performance could seem to be the voice of reason emerging through the travesty. Yet, to read the performance this way would be to believe too readily in Robin's critique. For, certainly, in *taking on* (by which I mean both 'adopting' and 'challenging') the form of the variety show – a form which we could describe as 'literalist' insofar as it acknowledges its own theatricality – *Spectacular* also pokes fun at a kind of theatre that resists making a spectacle. In doing so it also reminds us that this kind of antitheatricality – the kind that resists making a spectacle – is implicitly gendered.

While he stands there in his foolish costume and searches for his words, Robin also takes on an authoritative role as the one who describes and comments on the theatrical event. As Claire proceeds with her marathon act of dying, he gives voice to conventional rules of decorum: he implores her to do something 'with a bit more integrity', complains that her performance makes it seem that she's 'begging for their sympathy', and tries to control how she uses her body, telling her at one point to stop putting her bottom in the air. It is as though he is saying, 'Stop making a spectacle of yourself!' (and isn't making a spectacle of oneself something to avoid precisely because it is something that women and children supposedly do?). After forty-five minutes of Claire's 'dying', Robin expresses his disapproval in an extended assessment as she drags herself across the floor in continuing agony:

You know what, Claire? I think you're really milking it with this stuff now. Um. You know, I think you're pushing it, and well actually not in a

68. To see that that which is 'theatrical' is excessive from the start, one need go no further than the *Oxford English Dictionary*. See definition 3: 'Having the style of dramatic performance; extravagantly or irrelevantly histrionic; 'stagy'; calculated for display, showy, spectacular'. ('theatrical, adj. and n.', *OED Online* <http://www.oed.com/view/Entry/200230?redirectedFrom=theatrical> [accessed 10 November 2011].

69. On the association of melodramatic behaviour with women, consider for example that the *Oxford American Writer's Thesaurus* offers 'actressy' as a synonym for melodramatic. On the phenomenon of women performance artists being criticised for being too excessive, demanding and self-involved, see for example, Rebecca Schneider's discussion of Carolee Schneemann's explicit body performance art, where she notes that 'Schneemann was often dismissed as self-indulgent and narcissistic by the art establishment' (Rebecca Schneider, *The Explicit Body in Performance* (London and New York: Routledge, 1997), p. 31). Numerous commentators have noted the tendency to describe performance art by women as narcissistic and self-indulgent. Amelia Jones, for example, notes that 'body art, especially in its feminist varieties, has frequently been condemned (and occasionally exalted) for its narcissism'. See Jones, *Body Art*, p. 46.

70. For further discussion of the gendered connotations of antitheatricality, see Davis and Postlewait, 'Theatricality', pp. 17–19.

particularly helpful way, um. Cause, you see I think people have, you know, people have given you plenty of room, and you've taken it. Um, It's just that [...] I'm just not sure that you can really take them with you, you know, where you're going. I don't know, it's like everything you're doing is all down one track, you know? It's all down one track. It's like you're hitting them over the head with a hammer. [Claire lets out a huge howl.] Look, I just worry Claire [...] I think people have made the effort, you know. They've come with you, they've gone with you so far, you know? They've gone the extra mile for peace. [...] I just, you know, I worry. I think it's like, well actually sometimes I think it's a bit like you're punishing them. I don't know, I mean, you know, look, what you're doing, it is strong, it's very strong [Claire is crouched now, moaning quietly], it's just it's also a little bit upsetting, you know. It's just, well frankly, it's a little bit absurd, isn't it, because we all know that what you're doing is playacting. [Claire sobs louder.] It's just playacting.

Here, the single idea carried to extremes, so often a feature of endurance art, is linked to playacting: to histrionics and a lack of decorum, to not knowing how to act appropriately or when to stop. Claire's playacting is 'upsetting' not just because she is pretending but because she doesn't know when enough is enough. And isn't this always the problem with that which is 'theatrical': it's always already too much.[68]

Through Claire's prolonged act of dying, the categories of theatre and performance art, so often opposed, begin to appear to have more in common. On the one hand, Claire's performance of dying 'is what it is what it is what it is': a straightforward mimesis of dying that emerges not in relation to narrative expectation but according to a structuring rule. Claire approaches her extended act of dying with the single-minded focus of an endurance artist, committed to exhausting the task before her. Yet, within the meta-theatrical narrative that emerges in *Spectacular*, Claire's investment in the act of dying itself allows her to be positioned as a prima donna who demands too much of those around her. What *Spectacular* enables us to see, then, is that the rejection of theatrical melodrama and the rejection of the excessiveness or extremity associated with performance art can take similar forms. Importantly, these criticisms are often directed against performances by women: too excessive, too demanding, too self-involved.[69]

To notice that antitheatricality is gendered is certainly not a new observation.[70] But what *Spectacular* does in pushing that quintessentially 'theatrical' act – the stage death – to the point of endurance we associate with performance art, within a dramatic context that is gendered, is to remind us that sometimes, theatre and performance art are on the *same* side of the antitheatrical divide. Amidst all the discussion about distinctions, it's easy to forget that theatre and performance art are sometimes tarred with the same brush. They may both try in different ways to avoid association with a theatricality that is defined as excessive from the start, but they both continue to endure that taint. To take up the opportunity that Live Art offers as a third term bringing theatre and performance art together, isn't to overcome the problem of antitheatricality that seems to divide them, but to see theatre itself as something that all performance endures.

Come Closer: Confessions of Intimate Spectators in One to One Performance

Deirdre Heddon, Helen Iball and Rachel Zerihan

We have licked and plucked the ripe red strawberries held gently between his fingers, feeling the juice dribble down our chins.

We have had our eyes blindfolded and our skin teased with the seductive caress of her peacock feather.

We have pressed our ears against the metal grille to soak up the secrets of wrongdoing.

'One to One', 'One on One' or 'Audience of One' are all terms used to describe performances that invite one audience member to experience the piece *on their own*. In practical terms, the spectator books a performance slot during which they alone encounter the work. This formal shift in the traditional performer/spectator divide can, quite radically, reallocate the audience's role into one that receives, responds and, to varying degrees restores their part in the shared performance experience. In place of the metaphorical or imaginary dialogism that pertains to all acts of theatre (the spectator is always in some sort of relationship with what is seen), in One to One performance the spectator is actively solicited, engendered as a participant.

Demanding a more explicit and overt relational exchange, performers Adrian Howells, Sam Rose and Martina Von Holn are part of a wider group of UK-based Live Art and performance practitioners including Kira O'Reilly, Franko B and Oreet Ashery who have been drawn to utilising the form in their practices. In the last few years, early-career

1. <http://www.bac.org.uk/whats-on/one-on-one-festival/> [accessed 21 May 2011].

2. See Dee Heddon and Adrian Howells, 'From Talking to Silence: A Confessional Journey', *PAJ: A Journal of Performance and Art*, 97:33.1 (January 2011), 1–12.

3. Jacques Rancière, *The Emancipated Spectator* (London and New York: Verso, 2009).

4. See Lyn Gardner, 'I Didn't Know Where to Look', *Guardian*, 25 March 2003, <http://www.guardian.co.uk/stage/2005/mar/03/theatre2> [accessed 28 August 2011]; Emma Safe, 'Come into My Parlour', *Guardian*, 3 March 2005 <http://www.guardian.co.uk/artanddesign/2002/may/25/artsfeatures.books1> [accessed 28 August 2011]; Theron Schmidt 'Review: Helen Paris, Vena Amoris', *Writing from Live Art blog*, 24 June 2007, <http://www.liveartuk.org/writingfromliveart/index7e5b.html> [accessed 28 August 2011]; Alex Eisenberg, 'Becoming a Child or a Lamb? Review of Samantha Sweeting's La Nourrice: *Come Drink From Me My Darling*', *Spill: Overspill*, 12 April 2009, <http://spilloverspill.blogspot.com/2009/05/becoming-child-or-lamb-by-alex.html> [accessed 28 August 2011]; Lyn Gardner, 'How Intimate Theatre Won Our Hearts', *Guardian*, 11 August 2009, <http://www.guardian.co.uk/

artists can also be seen experimenting with the seemingly intimate at Live Art festivals and at the Edinburgh International Fringe Festival too. The Battersea Arts Centre in London has now hosted two 'One on One' festivals. Notably, the latest (in April 2011) presents spectators with a number of 'set menus', inviting them to make individual choices of what to see, according to – or framed by – appeals to personal taste: from the 'mind-bending' Menu One (for those with 'strong stomachs'), to the 'personal' Menu Two (which offers a 'spicy main with subtle nostalgia inducing sides').[1] One to One performance is employed as a tool for claiming and proclaiming individuality.

The concurrent popularity of both the One to One form and of digital 'first person' platforms for seemingly intimate displays is surely not coincidental. Both media suggest the possibility of connection and personal encounter via their forms. The intimacy proffered by live performances has previously been framed as 'real', and a deliberate intervention into and resistance to the 'virtual' relationships engineered via digital interfaces such as Facebook and Twitter.[2] While we would not wish to deny the differences that the sharing of time and space make to the phenomenological experience of an encounter between people, nor do we wish to presume it uncritically – or presume a total lack of intimacy in the virtual. Both forms share a potentially paradoxical promise of sociality through performances of 'self'. Crucial to this discussion, then, are the practices of *exchange* between selves enabled by One to One work. For this reason, we choose to use the term One *to* One.

Jacques Rancière argues in *The Emancipated Spectator* that all spectators are active irrespective of the form of performance being witnessed,[3] yet the prevalence of the One to One form and its particular dramaturgical-spectatorial structure prompts interrogation into what it means to be a literally performing spectator. The generic term One to One risks erasing the diversity of ways in which and degrees to which this work actively constructs participant-spectators, engendering different participant-spectator roles and the experiences that arise from playing them. As we suggest, in creating a space within the work for the spectator to become a participant, the perceived value of this form of performance hinges on the seeming authenticity of exchange, on the engendering of a relationship between performer and performer-spectator. This relationship – this performance of the *between* one and another – is intertwined with and inseparable from the sensitive, generous and demanding work of collaboration; collaboration makes the work. Claims of authenticity, though, are tricky to define in an environment of roles and masks, of script and improvisation, of being a performer and playing at being one. As we suggest, alongside the 'parts' created for us by the performers are other habitual, sticky roles, including that *of* spectator. What is it to collaborate *as* a spectator? And how does the collaborating spectator evaluate the – and their – performance? What and whose performance are we judging?

While arts bloggers and journalists use the Internet as a way of sharing experiences and opening discussion on One to One,[4] to date only a few detailed scholarly discussions have been published on artists' use of this form, perhaps, in part, due to the unappealing yet inescapable subjectivity

culture/2009/
aug/11/intimate-
theatre-edinburgh>
[accessed 28 August
2011].

5. See Rachel Zerihan, 'La
Petite Mort: Erotic
Encounters in One to
One Performance', in
*Eroticism and Death in
Theatre and
Performance*, ed. by
Karoline Gritzner
(Hatfield: University of
Hertfordshire Press:
2010), pp. 202–23;
Zerihan, 'One to One
Performance: A Study
Room Guide', *Live Art
Development Agency*,
2009, <www.this
isliveart.co.uk/
resources/
Study_Room/
guides/Rachel_
Zerihan.html>
[accessed 28 August
2011]; Zerihan,
'Revisiting Catharsis in
Contemporary Live Art
Practice: Kira
O'Reilly's Evocative
Skin Works', *Theatre
Research International*,
35 (2009), 32–42;
Deirdre Heddon,
*Autobiography and
Performance* (London:
Palgrave Macmillan,
2008); Helen Paris,
'Too Close for
Comfort: One to One
Performance', in
Performance and Place,
ed. by Leslie Hill and
Helen Paris (London:
Palgrave Macmillan,
2006), pp. 179–91.

inherent in such authored works, something we choose to embrace in this dialectical exchange.[5] The shame of scarce documentation is magnified when one considers the rich variety of One to One works made over the last ten years or so – Howells, Von Holn, Rose, as well as O'Reilly, Franko B and Ashery adopt vastly different strategies for making use of such constructed engagements. The decisions of seminal artists such as O'Reilly, Franko B and Ashery to work with the form reflects not only its lure for practitioners (as well as spectators), but also says something – still being put into words – about the genre's inclusion of and expansion into the form's possibilities.

The authors of this article are well practised participants in the circuit of exchange and desire that functions as the architecture for One to One performance. Our collective attendance at a symposium, *i confess...* (Glasgow, 2009), provided a forum for us to participate in the same One to One performances and then to share our experiences of that participation. Practice-as-Research (PaR) usually refers to making performance but, given that One to One is usually participatory, here the practice is located in the experiential processes of reception: PaR becomes SPaR (Spectator-Participation-as-Research). This acronym intentionally signals the relational dynamic embedded in the One to One form, a dynamic – or enfolding – that we unfold here.

i confess... was the culminating event of a three-year creative arts fellowship held by Adrian Howells at the University of Glasgow between 2006 and 2009 (funded by the Arts and Humanities Research Council). Howells' research project had practically explored the use of intimacy and risk in solo performance. *i confess...* afforded the opportunity to invite academic researchers (including Dominic Johnson, Roberta Mock, Helen Iball and Geraldine Harris) and performance practitioners to engage in discussion and debate around the use of intimate and confessional forms in performance. Reflecting on our participation in Howells' *Garden of Adrian*, Rose's *Bed of Roses* and Von Holn's *Seal of Confession*, in this article we individually and collectively explore the shifting dynamics of subject/object, gift/demand, performer/spectator and authenticity/performance, revealing the complexity inherent in playing the role of an intimate spectator. The intimacy of our individual encounters with each of the three practitioners is remembered as at times excruciating and at other times very moving. We begin to recognise here the ways in which these differences map onto acculturated expectations, and relate to personality traits and personal histories.

One to One proposes a dialogic and collaborative encounter, though as our discussion reveals, identifying and claiming the success of those encounters is not straightforward either. Our discussion also strategically staged another dialogic and collaborative encounter as in writing this article we devised a collaborative writing process. We spent four days together in a rented apartment, reflecting on our experiences, allocating writing tasks, reading aloud and sharing our draft writing and then agreeing a structure. In this iteration, we consciously retain both the dialogue and the collaboration that took place between us as we sought to make sense of what had taken place between us and the performers.

The Garden of Adrian

Dee Heddon: In *The Garden of Adrian* I am led gently and carefully by Adrian Howells through a woman-made garden (designed by Minty Donald), built inside a converted church that is now a theatre. Leading me by my hand, Howells softly tells me that if there's anything I don't want to do, I shouldn't do it. Over the next hour or so, I will place my bare feet into cool soil; gingerly pluck strawberries from Howells's fingers, letting the juice dribble down my chin; cradle Howells' head in my lap, holding him like a lover, like a mother; have my hands and arms tenderly washed, each one in turn; and lie on a blanket atop a perfect square of green grass, Howells spooning into me. Engaging with the five senses, I will travel through childhood reminiscences, prompted by tastes, smells, sounds and textures. My memories will be re-membered, re-inhabited, re-lived, re-stored, re-storied.

Rachel Zerihan: My dad, who I would do almost anything for, once tried to tempt me with a freshly picked ripe one on a trip to a 'pick your own' farm when I was a child. I squirmed and whinged until he reluctantly accepted my refusal. More recently my boyfriend brought a punnet of them onto a romantic picnic break. He sought to edge them into an erotic sphere of sensual delight, but my disdain for their hairy skins and mushy middles meant he eventually ate them all, my mouth remaining dry and berry-free. The twenty years or so in-between, I'd even tried to coax myself to eat a whole one yet failed each time, nibbling only a hamster's portion with winced eyes and screwed up-face.

I don't like strawberries, yet I ate one for Adrian Howells. Moreover, I ate two.

Howells' welcome hug was warm and inviting and it was a relief to see him after being stuck in the shed so long; a reward, it felt, for my time in isolation. We had not long left the first stage of the journey, the visual feast of looking at a beautiful white flower whilst wriggling fresh earth beneath our feet, when I saw the full punnet waiting for me at the next station. Howells held my hand as we walked towards the bench and gently led me to take my place.

I don't like strawberries. 'I don't like strawberries' was all I needed to say. He asks me if I like them and I lie, 'yes', though my eyes plead 'no'. Why lie? My will to please has followed me throughout my life, from asking my mother each night whether I had 'been a good girl' and only accepting her affirmation as license to sleep with ease (this lasted for years), to more recent decisions I've made to behave, do good, please others. My role as dutiful spectator in Howells' garden was led by my desire to please even though he had explicitly told me that I would not have to do anything I felt uncomfortable with shortly after the hug that marked my entrance to the garden space.

The sensation of tasting the strawberry, quite clearly, was intended to be a pleasurable one and I remember trying to fake enjoyment. Like receiving an unwelcome lover, I feigned delight and satisfaction.

One to One performance is an art form that both relishes and can be interrupted by autobiographical fragments. In other art forms this is the case for *reception*. One to One is unusual in that the artist's moments of

Image 1   Adrian Howells, *The Garden of Adrian* (2009): photo by Hamish Barton. Used with permission.

Image 2   Adrian Howells, *The Garden of Adrian* (2009): photo: Hamish Barton. Used with permission.

6. Sidonie Smith and Julia Watson, 'Introduction', in *Getting a Life: Everyday Uses of Autobiography*, ed. by Smith and Watson (Minneapolis: University of Minnesota Press, 1996), pp. 1–24 (p. 9).

7. Ibid., p. 10.

8. Ibid., p. 11.

9. Ibid., p. 17.

10. This phrase is borrowed from 'the character Adrian', played by Adrian Howells, a scripted 'audience member' in Tim Crouch's *The Author* (Royal Court Theatre London, 2009), who declares: 'I saw a play last year. And I remember thinking, "that writer has imagined me". I've been imagined! Poorly imagined! The audience has been badly written! We're all going to have to pretend ourselves!' (London: Oberon, 2009), p. 20.

production are inevitably affected by – entwined with – the participant's life experiences and senses of self. In its processes of signification, One to One performance presents as inevitably and unpredictably dirty; it is revealing to consider how readily participants protect the performance from the 'clutter' of personal baggage. The more we reflect on our spectator-participation at *i confess...* the more it is evident how, as spectator-participants, we so easily (though, often, not willingly, as you will see from the examples that follow) adopt 'ready-made narrative templates to structure experiential history' and thus 'take up culturally designated subjectivities'.[6] Indeed, One to One often piggybacks on everyday autobiographical practices. These provide a useful shortcut in behavioural acclimatisation, given that 'recitations of our personal narratives' are 'embedded in specific organisational settings and in the midst of specific institutional routines or operations: religious confession goes to church, psychological trauma goes to the counsellor's office or the analyst's couch' and so on.[7] We are aware that 'only certain kinds of stories need to be told in each narrative locale' and 'in this way, the institution writes the personal profile, so to speak, before the person enacts and experiences it as "personal"' and thus 'in everyday life, autobiographical narratives are part of a frame-up'.[8] Invited to offer some reflections at the *i confess...* symposium, Helen Iball recognised spectatorship as a process of conventionalised 'self-presentation and composition' that is 'largely unreflective',[9] an impulse that she identified as 'giving good audience', where there is a compulsion to participate in the normative assumptions that are a pitfall of One to One performance. So it is that coercion becomes a much more problematic issue than it might seem: it goes beyond the intentionally manipulative, because there is a (danger) zone where practitioner's assumptions meet the participant's desire to 'give good audience'. Rachel has assumed her response to strawberries is too insignificant in terms of the hierarchies of experience that experiential performance proffers; invoking the notion of an 'ideal audience-participant' perhaps. That Rachel had agreed to have her experience filmed for the archive probably heightened her sense of responsibility for the piece of performance to be realised. In fact, and for such reasons as Rachel *pretending herself*,[10] intimate spectatorship agitates for recognition that, as Helen has written elsewhere, 'to a greater extent than in other forms, no response is easily dismissed as inappropriate, over-sensitive or shallow because there can be no grounds to be frustrated with audience response'.[11]

In discussing our experiences of *The Garden of Adrian*, we talked a lot about Rachel consenting to eat the two strawberries. As Rachel has described above, she chooses to suffer this course of action in response to Howells' request because she believes she should be good. This is the sort of dogged observance of once prescribed and now habitual behaviours carried by us all: it is called introjection. Commitment to our 'introjects' ('I should be, I must be, I ought …') can be so strong that they often have the power to override our interest in our own well-being. Clarkson and Mackewn explain that introjection interrupts 'the individual's holistic functioning because' she is 'internally split between the original impulse':[12]

11. Helen Iball, 'My Sites Set on You: Site-Specificity and Subjectivity in "Intimate Theatre"', in *Performing Site-Specific Theatre: Politics, Place, Practice*, ed. by Anna Birch and Joanne Tompkins (London: Palgrave Macmillan, 2012 forthcoming).

12. Petruska Clarkson and Jennifer Mackewn, *Fritz Perls* (London: Sage, 2007), p. 73.

Rachel: I don't like strawberries
Helen: – 'and the introject':
Rachel: I must be a good girl to please others.

Rachel described how this introject interrupted her experience of *The Garden of Adrian*. Her dialogue with Howells at this point is based on habitual rather than honest responses.

The processes of Gestalt psychotherapy, such as this notion of introjection – along with perspectives from, for example, psychology and applied ethics – suggest themselves as useful ways of attending to responses that other critical methods might dismiss as incidental digressions. Using existing formulations of behavioural processes such as introjection enables the expression of blocks and digressions. These are part of the autobiography of the participant-spectator, as much as (maybe rarer, elusive) moments of meaningful One to One contact and dialogue.

Rachel: Stawberries aside, in the response that I wrote immediately after the event, I gushed at length about the need for everyone (not just the participants of the *i confess…* symposium) – and particularly vulnerable or dejected people – to be offered such a rewarding, nourishing and life-affirming experience. This intense response was caused by cumulative qualities including Howells' phenomenally caring presence, the Zen-like environment, the opportunities for sensual experiences and the natural materials used in constructing the garden path, yet most profoundly for me, was an action of cleansing that made me both incredibly sad and, quite simply, touched.

There's not much to say of the action involved – after asking me to roll up my sleeves Howells led each of my arms closer to a pool of water and gently dropped cool water over my hands, then my wrists, then onto my forearms. I've recounted the affect of this gesture and it seems out of proportion to the simple, solitary action but my response to Howells' gesture made me think about others: others in my life who deserve such careful attention, others I don't know who surely do too, others who are somebody's others, others who feel they have no other; re-connecting one with the human through contact is a skill Howells embodies in many of his

One to One works and is something he does with an openness that is often infectious. The completely self-less act of refreshing, cooling, bathing my lower arms inexplicably triggered a sense of gratitude that overwhelmed and moved me. If the camera hadn't been there I'm pretty sure I would have spilled tears.

13. See Jean-Luc Nancy, *Being Singular Plural*, trans. by Robert D. Richardson and Anne E. O'Byrne (Stanford: Stanford University Press, 2000).

14. Hélène Cixous and Catherine Clément, *The Newly Born Woman*, trans. by Betsy Wing (Minneapolis: University of Minnesota Press, 1975), p. 148.

15. Sara Ahmed, *The Cultural Politics of Emotions* (Edinburgh: Edinburgh University Press, 2004), p. 126.

16. See Adriana Cavarero, *Relating Narratives: Storytelling and Selfhood*, trans. by Paul A. Kottman (London and New York: Routledge, 2000).

17. See Felix Guattari, *The Three Ecologies*, trans. by Ian Pindar and Paul Sutton (London and New York: Continuum, 2008).

18. Lauren Berlant and Michael Warner 'Sex in Public', in *Intimacy*, ed. by L. Berlant (Chicago and London: University of Chicago Press, 2000), pp. 311–30 (p. 312).

19. Ibid., p. 322.

20. Lauren Berlant, 'Introduction', in *Intimacy* (Chicago and London: University of Chicago Press, 2000), pp. 1–8 (p. 6).

21. Ahmed, *The Cultural Politics of Emotions*, p. 201.

22. Berlant and Warner, 'Sex in Public', p. 324.

The current preoccupation with performances of intimacy is arguably contextually related to wider cultural concerns around inter-subjectivity, anxieties over how – in a world of inter-racial and inter-ethnic conflict and global inequalities and injustices – we might live together, better. Performances of intimacy, in their very staging, seem to demand performances of trust, mutual responsibility, mutual openness and mutual receptiveness. In this, they correlate with a critical understanding of subjectivity, of 'being' as 'being-together'.[13] The subjective is always inter-subjective, depending on identifying with the other *as* a subject. Understanding subjectivity as in process, our encounters with others have the potential to affect our selves and vice versa. Hélène Cixous, figuring this process of intersubjectivity, writes that: 'When I say identification, I do not say loss of self. I become, I inhabit. I enter. Inhabiting someone at that moment I can feel myself traversed by that person's initiatives and actions.'[14] Cixous' insights frame the duality of identification – a problematic process, perhaps, in that the other becomes transformed as much as the self. But what is clear, here, is that the self *is* transformed. Sara Ahmed also underlines the extension of self that results from empathetic identification. As she writes, 'Identification is the desire to take a place where one is not yet. As such, *identification expands the space of the subject.* . . . Identification involves *making likeness* rather than being alike.'[15] This expansion of the space of the subject is arguably enabled by the creation of a space *for* inter-subjectivity; a place for showing what Adriana Cavarero might call *who one is* – or, more simply, that one *is* one – to another *who is* and who is a singular one too (that is, unique and irreplaceable).[16] This creation of particular (One to One) inter-subjective space could be considered a site for 'resingularisation', set against 'mass-media manufacture' of homogenous subjectivity.[17] So One to One might fit Lauren Berlant and Michael Warner's account of 'queer social practices like sex and theory' that 'try to unsettle the garbled but powerful' project of 'normalisation that has made heterosexuality hegemonic';[18] performance might, then, be situated as a 'counter-public'[19] – a way of 'rethinking intimacy'.[20]

Rachel finds herself moved by Howells' gentle, giving gesture. Ahmed, in her critical revalorisation of the emotion of being moved, writes evocatively and usefully: 'Moving here is not about "moving on" or about "using" emotions to move away, but moving and being moved as a form of labour or work, which opens up different kinds of attachments to others'.[21] Berlant and Warner recognise that non-standard 'border intimacies' can 'give people tremendous pleasure'.[22] Howells' performance operates in ways that accord with such 'border intimacies', dismantling some of the 'conventionally based forms of social division' such as male and female, friend and lover, hetero and homo and also, by creating a personal encounter in a performance space, some of the 'taken-

23. See Berlant,
'Introduction', p. 3.

for-grantedness of spatial taxonomies like public and private'.[23] By such means, Howells consciously disentangles the intimate from the sexual. In his use of physical intimacy, Howells engages a process of identification, using touch as a means to impress the other into/onto Rachel, bridging the space(s) between. Howells moved Rachel beyond the space of their personal interaction into a wider social realm: is this perhaps to reconfigure the One to One as One to Two to Three, foregrounding social engagement through its 'rethinking' of intimacy', in contrast to the hegemonic model of intimate life sited in the '*elsewhere* of political public discourse, a promised haven' that 'consoles' citizens 'for the damaged humanity of mass society'?[24]

24. Berlant and Warner,
'Sex in Public', p. 317.
Emphasis in original.

Bed of Roses

Helen: Attending Sam Rose's *Bed of Roses*, I was aware of the play on words in the title. The bed belonging to a Rose: Sam Rose. I was invited to get into bed.

Dee: Rose and I are in a four poster bed, huddled under its voluminous, fluffy white quilt. Rose is wearing a long, black, thin, floaty nightdress. I am fully clothed, but without my shoes. Rose is wearing very red lipstick, her bottom lip pierced through with a ring. Rose is so close to me I smell not only her perfume but her make-up. I am hot and feverish – though not with desire but raging tonsillitis. It is true, I want to be in bed, but I don't think it's this bed I want to be in. This bed is set up in the black box studio of the department in which I work at the University of Glasgow. This basic, black box studio is where I teach undergraduate students every week. The studio is not, to me, a site of seduction. And I am not sure, in any case, that this is, really, a scene of seduction; though it might be a script of one.

Helen: I made a concerted effort not to objectify myself. I mean, lying there waiting for Rose to emerge out of the shadows of the studio, I arranged my body in a pose that appeared relaxed and that sent out no alluring signals. I felt corpse-like and hyper-tense simultaneously. I have lain in some bedrooms waiting for lovers in my time, and I have wanted to look sexually enticing: the object of their attraction. This remembrance felt very strongly to be my signal of what not to do or be with Sam Rose. What did she want with me? I had a pretty clear idea what was wanted and what I wanted with my lovers. But in a One to One with Rose, what did I want? What did she want? Who did she want? How did she want me? Did she want me?

I wanted her to think well of me. I wanted to appear collected, unfazed. Game to participate but sending clear signals about the performance of all this.

Dee: We may be lying closely together, but I do not feel close. I feel like the grin on my face is an act. I must also admit that I am a little anxious that Rose might think I am actually being seduced by her. That she might believe my performance? (Am I that good at faking it?) I can't quite dislodge the (internally homophobic?) thought that, as I identify as a lesbian, Rose might think I really do want to kiss her. And this thought is quickly followed by wondering whether Rose is awkward, being in bed with me? Is she performing differently, with me? But maybe Rose is a lesbian? It doesn't matter anyway, does it, because none of this is real? That this performance is fake is evident; but my hyper-anxiety and self-consciousness propose that the 'real' nevertheless keeps surfacing, troubling the performance; performance anxiety.

Helen: I felt caught in the duration and demands of the piece, and I did not want to be subjective because my subjectivity was taking me down roads that I had left behind. I could feel the pull of episodes in my life that I was not in a place – literally or metaphorically – to recall here and now in this bed with this person I did not know. We couldn't have taken it. The piece depended on a person but it mattered that the person wasn't being me.

Rose did not ask anything about me. I found it difficult to look at her and so, out of the three choices I am offered by Rose, I choose one that involves feathers and a blindfold. I found it difficult to look at her because I did not want her to see the vulnerability in my eyes. The vulnerability was produced by pushing against the memories trying to slip in.

Dee: I choose to be blindfolded, and rather awkwardly ask if I can remove my glasses (another passion killer) before I am plunged into darkness. My throbbing throat is momentarily relieved, tickled by a soft feather. It feels soothing rather than erotic. I lie back, relaxing for the first time – perhaps because I cannot see Rose? I can only feel the sensation of the feather on the skin of my neck, my arms, my face. Though I have selected my encounter, I am utterly passive within it, an object to be worked on and over. This fits with my mood. As symposium organiser, suffering from chronic tonsillitis, it is good to just lie here, to receive. Rose is silent. I can relish the softness of the peacock feather, in these brief moments of repose.

The feather is put away, the blindfold removed, the real world of the studio brought back into focus, alongside the fake world of Rose's seduction. The red lips, the wispy voice, the slight negligee, the crafted words, it's all carefully constructed, and whilst we might be literally close, I'm reminded of fourth-wall proscenium staging.

Helen: She was the show and, lying there on my back, legs overheating under duvet and in jeans, I wonder if I was the stage and the full auditorium for her.

Rose offers a performance of seduction, perhaps, but a tightly scripted one. One to One work engages with the dramaturgy of relations constructed between one and an other. This 'relational' dramaturgy is a recognised feature of contemporary arts practice, with Nicolas Bourriaud and Grant Kester just two of its most influential critics. As Kester writes, artists pursuing this aesthetic, if that is what it is, abandon the object of art in place of a more 'performative, process-based approach'.[25] These artists are 'context providers' rather than 'content providers'.[26] Kester's citing of 'process' signals a particular tradition of theatre practice – that of devising. In devising, the script emerges from the performance process, rather than existing prior to it. The performance text emerges through a range of activities, including improvisation, trying things out and chance procedures (though we should not forget the impact that habit has on the way things work out). A word typically associated with devising is

25. Grant H. Kester, *Conversation Pieces: Community and Communication in Modern Art* (Berkeley: University of California Press, 2004), p. 1.

26. Ibid.

collaboration and its surely not coincidental that both Bourriaud and Kester use this too: Bourriaud writes of likely aesthetic forms encountered in relational art, models of sociability that include 'various types of collaboration between people'.[27] Relational art extends the practice of devised theatre by moving it beyond the closed circuit of the practitioners to the spectators. In this context, no text exists in advance of the interaction between the artist and the spectator, or participant. As Kester writes, with a nod to educational theorist Paul Friere, relational artists 'replace the conventional, "banking" style of art [...] with a process of dialogue and collaboration'.[28] Collaboration is positioned as a political practice that engenders multiple authorship and multiple ownership.

Returning to Sam Rose's performance, *A Bed of Roses*, what becomes clearer is that its relational potential was foreclosed because the performance script was 'closed' rather than 'open', driven by the artist rather than via a process. This is in contrast to Kester's summary of 'dialogical aesthetics', which suggests an image of the artist 'defined in terms of openness, of listening [...] and of a willingness to accept a position of dependence and intersubjective vulnerability relative to the viewer or collaborator'.[29] While the spectator in *A Bed of Roses* was required to complete the performance, the performance was already written. The space was certainly intimate – a shared bed – but there was little inter-action, let alone intercourse. The spectator, then, as suggested by our accounts, figures more as an actor than a collaborator, but at the same time, also as a spectator gazing on Rose's performance. We were solicited to perform and spectate, but not to co-create.

If we agree with Bourriaud that relational work is a response to the lack of face-to-face encounters in an increasingly mechanised world, then Rose's performance's failure for us (if that's what it is) might be located in its *lack* of face-to-face encounter. In the face of Rose's seemingly fixed, theatrical facemask, it is not clear *who* it is that sees us, or even if she does see us. It feels like we are neither addressed nor responded to as individual subjects, which must mean that we function as objects; and interchangeable, undifferentiated ones at that.

> **Helen:** And yet... Sam Rose got to me the next morning. I opened my suitcase and crumpled inside was the shirt I'd been wearing the day before. The smell of roses was overpowering. All of those memories I had been suppressing in *A Bed of Roses* flooded in. Including the unpleasant memories, the regrets, the one night stands. Then Rose became fickle: a repetition of the performance to numerous others transformed into a vehicle for my regrets.

Our description, in relation to Rose, reveals that, even as Rose attempts – and as we, independently, separately attempt – to resist 'ready-made narrative templates to structure experiential history', we risk imposing those very narratives on ourselves, and on others, because we so easily (even though often if not willingly) adopt and thus 'take up culturally designated subjectivities'.[30] We have found that this happens even through participation in One to One performance, which would seem to offer an alternative and resistant space. Maybe, even in

27. Nicolas Bourriaud, *Relational Aesthetics*, trans. by John Howe (Paris: Les Presses du réel, 2002), p. 28. Emphasis in original.

28. Kester, *Conversation Pieces*, p. 10.

29. Ibid., p. 110.

30. Smith and Watson, *Getting a Life*, p. 9.

performance, intimacy's 'potential failure to stabilise closeness always haunts its persistent activity' causing a state of 'constant if latent vulnerability' which 'somehow escalates the demand for the traditional promise of intimate happiness to be fulfilled'?[31] All three of us have been quite harsh critics of those performances that do not make us 'happy' and that make us feel 'vulnerable'.

31. Berlant, *Intimacy*, p. 2.

Rose wears a mask; we attempt to wear our own masks, in response. The *play* we are engaged in here is clear; and if we were different players, we may choose to play our roles differently: what would happen if we chose to remove all our clothes? Or chose to kiss Rose? While it is suggested that relational art, dependent on a collaborative process, dislodges the artist from a position of authority, this cannot be taken as a given. Collaboration does not, in itself, guarantee equality or democratic process. As theatre makers we have learnt from the attempts at collaborative models of our feminist predecessors of the 1970s that simply providing the opportunity for everyone to speak does not ensure that they will. Such opportunity does not address the network of power relations that precede the moment. Personal histories and experiences make some more confident in speaking than others; and cultural bias means that some who speak seem to be more readily heard. There is a politics to participation and this sticks to relational, One to One performance practices (which is not to deny that one potential outcome may be the increased confidence of the participant-spectator).

Howells is a very experienced, professional practitioner. Where Rose perhaps fails to seduce us wholly, Howells succeeds. We are, indeed, disarmed by him. Where Rose prompts the putting on of a mask and the playing of a role, pretending to be seduced, Howells' performance of authenticity, of being unmasked, encourages us to unmask ourselves similarly, to give ourselves to him and the performance, to actually be seduced without knowing it. So we are unmasked while Howells *performs* (pretends) an unmasking. His performance is as structured, crafted and repeated as Rose's. But his skill is to disguise that skill, to try and persuade us that this is not performance. While Howells might function as a 'context provider' rather than a 'content provider', his skill and professionalism provide him with security, a script of sorts that he has constructed. The spectator, however, has no such safety net. We have not done this before. We know not what we do, what we might do, what we will come to wish we had not done. Howells' beguiling tone is not one to easily resist. Just as collaboration does not guarantee equality, so we must be careful not to confuse action and activity, or participation, with agency.

Rachel: I don't like strawberries. 'I don't like strawberries' was all I needed to say. He asks me if I like them and I lie, 'yes', though my eyes plead 'no'.

Seal of Confession

Dee: In the otherwise empty, subterranean basement room stands a bulky confessional box. A woman sitting behind a table takes my name, invites me to wait in the single chair, placed against the wall. Eventually, she instructs me to enter the confessional box. I close the red curtain behind me. The partition wall to my left is punctured with small round holes. I can see an eye peering through at me, then a softly whispering voice. I bring my ear closer, feel the breath on my face. She is telling me a tale, of a friend and a stolen ring. She is confessing to being a thief, to a betrayal, to deceit, to cowardliness, to shame.

She asks me to share a confession with her, to return the gesture; but what is this gesture she has performed? For it is clearly a performance; this is a well-rehearsed, carefully crafted narrative. In this respect, then, perhaps not so far removed from the habitual scripts of confession, the 'forgive me father for I have sinned' litany of small misdemeanours that is met with an equally habitual script of forgiveness, an exchange of Hail Marys for absolution.

It would be difficult to mistake this performance for the really performed confessionals though. We are in a crummy basement room of my university department, where the pipes from toilets flush persistently. The shabby confessional box, constructed of plywood, is clearly a stage replica, a stand-in. The red curtain signals theatricality as much as secrecy; open the curtain, step into the show and play your role.

Helen: Hearing the raw edges of scripting, recognising something as staged, is not to say that its impact is inevitably distancing. I say this because I found Martina Von Holn's confessional booth a standardised product and I might easily have felt objectified, depended upon to comply, part of a transaction. I did not feel this. I think there are two reasons for this. One is that on that day something very fresh had happened to me, I had discovered a part of myself I did not know and felt I probably should not like but was in some way rather excited by – and so the opportunity was so coincidentally and entirely fitting, it was so 'me' (though she clearly had no idea and no intention or practical capacity to facilitate such a happy accident). Thrilled at the sight of a burnt-out car near the hotel that morning, I realised I was a potential arsonist. I'm certain I shouldn't be telling you this. It's the sort of confession that comes back and bites hard. I did not feel objectified or judged by Von Holn. She responded positively to my story and corroborated my evidence. She was clearly staying at the same hotel, I see that now.

The other reason Von Holn's piece got away with stagey-ness has to do with novelty. The lack of comparable experiences of Catholic confession because I was brought up Methodist, had fuelled a sense that confession booths were something missing from my life. She also let me steal a cheap ring, a permission I granted to myself because I knew the ring wasn't authentic and that I wasn't really stealing it (but also it was thrilling because she hadn't told me I could take it, just told me where I would find it) and so I depended on getting away with something I have always been too afraid to do or too responsible or too aware of the likely consequences.

Dee: I slip it onto my finger. For the rest of the day, I look for others wearing a similar ring. It's become a badge of identity, a marker of shared experience. Before long, the cheap metal begins to leave a green imprint on my skin. I am doubly marked by my sin.

Rachel: I had seen other delegates wearing the little purple rings and what began as something like envy soon became mild contempt. I knew that Seal of Confession would provide me with my own opportunity for obtaining my very own ring though I was unsure what I would have to do to get one. And I wanted one – if only to feel part of the gang.

Dee: I have stepped into the shoes of confessant and confessor and played my part, taken and given. She has spoken and I have listened. I have spoken and she has listened. The stakes, the exchange, feel about equal, with nothing lost on either side; but nothing gained either. No, that's not true. I had an experience. I heard a story. I told a story. Here, now, I tell that story of listening and speaking.

Rachel: By the time my performance slot came through I was a bit disgruntled by my wait and put off by the superficial title of the piece. 'What to confess…' I thought as I walked to the room where the performance took place. 'What to confess…' I thought as I sat waiting outside the makeshift confession booth, covered with red velvet curtain to reveal only the confessor's shoes. 'What to confess…' I thought as the artist began to speak through the little hole between us. 'What to confess…' I kept thinking as our script played out. 'What to confess…' I thought momentarily, before answering that I had no confession to proffer though I was told I could take the ring anyway. 'What to confess…' I thought as I walked away from the piece frustrated, grumpy and dissatisfied.

The context of Von Holn's *Seal of Confession* – and indeed of Howells' and Rose's performances – was the symposium *i confess…* Such explicit framing inevitably prompted reflection on confession as an act of performance, and the 'I' that is constructed through that act. Heddon and Howells' choice to deny the first person singular in the symposium's title by deploying an 'i' signalled that the terms and their inter-relationship were open to mutual scrutiny and resistance. If, as Michel Foucault proposes, confession is a (self-)policing technology through which truth is produced and maintained then, as Heddon has written elsewhere, it also affords productive potential to be performed differently.[32] Rachel's performance was a determined refusal to confess to anything, to be a confessant.

Conclusion

Helen Freshwater notes that 'academic theatre studies continues to engage with hypothetical models of spectatorship', and her book *Theatre & Audience* asks some uncomfortable questions of that practice.[33] There is an interesting paradox in One to One: that the survey can cover 100 per cent of the audience, and yet the data are always partial and subjective and significantly incomplete. And that while the academic commentator might, for once, reasonably speak for the whole audience that is only because she *was* the whole audience and this makes it impossible not to confront the narrowness of that perspective and the inevitability of a spectrum of responses, many of them very different from her own (because that range is part of the point of the form and its popularity). The Spectator-Participation-as-Research that we have applied in this article has begun to reveal the usefulness of comparative study, based in

32. Michel Foucault, *The History of Sexuality, Vol. 1: The Will to Knowledge*, trans. by R. Hurley (London: Penguin Books, 1980), p. 59. See Deirdre Heddon, 'Personal Performance: The Resistant Confessions of Bobby Baker', *Modern Confessional Writing: New Critical Essays*, ed. by Jo Gill (Oxford: Routledge, 2006), pp. 137–53.

33. Helen Freshwater, *Theatre & Audience* (Basingstoke: Palgrave Macmillan, 2009), p. 29.

34. Petruska Clarkson, *Gestalt Counselling in Action* (London: Sage, 2004), pp. 30 and 181. In these terms, Clarkson draws direct comparison between the concerns of Gestalt counselling and those of qualitative research. She adds that, just as qualitative research is concerned with 'the examination of practice' and 'research into the qualities of [...] subjects, subjective experience, the phenomenological quality of experience unique and inimical as it is. So is Gestalt' (pp. 182–85).

phenomenological description and reflection and personal revelation between the three of us having experienced the same three performances, sometimes very differently. As a result of this research method, it has become apparent that personal insecurities and digressions have the potential to produce *more* intimate connections to the 'integrity of experience', through 'immediacy', 'relationship', 'awareness' and 'attention',[34] if we are able to sidestep the autobiographical subjectivities that we feel bound to (re-)produce. What is also revealed, in our eagerness to compare notes and discuss individual experiences, is our desire to know 'what it was like for you'; in the fragmented, singularised and often insecure space engendered by One to One, this shared desire is surely bound up with needing reassurance: 'That's what I did too.' It has not slipped our notice that our conscious collaboration between three has returned the 'individual' experience towards the 'collective'.

Index